Corporate Sabotage—National Security Threat

The front of the building was lined with cars labeled with the familiar logo of the security company. Several of the unmarked variety were double-parked next to them. Security guards holding shotguns stiffly across their chests flanked the floodlit entrance on either side.

"FBI," Alex told her, taking her arm. "They've assumed jurisdiction in this."

"In what?" she returned.

Karen's thoughts stopped abruptly when they approached the entrance to the lab where the research on Lot 35 had been confined, located in a separate section of the building to avoid intrusions by the curious. Another suited man stood guard at the door. Karen approached the threshold and felt her feet grow heavy. Her stomach churned. The floor wavered.

The Lot 35 laboratory was a shambles.

Tables had been turned over atop shattered glass. Filing cabinets had been spilled and robbed of their drawers. Computers lay in smashed heaps.

Strange, Karen would reflect later, on how those were the images she would always recall coming first. Not the blood. Not the bodies of her eight-person Lot 35 team who, as always, were working late.

She should have been here! On any other night she would have been.

Other books by Jon Land

KINGDOM OF THE SEVEN

JON LAND

FORGE ®

A TOM DOHERTY ASSOCIATES BOOK
NEW YORK

KINGDOM OF THE SEVEN

Copyright © 1994 by Jon Land

Cover art by Paul E. Stinson

A Forge Book
Published by Tom Doherty Associates, Inc.
175 Fifth Avenue
New York, N.Y. 10010

ISBN: 0-812-53435-2

First edition: December 1994

Printed in the United States of America

0 9 8 7 6 5 4 3 2 1

For Tom Doherty, who believed

ACKNOWLEDGMENTS

Thank-yous on this one have to begin with the wonderful family at Tor/Forge, starting of course with Tom Doherty but continuing right down the line. Linda Quinton, Yolanda Rodriguez, John Del Gaizo, Bob Gleason, and everyone else believe in people as well as books, and it is a pleasure working with them all. Natalia Aponte is a terrific editor who spares readers the pain of my mistakes and misjudgements.

But it was my miraculous agent, Toni Mendez, who found Tor/Forge in the first place, just another day in her devoted commitment to my work and my career. Ann Maurer, a creative genius in her own right, is prominently responsible for making sure that work continues to improve by refusing to accept anything even remotely approaching mediocrity.

I am also blessed with numerous people who keep my technology on the straight and narrow. Emery Pineo, still the smartest man I know, recently learned he was a finalist for the Presidential Award for Science Teacher of the Year award. He's the winner hands down in my mind. And I thank Walt Mattison for not only his expertise in weaponry and armaments, but also for introducing me to the world of the Special Forces, the true American heroes. Thanks also to the now retired Dr. Mort Korn for his typically insightful input.

Along the way I was also helped enthusiastically by John Signore, the Arizona Department of Public Safety, the Illinois Department of Corrections, the Daughters of the Republic of Texas, Mike Gonzales of the San Antonio River Authority, Jim Schmidt of John Deere. Thanks to Tom Walser for showing me Atlanta, Eric Darrow for introducing me to the Texas Panhandle, Matt Lerish, and Steve Frantz. And to Dr. Richard Greenfield for La Jolla and his beautiful new home.

A very special acknowledgement to Dr. Alvan Fisher for steering me through the medical aspects of this book. Advising me was no simpler a task than serving his station on the front line in the war against a deadly, insidious disease.

I finish with a sad note. My Brown University advisor and mentor, Professor Elmer Blistein, passed away last fall. Professor Blistein, who referred to himself as Dr. Frankenstein since I was the monster he created, made it a tradition to take me to lunch after each book was published. Sadly there will be no more lunches but, thanks in large part to this great man, there will be lots more books. I'll miss you, Professor.

PROLOGUE

GONE . . .

THE ARIZONA DESERT:
MONDAY; 1:00 P.M.

"What d'ya make of that?"

Officer Joe Langhorn applied the brakes and inched the Arizona Highway Patrol car toward the shape on the side of Route 181. At first glance he had passed it off as a Hefty bag discarded by some lunk in a Winnebago too impatient to wait for the next rest stop. But now he was thinking it could be a coyote or even a mountain lion. Roadkill of a bumper bending sort.

"Jesus Christ, Wayne . Is that a . . ."

His partner, Wayne Denbo, held a hand up to shield his eyes from the bright sun, then pulled it away along with his sunglasses.

"Shit," Denbo muttered. "Pull over."

"I'll call it in," from Langhorn, reaching for the mike stand that connected their cruiser to the highway patrol's southern headquarters a hundred miles away in Tucson.

"Wait till we're sure."

Denbo climbed out his door the moment the cruiser had ground to a halt on the gritty pavement. He redonned his

sunglasses and unsnapped his gun flap out of habit. Joe
Langhorn advanced a step past him and stopped. He
looked back at Denbo through a blast of windblown sand.

"I'm sure enough now, Wayne."

Denbo nodded and started forward. The shape suspended halfway over the shoulder embankment belonged
to a man. The flapping of a black shirt spilling out of his
pants accounted for the illusion of a discarded Hefty bag.
His outstretched, sand-caked arms were tawny enough to
look like the limbs of some unfortunate mountain predator.
Not a coyote, but roadkill quite possibly after all.

Langhorn waited, one eye on the cruiser, while his partner leaned over the body and felt about its neck for a
pulse.

"He's still alive," Denbo said, looking up.

"I'm calling this in now."

Denbo eased the man over onto his back. "The fuck,
Joe. Bring my thermos over."

It was a Dunkin Donuts jumbo, the kind that came free
with enough coffee to fill it. Except Wayne Denbo always
filled it with iced tea. Every day that Joe Langhorn could
remember since they'd been paired up on this route.

"He hasn't been here long," Denbo reported. "Couple
hours at most."

"Hit by a car maybe?" Langhorn asked from the cruiser.

"Nope. He's got no bruises or abrasions I can find."

Langhorn grabbed the thermos from the backseat and
gazed around into the emptiness of the desert that
stretched in all directions. "Where's his car? How the fuck
he get out here?"

The shape moaned. Denbo lifted the man's head and
tapped his cheek lightly.

"Mister? Come on, mister, wake up. Come on . . ." He
looked back at Langhorn. "Hurry up with that thermos!"

The ice had long since melted, and what contents had
survived the morning sloshed about inside. Joe Langhorn
handed it to his partner.

"You check for ID?"

With his free hand, Denbo flipped his partner a wallet he had pulled from the man's pants pocket. Langhorn bobbled it briefly, then grabbed hold.

"Name's Frank McBride," he reported, after locating the man's driver's license. "From Beaver Falls." Langhorn looked up. "Just off Route 10 north of Courtland, near forty miles away."

"Less than half that, walking 'cross the sand."

"You figure that's how he got himself here?"

"Look at him."

Langhorn didn't really want to. Whatever would make a man walk maybe twenty miles straight into the heat of the desert with only tumbleweeds and sagebrush for company was beyond anything he could conceive of.

Denbo had Frank McBride's head cradled in one hand, while the other lowered a half cup of brown-black iced tea toward his lips. He saw something tucked into the inside pocket of his jacket and reached for it, easing McBride's head briefly back to the ground.

"What's that?" Langhorn asked.

"Airline ticket envelope." Denbo opened it. "Empty." He lifted McBride's head up gently again and rested the rim of the cup against the unconscious man's lips. "Come on, Mr. McBride. It's okay now. You're all right. Wake up. Wake up."

The shape stirred slightly. His eyes opened, uncertain, wavering, frightened. He began to swallow the tea, trying to raise himself high enough to gulp it down.

"That's it. There we go. Not too fast now . . ."

Denbo pulled the cup away and McBride was left with dark brown droplets washing the sand off his chin. His lips trembled, then opened, moving.

"I think he's trying to talk, Wayne," pronounced Langhorn. "I think he's trying to say something."

Denbo moved his left ear closer. "Did you walk here from home, Mr. McBride? Did you walk here from Beaver Falls?"

The shape tried to force out a word and spit sand forth

in its place. His hand latched desperately on to Denbo's
sleeve and drew the patrolman's ear almost to his lips.

Joe Langhorn heard a muttered rasp, something like air
bleeding from a tire. The rasp came again and then Wayne
Denbo pulled away.

"What'd he say, Wayne?"

Denbo drained the rest of the tea himself. "One word."

"*What* word, for the love of Christ?"

Denbo looked up from the empty cup. "Gone, Joe. I
think he said 'gone.' "

By the time the officers got him into the back of their
patrol car, McBride was out again, eyelids jittering like a
dreaming dog's.

"What do you think he meant, Wayne?" raised Joe
Langhorn. "What do you think he meant when he said
'gone'?"

"Dunno." Denbo paused, frowning. "What do you know
about Beaver Falls?"

"Population of seven hundred, seven fifty maybe. A big
influx moved in once they got the water problems straightened out a few months ago. Only folks know Beaver Falls
even exists are the ones who pass by the signs for it on the
way south to Tombstone." Langhorn met Denbo's stare
and got the message. "Local jurisdiction, case I need to remind you."

The senior man's eyes flicked toward the backseat. "We
should run him home."

"Call it in's what we should do."

"Beaver Falls got a deputy sheriff on site?"

Langhorn was paging through a thick pamphlet he kept
on the visor listing all Arizona municipalities and the
names of their head law enforcement officials. "Yup," he
said. "Name is John Toulan."

"What say we drive into Beaver Falls and leave Mr.
McBride with him?"

Now it was Langhorn who stole a glance at the unconscious form in the backseat. "I was thinking maybe we just call for an ambulance and let them take over."

"An hour for them to get here, if we're lucky," Denbo told his partner. "We can have Mr. McBride home safe and sound in half that."

"Yeah, but—"

"Start the car, Joe," Denbo ordered. "Beaver Falls is barely out of our way."

Joe Langhorn never would have admitted it, but he breathed a silent sigh of relief when the town of Beaver Falls came into view three miles west of Route 10. A part of him deep within had feared it was going to be . . . gone. Melted into the ground or reduced to rubble, like in some thriller novel they sold in the discount paperback section of Wal-Mart. But it was there, faded storefronts baking in the midday sun.

A squat collection of buildings no more than three stories high formed the town center along a half-mile drag. There was a church on one side of town. A K–twelve school rested on the other. Two restaurants, a bar, post office, and bank. The parking lot adjacent to the grocery store was half-full.

Joe Langhorn snailed the squad car through the outskirts past some of the residents' homes and headed into the center of town. He pulled into a parking space in front of the sheriff's station marked RESERVED.

In the backseat Frank McBride shifted uneasily, threatening to come awake.

"Wait here," Wayne Denbo instructed.

"The fuck I will," snapped Langhorn, joining him on the hot pavement. They entered the sheriff's office one behind the other.

It was empty. A cup of coffee that had long lost its steam sat on a big desk with a SHERIFF JOHN TOULAN nameplate. A half-eaten doughnut rested next to it on a napkin. There were three other desks and a counter for the receptionist/dispatcher, all unoccupied.

"Musta left in a hurry," said Langhorn.

Wayne Denbo moved behind the counter and reached for the microphone attached to the communications base unit.

"Sheriff Toulan, this is the Arizona Highway Patrol. Come in, please. Over."

Silence.

"Sheriff Toulan, come in, please. Over."

More silence.

Langhorn and Denbo looked at each other. They started for the door.

"Maybe they're out looking for McBride," Langhorn offered.

Back outside, Denbo stiffened. "Look over there. 'Cross the street."

Langhorn followed his eyes to an old-fashioned diner called Ruby's, its interior dominated by a long counter.

"What do you see, Joe?"

"Nothing."

"Right. Even though it's lunchtime . . ."

Denbo started moving, and Langhorn followed in step. Bells jangled when the senior cop entered the diner lined by empty stools and unoccupied booths. Half of the stools had plates of breakfast food resting on the counter before them, most partially eaten. A blackboard advertised a western omelet special, and three orders with varying amounts left were set on the table in one of the booths.

Langhorn stuck his hand in a half-gone cup of coffee and swept his tongue across his fingers. "Hours old. Looks like they never got past breakfast, never mind lunch."

"Enough time maybe for Mr. McBride to walk himself across the desert?"

"What the fuck, Wayne? What the *fuck*?"

They backed out through the door. The bells jingling sounded so loud in the stillness that they startled Langhorn and he unsnapped the flap on his holster.

"Let's take a walk," Denbo suggested.

In the post office, four letters rested atop the abandoned counter. Four stamps waited nearby to be licked.

The bank, too, was empty, its floor dotted with stray forms, a few checks, and deposit slips.

At Beaver Falls' single filling station, a Chevy Cavalier waited at the pump with the nozzle from the regular slot jammed into its tank. The gas had come to an automatic stop. The Cavalier's driver's door was open, key still in the ignition and no driver to be seen.

Each window Langhorn and Denbo passed, each closed door they stopped to knock on, brought the same results: nothing.

Langhorn was palming his gun butt now, flirting with the idea of drawing it. "Where the fuck is everybody, Wayne?"

"Whatever it was musta happened fast. . . ."

"Let's just get the fuck out of—"

"If they were all together, where would they be?" Denbo asked out loud, his eyes drifting up the street toward the school.

"We got to call this in, Wayne."

"One more thing to check."

The school door closed behind them with a rattling clang. The main office was just on the right, and Wayne Denbo led the way in.

Beyond the front counter, a trio of secretaries' desks were empty.

The two highway patrolmen advanced down the narrow hall separating the offices of the principal and guidance counselors. The first three were empty as well. They continued on toward a fourth door, attracted by a dull hum emanating from a space-age Xerox machine with multiple paper slots protruding from its side. The top slot had overflowed and spit neatly printed paper everywhere. The machine's small LED readout flashed a continuous message:

PAPER OUT

The Mr. Coffee against the far wall brimmed with a steaming full pot. Three Styrofoam cups had been set out as if to await its contents.

"Nothing," Joe Langhorn said from the doorway. "Fucking nothing."

"You take the back end of the building," Wayne Denbo told him. "I'll take the front." He pulled the walkie-talkie from his belt. "Stay in touch."

Judging by the maps dangling from the front wall in the first classroom he entered, Denbo figured this must be the school's social studies section. Textbooks and notebooks lay open on unoccupied desks, some with pens dropped haphazardly upon them. What little of the blackboard the maps left exposed showed a sentence uncompleted, abandoned in the middle.

Denbo moved on to the next classroom.

Identical sheets rested atop each desk. Denbo stopped near one in the rear and hovered over the chair, as if the kid were still seated there. Social studies quiz. Twenty questions, all multiple choice. Junior high school stuff. Kid from this desk had gotten through the first nine. Denbo started thinking again about what it had been like for Frank McBride, coming home to find his whole town missing.

"Wayne?" Langhorn's voice called over the walkie-talkie.

"Here, Joe."

"I'm in one of the science labs. It stinks to high heaven down here. Got all kinds of stuff in vials and tubes left out. Instructions on the board saying what to do."

"Don't do anything. Don't touch anything," warned Denbo, worried about chemicals lingering atop desks for hours that should have been sealed tight.

"Wayne, you there?"

"Yeah, Joe."

"I'm heading your way. We're calling this in. I've had e—"

The sudden silence turned the walkie-talkie cold in Wayne Denbo's hand. He brought it back to his lips.

"Joe? Come in, Joe, come in. . . ."

No response.

"Joe!"

Denbo was already sprinting down the hall. The stink Joe Langhorn had referred to, like rotten eggs, drew him toward the science labs.

"Joe," he kept calling into his walkie-talkie. "Joe."

"*Joe.*"

His own voice bounced back at him, and Denbo looked through the door of the second lab on the right. Joe Langhorn's walkie-talkie lay faceup on the floor. Denbo backed into the corridor and drew his gun. His mouth felt like someone had papered it with Kleenex. He started running, heels clacking against the linoleum tile and contents of his gun belt bouncing up and down. He burst through the front door and reached the patrol car breathless.

In the backseat the slumped form of Frank McBride was gone.

"Jesus," he muttered, reaching in for the mike. "Base, this is Seventeen. Base, come in!"

"Go ahead, Seventeen," returned dispatcher Harvey Milkweed from the highway patrol's southern headquarters in Tucson.

Denbo breathed a quick sigh of relief. Another person's voice had never sounded so good. "I got a situation here, a major situation!"

"What's your location, Seventeen?" raised Milkweed. He'd been stuck at a desk since a brief visit to the Gulf War left him with part of a land mine stuck in his leg. Milkweed hated the desk, mixed situations. "Are you requesting backup?"

"Backup? We need the whole goddamn national guard down here in a hurry. We need— Wait a minute. . . . What the fu— Oh my God . . . Oh *my*—"

The hairs on Harvey Milkweed's neck stood on end. He leaned forward in his chair.

"Seventeen, what's going on? Seventeen, come in. . . . Denbo, what's wrong?"

He waited.

"Denbo? Denbo, come in. . . ."

There was no response, and Milkweed realized there wasn't going to be.

Wayne Denbo was gone.

PART ONE

SWITCH

CHAPTER 1

"Hey, mister, you gonna get in or what?"

Ahmed El-Salarabi moved away from the open window of the cab and clutched his briefcase against his thighs.

"In or out, okay?" the driver pestered.

El-Salarabi noted the driver's eyes drifting to the briefcase and backed quickly away from the cab.

"The hell with ya then!"

And the cab screeched off.

El-Salarabi's first thought when he saw the cab slowing toward the curb was that there had been a change in plans. But the driver must simply have mistaken the shifting of his briefcase from one hand to the other as a hailing signal. El-Salarabi quickly composed himself and began weaving his way south down a Lexington Avenue cluttered with pedestrian traffic toward Fifty-ninth Street. He had emerged from Bloomingdale's main entrance just moments before after spending the better part of the afternoon strolling the floors with apparent aimlessness. In reality, of course, his actions were anything but.

Ahmed El-Salarabi had been sent to New York with a specific task in mind: select and destroy a symbol of American opulence and power. Another group had tried to blow up the World Trade Center and failed miserably. Their failure was laughable. *Only six dead . . .* If El-Salarabi had been in charge, the outcome would have been vastly different. Successful demolitions required specialized knowledge of where to plant explosives to achieve maximum damage and effect. And his degree in engineering would have guaranteed that the charges were placed at the proper stress points to insure that the entire *building* collapsed. Any target could be brought down.

El-Salarabi's superiors had suggested the Statue of Liberty as that target, but he had persuaded them that to destroy such a symbol would only produce anger. To provoke true fear and terror, the target selected must be a highly visible part of everyday existence. El-Salarabi had spent four days last month considering various target options.

Office buildings.

High-rise apartments.

A Broadway theater maybe.

But every bystander he passed during that initial reconnaissance seemed to be holding a shopping bag. His inspiration had come when a rank, pockmarked vagrant with a Bloomingdale's bag clutched in his hand asked El-Salarabi for his spare change.

Bloomingdale's . . .

The perfect symbol of the opulence and decadence of Western society. In London the IRA had gone after Harrod's once with a similar notion in mind. Their mistake had been to leave the building standing.

Now, one month after his first trip, El-Salarabi had returned to New York determined not to repeat it.

Almost to Fifty-ninth Street, he fumed at the obtrusive presence of sidewalk salesmen hawking knockoff designer wares piled upon asphalt or tables, which further slowed his pace. El-Salarabi was thankful at least for the tinted glasses that kept the bright sun from burning into his eyes. Three straight hours strolling the floors of Bloomingdale's and mapping out the store's interior had turned them sensitive.

El-Salarabi forced himself to be patient and clutched his brown leather Gurkha briefcase closer to his side, as he prepared to follow the next stage of the plan. The briefcase contained twenty pages of jottings and sketches, scrawled hurriedly but accurately while he was sequestered in a number of rest room stalls. El-Salarabi had learned not to trust such crucial planning to memory, getting everything down while the building's layout and construction were fresh in his mind. Once his briefcase had been delivered to his liaison, his part in the scheme was finished. Others would carry out the actual bombing according to the specifications his pages detailed. Such men and women were interchangeable. They came and went. He alone was indispensable.

El-Salarabi grasped the case's handle even tighter.

He had phoned his liaison from inside Bloomingdale's itself. His instructions were to proceed south down Lexington across East Fifty-ninth Street to an outdoor fruit stand set up in front of the abandoned Alexander's department store just before Fifty-eighth Street. Rest the briefcase against his leg while he inspected the produce and his liaison would stealthily lift it away. Simple as that.

The force of sidewalk traffic shoving up uneasily against his back led El-Salarabi to disregard the DON'T WALK signal at East Fifty-ninth. He dashed across dodging traffic toward a cavalcade of hucksters pitching replicas of Louis Vuitton handbags, Gucci watches, and Armani ties.

Pedestrian traffic had thinned enough for him to slow his pace to a casual gait. The fruit stand was directly before him. The collection of oranges, grapefruits, apples, and grapes looked tempting even from this distance. Maybe he'd fill up a bag to improve his cover. Distract the clerk, if nothing else.

His part in the mission was about to come to an end.

* * *

"Shit!"

Blaine McCracken shielded his ear, as if afraid a passer-by might have heard the gravelly voice of Sal Belamo.

"Something wrong, Sal?"

"That fucker Salami just crossed Fifty-ninth against the signal, you believe that."

"Salarabi."

"Salami, bologna—it's all the same to me. Just splash on the mustard between some seeded rye and give me a pickle on the side."

"Where is he now?"

"Heading toward East Fifty-eighth, boss. Hold on, light just changed. I'm going across."

"Keep him in sight, Sal."

"He's slowing down."

"Where?"

"Fruit stand on the sidewalk at Alexander's. Just stopped in front of it," Belamo added, as he stepped back up on the Lexington Avenue sidewalk.

"Indian," McCracken called, from his position three blocks away on the west side of the block in front of a fountain.

"Moving now, Blainey," returned Johnny Wareagle, who was waiting in front of a combination deli and casual clothing shop between Fifty-seventh and Fifty-eighth Streets called Boogie's.

"Hang back, Sal. Keep your eyes on the briefcase. It's the man who picks it up we want."

"I played this game before too, MacBalls."

"Never the same way twice," McCracken cautioned. "Whoever picks up the case has got to come toward one of you."

The knowledge that El-Salarabi would surely recognize him from their last encounter forced him to keep back for now. Eighteen months before, he had been asked by a friend in Egyptian intelligence to help that organization stem the tide of terrorism that had been launched against tourists. Just hours after arriving, a report that El-Salarabi had been sighted drew him and his Egyptian escorts to Luxor. The terrorist emerged unexpectedly from a crowded mosque and came face-to-face with Blaine. Before McCracken could get a single shot off, El-Salarabi turned into a wild animal. His randomly fired bullets created a panicked rampage amidst the crowd as he bounced from hostage to hostage to keep McCracken from chancing a shot of his own. A repeat of that in the streets of New York today had to be avoided at all costs.

Two days earlier, McCracken had been contacted by an Arab informant with news that El-Salarabi had paid one visit to New York City a month before and was en route back for a second. The informant knew a major strike was about to be carried out according to the terrorist's specifications, but insisted he had no knowledge of the specifics. The only thing he did know was that El-Salarabi was staying at the Pierre Hotel. So Blaine had summoned Sal Belamo and Johnny Wareagle to New York to aid him in preempting the strike and apprehending all the parties working with El-Salarabi. Normally a dozen men would be required for such a complex task. Blaine figured the three of them together was close enough.

Belamo, the ex-middleweight boxer whose primary claim to fame was having his nose broken both times he lost to Carlos Monzon. Wareagle, the mystical seven-foot Indian with whom Blaine had fought in Vietnam and now summoned from his backwoods Maine home whenever the situation warranted. Belamo until recent years had still been active in the intelligence community, but he had freelanced once too often and been banished as a result. Fortunately for McCracken, he managed to take his contacts, which remained the best in the business, with him. Wareagle, meanwhile, never wavered from his stoic, leathery self. In the more than twenty years they had known each other, it seemed to Blaine that the big Indian hadn't changed at all.

El-Salarabi had emerged from the Pierre just before

noon and come straight to Bloomingdale's. His presence
inside for over three hours made the target for the coming
strike clear. El-Salarabi's briefcase would now contain the
building's structural layout and instructions on where to
plant the explosives for optimum effect. The plan at this
point was to wait for the pickup to be made and then en-
trap the courier in a classic bubble. If he headed north,
Johnny would move in from the rear while Belamo closed
and brought up the front. If the pickup chose south, the
roles would be reversed. Meanwhile, McCracken would
handle El-Salarabi personally after the exchange was complete.

"Salami just put the case down, boss," Belamo reported.
"Got it resting against his leg."

"Indian?"

"I'm coming up on Fifty-eighth Street now, Blainey."

"Talk to me, Sal," McCracken said into the miniature
microphone wired down his sleeve, frustrated at being detached from the action. The Motorola unit was a step
above those used by the Secret Service, featuring an independent earphone that used the jawbone as a pickup mike.
No wires that way. Secret Service men didn't care if they
stood out; McCracken could seldom afford to.

"Salami's at the fruit stand, boss," Belamo replied.
"Briefcase is still against his leg. Looks like he's picking
out oranges."

"Blainey," Johnny Wareagle whispered, "someone just
crossed Fifty-eighth Street ahead of me."

"Make him?"

"I did not see his face, only his briefcase."

"Briefcase?"

"Brown leather, high quality," the Indian explained.
"Identical to El-Salarabi's, Blainey."

"They're gonna try a switch, boys," said McCracken.
"It's show time."

Crossing East Fifty-eighth Street, Benjamin Ratansky
kept his pace slow enough not to stand out. He held his

neck rigid to keep himself from looking back so often as to draw attention. Sweat had long since soaked through his shirt.

Were they still there, lurking somewhere behind him?

Ratansky felt certain they were, although common sense told him they could not be. His lunge onto a bus just as it began to drive away should have been enough to lose *anyone*. A stop ten blocks later left him near the subway, and he rode the train to Fifty-first Street. The blocks since then had passed in a blur, his senses showing the effects of going forty-eight hours without sleep.

He had come to New York yesterday to deliver the contents of the briefcase, but his contact had failed to show up. Terrified, Ratansky had tried the phone number provided again and again without results. Then he spent the night in a run-down fleabag of a hotel on West Forty-sixth Street, sitting up through the neon-broken darkness, facing the door in a wobbly chair.

This morning the contact number continued to ring unanswered. Ratansky had elected to stay in the city, stay on the move. They might have gotten to the man he had come to New York to meet, but there would be others. His contact was not alone. Sooner or later the line would be answered.

Halfway across Fifty-eighth Street, he finally let himself turn to the rear. A pair of men had just stepped down from the curb and were weaving their way toward him. His stare met one of theirs and he swung back fast with his breath frozen in his throat.

It couldn't be, it just *couldn't be*!

It was *them*!

Not any he had seen before, no, but all the same he was certain. The briefcase trembled in his hand as he reached the other side of the street to find his progress stalled by a fruit stand that was sprawled across a good portion of the sidewalk. Would the men at his rear dare try for him amongst a crowd, or could he buy himself time by planting himself before the stand? This question at the forefront

of his mind, Ratansky's gaze captured a man bagging oranges who had laid his briefcase low against his leg.

A brown leather Gurkha, a virtual twin of his own.

His next move was decided upon in the shortest moment
his weary mind would allow. The contents of the briefcase,
after all, were *everything*. He recalled the long, torturous
minutes it took to make a hard copy from the disk. The
pages couldn't spill out of the laser printer fast enough.
His heart lurched into his throat every time the slightest
sound came from the corridor.

Ratansky had done it, though, pulled it off—all for
naught if they caught him now. The contents of the briefcase had to be salvaged, his own fate of secondary impor-
tance. If he moved fast enough, if he moved now . . .

He slid toward the tall, dark man bagging oranges and
knelt as if to retie his shoe. Barely brushing against him,
he placed his Gurkha near the man's leg and snatched the
twin case up in its place. The man looked down, and
Ratansky tried for a casual smile that wouldn't come. The
best he could do was bring his new briefcase toward him
and stiffly climb to his feet.

The switch complete, Ratansky started on again just as
his pursuers stepped up on the curb in front of the fruit
stand.

Ahmed El-Salarabi felt the slight nudge against his leg
and thought at first his contact had made the pickup. Gazing furtively downward, he saw a man fidgeting with his
shoes. Their eyes met and something about the man's stare
sent El-Salarabi's well-honed defenses screaming. He was
gone, on his way before the Arab could do anything other
than enclose his briefcase between both legs. But the damage had been done, he was certain of it.

He had been made! The enemy was on to him!

A pair of well-dressed, dead-eyed men glided through
patrons huddled before the fresh fruit. El-Salarabi dropped
his bag of oranges and lurched away from the fruit stand.

The oranges tumbled to the sidewalk. The terrorist

grabbed a wooden crate full of them and flung it at the
dead-eyed men. Not bothering to gauge the effects, he
lunged off the sidewalk straight into the center of Lexington
Avenue. Brakes squealed. One yellow cab slammed into another's rear end, forcing it into a shuddering lurch forward.
More cars screamed to a halt, and El-Salarabi rushed back
down the street between them, briefcase in hand.

"*What the fuck . . .*"
"Sal?"
"Our boy just jumped into the street, boss. Our boy's
running!"
"He made us!"
"No! It's something else, *somebody* else! Bastard emp-
tied a crate of oranges at a couple guys 'fore he bolted."
"Indian, did the man you saw with the briefcase make
the switch?"
"I couldn't see, Blainey."
"Stay with him in case. Sal, you stay on El-Salarabi."
"Already am."
"I'm on my way," McCracken said, and launched him-
self into a dash east across the center of Lexington, pre-
cious seconds ticking off in his head.
"Boss!" Sal Belamo's breathless voice cried.
"Here, Sal."
"Salami's off the street! Just ducked back inside."
"Back inside *what*?"
"Bloomingdale's," replied Belamo.

CHAPTER 2

Almost to Fifty-ninth Street, Benjamin Ratansky had turned to peer behind him when he felt the thump of impact against someone coming the other way down Lexington.

"Excuse me," he started, turning his head all the way forward just as the abominable stink assaulted him.

He found himself eye level with the chest of a man draped in a black canvas coat half-open to reveal tattered and soiled clothes beneath it. Ratansky gazed up, stunned by the man's stench, and nearly gagged. The giant's huge face was bearded and filthy. He opened his mouth for a smile that revealed rows of brown, rotting teeth marred by several spaces. He chuckled and his breath nearly toppled Ratansky over.

"Hey," Ratansky uttered when he felt the rank giant's massive hand seize his elbow. "Hey!"

The giant's hair hung in long, oily hanks across his face. The bushy clumps of his eyebrows topped yellow, jaundiced eyes; almond-shaped like a cat's. His skin was dotted with oozing boils, one of which hung at the very edge of his beaklike nose.

The giant squeezed harder, flashing what remained of his teeth.

And then Ratansky knew, felt his insides melt into powerless putty.

"No." A mutter. "No!" A gasp.

He glimpsed the dull, rusty brown blade coming forward, as worn and decayed as the giant who was wielding it.

"April is the cruelest month."

The opening line of T.S. Eliot's famed poem "The Wasteland" was recited by the vagrant in a raspy voice as the knife swished into Ratansky's stomach.

The huge figure's eyes rolled upward. As his hand jerked up on the knife to finish the kill, he spotted the shape of an Indian slicing through the clutter of the sidewalk en route to the street. The Indian's attention shifted suddenly from that path, drawn, it seemed, to the huge figure's stare.

Their eyes looked briefly, before the huge figure slipped away with his victim's briefcase clutched in his hand.

Johnny Wareagle froze for the briefest of moments, bewildered by the sight of the shapeless mass of a man twenty feet from him. He was looking into the sun and tried to blink away the impossible. In the scant few moments it took to recover his senses, the figure managed to vanish from the street.

Johnny bolted for the sidewalk, trying to determine in which direction the massive shape wrapped in filth and canvas had fled. He had caught enough of a glimpse to recognize who it was and to thus believe that his eyes must have deceived him.

Johnny was almost to the corner of Fifty-ninth Street when the bloodied figure of the man with the briefcase he had seen approaching El-Salarabi back at the fruit stand collapsed against him. Passersby lurched away, shrieking.

The man's dying eyes found Johnny's as his trembling grasp dug into the Indian's forearms.

"Judgment Day," he uttered, blood and entrails pouring from a tear straight down his abdomen. "Judgment Day."

He started to collapse. Johnny crouched to ease his drop.

"Stop them," the man rasped, eyes starting to fade as his clench on Johnny tightened. "You've got to stop—"

The man's mouth locked open, a last puff of breath emerging in place of words. Wareagle lowered him gently to the pavement. He searched the area for the brown leather briefcase and lunged back to his feet when it was nowhere to be found. He darted through the gathering crowd down Fifty-ninth Street, hoping to find the monstrous, tattered figure who must have made off with it.

Nothing. Wareagle continued his dash east, defenses sharpening at every stoop, building break, and alley.

"Johnny!" Blaine McCracken's voice shot into his ear. *"Johnny!"*

Wareagle stopped. "Here, Blainey."

"El-Salarabi just ducked back inside Bloomingdale's. Did you find the other—"

"He's dead, Blainey."

"The case, what about the case?"

"Gone."

Blaine pushed aside the confused disappointment that threatened his focus. "Well, we've still got this Arab son of a bitch, anyway. Get over here, Indian, fast as you can."

The two well-dressed figures stopped in the Sixtieth Street alley two yards from the huge man. They were frozen as much by an aura of menace as by the stench coming off him. He crouched with his head lowered, yet his yellow eyes peered up at them like those of a predator ready to pounce.

" 'Quoth the Raven,' " the voice said through dried and cracking lips. " 'Nevermore.' "

His left hand came forward with the briefcase, and one

of the figures extended his right to accept it. Both men turned away from the giant instantly. The one holding the case pulled open its zipper and yanked out the pages contained inside.

Drawings and scribbles. Schemas and plans like some disorganized architect's first draft. Utterly meaningless to them.

What had happened to the contents they had been sent to retrieve?

The two men looked at each other. At the same time they recalled the man who had without reason tossed the oranges at them back at the fruit stand and then fled with a briefcase that was a virtual twin of this one clutched in his hand. A chill surged through them.

Ratansky had managed to pull off a switch!

Whether the man who had fled the fruit stand was actually linked to him mattered not at all. What mattered was the contents of the briefcase he now possessed.

The two men scampered back to the head of Sixtieth Street in time to see some sort of commotion going on at the main entrance to Bloomingdale's directly to their left. They eyed each other briefly and then rushed for the door.

El-Salarabi's original intent upon bursting through Bloomingdale's main entrance on Lexington was to escape his pursuers by swinging to the right, down the stairs leading to the subway station that lay beneath the building. But the huge cluster of people jammed on the steps forced him to dart straight into the store instead.

He dipped down a brief set of stairs into the wood-lined Ralph Lauren Polo section of the men's department. On this and all the other floors, exits were plentiful and hiding places everywhere. He had spent the better part of the day walking the halls and aisles that separated the merchandise and individual departments. He knew every corner and crevice.

But his pursuers knew what he looked like, what he was wearing. Change those clothes and he would effectively change himself.

Yes . . . *Yes!*

Briefcase dangling from a tight grip, El-Salarabi hurried for the Levi's section, located on the far left. He had judged this to be the department's busiest area and therefore the one where he'd be least likely bothered by store salesmen. Sure enough, it was teeming with shoppers ambling about the brightly lit stacks of jeans twenty pairs high in countless styles and colors. To El-Salarabi the whole scene typified American excessiveness. How ironic that this very attribute was now going to figure prominently in his escape.

The terrorist grabbed a pair of stonewashed jeans off one of the stacks and a plaid shirt from a rack squeezed tight with them. Recalling from his schema the alcove where the fitting rooms were located, he hurried over and ducked into a cubicle.

He closed and bolted the door behind him, then shed his clothes frantically. He pulled the jeans and shirt on in their place and wedged his Browning nine-millimeter pistol into the waistband, making sure the plaid shirt covered it. He had stooped to retrieve the briefcase when the thump of footsteps racing his way made him draw his hand away from the handle and reach for his gun.

Sal Belamo was waiting just inside Bloomingdale's main entrance when Blaine McCracken charged through the door. Until less than two minutes ago, the operation had gone smooth as silk. Then, inexplicably, everything had turned into a jumble that had him fearing the worst was yet to come, his mind rife with memories of what had transpired in Luxor the last time he had crossed paths with El-Salarabi.

"Security guard saw a man looked like our boy head that way," Sal reported, eyes gesturing toward the men's department. "You ask me, he's looking to change his wardrobe."

Blaine nodded. "Let's see if we can catch him with his pants down."

He led the way through the Ralph Lauren Polo section of Bloomingdale's men's department, stopping next to Belamo just after the Joseph Abboud and Nautica displays.

"Where to now, boss?"

Blaine was about to suggest they split up when a trio of Bloomingdale's security guards in blue blazers charged past the stacks of Calvin Klein underwear and socks on their left.

"What the fuck?" Sal wondered.

He and Blaine fell in behind the group of guards and raced with them toward the Levi's section, where another three guards were approaching the alcove containing the fitting rooms.

"Shit," Blaine muttered.

He sensed what was coming an instant before Ahmed El-Salarabi emerged from a cubicle with pistol blazing. Two of the store security guards fell instantly. The others managed to dive aside as the terrorist surged into the blitz of customers scattering in all directions.

Pistols out now, Blaine and Sal shoved forward through the clutter of panic in their path. El-Salarabi was starting to angle for the nearest escalator when he saw them coming. Desperately he jammed the handles of his briefcase over his left hand so it dangled from his wrist, then lunged forward and grabbed the long hair of a young man who had tripped over a spilled pile of denim shorts. In the next instant, El-Salarabi's gun barrel was pressed against the youth's temple.

McCracken and Belamo froze when they saw him jerk the kid's head backward. The terrorist's eyes locked on Blaine.

"*McCracken!* I should have guessed it was you. . . ."

Blaine's SIG Sauer was trained dead on him, no reluctance to use it shown in the black pools of his eyes.

"Let him go, El-Salarabi."

The Arab had been about to drag his hostage a step sideways. Now he held his ground, yanked the hair closer to him.

"Stay where you are or he dies! I'll do it, you know I will."

McCracken shook his head. "This isn't Luxor."

"I'll kill him!"

McCracken held his ground and sighted down the SIG's muzzle. "Not this time."

In the instant before Blaine's finger pulled the trigger, a burst of automatic fire rang out, stitching a jagged design across the entire Levi's department. A mirror just to his right exploded, and Blaine dove to the floor. His first thought was that these unseen gunmen had come to the terrorist's rescue. But as he looked up, he saw that El-Salarabi had barely managed to avoid the spray from the same barrage. The kid he had grabbed for a hostage had been able to spin out of the Arab's grasp and dive to the side out of the line of fire. Clearly these gunmen weren't allied with El-Salarabi.

Then who were they?

McCracken's mind worked feverishly, assimilating his data. At the fruit stand, El-Salarabi had fled from two mystery men in a mad dash that had brought him back inside Bloomingdale's. Then, barely seconds later, the man who had switched briefcases with the terrorist had been killed on the street by person or persons unknown. A third party was obviously at work here, then, not just Blaine's and El-Salarabi's. What, though, was their stake in this? Beyond that, why was El-Salarabi still clinging to a briefcase that should have been nothing more than a prop?

Blaine chanced a rise in search of a bead on El-Salarabi. But another burst of automatic fire forced him to duck once more. This burst was instantly followed by a quick series of shots from the Arab. Sal Belamo spun out from his position of cover to answer that fire, but a bullet from the new parties in the rear slammed into his shoulder and pitched him sideways. He went down and took a hanging display of cotton shirts with him.

The pair of mystery gunmen burst forward, heavy steps clumping against the wood floor. McCracken twisted away from the partition to cover Belamo.

His eyes found Johnny Wareagle rushing out behind the mystery men. Johnny fired at the same time Blaine did, taking them totally by surprise. One's head snapped back and then forward as bullets blew it apart. The other man twirled away and fired nonstop in a wide arc that sprayed fire from McCracken to Wareagle. Blaine and Johnny rolled toward fresh cover, opening up a path for El-Salarabi to charge toward a Tommy Hilfager display with the surviving mystery gunman in pursuit.

Instinctively both Blaine and Johnny rushed to Sal Belamo. His left shoulder was dripping blood, and a grimace of pain stretched across his features.

"Go get the fucks, boss," Belamo huffed, kneeling in a splatter of his own blood to pop a fresh speed loader into his .44 magnum.

Blaine looked up at Wareagle. "Where'd they go, Indian?"

"Toward an escalator leading to the next level down, Blainey."

"The subway!" McCracken realized, back on his feet fast.

Ahmed El-Salarabi thundered across the women's department and through one of the glass doors leading into the subway stop beneath Bloomingdale's, briefcase flapping against his side. The jeans he had pulled on, even cuffed, were much too long, and they sagged low at the waist. His shirt, tags and all, hung clumsily over them. Confusion plagued him. The identities of the gunmen he had glimpsed on the street and then narrowly escaped upstairs remained a total mystery. El-Salarabi's initial thought upon confronting McCracken in the men's department was that they had been part of his team. But when their fire included the infidel in its spray, this assumption was proven wrong.

The terrorist hurdled over the turnstile without inserting his token, nearly snagging the bottoms of his too long jeans on steel in the process.

"Hey!" screamed a transit worker.

El-Salarabi turned only long enough to fire at the man before he could offer pursuit. A train was rolling to a halt before him. The doors hissed open. Before El-Salarabi could enter the train, though, a barrage of automatic fire shattered the subway car window just to his right. The terrorist dropped to his knees and tried to use the cover of the panicked throng about him to slide along the train's length toward the next door. It closed just before he reached it. The train started to move. El-Salarabi rose to a crouch and searched frantically for his assailant.

A stitch of automatic fire sliced into his midsection and jolted him backward. He slammed into the rolling train as it gathered speed and hung there briefly before the momentum pitched him back onto the platform. The gunman rushed over and reached down for the briefcase still in his grasp.

Before he could pry it from the terrorist's death grip, Blaine and Johnny burst into the station with pistols spitting fire. The mystery gunman tried to reach his Mac-10, but bullets from both their guns thumped into his chest and midsection before he could grab it. Impact threw him backward down onto the tracks. McCracken reached the edge of the platform and fixed his gun upon the figure sprawled limply ten feet below, keeping it steady until satisfied the man was dead.

Johnny Wareagle, meanwhile, had unzipped the briefcase peeled from El-Salarabi's death grip and withdrawn its contents. He scanned the first few pages before gazing over at McCracken.

"You better have a look at these, Blainey."

CHAPTER 3

"They're ready for you, Dr. Raymond."

Karen Raymond gathered the bound reports from her lap and rested the videocassette atop them. Steadying herself with a final deep breath, she rose and started for the conference room.

Gentlemen, the Jardine-Marra Company is now in possession of what may be the greatest discovery in the history of medical science . . .

She had considered a hundred different opening lines for her presentation and summarily rejected them all. This was a moment she, along with the entire pharmaceutical and medical communities, had been anticipating for more than a decade. Dashed hopes and unrealistic expectations had marred those years for hundreds of research teams working for dozens of companies and institutions that dwarfed JM, not to mention the government itself. The best scientific minds in the business had been applied to this problem. That the solution might come from a pharmaceutical company too small to make anything but the daily NASDAQ small-capital listings was nearly inconceivable.

Jardine-Marra was located, appropriately enough, diagonally across from the Salk Institute in Torrey Pines Industrial Park. Situated in northern La Jolla, in actuality a part of San Diego, Torrey Pines contains a large number of biotech firms of the cutting edge of current technology. JM was the only pharmaceutical representative in the group, and up until today, perhaps the most innocuous of all the occupants.

Halfway to the conference room, Karen caught her own reflection in a mirror-glass piece of modern art hanging from the wall. She had mulled over her choice of outfits today longer and harder than even her opening line, ultimately settling on a conservative gray tweed suit. She questioned now leaving her hair down and tumbling instead of tying it up in a more conservative fashion. Her normal hairstyle made her look almost too youthful, more a graduate assistant than a research head. She also thought it might have been wise to forsake her contact lenses for glasses. She reflected that perhaps even her athletic, well-muscled frame might work against her, a look achieved only by daily workouts on her exercise machines no matter how tired she might be after putting her two sons to bed.

Nonsense, she thought. This wouldn't be the first time she had addressed JM's directors, after all; only the first time she had been responsible for summoning them together.

The seven-man board, nary a woman, rose as their director of research and product development entered the room.

"I'm sorry we kept you waiting," the company president, Alexander MacFarlane, greeted, stepping over to meet her near the door.

MacFarlane seemed to have been chiseled out of this very boardroom where he held court. His suits were inevitably brown, olive, or taupe, the dominant shades of the walls, floor, furniture, even the Oriental rug on which the conference table was perched. He was tall and lean, graceful for his years, with teeth bright enough to be a school-boy's. The furniture in the boardroom was for the most part antique, any nicks and scratches carried as furrows of experience rather than scars, just like the creases on Mac-Farlane's face. The table itself was rich mahogany, the chairs squared and heavy.

Alexander McFarlane had picked each piece out person-ally, testaments to his belief in substance. He approached the hiring of personnel with the same commitment, which meant meeting with each potential employee. It was Mac-Farlane who had brought Karen into the company, and he had personally overseen her advancement. Any number of companies had expressed initial interest based strictly on her academic record. But a shaky personal life that left her rais-ing two small boys by herself turned all of them away from offering her a high-level position, with the exception of MacFarlane at JM. She had come to the company eight years before. Hard work and proven results had led to steady advancement, culminating in her being named chief of the research and development department eighteen months ago. Alex's refusal to consider any other applicant despite the board's recommendations was about to be vindi-cated.

Dr. Karen Raymond tightened her grip on the set of seven half-inch binders and curled her fingers over the boxed videocassette.

"Thank you for coming on such short notice, gentle-men," she greeted. "It couldn't be helped, I'm afraid. But in a few minutes I'm sure you'll agree the trip was well worth it."

Chairman of the Board Roger Updike, who had been the primary opponent to her promotion, shifted uneasily. Updike was a stocky, big-faced man who for some reason continued to comb hairs that looked to be in the single digits across the top of his head. The effect, coupled with the ever-present frown on his face, reminded Karen of the villainous Simon Bar Sinister character from the "Under-dog" cartoon her younger son watched daily.

Eyeing him subtly, Karen reached the head of the conference table and stopped. The VCR was set up immediately to the right on a shelf beneath a thirty-two-inch Sony Trinitron. She rested the videocassette atop it and distributed the black Velobound reports down each side of the table, one to every member.

"You have before you the results of five years of research I initiated and have continued to supervise in my new capacity," she announced.

The men, none of them chemists other than MacFarlane and having only a rudimentary understanding of the field, flipped through the pages, barely comprehending what was before them.

"My God," muttered Alexander MacFarlane, eyes bulging as he read the contents of the third page.

"Pages three through seven accurately summarize the results of the study," Karen continued. "In a nutshell, gentlemen, Jardine-Marra is now in possession of a vaccine for HIV, the virus that causes AIDS."

The men's mouths dropped as one. A few flipped quickly to the first page in question, adjusting their glasses. The rest simply sat there in dumbstruck amazement.

"Why weren't we advised of this earlier?" demanded Roger Updike.

"You were," Karen told him. "I have issued quarterly reports for the past four years on our progress with developing an AIDS vaccine. If you recall, my yearly report detailed the rather impressive results of our testing on chimpanzees."

Updike's eyes darted up from the summary material on page seven of the report before him. "Indeed. But at the same time I seem to recall that the federal government didn't think much of the direction you were proceeding and refused to fund the project further."

Karen swallowed hard. "I was able to find alternative methods to fund the preliminary human-stage testing."

"I'll take responsibility for that," Alexander MacFarlane interjected. "Dr. Raymond came to me with a bare-bones budget to pursue the project, and I approved it."

"Without our consent, obviously," Updike snapped.

"I didn't feel it was necessary to inform you."

"And neither did you feel it necessary to keep us updated on the progress of the project."

"On my insistence," Karen said firmly. "I elected to hold that information back from all of you, including Mr. MacFarlane, as a matter of security."

"Security?" raised Updike, veins pulsing along his temples.

"Until we were sure, you understand."

"No, Dr. Raymond, I don't."

"We had to avoid leaks at all costs," Karen told him. "Unwelcome scrutiny would have burdened us with more attention than we could afford as we took Lot 35 to the human testing stage."

"Lot 35?" Updike questioned.

"That's the clinical name we have given to the vaccine."

"Actually," Alexander McFarlane corrected, "vaccine *candidate* at this stage."

"A very good candidate, though," Karen said, a slight layer of defensiveness lacing her voice. "The results are all there before you, but let me summarize them. We gave the vaccine to thirty healthy volunteers. Twenty-seven of these developed antibodies that neutralized the AIDS virus in test tubes. Furthermore, we observed no significant side effects in the volunteers themselves."

Karen moved to the VCR and popped in the tape she had brought with her.

"Alex, if you could get the lights, please . . ."

MacFarlane flipped switches until the only light was the glow off the television. The screen went black briefly and then lit up with what might have been a scene from a science fiction film; dozens of pinkish gray forms battling for space amidst a black grid.

"What you are about to see, gentlemen, is a computer

simulation of how HIV invades the system," Karen narrated. "Each of the forms displayed before you represents a cell. The virus has to be able to bond to a cell in order to multiply and spread."

Suddenly on the screen small blue shapes appeared. They slid about between the digitized cells like characters in a video game, ultimately lodging themselves against the outer walls of perhaps a quarter of the pinkish gray cellular forms and then slowly penetrating them.

"We have known for some time," Karen continued, "that the HIV virus will bind to certain cell shapes before others."

"But all these look the same," interrupted Roger Updike.

"I was speaking of *molecular* shape and composition, Mr. Updike, not physical structure. It's nothing you can actually see and, until very recently, even were able to detect." She turned toward the screen, where all the blue invaders had found homes within the pinkish gray cellular forms. "We thought the invasion process was simply random. The discovery that something far more specific and identifiable was going on became the launching point for our research. As you can see in this computer-enhanced demonstration, the infection spreads by reproducing itself in the cell and then entering the blood once the cell dies. But if it were trapped in the receptor and couldn't get out, then the virus would be rendered impotent. And we know there are many more receptors than free virus in the blood."

As if on cue, the screen changed to a fresh scene of untouched cells. This time forms outlined in white had joined the pinkish gray shapes in battling for position across the black grid. Karen waited silently for another wave of blue simulated HIV viral capsules to make their appearance, repeating the same swimming dance as before. This time, though, the only cells they lodged against were the ones outlined in white.

"The white forms that the HIV has bonded to this time are modified human blood cells," she explained, "modified to contain attached receptors that mimic the molecular structure that HIV is unalterably most attracted to. But since they contain no DNA, there is no way for HIV to reproduce—a deadend. In essence, we defeat the virus by tricking it. Once injected, our vaccine produces the mimic receptors that attach to the red blood cells, which then act like magnets for any HIV cells entering the body. If infection does occur, it can't reproduce and thus it can't spread."

Karen hit STILL and the picture froze in place. "This is an offshoot of the Trojan horse approach that's been tried unsuccessfully in the past with AIDS vaccines, both preventative and therapeutic. Because the federal government saw our methods as just another variation, they refused further funding. I admit it was a long shot. All the hard work aside, the bottom line is we got lucky."

"So did Salk with polio," MacFarlane reminded.

"Are you saying Lot 35 is actually a therapeutic vaccine as well as a preventative one?" asked a third director, the youngest on the board.

"I'm afraid not. Our research has found that once HIV begins its rampant invasion of the body through the blood, its virulence is such that it is no longer limited to a narrow choice of receptor shapes. Any, in fact, will do, so the Trojan horse approach would have only a limited impact."

"But what you are saying," picked up a suddenly conciliatory Roger Updike, "is that Lot 35 never gives the virus a chance to get that far in previously uninfected subjects."

"In fact, Lot 35 never gives HIV a chance to get anywhere at all. Keep in mind, gentlemen, that this is a treacherous disease we're dealing with, treacherous because it doesn't play by the normal rules. A vaccine that tests positive in one person may not in another because of the infinite number of forms the virus is capable of taking on. But the principles Lot 35 was founded on suggest it will work on *all* of them, because Lot 35 lets, actually encourages, the virus in any form to do what it does best:

bond to the cells it is most attracted to." She paused long enough to swing her gaze about the men before her. "I called you all here today because, in spite of all this, we still lack the hard documentation needed to change the government's mind about further funding for this project. Proceeding thus means doing so on our own."

"Entailing . . ."

"Entailing, Mr. Updike, a large-scale study involving in the area of one thousand test subjects."

"Timetable?"

"Eighteen months before we could present the necessary documentation to the FDA."

"Cost?"

Karen didn't waver. "Seventy-five million dollars."

The members of the board of directors traded uneasy glances.

"That's a tremendous amount of money for us to come up with, Doctor," Updike said. "Failure on your part could mean the bankrupting of Jardine-Marra."

"And success could mean a hundredfold profits for the next decade. The seventy-five million is simply an investment."

"More like a gamble."

"The most lucrative investments often are."

Updike traded glances with the other directors and then with Alexander MacFarlane. "Could you excuse us briefly, Dr. Raymond? . . ."

Briefly turned out to be nearly an hour. Updike had taken the chair at the head of the table when Karen reentered the room.

"Fifty million, Doctor," he said, somewhat reluctantly, as she faced him. "That's the best we can do."

Karen Raymond left the boardroom physically and emotionally drained. It seemed as though a great weight had at last been lifted from her shoulders, a lifelong struggle coming to an end.

She had been struggling against something for as long

as she could remember. First there was the struggle to get the best grades in high school to win a scholarship to college. But when Brown University accepted her, she couldn't say no even though their financial aid offer came up significantly short of what she needed. Her next struggle became working to help support herself. As an undergraduate this meant several school-sponsored jobs, but as a graduate student she was offered a position as a teaching assistant to help her make ends meet.

Karen did her doctoral work at Columbia, and that was where she met Tom. She had been so lonely and starved for affection for so long that she must have worn her vulnerability like a collar, because he leashed her hard and fast. He was finishing his final year in the school of film when they met, certain that a brilliant future as a screenwriter and then as director lay before him. He was undeniably brilliant, but equally mercurial. His disordered thinking, the wonderfully creative chaos of his mind, drew Karen to him instantly. He was her antithesis, and that allowed him to bring alive in her a part she had forgotten could exist.

Karen fell hopelessly in love.

She did not lose sight of her work and career; she simply had something else in view as well. When Tom graduated a year ahead of her, she agreed to move with him to California and enrolled at UCLA. Its program wasn't Columbia's, but it would do. Besides, Tom was making good money doing freelance work: selling some options and a few television episodes. Making the right contacts. Seeing the right people. They lived spartanly enough in a nice studio apartment in Westwood, and on Sundays they would sometimes stroll about Beverly Hills trying to pick out the house they would someday buy. They got married six months into their life together. Making it big, all the way to the top, seemed inevitable. For Karen the constant struggle at last seemed on the verge of ending.

Instead, the most painful struggles were just beginning. Not long after their wedding, she returned home to find Tom cradling himself in the middle of the living room with a nearly empty bottle of Jack Daniel's between his knees. She had just come from the doctor's office, where he confirmed she was pregnant. She was thinking of putting off school for a while anyway. The timing couldn't have been better.

Or worse, as it turned out.

The truth emerged as Tom sat there rocking on the rug. He had not sold a single script or been paid so much as a dollar since they had come to Hollywood. All his achievements had been fabrications and lies. The money he brought home came courtesy of a trust fund left him by a grandparent. The parents he had tearfully told her had died years before were only estranged; they had thrown him out and cut him off years before. The trust fund had got him through school and financed his honest attempt at building a writing career. But now it was gone, all gone.

In retrospect, Karen should have ended things there and then. Except there was the baby to consider and, more, her own romantic ingenuousness. In spite of everything, the lies and tales, she convinced herself that Tom Mitchell was still the man she had loved and married. Her need for affection, coupled with the fear of being plunged once more into a life of aloneness, made her believe that she could salvage the relationship. In another year her doctoral work would be complete and she could begin what would eventually be a lucrative career. If in the meantime Tom could hold down any job at all, they could get by.

It was a good plan, but it was doomed from the beginning. For one thing, her difficult pregnancy forced her to postpone her schooling indefinitely. For another, she failed to consider the depth of her husband's problems. The lies continued. He couldn't keep a job for longer than a single month and dove headfirst into the bottle each time he quit or got fired.

She transferred to the University of California at San Diego and they moved south, first to a run-down apartment and then a trailer park in Sanpee, where their closest neighbors were the members of a motorcycle gang called

the Skulls. Hard chords and riffs of rock music dominated
the day and night, intermixed with the revving nightmare
of chopper bikes coming and going. Karen's first son, Taylor, was born in the spring, and eight months later, thanks
to a faulty diaphragm, she was pregnant again.

Again, in retrospect, she seemed so stupid. Why had she
put up with Tom Mitchell for as long as she had, long after
he revealed himself as a ne'er-do-well, a do-nothing? Just
having him there was a comfort, she supposed, although it
was difficult today to understand why. By the time her
second son, Brandon, was born, she was inching her way
through her doctoral work. She waitressed at a local restaurant to put food on her own table while Tom tried to get
back to his writing. His talent had never been in question,
and seeing him at least taking a stab at productivity made
the day easier to get through. The arrangement enabled
Tom to care for the kids, while she worked and studied.

The end came abruptly on a day she returned home to
the trailer to find both babies crying and her older son,
Taylor, bloodied and bruised. Tom tried to explain it away
with his usual lies, but this time she wasn't buying the
tale. The argument that followed must have risen above
even the Skulls' music, because the door burst open just as
Tom was about to strike her for the second time. A huge
shape decked out in black stood in the threshold, had to
duck to step up inside.

"This punk givin' you trouble, miss?"

The man's oversized lips barely moved as he spoke. A
black beret stretched tightly over his massive scalp, adding
to the menace of his bearded, bearlike face.

"Mind your own fucking business."

If Tom hadn't said that, he might have turned and left.
As it was, Karen saw the slightest of smiles cross the
biker's face. He advanced deliberately forward, his leather
chaps cracking and creaking, boots clip-clopping across
the trailer's cheap tile floor.

He was the biggest man she had ever seen!

Tom's eyes followed him meanly the whole way. Liquor fueled his courage and he wasn't backing down.

"Get the fuck out!"

"Sure, mister."

The biker closed the last of the way in a quick surge and fastened his hands over Tom's shirt. Tom was airborne in the next instant, looking like a rag doll. He slammed into the folding utility table upon which rested his useless Smith-Corona Typetronic, and spilled over it into a pile of crumpled pages lying in a heap on the floor.

When he staggered to his feet, the biker threw him against the wall. His back hit with a thud and he slumped down. The biker looked over at Karen.

"You want me to kill him?"

"No," she managed, the flatness of his question unnerving her.

The biker stole a glance at the two wailing babies in their cribs. "I throw him out, he might come back."

"No," she repeated. "No, I don't think he will."

The biker looked briefly at Tom. He smiled, showing gaps where some teeth had been. The smile was the coldest gesture she had ever seen. Karen shuddered.

"Yeah. I think you're right."

Tom made it upright again, using the wall for support.

"Get out," the biker ordered in that same soft, immovable voice. "Don't bother packing."

Tom's feet fumbled toward the door. He stopped to lean against a second utility table they used to eat their meals on, looked at Karen, but didn't speak. Then he pulled himself through the still open doorway and disappeared into the night past a crowd of bikers drawn there by sounds of the brawl.

It was the last time she ever saw Tom, but hardly the last time she ever saw the big biker. His name was T.J. Fields, but everyone called him Two-Ton. He'd been an Olympic-class power lifter until his knee gave out, after which he tried a stint as a professional wrestler. Trouble was, he didn't like losing on purpose. He put up with it for a time until a match he was supposed to tank to a little gymnastic squirt who called himself the Tumbler. The Tumbler hit him in the groin by accident, and when the crowd cheered, he slammed him there again on purpose. As soon as T.J. got his breath back, he took the Tumbler apart. Literally. Dislocated both his shoulders, redesigned his nose, and left him with a mouthful of teeth to spit out onto the mat. Then he stepped out of the ring without even bothering about the pin. The three-count just didn't seem important.

T.J. and the other Skulls, under the leadership of their limping, ageless founder, Papa Jack, adopted Karen and her kids as their own. After some coaxing, she agreed to let some of the women who rode with the gang take care of the boys so she could devote her time more fully to her studies. As a result she managed to finally complete her doctoral work and landed an excellent starting position at Jardine-Marra, thanks to Alexander MacFarlane. The Skulls never asked anything of her and refused to accept any form of compensation once she began to earn real money.

The day she moved out of that Sanpee trailer park for the first of their three real homes was one of the saddest of her life. She might have stayed longer, except Taylor was ready to start kindergarten and there was no nearby school decent enough to suit her tastes. Of course, the Skulls again offered their assistance, but the thought of her boys being chauffeured on the back of Harleys was a bit much for even her to take.

She stayed in touch with T.J. and the others regularly for a while. Lately, though, it hadn't been more than once a year, if that. Since her work on Lot 35 had come full circle, there had been little time to think of anything else. Yet somehow she had felt better about leaving her boys with leather-clad biker moms than with the endless succession of day-care centers and baby-sitters that had followed. The long hours her position demanded left her with few to be at home.

The baby-sitter of this month took her leave as soon as Karen stepped in the door of her house in the North City West sector of Del Mar, a bustling development of high-

end tract homes layered across private cul-de-sacs on the
east side of the freeway. The easy five-mile commute from
Jardine-Marra's offices in Torrey Pines inevitably made
her reflect back on the maddening rush-hour rides into
UCSD from Sanpee across divided highways and two-lane
dinosaurs that begged for accidents. And yet, and yet . . .

"Mommy!"

Ten-year-old Brandon's hug remained tight as ever, but
she counted herself lucky on those days Taylor had one for
her as well. Now that he was almost twelve, hugging his
mother was on the to-be-phased-out list. That in itself
wouldn't have been so bad if it weren't for how much he
looked like his father. He had Tom's dark eyes and sultry
features. Every time she looked at him lately, she saw his father and felt the vulnerability he had revealed in her. Taylor
knew how to wrap her around his finger, just as Tom had, to
get a third chance when he plainly didn't deserve a second.

My God, how many did I give Tom?

People don't really change, she supposed. She hadn't
and certainly Tom hadn't. Her greatest fear for ten years
now had been that he would walk back into her life and
she wouldn't have the courage to throw him out.

And T.J. Fields wasn't around anymore to come to her
rescue.

Get out. . . . Don't bother packing.

She sometimes wondered if it would come to that with
Taylor. She didn't approve of his friends, his clothes, or
the way he was letting his wavy black hair grow rock-star
long. Yet she hadn't been around enough these past few
months to voice her disapproval. Being fair under the circumstances meant trusting him. And trusting him meant
resisting the temptation to smell his shirts for the pungent
after-stench of marijuana, or inspecting the various zip-
pered compartments of his black leather jacket to see what
they might contain.

"Any homework?" she asked, while he sat perched in
front of the thirty-five-inch Mitsubishi.

"Done," he replied.

"Dinner?"

"Ate."

"Any of your answers gonna expand beyond a single word?"

"No," he said, wryly, the glint in his eyes showing for a moment before they returned to the television.

"You could ask me how my day was."

"Yeah." Still wry, liking it.

"So go ahead."

His barely twelve-year-old face changing, softening, looking at her as though the television at last weren't there. "I need a new computer."

"Really?"

"The new Mac. Color monitor. The one that talks."

"More than one word at a time, I hope."

"I'm being serious."

"And talking in sentences now ..."

"Mom!" Taylor slammed the arm of the couch in feigned exasperation.

"Oops. Back to one word at a time."

She left the room to help Brandon with the Ben & Jerry's he was scooping out. Somehow it was important for Karen to leave the den, if not in charge, then at least ahead. She supposed she would do anything to make sure Taylor didn't grow up to be like his father, but she was unsure of exactly what that "anything" should be. One thing she could do was trust him, yet first she had to trust herself.

Brandon still liked being read to, and exhausted, Karen dozed off in his bed to the mild strains of heavy metal coming from Taylor's room down the hall. She awoke finally with a start in the midst of what must have been a nightmare. She lurched upward, feeling as though she had brought it out of unconsciousness with her, heart pounding and breath caught deep in her throat.

Karen got up from the bed slowly and came alert. *Something* had awoken her, a sound, a voice. Taylor maybe, trying to sneak out to join his friends. She moved to

Brandon's window, which overlooked the front of the house.

Down on the lawn, both of the lights that automatically burned all night were out. They were photocells, no inside switches to be bothered with. Besides, she told herself, Taylor had never sneaked out of the house in the past anyway.

There had been a sound. That was what had woken her.
A thunk, light and crisp. Like glass breaking.

Karen pressed herself closer to the window, heart hammering anew. The outside lights were too far away to glimpse clearly, too far away to—

Something or someone was moving on the lawn, a mere shadow set against a background turned utterly black by the loss of light.

Standing at the window, Karen strained her eyes, trying to see through the dark. The night gave up nothing. The figure might have been there; it might not have been.

She crept away from the window and moved for Brandon's door. Wide-awake now, the adrenaline flowing. She moved into the hall and through the door to her bedroom, where a single light burned on the nightstand upon which she kept a phone. She snatched the receiver to her ear, fingers ready to pound out 911.

There was no dial tone.

The phone was dead.

CHAPTER 4

Karen jiggled the switch hook to no avail. Only silence came from the receiver.

Her backup was the house's elaborate alarm system, and she hurried to the keypad on the wall outside her room. Press the two bottom corner keys and a panic signal would have the police here in under three minutes. More, unlike traditional alarms, hers contained a backup power supply and radio transmitter that would insure its operation even after the phone lines had been cut or deactivated. Karen placed her fingers against the two symbols in the bottom corners and pressed, flinching involuntarily against the anticipated shrill piercing sound that would follow.

There was no sound; only silence again.

Karen's fear gave way to panic. She was still thinking, but her thoughts veered chaotically, tumbling against each other. The front door and lock system were also the best available. Not impenetrable to a professional but certainly presenting a difficult and time-consuming obstacle.

From downstairs came a soft noise like a click. Something working the door latch or scratching against window glass.

Karen stood absolutely still, her orderly mind taking over. First and foremost, there were the boys to consider. Get them to safety or the closest thing that amounted to it, under the circumstances. But there was no second-floor exit, no convenient tree to leap out onto through an open window. There was only the single staircase.

Back in Brandon's room, she cradled his sleeping form and raised it from the bed. He stirred slightly, moaning. Karen moved past the window and caught the shadow of more movement on the lawn below: several shapes this time, two at least.

Brandon came awake in Karen's arms as she hustled him into the hallway toward Taylor's room.

"Mom . . ."

As Karen opened Taylor's door, she heard several muffled popping sounds coming from downstairs, immediately followed by the distinctive crackles of glass giving way.

"Mommmmmmmmmm . . ."

Brandon fought her grasp, his voice cranky and whining.

"Shhh!" Karen followed, hoping he didn't notice her fear.

Taylor lay atop his bedcovers in sweatpants and a Metallica T-shirt, a pair of stereo headphones draped over his ears. Lowering Brandon to the floor, she pulled the headphones off and shook him awake.

"What?" he started.

Karen covered his lips. "Someone's downstairs. Take your brother and—" She was about to say hide in the closet, but her thoughts veered in midstream. They could not hide from what was invading their home; it was after them, it wanted *them*. Thieves did not usually disable phone and alarm systems before launching their intrusions. Thieves, in fact, most often fled if the front door would not yield quickly and easily before them.

"Take your brother and stay by the door. Keep it open a crack and wait until I call for you. Understand?"

After a moment, Taylor nodded. Karen couldn't remember the last time he had looked so innocent and childlike. She slid reluctantly away as he snapped upward in bed. Turning back one last time at the door, she pressed a finger against her lips. Taylor nodded as he tried to bring Brandon all the way awake.

Karen was back in the corridor, cursing herself for the fear and loathing she felt for guns. If she had a well-practiced one in the house, a means of defense would be hers. As it was, she needed something in its place, a weapon where none existed.

But weapons existed in every home, recognized by anyone who had spent a portion of her life around chemicals.

The sounds downstairs continued, soft and muted. Not even two minutes had passed from the first glimpse she had caught of the shadow on her lawn, to this moment when Karen entered the boys' bathroom and opened its vanity. The liquid drain cleaner was just where she remembered, the plastic container resting near a small white pail. Karen rolled the plastic container and found it to be just over half-full.

Plenty.

Working fast now, she emptied all of the drain cleaner into the white pail. Then she stuck the pail under the faucet and added a few ounces of water to create an acid compound, turning her face away to avoid the fumes.

She held the pail low by her hip for safety when she slid back into the corridor. She passed Taylor's room to find him staring out through a crack in the door, his brother a huddled, shivering form beneath him.

Mom, he mouthed.

Karen nodded as confidently as she could manage and kept going. Her eyes gestured toward the stairs, and the boy noticed the pail in her hand, grasping her intent when he caught a whiff of its contents.

She pressed against the wall near the top of the staircase. Moonlight shining down from the large skylight flickered off an approaching shadow. At least one figure was ascending, the sound of his steps swallowed by the thick Oriental runner that climbed the length of the staircase.

Karen neared the end of the wall and clearly heard the muffled sounds just passing the halfway point of the staircase. Above her the trees looming over the skylight shifted beneath the moon and a pair of shadows a step apart shifted with them.

Karen started to bring the pail upward and spun away from the wall. She faced the dark shapes of the invaders and tossed the contents at them, high for their faces. The great portion landed on target with a splashing sound that was instantly replaced by piercing screams of anguish, as the acid burned into their eyes.

"Taylor!" Karen cried out, turning back toward her sons.

He had charged into the hall with Brandon in tow when the screams began. She turned back to the stairs to find the two men staggering and stumbling, screeching horribly as they clawed about their faces. The guns had dropped from their hands. The men bounced madly from the wall to the railing on the staircase's open side. Their wails intensified, no relief found from the acid which was eating away at their flesh the same way it chewed through a drain clog.

Karen lifted Brandon in one arm and grabbed hold of Taylor's wrist in her free hand. They started down the stairs as a clumsy trio, trying to avoid the desperately groping hands of the now blinded men who had invaded their home. One of them managed to latch on to Taylor's ankle as he surged past.

"Mom!" he cried, pulling free at the expense of their balance.

Karen kept hold of Brandon but lost her own footing in the process. Her ankle turned painfully. Her shoulder rammed against the railing and she felt a fierce stab as though a nail had been driven through it. She touched down at the bottom of the stairs and nearly tripped again on one of the still-shrieking gunmen's silenced pistols. Still she clung to her senses, flailed out in search of Taylor with her good arm.

"I'm here!" he yelled. "Lean on me!"

She lowered Brandon to the floor, then, hanging on Taylor's shoulder, started for the front door.

Before they could reach it, his small frame gave under her weight, and they both tumbled to the hall carpet. The fall actually saved both of them from a three-shot barrage fired from inside the living room where the invaders had made their entrance. A third figure stormed forward, the muzzle of his semiautomatic gleaming dully in the darkness.

Karen heard Brandon sob, and sensed that Taylor had yanked him to one side as she dove to the other. She landed almost on top of the gun she had accidently kicked aside upon reaching the bottom of the stairs. Her experience with shooting was meager, limited to a pair of trips to a range when she had contemplated buying a gun.

Shoot and keep shooting. Don't stop. . .

The instructor's advice returned to her as she scooped up the nine-millimeter pistol. She fired before she was ready, before she could even aim. Squeezed the trigger and kept squeezing. The cartridges coughed back at her and stung her face. The first few shots had left her thumb sticking out behind the hammer, but Karen didn't feel the stinging pain until the muzzle locked open, the clip exhausted.

She realized at that point she had no idea where the third gunman was. The doorway he had owned for a dangerous moment was empty. Beyond it the living room was drenched in blackness. Karen let herself hope he lay shot and bleeding within it. Behind her the first two attackers had crumpled to the staircase, still writhing and clawing at their faces.

"Come on!" she screamed to her sons, pushing herself to the front door.

Karen had the dead bolt undone when she heard Taylor scream.

"Mom, look out!"

Taylor came around the side of her and intercepted the lunge of the bloodied shape of the man she had shot. The man threw him hard against the wall, and Taylor gagged with pain.

Karen shrieked. Lost in that instant was the hulking size and brute force of the killer. Lost was the blood spilling out of him from the two shots that had found their marks. She only knew she was the one thing standing between this animal and her children.

With a throaty, raspy shriek, Karen threw herself upon him. Impact nearly stripped both of them of their balance, and the result was to carry the pair in a bizarre twirling dance step back into the living room. Karen felt her sneakers crackling over shards of the glass broken when these men gained entry. The big man was going for her throat and she shoved forward, trying to force him off. But her twisted ankle betrayed her and she went down, the hulk landing atop her.

One of his massive hands found her throat and dug into her flesh. She tried to scream and only a gasp emerged as the breath bottlenecked. She tried to pry the hand off her, but it wouldn't budge. The pressure in her head was building, her ears starting to bubble. What little light the room gave up began to fade.

With a fierce yell, Taylor leaped atop the man's back and began tugging at his hair. He tried to shake the boy off, but his wounds, coupled with Taylor's feral determination, weakened his grip enough to give Karen back her senses.

Her right hand scraped desperately across the floor, feeling for the jagged remnants of the window. She closed her hand around some ground glass and drove it upward into the scarlet, raging face above her. The bloodied man tried to turn away at the last, too late to stop Karen from raking the shards across both his eyes. He howled in anguish as

Taylor's last determined yank spilled him all the way to the floor. Then the boy was helping Karen to her feet, starting to drag her back for the front door. .

"Get your brother," she ordered, aware of the blood dripping from the cuts in her palm for the first time. "Get Brandon!"

Her younger son was leaning against the doorjamb, his face a mask of shock. Taylor grabbed hold of him as Karen threw open the front door.

"Come on!" she rasped, reaching to grab Brandon's other side.

They ran together for the garage with Brandon in the middle. Karen had to bite down the pain in her ankle every step of the way. She led them through the garage's unlocked side door and helped her sons into the backseat of her rosewood Mercedes 300D, before lunging into the front. She reached across the seat and popped open the glove compartment. Concealed inside was a valet key she kept for those occasions when an attendant parked the car for her and she didn't want to leave him her house keys as well. Karen jammed it into the starter and turned, hitting the switch that activated the automatic garage door opener as the car jumped to life. She squeezed the steering wheel and felt the blood from her cut palm soak into the leather.

Swinging round, she caught a brief glimpse of her terrified boys before she started the Mercedes backward. The windshield had just cleared the door still churning up the rails when the shape lunged atop the hood. Karen's scream echoed with those of her sons as a burned and ruined face pressed itself against the glass. She accidentally turned on the windshield wiper and it snared the attacker in its sweep.

His face was puffy and blistered. His eyes were virtually closed, and what little emerged through the slits looked red and raw. Enraged, he swiped at the windshield wiper with a hand holding a pistol.

Karen jammed on the brake. But the man held fast to

his grip, teeth gritted and full of hate. His gun scraped against the windshield glass as he struggled to right it.

Karen shifted back into drive.

The Mercedes shot forward above an ear-wrenching screech that took all the tires would give it. The big car thumped back into the garage. The man bounced once on the hood and fought to steady his pistol once more. Karen felt the strange spasming of the antilock brakes when she slammed her foot into the pedal, but they merely cushioned the jolt when the Mercedes' bumper slammed into the wall, throwing the gunman forward and up. He crashed into an assortment of hanging yard tools that spilled with him to the garage floor when Karen shoved the car backward again.

She remembered hammering down on the buttons that automatically locked the doors and speeding from reverse into drive as soon as she hit driveway, spinning the Mercedes around toward the road.

She tore off, not daring to turn back. The rearview mirror told her all she needed to know. Her boys were there in the backseat, afraid to raise their heads, Brandon cradled in Taylor's arms.

"It's all right now," Karen tried to soothe, wondering if it really was, as the Mercedes surged out of her driveway and onto the roadbed. "It's over."

Wondering that too.

CHAPTER 5

"Doc says I'll be good as new in no time," Sal Belamo told McCracken and Wareagle from atop the bed in one of the Grand Hyatt's suites.

Of course, that same doctor had told him to stay overnight at the hospital, advice to which Sal had nodded politely before he checked himself out.

"No way I'm cutting myself off from the action," he'd said by way of explanation.

"Most of which took us by surprise today," McCracken added. At the hospital he had given the doctor a number in Washington to call. As a result of the brief conversation that ensued, no report of Sal's gunshot wound would be filed with the police and no record of his ever being treated would exist.

"Gonna need me to help sort things out, boss."

"This one might be beyond even you, Sal."

All told, Blaine could never recall a more confusing episode. Surprises were nothing new to him; usually they were simply the residue of incomplete planning. But today

was different. Today they could not possibly have planned
for what ultimately confronted them, a fact that first came
clearly to light when Blaine at last had an opportunity to inspect the contents of the briefcase Johnny Wareagle had salvaged from the subway platform beneath Bloomingdale's.
Each page contained names and addresses; single-spaced,
sometimes taking two lines to get all the information down.
McCracken recalled the apparent involvement of a third
party: the pair of mystery gunmen and the man, dead now
as well, whose briefcase El-Salarabi must have ended up
with.

The terrorist must not have realized the switch had been
made! He thought he was still holding his plans for the destruction of Bloomingdale's to the very end.

"Say what?" Belamo snapped, after Blaine had laid it
out for Johnny and him once they were inside the suite's
bedroom, Sal resting as comfortably as he could manage
atop the bed. "You're telling me those two guys you
whacked were after a guy with a briefcase at the same
time the three of us were after *another* guy with a briefcase?"

"And then the briefcases got switched."

"Only Salami didn't know it. . . ."

"While we figured everything was just going along as
planned," Blaine completed. "Now we know otherwise."

"Enlighten me."

"The man Johnny found dead in the street who pulled
the switch knew he'd been made by the two gunmen we
killed in Bloomingdale's. He knew he couldn't save himself but figured maybe he could salvage the contents of the
case."

Belamo was nodding. "So after the two shits he was
running from realized they had the wrong case, they came
after the right one."

"Which ended up with El-Salarabi," Blaine affirmed.
"Inside Bloomingdale's."

"You ask me, they musta known exactly what was inside it and wanted real bad to make sure nobody else got a look."

"Only now we've got the pages."

Belamo gazed at the stack of papers piled on his lap. "Goddamn mailing list what it looks like."

"Three people died because of it today, Sal; four if you count El-Salarabi."

Belamo nodded. "You get me a computer terminal, soon as I get off this bed, I'll tie into the national database, see what I can learn 'bout the people who belong to these names. See what holds them together." His face paled suddenly and his head lopped low toward his chest. "Uh-oh . . . Looks like those last painkillers are starting to kick in. . . ."

"Get some rest, Sal."

He flapped the salvaged pages in his good hand. "Nod off having another look at these . . ."

Blaine led Johnny out of the suite's bedroom into its living room.

"You were awful quiet in there, Indian. In fact, you've been awfully quiet since this afternoon."

"There's something I haven't told you yet, Blaincy."

"That much I figured."

"The man on the street spoke before he died." Wareagle paused. " 'Judgment Day.' "

"That's what he said?"

"There was more, but the words do not matter so much as what was in his eyes: fear, not of death, but of what life was going to become—for everyone." Johnny's eyes were full and cold. "He knew something, Blainey, something linked to that list of names."

"In the Book of Revelation, Indian, Judgment Day refers to the end of the world."

"I know, Blainey. So did he."

"Then this list of names . . ." McCracken could see Wareagle's expression was wavering between uncertainty and uneasiness, a stark contrast to his usually stoic self. "What else?"

"It . . . does not matter."

"Who killed our mystery man with the briefcase? You saw him, didn't you?"

"Yes and no, Blainey."

"What do you mean, Indian?"

"I saw the killer . . . yet I couldn't have. Because he is dead." The uncertainty vanished from Johnny's face, but the uneasiness remained. "I killed him."

Wareagle moved to a window overlooking Forty-second Street more than thirty stories down. He spoke without turning away from it. "After the hellfire, Blainey . . ."

"We were both sent to Israel to lend a hand in the Yom Kippur War of seventy-three."

"And then . . ."

"I went to Japan. You retired to the backwoods until I came calling again eight years ago."

"No." Johnny turned slowly, noncommittally. "There is something I have never shared with you, Blainey. When I returned from Israel, they were waiting for me."

"They," McCracken repeated.

He stared at Wareagle long and hard until the big Indian was ready to speak again.

"There was a mission. . . ."

The mind-control and altering experiments carried out in the late sixties and early seventies, mostly under the auspices of the CIA, were common knowledge now. Only the most clandestine experiments and their devastating results had somehow been kept secret. One of these concerned a variant of LSD designed to increase sensory perception that was tested on a number of willing volunteers from maximum security prisons all over the country. Full disclosure of what the prisoners were actually signing up for was never made. They were told simply it concerned brain enhancement testing.

Three of the volunteers died horribly within hours of the initial injection, another pair after the second and final one. The surviving eleven were scrutinized minute by minute, put through a battery of tests to see whether the new drug could actually hone their senses of sight, hearing, and smell, too. Even a moderate improvement would be call for celebration in the search to provide an edge for the soldier in heavy combat.

The experiment could not have been more of a disaster.

Not a single tangible, measurable improvement could be confirmed. Meanwhile, the minds of the test subjects were slowly and inexorably destroyed. Paranoid psychosis, schizophrenia, and sociopathic behavior were the most commonly observed results.

The plug was pulled on the project, but it was too late. Three of the surviving test subjects murdered their guards and escaped into the thick woods of Northern California containing the Redwood Forest, not far from where the research lab was tucked away. One of them was a hulking graduate student specializing in poetry and a conscientious objector to the war effort in Vietnam who'd been imprisoned for smashing a rock over the face of a policeman. At the time the cop had been trying to bodily remove the objector's girlfriend from a protest at U-Cal Berkeley.

The man's name was Earvin Early.

The blow broke every facial bone from the cop's eye sockets across the underlayer of his cheeks. His nose had been flattened like a pancake, looking bulbous and squat beneath the flow of blood.

The cop ended up a virtual vegetable, and Early was ultimately sentenced to twenty years to life. The promise of early parole led him to volunteer for the experiment, but a more careful screening job by the overseers would have eliminated him from consideration. Earvin Early was a borderline psychotic even before voluntarily ingesting a mind-altering drug that turned normal men crazy.

"I killed him, Blainey, and today I saw him again."

"Back up, Indian."

"They asked me to track the three men down. They showed me pictures of what Early and the two others did

to a pair of families who were camping out in California's
north woods." Johnny stopped, his eyes wide yet distant.
"I wasn't the first who tried to catch them. Another team
had already failed. Some of its members were found.
Some weren't."

"They let you go in alone?"

"They wanted to give me a team, but a second team
would have been as useless as the first."

"You went in because of what Early and company did
to those families."

"Future deaths would be on my conscience if I refused.
It was before I learned separation."

"You found them."

"At night, deeper in the same woods. The first one went
fast, the second a little harder. Early was the last. I trapped
him on the edge of a ravine. Put two arrows in him. He
fell over. I saw him."

"But today . . ."

"It was him, Blainey," Wareagle insisted, thinking of the
hulking shape of a vagrant cloaked in a patchwork canvas
coat, face a nightmare of boils and grime.

"Resurrected."

"I failed. He tricked me."

"And now he's joined the ranks of whatever our mystery man with the briefcase was running from. . . ."

"Judgment Day is coming, Blainey, and Early is a part
of it. I will track him down again. Finish what I failed to
finish all those years ago."

"And maybe figure out where it leads?"

Johnny's silence provided his answer. It continually
amazed McCracken how similar they really were, taking
different routes toward the same destination. That thought
made him realize something now for the very first time.

"After what happened in the woods, Indian . . ."

Wareagle looked at him, nodded.

"That's when you pulled out, withdrew. Gone, no for-
warding. Not even rural free delivery in the Maine backwoods."

"I had seen enough."

"I know the feeling. You see results like Earvin Early and you wonder maybe if we had it wrong the whole time. If those above us could be that far off about one thing, maybe they could have been that far off about *everything*. Then you begin to believe that you and all you stand for were manufactured the same way Early was made into a monster. And that takes away the only thing they gave us, the only thing they left us: pride, dignity."

Whatever reaction Blaine might have expected from Johnny Wareagle, the very slight but firm smile was not among them

"Our roles have reversed, Blainey. The counselor has become the counseled."

"It's just that I know what it feels like, Indian. I was there too, remember? Just a different place. For me the reality check came in London. . . ."

McCracken, of course, was referring to the most infamous incident of his career. Back in 1980 the tempers of some very mean hijackers at Heathrow Airport were left to smolder while British officials argued and the Special Air Service twiddled their thumbs in sight of the tarmac. Blaine was working with the SAS at the time and was lying prone next to the commander when the plane turned into a fireball. No one was ever sure whether it occurred out of accident or exasperation over another deadline passing. The point was it happened, and the entire planeload of hostages was senselessly lost.

Blaine took out his frustration for the way the whole episode had been botched on Churchill's statue in Parliament Square. Specifically, he shot out the section of it he was convinced the British were lacking. The incident won him instant ostracism and the nickname "McCracken-balls." The nickname stuck for good, the ostracism for only five years.

"If they hadn't buried me in France, Indian," Blaine confessed, "I probably would have walked. Difference is, if I had walked on my own, I'm not sure I would've ever come back."

"I wouldn't have if you hadn't called upon me, Blainey."

"But getting out for a time made both of us see things clearer, for what they really are. We came back in, we weren't doing it for the same reasons as before."

"For ourselves, then?"

"For those who matter. We don't cut into El-Salarabi's network, how many people die when Bloomingdale's becomes a parking lot? There's a lot of shit in the world, Indian. Difference is, we used to be part of it. Now we sweep it aside."

"Like I said," Johnny followed, smile even tighter, "for ourselves. We are hunters, Blainey, preying on the vermin which thin the herd while the shepherds sleep. For us, the hunt is everything."

"Better hope we haven't lost the scent, Indian," McCracken said, thinking of the force behind Earvin Early and the list of names Sal Belamo would soon be going to work on, "because this might be the most important one yet."

"Judgment Day, Blainey."

"Not if we can help it."

Earvin Early sat huddled against the building, knees tucked against his chest. The name of the building, he did not know. The name of the city did not matter. They were all the same; interchangeable pieces in a puzzle he cared nothing about.

Early shifted his great bulk, twirled his canvas coat tighter against him to provide further obscurity. Not that he needed to.

He could, after all, make himself invisible. He could do lots of things if he really put his mind to it. Could go places just by closing his eyes, anywhere he wanted. Do anything he wanted when he got there.

Earvin Early lived in his mind. The body was nothing to

him; a ragged shell the only purpose of which was to shroud the vast temple of his being. For this reason a bath for Early consisted of being caught in a downpour. He liked the stink that rose from his soiled clothes and frame because it kept him in touch with his physical self. So did the pain rising off the boils and open festering sores that dotted his face, neck, and shoulders. The pain kept him from slipping away permanently into one of the worlds his mind created.

Early suddenly saw rats rushing down the sidewalk, clustering around him, rising on their hind legs and sniffing at him. Early reached out to pet a few and they nuzzled against his fingers, purring. Early blinked his eyes.

The rats were gone.

He saw lots of things that didn't last very long. Long ago he had stopped trying to figure which was real-world real and which was the product of his mind that could do anything. Instead he just assumed everything was real-world real; a kind of compromise.

Early's revulsion for his consciousness was what caused him to become a vagrant. But the role evolved into the ultimate disguise. Wherever he went, wherever they brought him, he fit in. He could disappear without really disappearing at all, and that was good because becoming invisible took a great deal of energy, energy better saved for his Freeings.

That's what Early called what he did best. He used to know it was killing, but if all he was ridding his victims of were the consciousnesses that chained them to mediocrity, then he was actually doing them a favor.

Freeing them

Early had Freed a man earlier that day. He had made himself not there when he did it so no one would see him.

But someone did. Early saw the man and recognized him in the flash of sight he allowed himself before he made himself gone.

The Indian . . .

The Indian was one of the last memories he carried be-

fore they gave him the power and the real world grew all
fuzzy and misted over. When he had survived the fall off
the ravine with two arrows stuck in him, he knew he had
passed into a higher plane of existence. Great powers had
saved him, great powers that were certain to expand beyond his wildest dreams inside him. A world was born
only he was fit to inhabit. He let himself grow dirty on the
outside while the rest of humanity grew soiled on the in,
prisoners of their own consciousness and bodies.

No matter. Given time, Early would be more than happy
to free them all.

He knew his great powers would serve a purpose, and
waited for that purpose to be revealed to him. When the
Others found him, he knew right away it would come from
them.

He did not work for them in the traditional sense of the
word. He only performed an occasional Freeing when the
need arose and then he disappeared once more. The fact
that they always knew how to find him proved they could
direct themselves anywhere, just as he could. The missions
they selected for him, the subjects they selected for Freeing, were part of a much larger program he knew little,
and cared nothing, about. He kept his special gifts secret
even from them. No one who lived in real-world time
could know about those, no one!

But the Indian had known; the Indian had seen him, recognized him, looked at him, and known everything.

Earvin Early sat crouched against the building, rocking
himself now as he tried to send his mind to find the Indian. The Indian, though, must have known enough to put
his psychic shields up, and the efforts of Early's mind
went for naught.

Of course, Early hadn't told the others about the Indian;
he wouldn't have even if he still spoke in the words of the
many prisoners who needed Freeing. He spoke only in
lines of poetry learned in the days before his wondrous
changing. In doing so he never let *his* words give away his
true self; the words he spoke were all other people's.

But the absence of words did not change things so far as the Indian was concerned. He relied on them no more than Early did, and Early was glad the afternoon had ended without their inevitable confrontation. Early knew fear only for those who saw him as he was.

Earvin Early would wait for another time, another place. Twice their paths had crossed. They were certain to cross again.

"What fates impose, that men must needs abide. It boots not to resist both wind and tide."

Early quoted Shakespeare out loud to the night and then returned to the inner reaches of his mind, where it was even darker.

CHAPTER 6

"You understand why I have summoned you," the man in formal priest's robes said to the figures kneeling on either side of him, slightly offset so a slight twist of his gaze could capture both of them.

The figures nodded, in unison.

Unlike the priest, they were cloaked in the garb of a novice or a monk: brown robes stitched of scratchy burlap held at the waist by a rope belted as a sash. Their hoods threw dark shadows over the tops of their faces, leaving only their mouths partially visible in the dim light.

The church around them was huge and dark, unseen recessed lights casting their meager glow from the ceiling far above. The wood of each pew was hand-carved, smoothed and darkened from years of experience and wear. The altar before them stood as it had for over two hundred years. The stained-glass windows, scratched and battered and left to the elements, kept the light out and secrets within. In the background a youthful choir could be heard chanting softly in traditional Latin.

"Ratansky was killed," the priest continued. His exposed face was long and drawn, worn by fatigue and strain. The deep blue of his eyes had faded. His graying hair hung limply to frame a right ear that angled into a sharp tip and left ear that angled into no tip at all.

The lobe on that side was missing.

"We have lost contact with all those forming the chain set up to aid him." The priest rotated his eyes from one of the figures before him to the other. "The network has been compromised, rendered useless to us."

"Are we safe *here*?" The voice from the figure on the left was young, masculine; fearful and excited at the same time.

The priest nodded. "I have kept this place a secret even from our most trusted contacts. Now, beyond these walls, trust no longer exists." He looked at them both. "Remove your hoods."

The robed figures did so in perfect simultaneity, revealing soft faces pale with strain and worry. Each had long, sandy brown hair; the boy's shoulder length and the girl's a half foot longer. Their eyes were an identical shade of piercing crystal blue, perhaps too large for the rest of their elegantly chiseled, statuelike faces. Their noses were long and slender, narrow chins centered between angular dimples grooved into both lower cheeks. Too perfect and unmarked, too beautiful to be real, and yet so perfectly matched that anyone seeing them would know instantly they were twins.

"It is only us," the priest continued.

"Then we have lost," said the boy.

"No, Jacob!" his twin sister insisted, her voice slightly smoky while Jacob's rose a bit too high for a male's. "There are still the three of us!"

"Yes," the priest acknowledged, and they both turned his way. "But Ratansky had what we so desperately sought."

"Then we must retrieve it," Rachel said staunchly. "Whatever that takes."

The priest shrugged. "That may be the only way to stop them. They have the means; we've feared that all along. But I never believed they would be in position so soon to bring it off. . . ."

"As I said," Rachel picked up, "whatever it takes."

"But," the priest started, and stopped just as fast, "I *can't!* . . . *I can't!*" The words stretched a grimace across his tortured features.

The twins looked at each other.

"We will do it," said Rachel, her twin, Jacob, nodding his agreement.

"If there was any other way," the priest followed, his voice dry and pained.

"There isn't," Jacob told him. "And there is no place to run to. At least there won't be. Not in this world."

The priest's face bent in sadness. The haunting melodic chants of the young choir echoed in the background and turned the sadness to grief.

"Children," he said softly, "all that remains are children. . . ."

"*We* are not children," Rachel insisted.

The priest looked at them. "You have not yet seen your eighteenth birthdays."

"But we have lived this war with you for half of them," Jacob remained. "And for the last four years we have trained with the other soldiers, who have now abandoned us. Taken the courses over and over again, *mastering* the skill sets—you said so yourself. And now you know there is no choice, for any of us."

"If we are as good as you always said," put forth Rachel.

"You are better."

"Then we will go to New York. Ratansky must surely have left *something*."

"The challenge lies in finding it," added her twin. "Perhaps picking up where he left off."

"The risks," from the priest forlornly. "Lord in heaven, the risks . . ."

"Whether we go or not, they remain," said Jacob.

"Only different," added Rachel. "This is our last chance, the *world's* last chance."

The priest nodded slowly, reluctantly. He rose from his crouch, knees and back creaking, and waited for the twins to join him. When they did, facing him with bowed heads, he performed a brief blessing that ended with the sign of the cross drawn in the air before their foreheads.

"May God be with you," he said finally. "May God be with us all."

Captain Ted Wilkerson of the Arizona Highway Patrol strode down the corridor of Tucson General Hospital quickly, causing Dr. Lopez to break into a trot to keep up.

"We got him here as fast as we could, Captain," Lopez explained, trying to plead his case.

They had come to the elevator. Wilkerson pressed the up arrow.

"Just give it to me again, Doc, and make it quick."

"Your man Denbo—"

"He's not just *my* man. He's a man with a family who are gonna want to know what happened to him."

"Well, as you know, he was found by one of your patrols four hours ago halfway between Tombstone and Mexico. He had driven a good ways across the desert, by all indications, and was suffering from severe heat prostration and dangerous dehydration. I think we got him here in time, but the next twenty-four hours will be the key."

The elevator doors opened and Captain Wilkerson stepped in without waiting for those inside the compartment to step out. Dr. Lopez squeezed through the crowd to join him.

"I want to prepare you for what you're going to see," Lopez continued as the elevator hummed toward the third floor.

"I seen lots of men been in the desert longer than Wayne Denbo, Doc."

"It's not the desert that accounts for what I'm talking

about, Captain. It's whatever happened to him before he drove himself out into it. Shock's not unusual in these cases, but Officer Denbo is totally unresponsive and incoherent. He hasn't said a word since we brought him in here, and we're not sure he can hear what we say."

On the third floor Lopez lunged out of the compartment ahead of Wilkerson and led him toward Wayne Denbo's room: a corner private with a view of the night-lights burning in the hospital's parking lot. When they got to the door, Lopez felt his progress stopped by a beefy hand in his chest.

"I'll take it from here, Doc."

"But—"

"Call ya if I need you."

Wilkerson closed the door in Lopez's face and turned to find Sergeant Bart Harkness standing vigil over Denbo's bed.

"Jesus," muttered Wilkerson.

Denbo lay there spread-eagle on the bed with his unblinking eyes staring at nothing. The heat blisters that had pocked his face had all been swabbed and bandaged, giving him the look of a man who had gone crazy during his morning shave. The flesh Wilkerson could see was sunburned red.

"Anything?" the captain raised.

"Not a word," said Harkness.

Wilkerson reached Denbo's bedside and looked back at the sergeant. "What the Christ happened?"

Harkness let his eyes fall on the still form lost in the air-conditioned cool of the room. "He makes a crazy distress call to dispatch, but before he can say where he is, the message just cuts off."

"Like that? Nothing else?"

"When we found the car, what was left of the mike was on the passenger seat. Looks like he crushed it apart. Tore up his hand in the process," Harkness explained, gesturing toward the bandage covering Denbo's right palm. "Anyway, he left wherever he was in a hurry and drove straight into the desert. Didn't seem to matter where he went, 'long as he got away. Chopper found him just before dark. He was sitting by the front fender, the car out of gas, looking just about like he does now. We airlifted him here."

"What about his partner? What about Langhorn?"

"Not a trace. We figure maybe Denbo left him off somewhere between where he ended up and where he started."

"Any idea yet where on their patrol that was?"

"We're sweeping a widening perimeter around Joe and Wayne's last known position. Lots of square miles, though. Size of Rhode Island, maybe."

Captain Wilkerson took a long look at Wayne Denbo's blank face before continuing. "What was it you couldn't tell me over the radio, Bart?"

"Wayne and Joe had someone in their backseat. We found hair that don't match neither of theirs and fresh blood."

"Blood . . ."

"Not much. Enough to tell us it wasn't Wayne or Joe's, though."

"Where's Langhorn?" Wilkerson asked out of frustration. "What the Christ happened to him?"

The question drew a shrug from Harkness. "Wish I knew, Cap."

"Then try answering me this, son: What is it can make a man drive himself into the desert and leave him like . . . that?"

The two men looked down at Denbo's still form and then at each other.

"What the fuck did he see, Bart?" asked Wilkerson "What the fuck did he see?"

CHAPTER 7

Alexander MacFarlane arrived ninety minutes into Karen Raymond's stay at the San Diego County Sheriff's Department substation ten minutes from her house in Del Mar. He hadn't been home when she had called, but the answering service promised to track him down. When a half hour passed with no results, she tried again, waited another twenty minutes, and dialed once more. The results were the same: none. Finally he called her at the station and said he was on his way. He sounded harried and strained. Now, as he hurried down the hall toward the back office where they had stowed her and the boys, he appeared to her to be frightened. Behind him strolled a trio of men she recognized as part of the private security force Jardine-Marra utilized.

"My God, Karen," he said by way of greeting, "my God . . ."

She moved to him and took his outstretched hands in hers. MacFarlane drew her in for a hug. It hurt putting weight on her twisted ankle, and the bandage a paramedic had wrapped around her torn hand made it impossible to close her fingers.

"We've got to leave here," MacFarlane said softly as they separated. "We've got to leave now. We're going to take you and the boys to my house. There's plenty of room. And—" he cast another glance the way of the armed guards "—we won't be alone."

Karen's expression was ashen, expressionless. "The police didn't find them, Alex. The police got to my house and they were gone. But they couldn't have made it out and away on their own. They just couldn't. That means others must have come for them. There had to be *more*!"

"We've got to leave, Karen. Please."

She stood her ground. "You see what I'm saying, Alex. The attack wasn't random. They weren't just after me." She lowered her voice. "It's Lot 35; it's got to be."

"I know," he said grimly.

The remark, together with its tone, froze her thinking. "How could you *know*, Alex?"

MacFarlane's gaze tilted briefly toward the security guards who had accompanied him. "Let these men take your boys to my house. There are two others outside who will accompany us."

"Accompany us *where*?"

"Where I was when the answering service reached me: the plant."

Karen Raymond was only vaguely conscious of Alexander MacFarlane's limousine sliding past the Salk Institute and through the Torrey Pines Industrial Park en route to Jardine-Marra. The front of the building was lined with cars labeled with the familiar logo of the security company. Several of the unmarked variety were double-parked next to them. Security guards holding shotguns stiffly across their chests flanked the floodlit entrance on either side. When she stepped out of the limousine, Karen could see a man in a suit standing just inside the lobby.

"FBI," Alex told her, taking her arm lightly. "They've assumed jurisdiction in this."

"In *what*?" she returned fearfully. "What's happening?"

Before MacFarlane could answer, the FBI man emerged through the door.

"Quantico's sending a pair of forensic teams out on the first flight this morning, sir," he announced professionally.

"What about my house?" MacFarlane asked him.

"Supplemental teams have already been dispatched."

"I don't want them supplementing, damnit, I want them supervising!" His eyes gestured toward Karen. "Dr. Raymond's children will be arriving there shortly."

"They'll be safe, sir."

"See that they are."

The FBI man spat out some instructions into a walkie-talkie pulled from his belt, while Karen and Alexander MacFarlane started through the JM lobby. The agent caught up with Alex and they exchanged hushed words that Karen couldn't decipher.

It made sense, each and every piece of it. If the attack on her house had come for the reasons she suspected, it figured the force behind it wouldn't have stopped there. She was only a part of Jardine-Marra's miraculous work with Lot 35; an important one, yes, but a part all the same. Other parts, together or alone, were equally important.

Karen's thoughts stopped abruptly when they approached the entrance to the lab where the research on Lot 35 had been confined, located in a separate section of the building to avoid intrusions by the curious. Another suited man stood guard at the door. He saw MacFarlane and the FBI agent approaching and slid stiffly aside. Karen approached the threshold and felt her feet grow heavy. Her stomach churned. The floor wavered.

The Lot 35 laboratory was a shambles. Tables had been turned over atop shattered glass. Filing cabinets had been spilled and robbed of their drawers. Computers lay in smashed heaps.

Strange, Karen would reflect later, on how those were

the images she would always recall coming first. Not the
blood. Not the bodies of her eight-person Lot 35 lab team
who, as always, were working late.

*She should have been here! On any other night she
would have been.*

The bodies of her team lay scattered randomly throughout the lab, dropped in the positions they had been working. She had shared the better part of the past two years
with these men and women, the significance of their discovery bringing them especially close over the past six
months. They savored every second, coveted that final
mad, sleepless dash to the finish line. They cried, they
hugged, they ate Chinese food, and, finally, they cele-
brated.

"They were shot," Alexander MacFarlane said softly.
"All of them."

"One team sent to my house," Karen muttered, "the
other . . ."

"Here," he completed for her, swallowing the pause.
"The killers took everything: notes, computer disks, samples, even the test animals."

She grabbed his arm. "Get me out of here, Alex."

"I think we—"

"Now!"

Karen felt a sudden desperation to be with her sons. No
matter how deep her pangs of sadness and loss might be,
they paled next to the very real possibility that Taylor and
Brandon might still be in danger.

"I want to be with my kids."

"Karen, you and I really need to talk."

"Take me to my boys, Alex."

"They're safe."

"Now!"

"You're all that's left," MacFarlane said in the limo. "If
they had . . . been successful at your home as well, we
would have lost Lot 35."

"Who are *they*, Alex?"

"Quite obviously someone who does not want our vaccine to ever reach the market."

Karen tried to stop herself from shuddering and couldn't. "That means there was a leak. You know that."

He looked at her through the darkened cavernous rear of the limo. "But I don't know at what level, not yet."

"Yes, you do. And so do I. One of our board of directors is responsible for this. One of them must have a pipeline to someone who wants Lot 35 buried forever, someone at *another* pharmaceutical company!" she finished, the realization striking her hard and fast.

"Karen—"

"Hear me out, Alex. Say this other company is as close as we are to a vaccine, maybe even closer. There's billions of dollars at stake here, *tens* of billions, and there's only room for one AIDS vaccine."

"You're moving too fast."

"So did whoever it was on our board who leaked Lot 35's existence."

"They weren't the only ones with access to the information you're referring to," MacFarlane cautioned.

"No, but they were the only ones who learned of Lot 35's existence *today*. Everyone else in confidence has known for at least several months. The fact that all this happened tonight can only mean . . . Tell me I'm wrong, Alex. Go ahead and try."

MacFarlane sighed. "The FBI reached the same conclusion."

"And what do they intend to do about it?"

"Investigate each of the board members thoroughly."

"Tell them to try Merck, Ciba-Geigy, Pfizer, and Van Dyne as well."

"I'm sure they intend to." MacFarlane fidgeted, drew himself closer to her. "Our problem now is one of recreating your work under tight security, probably in a different location. You can do it, of course. You always insisted on keeping all the backups yourself."

She nodded, but the nod gave way quickly to a shrug. "It's just difficult to think in those terms now."

"Of course. I'm sorry."

"You don't owe me any apologies, Alex. You lost as much as I did tonight."

He touched her arm. "We'll put it back together, Karen, the two of us. I promise."

The mere mile-and-a-half distance to MacFarlane's home in the three-car convoy, the limo sandwiched by vehicles manned by the security force, took barely five minutes. Set upon the cliffs of La Jolla three hundred feet above Black's Beach, his house was a sprawling, three-story geometric marvel of circling layers and triangles locking around limestone patios. Steel frame with a 90 percent glass exterior that allowed for an open ocean view for hundreds of miles from most rooms, and Black's Beach from all of them. Called that for the volcanic sand that caked it, the beach was accessible either by a treacherous descent down the face or the elevators that many of the residents had installed which angled down over the cliffs. Karen's boys were probably the only ones to have used Alex's when they visited in the past few years, since MacFarlane's kids had long grown up and he hadn't been to the beach himself since his wife died.

The activation of every floodlight on the property had turned the front yard to near daylight brightness, enough to cast shadows for each of the uniformed figures shifting about on the grounds. The single guard posted before the front door moved toward the limousine as it snailed to a halt.

"Dr. Raymond's boys," was MacFarlane's greeting to him.

"They're under guard upstairs as instructed. They insisted on taking one room instead of two. I believe they're asleep."

"There," said the president of Jardine-Marra to Karen. "See."

"I want to see them."

"Why wake—"

"Now, Alex." Then softly, firmly. *"Now."*

The sight of her sleeping boys lifted a great weight from Karen's mind. She did not wake them up, though it took all her willpower to keep from doing so.

Karen closed the door behind her and didn't turn on the light, leaving the room's sole illumination as that which slipped through the drawn vertical blinds from the floods positioned in a tree across from the window. Her thoughts turned to tomorrow and beyond. Alexander MacFarlane was right: They had to put Lot 35 back together, assemble a new team and work round the clock if that's what it took, because only winning publicized approval for formal testing could make her feel safe. Once they went public, the enemy that had struck tonight would have no reason to go after her.

Or her boys.

Karen looked at them sleeping peacefully in the same big bed, faces awash with the light of the floods from outside. She wanted to lie down between them, take her sons in either arm and surrender to the dark for a time. Afraid to disturb them, she didn't. Just stood there thinking about it with the stars, the sky, and the ocean peering in at her through all that glass.

Then, as her mind returned to the events of the night, a sobering thought struck her, chilling in its message: according to Alexander MacFarlane, the killers had struck with virtual simultaneity at the lab and her home. But the attack at her house hadn't come until nearly midnight, long after at least a few of her co-workers would have called it quits for the night. There was no way, no way at all, that all of them would be present in the lab as late as twelve o'clock. Which meant, which meant . . .

Alexander MacFarlane had lied about the timing of the massacre. It must have been considerably earlier, several hours at least. Only when it was discovered she had been missed was the attack mounted on her home. The men had come with incredibly accurate intelligence. The invaders knew *everything*, about the alarm, the layout.

Alexander MacFarlane had an identical alarm in his home. She had bought her house from a friend of his two years ago.

Not Alex, never Alex. Anyone but Alex . . .

And yet, and yet . . .

He had her where he would have wanted her: in his domain, frightened and subservient. Along with Taylor and Brandon.

He had her sons.

The problem now is one of re-creating our work under tight security, probably in a different location. You can do it, of course. You always insisted on keeping all the backups yourself.

Was that what he wanted, *the backups*? Was he afraid that somehow Lot 35 might endure beyond her?

It made a terrifying kind of sense. And yet it didn't, because she trusted Alexander MacFarlane. And if she couldn't trust him, then who could she trust? Beyond that, there were more people involved than just him. The FBI, for example.

But, in fact, she couldn't be sure the men in suits were actually from the FBI. And why weren't authorities from the San Diego Sheriff's Department represented at Jardine-Marra in any form?

Perhaps because they had never been summoned. Perhaps the whole show had been put on for her benefit.

A soft knock rattled against the door behind her, and she jumped.

"Karen?" Alexander MacFarlane's voice called. "Is everything all right?"

Why don't you tell me? she wanted to shoot back, but instead said softly, "Yes."

Her decision was already made by then, her children the only concern.

"I told you they were fine," MacFarlane reassured when

she stepped out of the room and closed the door carefully behind her.

"Thank God."

"They're safe here. So are you."

"I know."

She waited until after 3:00 A.M. to make her move. The bedroom Alex had given her overlooked the sloping cliffs and the ocean beyond, a stretch of Black's Beach visible in the day. The floodlights were still burning when she arose, the guards continuing to methodically patrol the grounds. Either the illusion of security was being maintained for her benefit, or MacFarlane's intentions were genuine. The thought crossed her mind that the guards might also be there to make sure she didn't leave. If that was the case, the next few minutes might go very badly indeed.

Fortunately, MacFarlane had not stationed guards inside the house, which would give her the run of the interior for as long as she needed it. Karen crept into the hallway and padded toward the boys' room. The door opened soundlessly and she moved to Taylor's side of the bed. She stirred him from sleep with a hand cupped over his mouth. His eyes regarded her sleepily, then gratefully.

"Mom." The word muffled, sound absorbed by her palm.

"Shhhhhhhhhh," she counseled. "We've got to leave."

His eyes looked at her questioningly.

"I'm not sure we're safe here. We may be, we probably are, but I can't be sure."

Where they would be safe, where they would be going from here, was a problem she had not yet confronted. First things first.

Taylor slipped into his sneakers while Karen roused Brandon, who fought determinedly against coming awake. She had to nearly drag him into the corridor and then support him as they started down it.

"This way," she whispered, leading them toward the stairway.

She knew where Alex MacFarlane kept the keys to his three cars: a Rolls Corniche, a rare Porsche, and a Cadillac. The garage in which they were stored was attached to the house, accessible through a small hall off the kitchen. In that same kitchen, Karen found the keys in a drawer and grabbed the ones attached to a chain bearing the Cadillac logo. Still in silence, using only the light the outdoor floods gave them, she led the boys into the garage and eased the door closed behind her.

The most difficult part remained ahead. The grounds were still swimming with security men. They wouldn't be expecting what was about to occur, but that didn't mean they wouldn't be able to respond to it rapidly. Her sons stowed safely in the Caddy's backseat with instructions to keep down out of sight, Karen stuck the keys into the ignition and turned.

The Cadillac purred to life.

Karen reached up and touched the button on the visor that activated the automatic garage door opener. Instantly it began to churn upward. A light snapped on above and she cursed herself for not removing the bulb prior to entering the car. The soft whir of the garage door's machinery might escape the patrolling guards' attention, but the light would be noticed with a turn of the next head.

Karen eased the Caddy into reverse. The big car slid onto the dark macadam of the circular drive and nearly collided with a pair of the cars double-parked along it before Karen found the brake. She kept the Caddy's lights off as she started toward the main entrance. She didn't screech away, keeping her pace normal, hoping to make those on the grounds think the exit was expected, planned for.

The one at the front gate didn't bite. Karen saw the gun holstered on his hip as he came toward the car in a trot. There was no choice. She floored the accelerator and the Caddy shot forward with a burst of dirt and debris kicked behind it. The man lurched away at the same time she jerked the wheel to avoid him. The car jumped onto the grass and sideswiped an ornamental boulder set at the entrance as it swept through. She righted it quickly and tore off, barreling down the street.

"Awright, Mom!" congratulated Taylor, elated by their screeching getaway.

As had been the case earlier the same evening, Karen's eyes flirted nervously with the rearview mirror. As before, though, no unfriendly sights appeared. No sights at all, for that matter.

Lights on now, she drove into the night. Gone from the place that might or might not have been her prison, Karen turned her focus on possible destinations. The local police were out, those of the state variety made up by the California Highway Patrol a good possibility. Yet she had no idea where the nearest substation could be found, never mind what would happen once she got there. Again her decision might have been different if not for her sons. Wherever she drove, it had to promise sure safety and real refuge for Taylor and Brandon, perhaps for an indefinite period.

Only one place fit that bill, and Karen pushed the Caddy further into the night toward it.

CHAPTER 8

"That's it, sir," a voice said from the dark of the small theater when the tape reached its conclusion.

"And they are all here now, Major?"

"Still being settled in when I last checked, sir. It's a rather complicated process, given the situation."

"But we are equipped to handle it, I trust."

"We are now, sir."

"And what of the state trooper?"

"He never should have gotten away, of course. It was a fluke, sir."

"A rather ominous fluke."

"Not according to present reports. He was picked up in the desert several hours ago in a near catatonic state. I doubt very much he'll be talking to anyone anytime soon, sir."

"We will have to make sure that is long enough, won't we, Major?"

The man in the rear grasped the back of the crushed red velour seat before him. Every detail of the small theater had an ornate look and feel to it, as if an old-fashioned movie house had simply been shrunk down and placed here. Rich wood paneling with hand-carved pilasters and moldings covered the walls. The ceiling was painted in neo-Pompeian style, with arabesques and ropes of flowers intertwined with gods and goddesses.

"And what of the site itself?" he resumed.

"All reports indicate it's clean, sir. Not even the slightest trace. The tests carried out were remarkably thorough. I don't think we have anything to fear on that account."

"We have that much to be thankful for, I suppose. What about security, containment?"

"We're monitoring the area closely, sir, but so long as we are able to move the replacements into the town before the highway patrol happens to return, I think we'll be all right."

"And how long do you expect that will take, Major?"

"Tomorrow afternoon, sir, at the latest."

"Very good. Keep me informed." He seemed finished until something else occurred to him. "Of course, the other events of the day do now allow us to eliminate a problem that has been vexing us for some time. You know of what I speak, Major?"

"I have issued the appropriate orders, sir."

"By my specifications, I trust."

"Of course, sir. To the letter."

"I want her to have a chance to atone. I owe her that much." The figure rose in the back of the dark theater, silhouetted by the dim ceiling lights. "Very well, then . . ."

"Sir?"

"Ah yes, Major, there was something else." He sat down again, reluctantly.

"Something else rather pressing, I'm afraid, sir."

On signal, the lights in the small, plush theater were snapped all the way off once more. On the eight-by-twelve-foot screen encompassing the center of the front wall, a picture came to life portraying a narrow slice of Lexington Avenue in New York City. A number of pedes-

trians were stepping past a tight throng gathered before a
fruit stand set up in front of the abandoned Alexander's
department store.

"We confiscated this tape from a bystander who happened to be filming at the time of the attack."

"An attack that was most poorly executed, leaving the
material we sought to acquire potentially in dangerous
hands."

"Erase potentially."

"Major?"

"I believe we have located the material, sir. I'm going
to fast-forward here to the spot in question."

"Please," returned the voice from the very back row,
sounding disturbed.

The action on the screen returned to normal speed. A
woman and three children were smiling and waving at the
video camera. Their lips moved, but he couldn't hear what
they were saying. Suddenly a figure crossed in front of the
lens, obscuring the family. At the front of the theater, the
major froze the tape briefly on the befuddled looks of
the family members. Then he rewound it and ran it again
in slow motion, freezing the frame when the intruding figure was centered on the screen, visible from only the waist
up. Even through the blur, it was clear he was broad and
had a beard that looked more the result of a week gone
without shaving than careful grooming.

"Sir, this man meets the description of one of the surviving gunmen from inside Bloomingdale's who eliminated our people. We have now been able to obtain a
positive identification based on a computer enhancement
of this frame." The major paused. "The man's name is
Blaine McCracken."

The figure in the theater's rear rose to better his view,
but the screen denied it, refusing to let him gain a clear
glimpse through the blur. "Is that supposed to mean something to me, Major?"

"Indeed it is, sir," said the man in the theater's front,
and then he began to explain.

PART TWO

THE KEY SOCIETY

NEW YORK CITY:
TUESDAY; 9:00 A.M.

CHAPTER 9

Sal Belamo arranged the meeting for McCracken from his bedside. The effects of the bullet wound suffered the previous afternoon had left him stiff and uncomfortable after a restless night. He grimaced and dry-swallowed a pair of Percodans in the bedroom of the Grand Hyatt suite.

"You ask me, a guy could get to like this shit too much, he gets the chance."

"What'd your man say about the bodies?" McCracken asked him.

"Nothing. Won't talk on the phone, even after I tell him that's the way it's gotta be. He says in person or I can go fuck myself."

"You tell him I was coming?"

Belamo smirked, eyes starting to grow glassy as the Percodans took hold. "I told him to look for a guy 'bout as pretty as me only ten years younger."

McCracken walked the short distance from the Hyatt to the Broadway Deli on Forty-second, where Sergeant Ed Reese would be waiting for him. Blaine didn't need

Belamo's description to spot the cop; a fat man in a cheap
khaki overcoat was sitting with his counter stool half-
cocked toward the door when he stepped into the deli. He
gave McCracken a disinterested glance and went back to
a jelly doughnut which leaked all the way to his lips. Took
a big slurp of coffee next and left what didn't reach his
mouth pooling in the saucer. Reese had hair that was
slicked down in the front and stood upright in the back.
His eyes looked tired and drained, but confident.

McCracken was a yard away when Reese threw him another cursory glance and then started talking.

"Old Sal got himself shot, did he?"

"He did."

"It's happened before."

Reese shifted his bulk enough on the stool to make it
wobble.

"Got hit myself in Korea," he explained, and slapped
the upper part of his left leg. "Took it right in the hip. Part
of the slug's still in there. Bastard doctors couldn't get it
all."

"You know Sal from Korea?"

Reese shook his head demonstratively. "Hell, no. He
was into a whole different game and a lot better at it than
I was. You?"

"Nam."

"So I figured. Anyway, I got to know Little Sal after,
while he was boxing. Bet on both Carlos Monzon fights."

"Must have lost your shirt."

"Nah! I took the odds and went with Monzon. What the
hell, I figure. Guy's never lost, it's not gonna be Little Sal
puts him on the mat." Reese stuffed the rest of his doughnut into his mouth, chewed rapidly, and swallowed before
he checked his watch. "You don't mind, I want to be out
of here fifteen minutes ago."

"You ID those two shooters we iced?"

"Nope, and we're not going to neither." Reese stopped
and looked around to see if anyone was watching before
he took another doughnut from inside the glass container.

" 'Cause the bodies are gone. Somebody lifted them right out of the ME's office. Knocked the guard out and that was that." He reached a hand into his sport jacket and it emerged holding a folded, coffee-stained envelope. "Preliminary report on the two stiffs is in here. Best I can do. Hey, they got something in common."

"Other than having been stolen?"

"Try this out: Both of them were missing the lobes on their left ears."

Blaine thought about that briefly. "What about the body found back on Lexington near Fifty-ninth Street?" referring to the man who had uttered a dying message to Johnny Wareagle, after switching briefcases with El-Salarabi.

"Had both his lobes still intact, that's what you're asking."

"At least you didn't lose his body too."

Reese frowned. "Yeah, well, that guy lost most of his guts to somebody who knows how to use a killing knife." Reese reached into his pocket and came out with a notebook. "On account of we didn't lose the body, we did a little better with this one. Got a make on him off the fingerprints. Stiff's name is Benjamin Ratansky. Age fifty-three from Aldrich, Illinois. Funny thing is, according to the make we ran on him, he ain't dead at all. Computer insists he's serving out a ten-year sentence for computer fraud at the Taylorville Correctional Center in Taylorville, Illinois."

Johnny Wareagle was walking the streets of New York. He had no precise destination in mind, no specific route to follow. Anyone watching him might be reminded of how a hunting dog circles the woods in search of the right scent.

His sighting of Earvin Early the previous afternoon had brought him face-to-face with failure, a condition he was not used to and disliked intensely. His Sioux heritage counseled that the entire universe was composed of a single interconnected and interdependent chain. Some men's actions are explicitly tied to those of others, and the responsibilities must be shared. In Wareagle's mind, this meant that his failure to kill Early twenty years before cast him with a measure of the blame for all those the madmen had subsequently killed. And there had been many—of that, Johnny was sure. He could see it in Early's yellow eyes even from the distance he'd caught his glimpse of him yesterday.

The morning air grew warmer. The city turned alive.

"Hey, giant. Hey, big giant."

Johnny stopped and gazed downward at the origin of the voice. The speaker was a one-legged vagrant sitting on the pavement with his single leg crossed beneath him. The cool slate supported his shoulders and helped keep his torso from toppling. From around his neck dangled a handwritten sign that read DISABLED VIETNAM VETERAN. He thrust toward Johnny a Styrofoam cup that still smelled of coffee.

His sunken eyes lost their hopelessness for a moment as Wareagle met his gaze.

"You was there, too. I can tell it for sure, you was there, too!"

Wareagle stared intently at the derelict, and the sight taught him much about Earvin Early. Early, after all, had looked almost the same way yesterday. Johnny knew it was not a disguise. The material, anything physical and thus transitory, bore no meaning for the mad giant. Early lived in his mind, and in his mind anything could happen. The experiment he had subjected himself to while in jail had done something to that mind, turned a man into a monster. But it had been Wareagle's misjudgment that had set the monster free in the north woods of California twenty years ago.

In the thick forest that night, Earvin Early had survived a tumble over a steep ravine with two arrows stuck in him and had lived to begin a new existence. More than anything else, that new existence concerned Wareagle. Indeed,

this hunt wasn't so much about Early as what he was now
a part of—what Johnny had *let* him become a part of:

Judgment Day . . .

Early had killed the man who held its secrets, killed the
man to *protect* those secrets. Find him and the next stage
of the chain would follow.

Judgment Day had to be stopped.

And Earvin Early was going to help Johnny do it.

Sal Belamo returned the receiver to its cradle and
looked disparagingly at Blaine from the chair in the suite's
bedroom. "And you thought a contact of mine coulda been
this far off. . . ."

"Ratansky?"

"According to Illinois prison records, he's in the
Taylorville Correctional Center, all right. Cellblock D, cell
twenty-seven. Transferred there from the medium security
facility up in Sheridan."

"Except he's lying on a slab in the New York City medical examiner's office. Funny how a dead man can still be
serving time in prison."

"Beats me, boss."

"I guess I'll have to go ask him in person."

"You sure you wanna do this, Indian?"

Wareagle looked up from the small shoulder bag he was
packing on the couch in the suite's living room section. "It
is not a question of want, Blainey. It is a question of
must."

"Because you missed this Earvin Early the first time
around."

"And because he is a part of what we are facing now."

"Early falls off that ridge, survives somehow, and
makes his way out. Trail's cold, Indian. Twenty years
cold."

"The scent will still be there, Blainey."

"Just stay in touch, Indian."

* * *

"Sorry about your uncle, miss," Sergeant Bob Hume said compassionately. He looked up from the paperwork on his desk to meet the stare of the young woman seated across from him. Her blue eyes were cold and hard. Hume had seen lots of different looks on the faces of those who only minutes before had positively IDed the remains of loved ones. No two were the same, but Hume had seen few to match this particular gaze. In any case, his job was only to fill in the spaces on the report beneath him with the proper information to allow her to claim possession of the body.

"You were Mr. Ratansky's niece, then," Hume said, getting to that line on the requisite form.

"Yes," Rachel replied. Playing the part of someone older came easy for her; a smartly styled suit, some heavy makeup, and hot-iron tousling of her hair created the effect. She had considered acting more grief-stricken, but rejected that role for fear it would offset her subtle disguise.

"We can release the body once the autopsy report is complete," the policeman continued.

"Were there any . . . personal effects?" Rachel raised.

"A few," Hume told her, noting the small list clipped to the back of the case report. "We can turn them over to you as soon as we're done here."

"I'd like a copy of that file," she requested, eyeing the folder.

Hume fingered it, as if to question if that was what she was talking about. "There's really nothing—"

"For my own benefit."

"It's against procedure."

Her face softened, just a little. "My father's a police officer, too. He asked me to—"

"I understand. I'll make you a copy."

Hume started to rise to do just that when the young woman's voice stopped him.

"Sergeant, I was wondering about something else. My uncle always carried a brown leather briefcase with him. He moved around a lot and had gotten in the habit of never letting his most personal papers get too far away from him. I was wondering if something meeting its description might have been found near the scene."

Hume again scanned the personal property sheet. "Not according to this list. But I'll be happy to check for you, miss."

"Thank you."

"Now, if you'll just sign here, I'll go make you a copy of this report. . . ."

Jacob was waiting for her in the small asphalt park just down the street from the precinct. He noticed her small handbag bulged slightly with new contents.

"Nothing in his personal effects can help us," Rachel started, taking the seat next to him on the bench.

Jacob's gaze moved from the bag to her eyes. "Are you certain? Ratansky was very clever. He could have— "

"You didn't let me finish."

She extracted a set of crumpled pages from her handbag. "When the sergeant went to make a copy of the report, I grabbed this off his desk." She handed it to her twin. "It's the complete police report on the events that followed Ratansky's murder."

"What events?"

"Read it."

Jacob scanned the pages quickly, stopping when he came to the notation of the missing earlobes on the corpses that had disappeared. "They were *killed*?"

"Keep going."

Jacob read on through the sketchy details of a shootout that had taken place inside Bloomingdale's between the two unidentified corpses and at least three additional men. One of these had been identified as a Syrian national with suspected terrorist ties. He, too, was dead. All that the report offered of the other two were general descriptions compiled from terrified witnesses at the scene.

"This makes no sense," Jacob said when he was finished. "Who *are* these men? What brought them into battle with the soldiers?" His eyes widened hopefully. "Allies of Ratansky, perhaps. Help we're not even aware of!"

"Even so, that doesn't mean he passed the material on to them. And if he did, the fact that they have yet to make contact indicates they are pursuing a different agenda."

"One that intersects with our own, apparently."

"And unknowingly from their perspective."

"Leaving us with nothing more than their descriptions."

"A bearded man and a giant Indian," said Rachel, highlighting the most repeated phrases used by the witnesses trying to describe the mystery men.

"Not much to go on," Jacob conceded, his youth showing in his disappointment.

"But all we have for now."

CHAPTER 10

"Karen, what's gotten into you? Where in God's name are you?"

Alexander MacFarlane's voice blared into Karen Raymond's ear through the receiver of the pay phone in Modesto.

"It doesn't matter, Alex. And I don't plan on talking long enough for anyone who might be listening in to find out."

"*What?* What are you talking about? I was worried to death last night. I thought someone had kidnapped you. I couldn't believe it when the guards said you were alone in the car."

"Not alone. My boys were in the backseat."

"My God, they could have been hurt. . . ."

"Or maybe shot, Alex, by men who didn't want me off your property, out of your sight. Beyond your control."

"Make sense, Karen!"

She checked her watch, careful not to give MacFarlane

enough time to have the call traced. "Not this call. Suffice it to say I'm playing things safe."

"Last night, Karen, think about what happened last night!"

"I am."

"Talk to me, Karen! God help me, I don't know what's gotten into you, but we've got to talk."

"Soon," Karen finished, and hung up the phone.

She had abandoned MacFarlane's Cadillac the night before with the certainty that law enforcement officials all over the state would be watching for it and her. It had taken her twenty minutes to drive ten miles, far enough, she hoped, to give her a sufficient head start. From there she had called six cab companies before finding one willing to make a drive at that time of the night to Sanpee and a trailer park from her past.

Of course, she had no cash to pay the driver and informed him of this fact at the outset, promising to get the money as soon as they reached their destination. The man took another look at her kids, shrugged, and relented.

The drive toward Sanpee took just under a half hour. The boys had drifted off to sleep almost instantly. Every time Karen nearly joined them, a pair of piercing headlights or a horn would jolt her alert. She saw enemies everywhere; around the next turn, hidden on the embankment just up ahead, following in the minivan flaring its high beams into the rearview mirror.

They passed into Sanpee and reached the outskirts of the trailer park just before 4:00 A.M. It looked unchanged, the trailers just where they had been when she had left eight years ago. There weren't many lights on at this hour, other than the sporadically placed weak floods which the management called security. The cab weaved its way through the mazelike confines toward the rear, Karen straining her eyes through the darkness.

A dog barked. Then another.

The driver hit the brakes. Karen and the boys lurched forward.

"Holy shit," the driver muttered.

The dogs, all pit bulls, surrounded the cab and barked at it, jumping up and snapping at the tires and grille. The driver instantly closed his window. He turned round toward Karen with fatigue replaced by fear on his face.

"Were you expecting this, lady?"

Before Karen could answer, a familiar voice rang out.

"Looks like we got us some visitors. . . ."

T.J. Fields stepped into the spill of the cab's headlights, twelve-gauge shotgun in hand. The white glow shrouded him, and he didn't as much as blink it back. He was just as big as Karen remembered him, even bigger now in the gut. His hair had grayed and been trimmed much shorter. But besides that, he looked the same as the first night they had met when he saved her from Tom Mitchell's wrath, right down to the leather chaps, biker buckle boots, and leather vest with the Skulls logo embroidered on its rear. Karen imagined she could hear the chaps creaking as he started forward.

"That'll be enough, boys," his stern, powerful voice ordered. Instantly the pit bulls went silent, save for a lingering whine. "Dr. Raymond, I do believe you can come out now."

"Mom," started Taylor, wide-eyed, "who is—"

"A friend. Someone who's gonna help us."

"That guy's your *friend*? You know *him*?"

Instead of explaining to Taylor that T.J. Fields was his friend as well, Karen simply eased herself over Brandon and out the cab's door into the night. Two-Ton strode toward the car, the twelve-gauge balanced over his monstrous forearm. The dogs swarmed aimlessly about him, panting and whining. A few bored ones sauntered off.

Karen leaned against the open door.

"Come into the light and lemme take a look at you," the big man ordered. "Well, ain't you a sight. Still as pretty as the day is long."

T.J. eased the twelve-gauge away from him as if it were

a toothpick, then opened his arms. Karen took another step forward, and he swallowed her in a tight hug.

"Been too long, girl."

"I know. I'm sorry."

"Fuck sorry. Sorry's for losers. We got lots of people call this home who are just passin' by." He moved her away, holding her still at the shoulders. "Not many call themselves 'doctor,' though. Some of the boys thought you were the examining kind when I told them you was coming. They forgot."

"You didn't."

"Never forget my friends, doll. We drift apart sometimes, yeah, but getting back together always makes it seem like nothing's changed."

"Plenty has. Recently."

T.J. looked into the backseat at the two boys. "So I gather."

"I'm in trouble."

"Sounds familiar. We did this dance before, 'member?"

Karen started to reach into the backseat for Brandon. Taylor slid across the seat after him.

"Can you pay the driver?" she asked T.J. "I had to leave in a hurry."

T.J. already had pulled a wad of cash from the pocket of his jeans. He wet his finger and began separating the bills, holding them in the hand still helping to cradle the shotgun.

"How much?"

"Thirty-two fifty," the driver told him.

T.J. pealed off four twenties and handed them to him through the window. "Rest is keep-quiet money. You were never here."

The driver took a quick glance at the impatient pit bulls. "Never even knew the place existed." The relief was plain in his voice.

After the driver had swung around and started his cautious exit out, T.J. turned back to Karen. The fading glow off the cab's brake lights was enough to show the lingering fear in her face.

"You and a bunch of dogs," she said wryly, holding the sleepy Brandon against her. "I was expecting a bit more."

T.J. Fields grinned and jammed his thumbs into the corner of his mouth for a high-pitched whistle. Instantly from behind trees, from under, around, and atop trailers, a dozen armed figures appeared in the night.

"This enough for ya?" asked another familiar voice from the darkness.

Karen swung left in search of the speaker and saw an old man step out of the night. "Papa Jack?"

"None other."

She ran forward and hugged him.

"Easy," he sighed, "or you'll be crushing what's left of my bones."

Papa Jack, spiritual leader of the Skulls, had claimed to be on the near side of sixty since she had known him. The Korean War had left him with a black patch over his left eye, and a motorcycle accident years later was responsible for the eight steel screws in his right leg. His gray hair was tied back in a ponytail, and his single blue eye regarded her with a hint of amusement.

"Suppose you'll be wanting your old trailer back."

"Only if you got the hot water fixed finally."

"Next on my list, babe." He winked. "A little influence in the right place might speed me up a mite."

"You're too fast for me, Papa Jack."

He seemed to notice Taylor and Brandon for the first time. "These couldn't be *your* boys. Please tell me I ain't gotten that old, babe."

"They're mine, Papa Jack. But that doesn't make you any older than fifty-nine."

He tugged on his eye patch. "Music to my ears, babe, music to my ears."

That had been hours before. A brief interlude of relative respite followed before the time came to call Alexander

MacFarlane. She had made that call from a phone booth outside a convenience store a few miles from the trailer park. After hanging up, she drove an ancient Ford Galaxy belonging to one of the Skulls another twenty minutes down the road to a second Sanpee convenience store, where she called MacFarlane again on his private line.

"Karen," he said, without waiting to be sure it was her.

"I'll meet you, Alex, but it's got to be on my terms."

"Karen, let's talk this out now. I know how you feel...."

"Then you should be all the more willing to follow my instructions." Karen had already worked out the logistics in her head, having discussed them with T.J. The Skulls would be her ace in the hole neither MacFarlane nor anyone else could know about. "Torrey Pines State Park. The Overlook, ten P.M. tonight. Park your limousine on the south side of the ranger station. No one else but your driver."

"I'll be there, Karen."

"So will I."

Blaine McCracken arrived at the minimum security Taylorville Correctional Center in Taylorville, Illinois, for his appointment with the warden a half hour early. The guard inside the front entrance inspected the identification he had produced and looked up from it impressed.

"I'll call the office and tell them you're on your way," he said.

Ten minutes later Blaine was seated in Warden Warren Widmer's office. Widmer was a surprisingly dapper-looking man with an easy, conciliatory manner who treated every man, inmate or not, with respect. Now he listened to Blaine's tale of Benjamin Ratansky in utter astonishment.

"What you're telling me, Mr. McCracken," came his response when Blaine had finished, "is that one of our present inmates was murdered in New York City yesterday."

"That's right, Warden."

"Could you spell his name, please?"

Widmer turned his chair to face his computer terminal, entered the name as Blaine recited it, and typed in the proper instructions. He studied the results briefly and looked back at McCracken.

"It seems you're correct. Benjamin Ratansky does indeed reside here in cell twenty-seven of cellblock D."

"Resides there *now*?"

"Apparently not, I'm afraid. You see, cellblock D only has twenty-six cells."

The strain in the priest's voice was plain to the twins as he repeated his question to them over the speaker phone:

"Are you sure the descriptions you forwarded me are accurate?"

Jacob and Rachel looked at each other.

"Yes," said Jacob.

"Straight off the police report," added Rachel.

"I've managed to identify them," their father explained after a long pause. "It wasn't terribly hard. They're rather well known in certain circles."

"Who are they?"

As their father explained to them exactly who the bearded man and the Indian were and what could be expected of them, the twins grew more and more agitated.

"How could such men be involved in this?" Rachel wondered.

"They may well have stumbled into it. My information indicates this man McCracken had a prior experience with the Arab terrorist who was shot. Equally unpleasant."

"That doesn't explain the presence of the soldiers," Jacob reminded. "They should have fled the scene after dispatching Ratansky."

"We must assume they had their reasons for doing otherwise."

"McCracken's unwitting involvement? Something he did or . . . or even *learned*!" Rachel said, getting excited.

"Possibly. But only McCracken himself would be able to tell us."

"So we must find him!"

"But where to start?" Jacob raised despondently.

"Where would *you* start?" the priest challenged. "Think as outsiders. Detach yourselves."

"Ratansky," Rachel muttered.

"By now, McCracken will have identified him," Jacob added.

"And gone where with the information?"

The twins looked at each other. Rachel said exactly what Jacob was thinking:

"Where we must go next."

"Was the transfer unusual?" McCracken asked.

"In and of itself, not at all," Widmer replied with a hard copy of Ratansky's records before him. "Ratansky was a model prisoner, but wouldn't have been eligible for parole for another two years under the terms of his sentence. Transferring him here to a minimum security facility was the next best thing."

"Only he never made it to Taylorville."

Widmer leafed through the rest of the pages he was handling and then reached for another file that had just arrived via computer modem from Sheridan. "By all indications, his presence here was a sham perpetrated on the system and the state by someone who had tapped into and tampered with both prisons' computer systems. Sheridan's records, as well as ours, have been altered so everything appears as it should be."

"Ratansky was convicted of computer fraud," Blaine recalled.

"I see the connection didn't escape you, either."

"Along with the fact that he could never have accomplished all the logistics alone."

"Agreed. In fact, regular updates on his status have been entered into our system here in Taylorville, just in case anyone bothered to check."

"Any way of tracing them to a source?"

"Not with any high degree of confidence, under the circumstances. There's no paper trail to follow, remember. Everything was done with computers talking to other computers."

Blaine thought briefly. "Do you have a list there of his visitors while he was in Sheridan?"

"I should."

Again Widmer ruffled through the pages of the top manila folder. The diary-form visitors list for Ratansky's three-year stay was four stapled sheets long.

"Family members, mostly," the warden recited. "His lawyer, too."

"What about in the last few months he was in there? Any new names?"

Widmer looked up slowly. "Several of them. No two repeat."

"My guess is it was the same person using different identifications," Blaine concluded.

"Four visits over the course of Ratansky's final three months," the warden intoned skeptically. "Not much on which to base a conclusion."

"Unless there was a setup inside Sheridan passing him information as well. See if Ratansky was part of any group during his stay. See if he happened to join one during his last few months."

It took a few minutes of scanning through a second manila folder faxed from the Sheridan Correctional Center for Warden Widmer to find the answer. "Yes and no. He never joined a group, but there are several notations linking him to one, starting with those months in question. Something called the Fifth Generation. My Lord," the warden realized, "there was a group by the same name up at Menard when I was deputy warden there. It's a religious group, fanatical evangelists, I believe. I hadn't realized they were anything but local."

"No chapter here at Taylorville."

"Fortunately they're not the minimum security type, not even the medium really. But Sheridan maintains a small maximum security wing to help handle the overflow."

McCracken leaned forward, the hairs on his neck stiffening. "These Fifth Generation members, would you classify them as troublemakers?"

"No. Keep to themselves mostly, except when one of them is crossed. They take care of each other. Not unusual for prison. In fact, there's very little about them that is unusual, except maybe their claim to be religious zealots."

"You called them fanatics before, Warden."

"An unfortunate stereotype, I suppose, because they do have one strange tradition the penal system's been unable to stifle despite making a rather concerted effort."

"Why bother making it?"

"Health reasons. See, the members slice off their left earlobes, Mr. McCracken. Each and every one of them."

A connection established with the missing corpses of the gunmen in New York, Blaine called Sal Belamo from Warden Widmer's office to ask him to find out all he could about the group that called themselves the Fifth Generation. McCracken was an hour into his drive north toward Sheridan, and the prison Benjamin Ratansky had managed a brilliant escape from, when the cellular phone in his rental car rang.

"What'd you come up with, Sal?" McCracken asked by way of greeting.

"It's like this, boss. Fifth Generation got off the ground between prison walls, all right, but it's not limited to them anymore. Made up of extreme Christian fundamentalists, and I do mean extreme, who are big into the area of rebirth and redemption. Was started up fifteen years ago in San Quentin by a priest named Preston Turgewell. Thing is, Turgewell wasn't just visiting at the time; he was imprisoned there."

"For what?"

"Turned out this holy father was leading a double life, which he financed by stealing from the parishoners' donation baskets every Sunday. Made the best of his token two-year stay in the slammer, by all accounts. Became a new man and took plenty of other convicts with him."

"The Fifth Generation . . ."

"Damn straight, boss. Soon as he got out, he took his show on the road. Became quite the soul saver with branches in every big lockup across the nation. His people get out, they open or join Fifth Generation branches back in their hometowns, and the fucked-up former Father Turgewell used to hold the paper on each and every one. We're talking lots of ex-cons here, drawn from just about the most violent available. Leastways we were."

"Past tense."

" 'Cause the fucked-up former father has done gone to his Maker. About a year ago in a private plane crash. Suspicious circumstances, 'specially considering his kids disappeared round the same time."

"Kids?"

"I forget to mention that? Yeah, in addition to everything else, before he found the Lord for real, Turgewell found some pussy through which he ended up with two kids." Sal paused long enough to consult his notes. "Twins, a boy and a girl. They'd be almost eighteen now."

CHAPTER 11

The rain pounded the huge tent. The wind slammed vast torrents of water against the flapping canvas, threatening to tear it loose from its ropes and poles. For twenty-four hours now the water had poured down its sides into ever-deepening pools atop the grass. Where the grass choked off and died, oozing puddles of mud formed, determined to force their way beneath the bottom flaps that thus far had held the onslaught back.

Inside and outside the tent, dozens of sodden workers toiled feverishly to keep the canvas tied down. Fresh stakes were driven where the ground would take them. And when no ground could be found, the workers did their best to shore up the supports already in place.

Inside, though, the capacity crowd was spared the storm. They sat upon folding row chairs atop ground that had remained dry. The rain bursts thwacking at the tent top sounded like monotonous drumbeats that simply became part of the atmosphere. They noticed them not in the slightest, although the sudden flashes of lightning visible through the olive-khaki canvas did draw an occasional stir and sent a muttering through the makeshift pews.

"Are we to fear nature, my brothers and sisters?" challenged the woman from the lowest tier of a three-level stage set near the front of the tent. "Are we to fear our collective ends in this place tonight, victims of a terrible tragedy? Are we to fear our helplessness before the might of the Lord?"

The murmuring through the crowd intensified. Eyes swept the recently erected tent, as if to check whether the tower-high supports were strong enough to withstand the storm's power.

"I say, no! I say *we are not* to fear it!"

Sister Barbara was awash in the spill of bright white and blue spotlights that shone down from a trio of scaffolding towers. Her pearly white sequined dress seemed to both absorb and reflect the light, casting her as one with it. She cut a tall, graceful, and elegant figure striding across the stage, high heels clacking between the bolts of thunder. Behind her, seated in a semicircular erection of bleachers, a blue-clad choir a hundred strong followed her every move. She was wearing a wireless microphone that hung down unseen from her left ear. She came to the very edge of the stage and lowered her voice into it.

"There are those who stand on pedestals like this who say there is no hope. They tell you to forget hope. They say you must change your ways and accept their word, or risk not being saved when Judgment Day approaches."

As if on cue, a bristling thunderclap erupted, just before another flashbulb-bright flash of lightning. A collective gasp moved through the increasingly jittery audience.

"Well," Sister Barbara continued, "I am here tonight to tell you not to put your faith in them, these doomsayers who have given up on the world and on you. Have faith in yourselves to endure, to survive in spite of what is thrown in your path. Those who have been here before me have passed around their baskets and asked you to give in order that you might be saved. But it is faith in yourself

and in God Himself that saves you, not faith in the inter-
preters of His word. No baskets will be passed around tonight. No money will be collected, nor will it be accepted.
God does not charge for the benefit of His word."

Sister Barbara held both hands out to the crowd, reaching as if to touch them all. This time, when a thunderclap
and burst of lightning filled her pause, the crowd remained
silent and still.

"Are there those who have come to be healed tonight?"

"Yes!" a segment of the crowd shouted back at the
stage.

"Are there those who are sick in the body?"

"Yes!"

"Are there those who are sick in the mind?"

"Yes!" Considerably less resounding.

"Are there those who have lost hope . . ."

"Yes!"

"Forgotten how to love . . ."

"Yes!"

"Down on their luck, lost in their faith, faced with demons in the form of the bottle or the pill . . ."

"Yes! . . . Yes! . . . Yes!"

Sister Barbara brought her hands together before her in
a mock position of prayer. "What are we to do about these
cancers that eat away at our bodies and our souls? We
come here seeking salvation from the only force we have
left to turn to. And if we leave here as we came, what happens then? What happens tomorrow when the alarm goes
off and the pain of another day sets in?" Her eyes swept
the crowd, hundreds believing they had met her stare and
each of these feeling a strange shudder pass through them.
"We lose hope, and when we lose hope the hole we dig
grows deeper. When we lose hope our lives become a
quagmire in which our emotions have been lost. So all of
you who have come here for salvation must look into your
own souls before you can expect God to notice you."

"Amen," chanted the choir with upraised palms shaking.

"Amen," followed the crowd.

"But it isn't to find God that you've come here tonight," Sister Barbara continued, "it's to find yourselves. To find meaning, to find, yes, hope. And I will show you how to find it. I will be your guide because I've been there myself. I've sunk to the very depths. I've known what it's like to give up on the world, and when you give up on yourself, that's what you're doing."

Sister Barbara squeezed her eyes closed. Her whole face squinted up into a pained scowl. She bowed her head slightly and touched her hands to her temples.

"There's a woman out there who hasn't seen her son in five years. He ran away when he was thirteen—"

"*Ohhhh-ahhhhhhh,*" came a sobbing scream from somewhere in the middle of the rows.

"—because his father beat him." Sister Barbara's eyes opened. "And the woman threw the father out of the house when she learned what he had done. Too late to save her son, but not too late to save herself and her soul. She blames herself, because she was afraid to stop the father, tortures herself because her son is gone."

"*Please,*" the same voice from the middle pleaded, its echo swallowed by a thunderclap.

"Come forward," Sister Barbara instructed.

And the huge crowd turned en masse toward the center of the tent. Some rose slightly, stiff from the sitting. Others squinted. The murmur was deafening as a slovenly woman in a nondescript blue print dress made her way slowly down the center aisle toward the stage. Her hair hung uneven and limp. Rolls of fat pushed the dress outward at the sides and threatened to split the seams. She was sobbing quietly, eyes glazed in shock.

Sister Barbara knelt at the edge of the stage and reached down to take the woman's hand in one of her own. "You fear you will never see your son again. You want me to tell you if he will ever come back, tell you where you might find him."

"Yes! *Please . . .*"

"What reason have you given him to return?"

The woman looked up questioningly. Her grip on Sister Barbara's hand slackened.

"What have you made of yourself since he left, since your husband left? What has the boy to return to?"

"I, I, I—"

"Fear drove him away. If there is no hope, no faith, he will never return. You must make a life for yourself before you can make one for anyone else."

Sobbing horribly, the slovenly woman began to sink. Sister Barbara latched her second hand over her first and wouldn't let her drop.

"You want to quit. So many of us have wanted to quit, and at times we do. We fall into a grave we make for ourselves, hoping someone will pull us out. Ultimately, though, that task is left to us, and if we fail to perform it, we sink deeper until one day we can no longer see the surface. Can you see the surface now, sister?"

The woman's lips trembled.

"Can you see the surface?"

"No. God forgive me, no."

"Close your eyes, sister. Close your eyes and let your mind take you back to when the surface was there. See those years when you thought you had a chance to be happy. If you hadn't fooled yourself, you wouldn't have fallen. Can you see your wedding day, your child being born? . . ."

The woman's tears had turned joyous. A smile so long in coming that fresh dimples were carved in her cheeks stretched wide and mighty. "Yes! Yes! Praise the Lord, yes!"

"Don't praise the Lord, sister. Praise yourself. See yourself back then and make yourself into that person once more. Climb back to the surface."

The woman's smile vanished, pain replacing it across her features. "I—I—I . . . can't!"

"You can!"

"I can't reach it!"

"Then I'll pull you up. Bring your other hand to mine and I'll pull you up!"

"Yes—yes—"

"Give me your other hand, sister. Take mine with it!"

The woman's fingers flailed blindly until they brushed against the right hand Sister Barbara had locked over her left. Instantly Sister Barbara released it, feeling the clammy grasp close into her own as she interlocked all ten of her fingers into the woman's.

"Now use me to help pull yourself upward," she instructed.

"I'm too weak!"

"You're not!"

"Pull!" the crowd chanted, on their feet now. "Pull!"

The woman seemed to hear them and stretched upward, trying to lift herself.

"That's it!" Sister Barbara coaxed. "Try a little harder now. Just a little bit harder."

And when the woman obliged, Sister Barbara hoisted her atop the stage in one incredibly swift and strong motion, showing no sign of exertion whatsoever. A gasp of wonder for the apparently effortless feat passed through the crowd. The slovenly woman, meanwhile, stood next to her shaking. Her wrinkled dress clung to her, its bottom hanging stiff and uneven.

"Thank you," she sobbed, tears running races down her face. "Praise the Lord, thank you."

Sister Barbara was still holding her hands, but lower now in a tender grasp. "You know what you must do, don't you? You know what you must do if your son is ever to return."

"I have seen it."

"Don't let go of the sight, sister. Don't let go of it as you have let go of hope in the past, because the sight represents hope; the sight *is* hope!"

The woman slumped against her, and Sister Barbara eased her frame to the floor.

"This woman's spirit has been slain, her demons excised," she told the crowd. "Some of our demons are stronger. The demons of disease, of failure, of guilt, of missed opportunities. But they are demons all the same, and with the acceptance of hope comes the strongest weapon of all to banish them forever."

With that, Sister Barbara descended the narrow set of stairs to the floor. Thousands of eyes strained to follow her as she started down the aisle, reaching her hands outward to close upon random foreheads as she passed. Without fail or exception, those she touched crumpled to the ground and lay there. Some pushed into the aisle, waving to get her attention.

"Don't let anyone tell you there is no hope," she spoke on her way down the aisle, fallen bodies left in her wake. "Don't believe the doomsayers who have given up on the world and believe it cannot be salvaged. Don't believe them when they speak of a time coming soon that will see a new dawn of man with only those worthy to be saved in the populace. Don't believe them, brothers and sisters, because we are all worthy to be saved, each and every one of us. And your faith in that simple belief is what will stop their Judgment Day from sweeping us aside into a netherworld where hope lies suspended. You can find it," Sister Barbara said into the eyes of a man who folded up before her and dropped under her touch. "We can *all* find it, brothers and sisters. We—"

She cut her words off when she caught sight of the pair of well-dressed men standing near the aisle. Their smiles were wooden. They made no effort to draw closer to her healing hands. And she knew who they were, she knew even before she saw that each was missing the lobe of his left ear.

"They are among us even now, brothers and sisters," Sister Barbara started again, afraid to take her eyes from the pair of men. "We cannot escape them, no, but we *can* defeat them. We can, indeed."

She hoped.

* * *

Sister Barbara unlocked the door to her trailer and stepped into its welcome darkness. She was not surprised to see her small desk lamp on, even though she remembered turning it off. Nor was she surprised to see the two well-dressed figures she recalled from inside the tent sitting in the pair of matching chairs.

"Good evening, Sister Barbara," the one with dark hair greeted. "It is time to come home."

"Return to the kingdom," the light-haired one followed instantly. "Return to the Seven."

Sister Barbara didn't know where the gift that had made her what she was had come from, or when she realized she possessed it. She remembered playing guessing games as a child that she always won. Back then she learned to dissemble, to hold back her answers, so her friends would continue to play with her. She had never been able to foretell the future; in fact, she couldn't even have told the woman in the tent tonight where her son actually was. She had only heard the familiar voice in her head describe her wretched plight.

Thanks to that same voice, Sister Barbara could look at people and know what was in their thoughts, what was troubling them. Things came into her head when she opened up her mind, whether she liked it or not. She couldn't help it. She wanted to help people; anyone, *everyone*.

With that in mind, after college she had become a teacher. But her inclination to get personally involved in the lives and problems of her students cost her job after job in both private and public schools. She was always told she made people uncomfortable: parents, students, other teachers, *everyone*.

Only out of that series of disappointments had she found her true calling. She began speaking to small groups in clubrooms and libraries, focusing on how people could help themselves. The self-help craze was just catching on, and she rode the wave of it into publication and talk radio.

Her appearances grew from kaffeeklatsches to capacity crowds in large auditoriums. Her early reviewers likened her talks to old-fashioned revivalist sermons. There had been a lot of publicity, and she supposed that, more than anything, had eased her into the evangelical field, where her beliefs and teachings fit quite nicely. She became one of the most sought-after guest speakers in the entire country. Her following grew as vast as it was devoted.

And then suddenly and inexplicably, it was gone. Her Sunday television show, her million-name-strong mailing list, and at least that many regular donors had all been forsaken, replaced by an eight-truck traveling revival troop that set up shop quickly for one- or two-night stands in any town that would have it. Spreading the word to ever fewer, hoping it would pay off in a way only she understood. The media had for a time demanded to know why. But she never told them, because she was convinced they'd never have believed her and could have no role in this anyway.

The battle she was fighting was hers to wage, without the aid of the very implements that had necessitated it. No television, no share points and huge big-ticket donors. To preserve the future, Sister Barbara returned to the methods of the past, her endless tour undertaken toward preventing something she had nearly been a party to formulating:

Judgment Day.

It was a race between her and the other members of the Seven she had abandoned. As for the Seven, they would leave her alone. They had no choice. She had them, and they knew it. Taking out a little insurance policy before she had departed their kingdom had seen to that. Because of that insurance, the presence of the men in the tent and now in her trailer astonished her.

"Return to the Seven," the dark-haired one repeated.

"There is still a place for you in the kingdom," added the light-haired one.

"We have come to escort you."

"One final chance."

"I made it plain I had no intention of returning," Sister Barbara told them, "when I made my departure."

"The situation has changed," the brown-haired one retorted, "and the Reverend desires the return of your company."

"Sacrificing yourself would be a waste," added the blond.

Sister Barbara wasn't frightened. "Perhaps the Reverend is forgetting that I hold something very near and dear to him."

"A man entered your employ some months back," said brown hair.

"A computer wizard named Ratansky," picked up blond. "He was planted by Turgewell. When he left, he took your insurance with him."

"Turgewell is dead."

"We thought so, too," said the blond. "We were both wrong."

"And now all of us must pay the price for our mistaken judgment," elaborated the brown-haired one. "But for you that price is a blessing. You may return to the kingdom, Sister."

"And the Seven," from blond hair. "The Reverend will still have you. He still wants you to stand by his side."

Sister Barbara tried not to show the fear she now felt. Yet the revelation sent a numbness surging up her spine. Her mouth and throat felt as if she were trying to swallow cotton. She remembered the strange circumstances surrounding Benjamin Ratansky's abrupt, unannounced departure. Now she understood what accounted for them.

He had been planted by Turgewell, the other member of the Seven who had fled the kingdom even before her, whose overtures to join him in waging war against them, she had continually ignored right up until his supposed death a year before. Obviously he had faked that death to better enable him to strike back at the Seven, the list of names that had kept them from striking at her no doubt paramount in his plans. In Turgewell's hands that list would end up being put to violent use indeed, rendering it useless to her as a guarantee of her own safety against the mere threat of exposure.

"The time grows near," the blond one was saying.

"To what?" Sister Barbara asked him.

He looked at her calmly. "To accomplish our purpose."

"Judgment Day is upon us," the other one followed.

Sister Barbara went cold, a numbness slipping over her. Could it be? Could the Reverend actually have found a means to fulfill the mad dream that had led her to break with the Seven?

"We are waiting for your decision," the blond one said, interrupting her line of thought.

"Leave me," Sister Barbara ordered them both.

"As you wish." The brown-haired one nodded.

The two men climbed to their feet, hands rigid at their sides. When they reached the door to the trailer, the blond one turned back.

"Hell awaits you, Sister Barbara."

"No, I already left it once," she told the two of them from her desk. "And I don't plan on going back."

CHAPTER 12

It was a four-hour drive to the Sheridan Correctional Center, where Benjamin Ratansky spent his only three years of incarceration. McCracken would be arriving late into the night, but the gravity of the situation led prison officials to skirt the rules. In this case that meant setting up a meeting for Blaine with Arthur Deek, the inmate in charge of the Fifth Generation chapter Ratansky had been linked to.

The missing-earlobe trademark had drawn an obvious connection between the religious group founded in prison by Preston Turgewell and the two dead gunmen who had disappeared from the New York City medical examiner's office. Benjamin Ratansky's place in all this remained a mystery, though Blaine hoped his visit to the penitentiary would shed some light on it.

"Nothing unusual about them," noted the guard captain named Neal in reference to the Fifth Generation as he escorted Blaine to a private consultation room in the visitors' area. "Place like this, you gotta be part of something to survive."

"Do all the groups cut off pieces of themselves?" McCracken asked him.

"No, some wear tattoos, rings, bandannas, colors—anything to advertise that there are others who will fuck with you if you fuck with them."

"Does it work for the Fifth Generation?"

"They keep to themselves."

"How do you join?"

"You don't; you set selected. Criteria vary. Usually it's the most violent types, the most unsalvageable. Fifth Generation picks who they want. Only thing, candidates got to really want to be saved."

"From who?"

"Themselves mostly."

"And their leader here, the one I'm about to meet?"

"Par for the course," Captain Neal told him. "Maybe a little worse."

Arthur Deek had been imprisoned for life after the kidnapping and subsequent sodomizing of three junior high school students. Deek tempted them into his car at a bus stop with a simple promise of a ride home from school on the rainiest day in months. It was another month before the police tracked him and his prey to an isolated mountain cabin. One of the boys hadn't spoken a word since. Another would likely be institutionalized for years to come. A third had not yet started sleeping again.

Meanwhile, Arthur Deek found God as the penitentiary's latest leader of the Fifth Generation. He was six-foot-one, same height as Blaine, and just as powerfully built, although it was impossible to tell from his seated, slumped frame. His head was shaven and his face carried a smirk worn whenever out of the presence of his devoted followers. He had been awakened from a sound sleep and resented it. He didn't so much as turn Blaine's way when Captain Neal escorted McCracken into the private visitor's room. The room was a simple, windowless square dominated by gray, peeling walls. A table and four chairs made up the only furniture. Blaine could see the unused fittings where a water fountain had once rested.

"You can leave us alone," McCracken said when Neal started to back himself against the wall.

Neal gestured Deek's way. "He ain't wearing cuffs, mister."

"Neither am I, Captain."

Neal looked Blaine over once and then reluctantly took his leave. Only then did Arthur Deek turn his way. McCracken had never seen a stare any colder.

"Bad idea," Deek said, glowering.

"Thinking about saving my soul, Deek?"

"Killing you, actually."

Blaine frowned at him. "Both difficult tasks. I doubt you're up to either. You're welcome to try the latter anytime you want. Careful, though: I'm likely to put up more of a fight than those thirteen-year-old boys."

Deek's milk white face reddened slightly. "Another man's crimes, not mine."

"Too bad you were the one they put away."

"They put away my body, not my spirit. My soul lives. My soul runs free. Into the universe. Into infinity. My consciousness roams. My body means nothing."

"Tell that to all the people who are scared shitless of you."

Deek gripped the edge of the table with his hands. "Heathen swine who will not be saved come Judgment Day."

McCracken bristled at mention of the phrase. "What do you know about Judgment Day, Deek?"

"Nothing, other than it's coming. Soon."

"Based on reliable information, I presume."

"Most reliable," Deek responded, and turned his eyes upward.

"Sorry, Arthur, wrong direction."

"Only those who possess the key will be saved . . ."

"Like the one that got thrown away when the feds stowed you here?"

". . . the key to the better life that lies ahead."

"Which you, of course, have."

"All who seek the one real truth may possess it if they are worthy."

"And just what is that real truth?"

"The pursuit of rebirth and salvation above all else. A new beginning etched over a merciful end that will overcome the world as it lays dying. Then we will rise from this hell to claim it."

"Need a different key to manage that, Arthur."

"No," Deek answered, with chilling menace lacing his voice. "Only one."

"And where does Benjamin Ratansky fit into all this?"

"The former names of those who seek the truth hold no meaning for me."

"Let me jog your memory. This was an average, nondescript guy. Early fifties, heartbroken family waiting for him at home, probably." When that failed to bring a response, Blaine continued, "Anyone waiting for you, Deek?"

The flush of anger returned to the Fifth Generation leader's face, and Blaine sat down in the chair across from Deek before seizing the advantage.

"Computers were his specialty. You have a need for computers?"

"I have need only for God."

"The need I suggested better explains why you decided to make sure he was protected. A man came to see him a couple times in the month before you made contact. That same man came to see you."

Deek wet his lips with his tongue. "Interesting conclusion."

"Obvious is a better way to describe it: The handwriting on the sign-in diaries matched."

Blaine watched Deek's heavy hands creep over the top of the table.

"Here's how I figure it," he continued. "Someone in your movement on the outside decided they could make use of Ratansky's skills. Contact got made and all of a sudden you put out the word that this man is off limits. Not only that, the man needs a few able bodies to help him walk out of here. Logistical stuff, access to the right room containing the right computer maybe. Then, not too long after, he checks himself out of Sheridan and into a nonexistent cell in Taylorville. How'm I doing?"

Deek looked away from him.

"Only you got fooled, Deek. You thought it was your own people on the outside who wanted Ratansky walking free. Turned out it was somebody else, one of your many sworn enemies," Blaine said, filling in the gaps as he figured them in an attempt to draw a rise from Deek. "You find out and dispatch a couple goons who graduated from your school of madness to send Ratansky to his Maker, only they don't catch up with him until he's figured out what whoever's backing you is really up to."

Deek still wasn't looking.

"Thing is, though, Ratansky came away with evidence. I've got it now, Arthur."

Deek turned his head and met Blaine's stare.

"Maybe has something to do with Judgment Day. Maybe will tell me what I need to stop it."

Deek's smirk stretched into a smile. "You can't stop it. No one can stop it."

"You help me, maybe I can do you a favor God can't: reduce your sentence."

The smirk returned. "My sentence here matters not at all, not in the face of what is coming."

"Then why not tell me where Ratansky got those names I've got now? Tell me what they mean, what connects them. The computer fraud he pulled off that landed him here was called the most brilliant crime of the decade, and then he follows that up by having himself transferred to a nonexistent cell in another prison. Even a heathen like me can tell he's special. Man like that can make a lot of things happen." He hesitated. "And the man who got duped could be in some deep shit."

Deek rose with his fists clenched by his sides.

"Might even prevent you from being saved come Judgment Day," Blaine taunted.

Deek was sweating now, big rivulets crawling down his face on a collision course with each other. Blaine joined him on his feet. For a few long moments neither spoke or moved.

"Tell me who's behind whatever Ratansky uncovered," Blaine said finally. "Help me and I help you—believe me, it won't be easy."

Deek was starting to show his teeth now, like a dog on the verge of a pounce.

"Last chance," Blaine told him. "You got a move to make, go ahead."

His shape stayed frozen.

"Thanks for your help," McCracken said, and moved the rest of the way out the door.

In the hallway Captain Neal was gone, a burly monster of a guard in his place.

"Sergeant O'Malley," the man said, rigid at attention. "I'm to escort you out."

"Your captain have other business?"

"Some trouble in one of the cellblocks, sir." O'Malley hesitated, swallowing hard. His eyes fixed on the door to the visitor's room. "Was he helpful, sir?"

"You scared of Deek, Sergeant?"

They started down the hallway.

"Don't know anyone in this place who isn't, sir."

"I'm going to tell you something about men like him, Sergeant. I'm going to tell you something about—"

O'Malley shifted his frame slightly when they swung left at the end of the hall. The motion made him cock his head and gave Blaine a glimpse of the left side of his face.

The earlobe on that side was missing.

O'Malley must have caught the flash of recognition in McCracken's eyes because he spun toward him an instant before Blaine had thrown himself into motion. Blaine's initial blow grazed off the bigger man's cheek and kept him spinning. O'Malley tried to right himself, but Mc-Cracken slammed into him, grabbing a fistful of hair. Blaine pushed forward toward the wall, and O'Malley's face made the first impact. He ignored the crunching sound that followed and rammed O'Malley's face against the concrete surface again.

O'Malley started to slump. Blaine swung toward the sound of feet thudding his way.

The members of the Fifth Generation rushed him from both ends of the hall; some bald, some bearded and hairy. All missing their left earlobes. Blaine knocked the first few lunges aside and felt stupidly for the pistol no longer holstered back on his hip since regulations insisted it be left at the security desk. Another assailant lashed at him from behind, and Blaine threw him up and over his own body. The move took him to one knee, and before he could recover, a pair of men launched themselves atop him. He was pinned down. A shadow loomed overhead as he struggled to twist free. Something like a whistling blur whirled down at him.

Then nothing.

CHAPTER 13

Johnny Wareagle had not been to the north woods of California that encompassed Redwood National Park a single time since his pursuit of Earvin Early and the two other killers two decades earlier. Tonight those woods looked mean and foreboding, an unfriendly wild barrier that defied all efforts of man to tame it. Johnny stood staring at the forest for some time, his pack resting at his feet, as if seeking permission to enter. The darkness of the night was broken occasionally by the moon pushing its way through the dense cloud cover above.

Johnny checked his watch. It was coming up on 10:00 P.M., the same time he had entered the woods in this very spot twenty years before. The woods had grown larger, the trees thicker and the undergrowth more tangled. But the trails would still be there. Even if Johnny could not see them, he would be able to sense their presence and the direction they broke off in.

The woods swallowed him as he entered, wrapped him in their branches and reached for him with their vines.

Wareagle gave himself up. Part of his mind saw what lay ahead now. The other recalled the sights from two decades earlier. The trees and undergrowth had buried the signs of the trail Early and the others had left in their relentless, unchecked bloodletting.

But not the memories.

The spirits helped rekindle them, and they came with him every step of the way. For Johnny it was like walking into a mirror. The sounds from the past mixed with those of the present. The man Earvin Early was now had been born in these woods. The spirits' counsel had brought Johnny here on a trail he knew would lead to Judgment Day for reasons only this trek could reveal.

Time grew distorted, at times seeming frozen, appearing to fly at others. Johnny forgot about his watch, forgot about everything. He took no water, felt no thirst.

Twenty years ago he had been dispatched to find three men, three killers. Those who had retained him showed him the pictures of the killers' most recent handiwork. Johnny had known then he had no choice. Earvin Early and the others had to be stopped, and he was the only one who could do it.

On this night, just as on that night, Wareagle came to the campsite in the north woods where the bodies had been found. The forest had swallowed the sites now, leaving no sign. The picnic tables had been carted away or left to rot into the ground. The clearing had been filled in as deftly as if someone had transplanted another part of the forest over this one. The path to the nearby pond was gone, and so, too, was the pond, lost long ago to drought and no more than a wide brown strip cut out of the woods that grew narrower each year.

But Johnny could look through the darkness and see the site tonight as he had seen it that night.

The three killers had come upon the families not long after dawn. The bodies of the boys were found near the water. Two fathers, savagely mutilated, lay halfway between the pond and the camp, as if responding to the screams of their boys.

Early and the others saved the women and girls for last, cut parts of them out when they were finished, parts that had never been found. The government experiment they had been subjected to had been meant to enhance their senses. It had done that and more, creating monsters driven to fill whatever insatiable needs struck them. Psychotics who lived in a surreal state that, as in dreams, bore no real consequence for any action.

Johnny continued on through what had once been a clearing.

Screams. He heard screams. . . .

Even though they were the products of the past, the screams chilled him to the bone. Twenty years ago, Johnny had picked up on the fear and hate, enabling him to follow the trail of the killers into the night. He used the borrowed emotions when he came upon the first of the killers covering the traces of their camp in the last hours of dark.

A knife for that one, throat cut fast and neat.

He set out after Early and the other, climbed a tree when he sensed one of them returning up a path. When the short, muscular man passed under him, Wareagle pounced, the knife working again, not stopping until he was sure.

And then he went after Early.

He found the huge man standing on the edge of a ravine located at the far side of a clearing about fifty feet from Johnny. Early was standing frozen, his back to him. A massive knife glinted in the moonlight by his side. Johnny imagined it was still soiled with the blood of the families.

Johnny unshouldered his bow and unsheathed an arrow. Pulling back on a string packing 125 pounds of pressure, he sighted.

Early turned, the moonlight enough to catch the mad rage feasting in his eyes. He started forward.

Johnny released his hold. The string snapped taut with a twang, arrow slicing the air. He watched it thump home.

Early was still coming.

Johnny unleashed another arrow and placed it no more than an inch to the right of the first, just missing the heart. Early staggered, backpedaled, losing all the ground he had gained from the edge of the ravine.

Johnny had held his ground, another arrow at the ready. Early's eyes sought his out in the wind-whipped darkness. Then he was gone, falling backward over the edge of the precipice into the ravine.

Wareagle stood now in that very spot, Early's footprints long lost to time, but not the vision of his memory. The river currents one hundred feet below churned more slowly, fed now by diminished streams of water. The trail stopped here. Earvin Early had dropped down into the dark and was gone. Yet what he had become, what he was today, was birthed.

Something was down there. Something awaited Johnny tonight as it had awaited Early twenty years before.

Wareagle stripped the pack from his shoulders and withdrew what he needed. Rappelling without a belay down a sheer cliff was a daunting task at night, but Johnny felt impelled to follow where the spirits led him.

He tied off his two-hundred-foot coil of climbing rope to the base of a tree twenty feet from the edge, using an assortment of webbing and carabiners. Satisfied it would hold him, Johnny pulled himself into his harness. Then he threaded the rope through the appropriate slots on his figure eight device and pulled to take up the slack. Then he backpedaled to the edge and eased himself over the rock face, feeling the tight rope spooling through his gloved hands as he began his drop.

Johnny's first two bounds were met unforgivingly by the rock face, but he quickly settled into a rhythm as his rustiness with the process wore off. He discovered that what had seemed a sheer face was in fact partially a ledge. It jutted out far enough to slow or even stop a fall. Early could have flailed out in his descent and in his desperation managed to latch on to one of the thick plants growing out of the face. From there, even gravely wounded, he could have lowered himself down the cliff.

But something else had awaited him at the bottom, something that had allowed him to survive to become whatever he was part of today. It was a feeling in Johnny that grew stronger with each bound off the rock and sharpened every time his boots clacked against the hard face with the rope threading comfortably through his gloved hands and harness.

At the bottom a trickling stream gurgled where the churning river had been. Johnny left his rope hanging and returned his harness and gloves to his pack. The night glow showed the water to be barely up to his boots.

His instincts told him to cross the stream to the other side, where the foliage was thinner and more easily navigated. He found himself on a path that, unlike those in the woods above, remained clear of intrusive vines and branches.

Johnny leaned over and first felt the ground, then sniffed it. Men had been down this path fairly recently, a week before at most, a few days even. He rose slowly.

One of the tracks was fresh. Last-half-hour fresh. Someone out in the night who may have seen him in the midst of his rappel down the cliff face.

Johnny moved on down the trail. His pace was slow at first, methodical. But soon, before he knew it, he was trotting. Branches whisked by his face. The night meant nothing.

A few hundred yards later, the trail widened to almost road size. Soon after the woods receded altogether and a clearing appeared, carved out of the forest. Johnny stood very still, all his senses alert for any sound or movement signaling a human presence. Reassured that he was alone, he reached back into his pack and pulled out his flashlight.

Its beam fell on what had been a small nest of cabins. Now there were just blackened shells and dark patches incised into the ground to mark the spots where homes had once been.

The cabins had been burned to the ground, each and every one of them. Slabs of petrified wood and blackened hunks that had once been heavy base lumber were all that remained, taking the form of gravestones. Johnny reached down and picked up a charred chunk of black. A single squeeze turned it to powdery dust in his hand. The fires that had done this had burned long ago. Eerily, the clearing smelled of nothing, not life or death. Only the night.

Johnny continued to move about. The burn pattern was incredibly even. The buildings had frozen dark and dead in the midst of uniform smoldering. The flames could hardly be considered the result of an accident. Almost certainly they had been set, nurtured, coaxed. Wareagle shuffled his feet through some of the black-soaked earth.

Was this where Earvin Early had ended up? Might he have been responsible for the fire that had destroyed this place?

No. The fire had been years ago, but not twenty. The first question, though, remained open. Early could have found his way here after salvaging himself from the river. It made sense.

Crack . . .

Something still whole had given way underfoot. Not ahead of him—behind. Johnny turned off his flashlight.

More rustling sounded, some distant, some close. Ghosts rising out of the black soot to bid him welcome, maybe Earvin Early himself come back to pay his respects. There was a louder snap and Johnny swung to find a burly figure with purposely blackened flesh standing there grasping a leveled shotgun. In the next instant similar shapes appeared in the darkness, surrounding him while keeping their distance safe.

"Be a good idea," started the first figure he had glimpsed, as the others began to advance, "if you just stayed right where you are."

CHAPTER 14

The first thing Blaine felt when he began to come around was water dripping onto him. His initial sensation was to cough out a pool of it that had slid into his mouth. He tried to wipe the remnants from his chin, but his hand wouldn't move. Then he remembered. His eyes opened and cleared slowly to the memory of being overcome by an endless wave of members of the Fifth Generation. He wasn't dead; that was something, however little for the time being.

His vision sharpened to find a grinning face not more than a yard from his own. The face was still sweating, the eyes dark and malevolent. The bald head glistened.

"Nice of you to join us, heathen," greeted Arthur Deek.

Blaine gazed around him. The water dripping down on his face came from a rusted showerhead directly above. His hands were suspended over him to exposed piping, a pair of chains dangling down that had been fastened around his wrists. His unshackled legs were spread at shoulder width, his toes barely able to touch the floor. He was naked except for his briefs. His beard itched and he couldn't reach it.

Besides Deek, another dozen or so of the Fifth Generation were present in the shower room, approximately one for each of the ancient heads that dripped water to varying degrees. It pooled on the filthy tile floor and slid toward the drain. The continued plopping sounds of the drips provided an incessant backdrop, until someone turned the nozzle activating the shower directly above McCracken. An irregular spray of scalding water singed his flesh and made him arch involuntarily.

"You will tell me who sent you," Deek demanded, through the steam that floated between them.

"No one."

"You lie! *They* sent you. I know. Admit it and you die easy."

"Why don't you tell me who *they* are?"

Deek drew a bit closer. "This is our world. You don't belong."

"Let me go and I'll be glad to—"

Deek backhanded him, and Blaine felt blood pooling in his mouth.

"The traitors sent you, but you die knowing nothing."

"What traitors? Traitors to what?"

Deek nodded toward one of the figures behind him. The man slid forward and handed him some sort of electrical device formed of twin prods wired to a base station farther back. Deek took one in either hand and held them out to Blaine so he could see they looked like those of a portable defibrillating machine.

"We must know the identities of all our enemies." Showing the prods now. "Why did you ask me about Ratansky?"

"I told you why, scumbag."

Deek's eyes flared, the prongs raised to their level, close enough for Blaine to smell. "Where are the contents of his briefcase? Where is the list he stole?"

"Stole from who?"

"Tell me where it is!"

"Where do you fit into Judgment Day, Deek? What's your stake? What have you been promised?"

Deek jabbed the prongs forward. Blaine heard a buzzing sound an instant before the pain rocked him. A spasm shot through his body and slammed his teeth together. His eyes faded to darkness, then slowly found the light again. He couldn't stop shaking. The spray of hot water pounding him from above was what kept him from passing out, he figured.

"The lowest setting," Deek told McCracken. "Four more to go before we reach the highest. Your choice."

Blaine resisted the feeling of hopelessness that threatened to overcome him, analyzing his options. Since the jolt-induced spasms, something seemed different about his bonds. His wrists enjoyed a bit more slack. Ever so subtly he tried to move his hands and felt the exposed pipes they were chained to wobble.

Weakening! The pipes were weakening!

"You stood smug as my conqueror in the visitor's room," Deek taunted. "But none who know the true purpose of our existence can live."

"Judgment Day," Blaine muttered.

This time he saw the prods coming and tried to brace himself. It was no use. An even greater burst of fiery pain surged through him from toe to scalp. He wanted to kick himself out of his skin. His head whiplashed back and banged off the tile. Hot needles of water burned his scalp. He gasped, forgetting how to breathe for a lingering moment.

Above him the pipes his wrists were attached to were creaking from the strain.

"You will tell me where I can find the contents of Ratansky's briefcase!" Deek demanded. "You will tell me who you have shared them with!"

Blaine looked at him, having trouble keeping his head up. His legs were beginning to throb now from the strain of resting his weight all on his toes. He had to keep it that way so that the Fifth Generation members wouldn't notice the slack the pipes above were giving.

"Who has the list Ratansky stole?"

McCracken couldn't have answered even if he had wanted to. He could barely feel the steamy heat of the water flowing upon him now.

"Who sent you?"

Just getting all his breath back now.

"Talk!"

Blaine screamed an instant before the prongs hit this time. His whole body jumped, his spine seeming to sizzle. When the jolt ended, he had no feeling anywhere in his body. Everything was numb and tingly. His leg muscles had cramped and the pain was awful.

"Scream if you want!" Deek suggested gleefully.

McCracken still couldn't breathe.

"Scream!"

And the prongs came forward again.

This time Blaine felt almost nothing. The world before him turned black with agony. A cut on his tongue dribbled blood through his mouth and it leaked out with his saliva. His knees buckled and vibrated. He would have screamed if he could have, but the breath to manage it wasn't there.

Above him, though, the pipes had all but come free of their worn fasteners, the ceiling ready to give them up. Blaine knew he couldn't take much more, perhaps not even one jolt. The next setting was the highest, and if he managed to survive it, the effects might well leave him unable to respond further.

"You are weak," Deek told him. "Your strength is only an illusion, an illusion you share with so many others. All the weak will perish when Judgment Day comes. The weak will perish, and the strong—the deserving—shall rise to take our rightful place. We have the key." Deek came forward and jammed Blaine's face to him. "Do you hear me? We have the key to the door into the new world. We will be reborn into it, and in our image it shall be remade."

He stepped back and readied the prongs. They hummed slightly.

McCracken tensed his wrist muscles and willed the con-

trol back into them. He let the hot water run down his
face, using the pain to recharge himself. His hands tightened on the chains affixed to the loosened pipes.

Loose enough . . . They had to be.

"In the name of God," said Deek, and the prongs started
forward.

McCracken yanked on the pipes. The flood of water that
came when they jerked free of the wall soaked him exclusively. Deek noticed it too late, along with the corrugated
steel flashing between him and his target. The prongs
wedged up against the steel and sizzled. Deek's scream
was deafening but brief, giving way quickly to a raspy
gurgle that hung in the air while he jittered and juked. One
of the Fifth Generation disciples had grasped his leader at
the shoulders to try and pull him free. The result instead
was his simply joining in the death dance, a bizarre duet
now, one virtually mirroring the other.

The lights in the shower room flickered once and then
died, plunging it into a darkness broken only by dull rays
sneaking in around the corner leading toward the sinks and
toilets. The darkness, coupled with the Fifth Generation
members' shock, gave Blaine the freedom to slide his
chains all the way from the pipes' hold. His legs were still
unsteady and he nearly collapsed when he tried to put all
his weight on the two of them. He remained jammed
against the wall, willing the strength back into his limbs.

The water from the pipes he had split was the same scalding temperature as what had been coming from the shower,
and the result was to cast a steam cloud over the entire
scene, further hiding him from sight. But neither the near-
darkness nor the steam would keep him camouflaged forever,
not even long enough for the prison guards to come to his
rescue. He had to seize the advantage while he had it.

In their boldness none of the Fifth Generation had entered the shower carrying a weapon, and that made the
chains still laced to Blaine's wrists all the more effective.
His eyes were able to make out shapes in the steamy darkness and he lunged toward the first ones he saw, whirling

the chain still laced to his right wrist from left to right. The gnarled links surged across the prisoners' faces and eyes, blinding them.

McCracken jumped forward and looped one of his chains around the neck of the next nearest disciple and joined his free hand to it. He took the slack out and caught the man's windpipe between two of the links. The man stiffened, flailing away before his windpipe snapped, and Blaine dropped him off to the side.

Two of the surviving members of the Fifth Generation adjusted enough to the dark to charge at Blaine through the steam. McCracken twisted from their path to position one between himself and the other. He reached for the nearest and jammed his thumbs into both the man's eyes. The man's agonized howl rose over the rush of spilling water and panicked cries of those still milling about. The other man had a knife, more of a prison shank in truth, and Blaine twisted his blinded fellow into the path of the first wild strike he launched. The blade tore though the disciple's windpipe and splashed blood all over the rising steam.

"Where is he? Where is he?"

The desperate call repeated again and again. The man with the shank knew, or at least thought he did. He launched the shank forward at a shape lost to the dark. But the shape was gone, melted, and when he lunged to follow, the body of the blinded disciple still gurgling blood caught his foot and nearly spilled him. The man was trying to recover his balance when a hand latched on to the wrist holding the shank and twisted it totally around. The snap was as audible as a gunshot. The man's scream would have been as well, had not a hand clamped over his mouth and twisted his chin with sufficient force to snap his neck.

The remaining disciples had at last gathered themselves, the terrible calamity that had befallen them suddenly clear. They fanned out through the shower room, careful to dodge the bodies of their fellows. Inspecting the ones they encountered to see if one of them might have been McCracken's.

None were. He was nowhere to be found.

"He's out!" one cried.

"He couldn't be!" another followed.

"The door!"

"Covered!"

"But *where* is he?"

"Get the lights back on! Someone get the lights back on!"

From his perch above them, lying atop the exposed piping that ran a yard beneath the ceiling, Blaine heard footsteps shuffling. According to his count, six more of Deek's charges remained for him to contend with. Two of these passed directly beneath him. McCracken tightened his hold on a different pipe and his hand snapped away singed. The motion nearly toppled him and he felt something rubbery when he altered his grasp to hold on.

It was an electric cord, the power supply for the prods that had tortured him and killed Deek. The cord had been snaked up through the piping and plugged into an outlet somewhere high in the wall or even through the ceiling. He couldn't see the twin prods in the thickening, virtually foglike darkness, but followed the cord three or four feet down from the labyrinthine extensions of piping. If he could pull the prods up to him . . .

Yes! It might work!

Blaine steadied himself and carefully leaned his body forward to grasp the cord. Once he had it, he began to tug, slowly at first, and then snatched the prods to him in a quick burst when he encountered no resistance. As expected, they were operated by a simple setting switch on the power pack connected to the base unit. Once the arrow was moved to any of the five settings, the cuplike prods were automatically activated. As soon as the plastic casements were compressed slightly by pressure, the electricity would surge outward. The remainder of the enemy, meanwhile, collectively stood within the steadily pooling water that made for the best conductor of all.

Easy targets, if Blaine could make the prods work for him

once they got the power back on. The machine's electrical potency still set to the highest level, McCracken let the twin prods dangle below the pipe he was perched upon.

"Up there!" a voice called from below.

"Something moved!"

"It's him!"

Blaine let the prods drop still lower. One of the disciples fighting his way through the fetid mist and near blackness smacked into them.

The lights flashed back on, creating a dull haze through the thickening steam.

McCracken dropped down from the pipe, arms cradled above it to keep himself from reaching the floor. He swung his legs hard and caught the man nearest the prods in the back. The blow stripped the disciple of his balance and sent him over face-first into the deepening pool.

The electrified prods were pinned beneath him.

The hiss that came when the plastic activators compressed upon striking the floor under the water was brief. The screams and wails that followed were not. Blaine heard them as he hoisted himself back up upon the piping. The shower became one vast electric pool, pouring thousands of volts through all the men standing within it. Blaine could barely make out the shaking, twisting, writhing forms that toppled like dominoes one after the other.

A sizzling hiss preceded a shower of sparks from the area of the ceiling outlet where the cord had been plugged in. A pop sounded with a bright flash as power in the entire cellblock shorted out, and the shower room was plunged into darkness yet again.

McCracken dropped down from the pipe, and his feet sloshed into the steaming water. He eased forward, doing his best to avoid stepping on bodies en route to the door. Blaine found the latch and threw it open.

He emerged into the darkness of the cold corridor and hurried to the nearest guard station.

* * *

Wayne Denbo loved being in the dark. In the dark he felt in control. As soon as the light began to intrude, and the voices started to reach him, the control was gone, letting the fear return.

He had no idea of exactly how long he'd been where he was, only that more and more of the dark was receding. He'd reached out to keep it, but it was getting harder and harder to grasp. And the more it receded, the more he could see the shapes coming at him out of the dust in Beaver Falls. Coming at him like they'd come for the others.

Only he'd gotten away. Eyes glued more to the rearview mirror than the windshield, he'd quickly lost his sense of direction, cared only that he wasn't being followed. There seemed to be nothing to do but drive, although he did keep squawking into his mike for a good five minutes before he realized that he'd crushed it. Didn't even notice the blood seeping out of his hand until he smelled its coppery stench, and even then he'd been afraid to spare the time to bandage the wound.

Twice in the past day he'd seen the figures from the dust coming for him in the hospital room, and woke up screaming both times. It took three men to hold him down while a nurse gave him a shot that brought the blessed darkness back for a stretch, though not long enough. Got to the point where he knew if he screamed loud enough, they'd give him a shot and he could have the darkness back, because that was all he had wanted.

Denbo knew he could speak if he really tried, but he chose not to; they wouldn't let him have the darkness again if he did, and the darkness was his only refuge. There none of it had happened. There he had never gone to Beaver Falls. There Joe Langhorn was still sitting next to him in the car.

But Joe was gone now. Wayne was alone.

No one else would listen. No one would believe. He had nowhere to go.

Except the darkness.

* * *

The twins were like chameleons, able to become part of any situation they entered and appear as though they belonged. It was a skill long mastered and well practiced. The news that a number of inmates had been killed brought scores of relatives out to the federal penitentiary. The twins mixed easily among them, and according to plan, it was Jacob who slid inside the Sheridan Correctional Center's gates along with representatives of the media.

"Interesting," was his first comment when he emerged just under an hour later.

"What were you able to find out?" Rachel asked him.

"Fourteen inmates are believed to have been killed. The rumor is, a single man was responsible."

"Rumor . . ."

"There's more. Apparently all the victims were members of the Fifth Generation, including their leader."

"Then it was McCracken! He was *here!*"

"Just as we would have been, given the same information he had."

"Please don't compare yourself to—"

"I was comparing *us.*"

"Never mind." Her gaze drifted back to the prison yard, where revolving lights continued their red spin through the night. "Could he still be inside?"

"If he is, he won't come out through the front."

"Then there's a chance! If we keep moving about the other exits, if we get lucky . . ."

"It's worth a try," Jacob said with little enthusiasm.

"You think he's gone."

"We would be by now."

"Comparisons again."

"If we're going to find Blaine McCracken," Jacob told his twin sister, "we'd better learn to think like him."

CHAPTER 15

The rifle-wielding figures enclosing Johnny Wareagle started to move forward, looking more scared than angry. If they were going to shoot, it seemed to Johnny, they would have already.

"Is he one of 'em?" a new voice blared. "I think he's one of 'em!"

"Then let's kill him."

"Hush up!" ordered a new, gravelly voice. "He ain't carrying a gun. They ever come, it'd be with guns."

"What'd ya call that thing on his chest there?"

"A knife."

"Biggest one I ever saw. Killin' is killin'."

"Never mind that," noted the gravelly voice. "We know he's alone. They'd never come alone."

"Who?" Johnny dared to ask.

"Shut your trap!" ordered the original voice.

The gravel-voiced speaker came closer to Johnny in the darkness. "You lost?"

"No."

"Looking for us, then?"

"Looking for . . . something."

The man with the gravel voice scanned the others with his eyes. "I say we talk to him."

"I say we kill him!" from somewhere in the tight pack of his captors.

"Might not be as easy as it seems."

"He's seen us, goddamnit! Even if he ain't one of them—"

"They did this," Johnny said suddenly, calmly.

The men enclosing him looked at each other.

"What?" the man who wanted to kill him asked.

"Whoever you fear I am a part of, they burned this village."

The man with the gravelly voice finally stepped forward, into the moonlight. The right side of his face was a mass of patchy scar tissue, the eye on that side no more than a shriveled socket sewn closed by the years.

"You come here lookin' for us?" he asked through the perpetual grimace his mouth had been turned into.

"No," Johnny told him, starting to realize. "I think I've come here looking for them."

The walk deeper into the woods took all of a half hour. Johnny towered over his dozen or so captors and made sure his hands were always in plain view so they would have no reason to fear he might be hiding another weapon. They brought Johnny to a settlement nearly indistinguishable from the woods containing it, the decently built cabins shrouded by trees and brush. He couldn't tell exactly how many cabins there were. A row of ten or so lined the front. However many lay amidst the woods beyond these was indiscernible. The settlement's only clearing contained a central hearth around which rock seats had been placed. Tonight Johnny could see that no fire burned in that hearth. Almost to the clearing, the man with the scarred face turned on his flashlight and poured its beam over Johnny.

"You're an Indian."

"Yes."

"You said you thought it was them you were after," the scarred man continued to Johnny. "Mind telling us exactly how you came to that conclusion?"

"I was in these woods before. Twenty years ago."

"So was we," a voice Johnny didn't recognize put forth.

Farther back from the circle, new figures had gathered at the rim of the clearing. Wareagle tried not to let his stare linger on them long, but a few seconds were more than enough for him to identify a number of women and a few older children. What little he could glimpse of their faces showed the same trepidation and uncertainty that had laced the voices of his captors.

"I killed two men that night," Johnny told the men. "I thought I killed three. The third survived, fell off the cliff and into the river. His name was Earvin Early."

The scarred man's expression turned even more pained. "Little late to come after him, ain't it?"

"I only learned Monday afternoon that he was still alive. To me that makes the trail barely thirty-six hours old."

"You a bounty hunter, something like that?" the scarred man wanted to know.

"In a manner of speaking, I was back then," Johnny told them all, and summarized the events of twenty years ago as best he could.

The scarred man was nodding in the end. "These, er, people who sent you after the killers. They musta had their reasons for choosing you."

"They did."

"Knew you were the kinda man got a job done right."

"Until yesterday, I thought I had."

"Those three the only ones you were looking for?"

"Back then, yes."

"And now?"

"Wherever Early's trail takes me," Johnny said, leaving out mention of Judgment Day.

"But it took you to us." The moonlight caught the good side of the scarred man's face, showed it to be creased and wrinkled, the single eye a pale gray color set in a grim countenance. "See, here's the problem. You say this Early and the two others were what brought you to the woods originally. Thing is, it coulda been any of us, Injun, 'cause the truth is, we're not much different. We're all criminals and we were all on the lam when we got here."

The moon peeked out from behind the clouds and caught the whole of the scarred man's face, now concentrated intensely his way. Johnny gazed down at him. "And yet you weren't worried that was what brought me to you tonight."

The scarred man's jaw clenched tight. His eye narrowed into a determined slit, and Johnny could see in it the memories of the burned-out settlement they had left a few miles back in the woods. "They'll be back. Just a matter of time, and time's the one thing we fought to keep our control over."

"Who are *they*?"

"The rest of us, Injun, the ones that got away. The rest of the founding members of the Key Society."

"Man who brought us here called it that 'cause he figured he had the key," the scarred man continued, after introducing himself as Hodge and inviting Johnny to take a seat across from him on one of the rocks that enclosed the cold hearth. Most of the others joined them in the ragtag circle, the rest hanging back on foot or crouched on their haunches. The women and children had vanished from the clearing, at least from sight. In the wooden cabins that rimmed it, Johnny caught occasional flashes of dim light that came and went quickly in the darkness. "What we're talking about here is second chances, a kind of rebirth, or as Frye called it, the key that would unlock the door to a better world for us."

"Frye?" Johnny questioned.

Hodge's eye swam about the others in the circle before responding. "You never heard of him?"

"No."

"The Reverend *Harlan* Frye?"

Wareagle shook his head.

"Television preacher, rich as sin now. Founded the Church of the Redeemer. Worth maybe a billion dollars."

"I don't see any television antennas in the area."

"We got our sources. Got to keep abreast of the son of a bitch. Anyway, these woods was where he got his start. You're looking at some of the original disciples he was determined to save by opening the door to a better life—his jargon."

"I understand."

"Well, what else you got to understand is, those of us came here did so with the law sniffing at our tails. Had nowhere else but the road and where it led. Word was out about this place, a refuge for those down on their luck who'd tried to change it the wrong way. Musta been fifteen or so here when I pulled in. Came with three others I met up with 'long the road. All dead now, all killed that night."

"The fire?"

Hodge didn't respond. "Frye welcomed us all with open arms. Said we were welcome to stay 'long as we wanted, so long as we were willing to leave the men we were at the start of the woods. Oh, he wasn't talking about rehabilitating us. He was talking about making us realize we were worth something, that he had the key to open up a better world for us, and all we had to do was listen for him to use it. Son of a bitch honestly believed he could save the world one person at a time, starting here."

"How did you find out about . . . this place?" Johnny wondered.

"Word gets passed along the road, rumors and stories. At first you don't believe 'em. Then you figure, what the hell you got to lose, and you come out this way. New men—and some women—started arriving not long after

we did, pretty regular flow. The work of building that settlement back there in the woods kept us busy. Frye kept us
in line. Don't ask me how neither. I mean some of these
boys were ornery sorts who'd slit your throat as easy as
shake your hand. But they never moved on the Reverend.
Like he held some kind of power over 'em."

"What about you?"

"Me, too, I guess. I was just a house burglar who got
clumsy with a club when the owner came home early.
Plenty of the others was different."

"Like Earvin Early."

Hodge's one eye widened briefly at that. "What'd he do,
anyway? All these years, I never knew that."

"Murdered two families," Johnny replied, figuring that
was enough.

The one eye closed briefly, then looked back up. "I remember the night some of the others found him dragging
himself out of the river. Big mess of a man, scary to look
at it." The eye sought out Johnny's. "Still?"

"Worse."

"Things had already started going sour here by then.
Frye had gone loony. We had maybe two hundred in our
number, more than we could handle as it was, and the flow
had started slowing down. But that wasn't enough for the
Reverend. He didn't figure it was enough anymore to save
only those who showed up here. He wanted to go out and
find them that were in need. Thing was, he wanted us to
go with him as his messengers, spread the word of his key
to a better world. That was fine for the men who didn't
give a shit about showing their faces where they plainly
didn't belong. But those of us that still had our marbles
knew better than to be seen again. We liked what we built
here, wanted to stay. Frye was disappointed, but he agreed
to let us."

The wind whipped up, rattling the trees above them. It
was a warm wind that nonetheless drew a shiver from
Hodge as he grabbed a stick and began poking it into the
dirt. The moonlight continued to light the clearing.

"Then one night, not long afterwards," he continued, "Frye had your friend Early cut the throats of some of those that had spoken out against leaving and elected to stay. One of them managed to get away and run back to warn the rest of us."

Hodge's words were slower and more deliberate now. He poked the ground even harder, bending the stick, threatening to break it. Johnny looked into his one eye and knew for him it was that night again. Hodge turned his face away and concentrated on the ground between his feet.

"We fought back, then tried to run. They caught most of us and tied us inside the buildings before lighting them on fire. I was in the last house they set. Could hear the screams of the dying, smell the stink, 'fore they even got to me. The rest of Frye's people were hootin' and hollerin' up a storm. They ran off, left me for dead. But the ones of us they didn't catch came back. Managed to get me and maybe five others freed." Hodge touched the mangled side of his face with his free hand. "Little late in my account, but least I was alive. Plenty of men died in that burned-out settlement we found you in tonight. I won't tell you they were good men, just better than those that killed 'em." Hodge's one-eyed gaze came back up, reflective. "Eighteen years ago that be now. We ain't seen sign of Frye or the others since."

"But still you take precautions. The men who spotted me enter the woods must have been on a regular shift."

"Thing is, if you'd known we were here and came after us, would they have seen you?"

"No," Johnny said.

"That's what keeps us fearing the nights. We figure sooner or later Frye's gonna come back to finish the job he started. He ain't the sort to leave things uncompleted, no matter how long it takes." Hodge took a long, deep breath. "As for us," he resumed, taking in the whole of his domain with a quick sweep of his one eye, "what you see is what you get. Word about this being a haven for those on the lam don't get spread no more, and that suits us just fine. There are children here now, families. We ain't got much, but we get by." Hodge gave Johnny a long look. "Man like you could spoil it."

"Could, but won't."

The look became knowing. "You come here after Earvin Early, maybe you're after Harlan Frye too. Early worshiped him, that much I remember. He done something that set you on his trail, you can bet the preacher wasn't far behind him. That being the case, I'd watch myself, I was you. Frye don't take kindly to people disagreeing with him." Hodge touched the ruined side of his face. "And he's got a fondness for fire to go with it. Burn the world if that's what it took to do in those against him."

"Judgment Day," Johnny muttered, just loud enough for Hodge to hear.

"Every time the sun comes up, if you're Harlan Frye."

It was well after midnight before Blaine McCracken was permitted to leave the Sheridan Correctional Center in Illinois. Shortly after exiting the shower room, his nearly naked figure had been illuminated by the flashlights of guards responding to the power failure in the cellblock. The shocking sight of his handiwork in the shower room led to his detainment, the guards not caring to accept his explanation. The warden was summoned to the scene, and even with help from the proper contacts in Washington, McCracken had a tough go at gaining his release after being responsible for the deaths of over a dozen prisoners. A thorough search of the premises had turned up his clothing, piled into a corner of a storage closet adjacent to the shower room.

This time he waited until he had checked into a roadside motel fifteen miles away before calling Sal Belamo.

"Been a good day, boss."

"Ratansky's list of names?" Blaine questioned, expectations rising.

"Crazy nuts. I ran these names for hours, looking for

something that links them together. Came up with diddly-squat till I logged into a data bank even I never dare fuck with: the IRS."

"Keep talking."

"Turns out almost seventy percent of the names on the pages you salvaged have something in common in a big way: major donors, boss, and I do mean major. To the tune of over a billion dollars total."

"And just who's the lucky recipient?"

Belamo sounded like he was enjoying himself. "This is where things start getting interesting. That billion all went to something called the First Church of the Redeemer. But don't look for the typical steeple and stained-glass windows. The First Church of the Redeemer is strictly a television ministry, and the names in question are its primary benefactors. Charter members of something called the Key Society."

"Never heard of it."

"You wouldn't have, 'less you got nothing else to watch on Sundays, boss, or any other day of the week, for that matter. These boys don't just sponsor their own TV ministry; they got their own TV network called the Future Faith channel. Ain't theirs really, though. Belongs to a dude comes into fifty million homes with a touch of the channel changer.

"Dude by the name of Harlan Frye."

CHAPTER 16

The limousine's engine was still purring when Karen Raymond stepped into the clearing that leveled off before one of the many sharp drops in Torrey Pines State Park. She had huddled amidst the trees that had given the park its name while awaiting MacFarlane's arrival. Part of her breathed easier that Alex had at least lived up to this part of the arrangement, while another part remained wary of the man who was somehow part of a plot that had nearly killed her.

Trust no one.

That was easy: She had no one left to trust, except T.J. Fields and the Skulls, of course. A number were here with her now, all personally selected by T.J. He had wanted to come himself, but Karen reminded him of a greater responsibility she had entrusted to his care: her sons. The team he had selected had arrived hours ahead of her. They would be in position now, although Karen could see none of them through the thick tree cover rimming the area.

Karen stopped fifteen yards into the coarse expanse and

waited. As instructed, the limousine flashed its high beam
twice. She watched its rear passenger door open and the
shape of Alexander MacFarlane emerge. The night wind
blew his shock of white hair this way and that, disarrang
ing his careful coiffure. He approached her with hand
stuffed in his overcoat pockets. Karen waited until he wa
twenty yards from the limousine and then started forward
They met in the open center of the grove encompassing
the Overlook, alone in the dark with only the limo's high
beams and some stray light from the ranger station for il
lumination.

"Take your hands out of your pockets, Alex."

"What?"

"You heard me. Your hands, let me see them."

MacFarlane removed them from his overcoat, shaking
his head. "This has to stop, Karen."

"I'll say."

"You're in danger."

"That's why we're meeting here."

MacFarlane took one step closer. "What you did las
night was foolish."

"Prove it, Alex. Tell me what's going on. Tell me why
my lab team had to die. Tell me why my kids almos
joined them. *My kids!*"

His mouth dropped. "You don't think I could have had
anything to do with—"

"I know you did." Karen hadn't been sure until tha
very moment. Something about MacFarlane's tone con
vinced her, something about the way he held his eyes
"Don't bother denying it. If you do, there's no reason fo
this discussion to go any further."

MacFarlane frowned. "I never would have hurt you
kids. I never would have hurt you. That much is true."

"What about the rest?"

MacFarlane's eyes had grown sad, conceding. "I told
them to let me handle it. They agreed, Karen. Do you hea
me? They *agreed*."

Karen could feel her heart thudding against her rib cage. "Who, Alex? Tell me who."

"The who doesn't matter. It's the what." MacFarlane paused. "Your discovery."

"Lot 35. The AIDS vaccine. Keep going, Alex."

"This is so damn hard. . . ."

"I can wait."

"It's about power, Karen, it's all about power. I'm talking about Lot 35."

She glared at him. "Who wanted it buried? Who killed eight people and nearly three others to keep it from reaching the market?"

MacFarlane let out a long sigh. "Van Dyne."

Karen heard the words again, a heartbeat after MacFarlane spoke them.

Van Dyne . . . One of the largest, most powerful pharmaceutical companies in the world.

"I work for them," MacFarlane continued without any prodding. "So do you. They own Jardine-Marra."

The revelation hit Karen like a hammerblow. Disgusted, she looked away from MacFarlane briefly to disguise her emotion before her gaze was drawn back to him as he continued.

"Van Dyne's the biggest in the world now, Karen. Their biggest concern isn't their competition, but the government itself. Managed health care, price fixing, regulation—they knew their profit margin was headed for the shredder. They needed to expand quietly, buy out companies who weren't in direct competition with them."

"Like Jardine-Marra . . ."

"Because of our mail-order business primarily. Their buy-in was all done quietly, stealthily. Everything was perfect."

"Perfect? Listen to what you're saying!"

MacFarlane's voice took on an edge. "*You* listen, Karen. Where do you think the money came from to finish your project? That's right, without the cash acquired through Van Dyne's buy-in, Lot 35 never would have happened."

Karen stumbled over her thoughts briefly, then righted herself. "But they knew about it, didn't they?"

"They knew it was a long shot. Knew the government had already rejected your request for further funding."

"You told them," she said flatly.

"I had . . . no choice."

"When? When did you tell them?"

"At the beginning of our conversations. Well over a year ago."

"Then they've known about my work that long and yet they waited until yesterday to strike?"

"We—I—had no idea Lot 35 worked until yesterday. You did a superb job of keeping your progress secret, even from me."

"Makes us even, since you never told me I was working for Van Dyne."

"And if I had?"

"I would have taken my work somewhere el—" Karen stopped herself, having made MacFarlane's point for him.

"Exactly." He nodded. "They couldn't afford that."

"Why?"

"Because they've got their own vaccine, Karen. Hundreds of millions of dollars already invested, final testing toward gaining approval well under way. Lot 35 would have offered them competition they couldn't afford."

"Then so long as it didn't work, they had nothing to worry about. But once I revealed our success with the project at the board meeting, you informed your friends at Van Dyne, and they responded just like you knew they would."

"No! No! I told them I could handle it. I told them it was under control. They agreed."

"They lied."

"But there's a way out of this. I can save you. I can save your kids." MacFarlane took a step toward Karen. "Lot 35. They want it. Give it to them and—"

"What do you mean they want it? After they destroyed *everything* last night . . ."

MacFarlane seemed about to speak, but didn't.

"Wait a minute," Karen said, realizing, "not destroy—steal. That's what last night was about. They destroyed evidence of my research only after they thought they had stolen it."

"The computers," MacFarlane started.

"No single disk contains more than fragments that are virtually impossible to make sense of independent of each other. It would take even the most advanced technicians months. I alone possess the ones that contain everything. Only they didn't know that. They *couldn't* have known that." Her expression tightened, confusion twisting it taut. "But according to you, they've got their own vaccine. What could they possibly need Lot 35 for, Alex?"

"It doesn't matter. All that does is that it gives us a bargaining chip. If you agree, I can get them to guarantee your safety in return."

"Like they did last night."

MacFarlane's face was expressionless. "This is the only choice we've got, Karen."

"And accepting it means the killers of my team, my *friends*, go free."

"If it means you and your kids stay safe, yes, absolutely." MacFarlane swallowed hard. "You've got to trust someone, Karen, and I'm your best bet." He extended a hand toward her. "Come with me to the car, Karen. Let's walk out of this together. Now."

"To the police, Alex? Will we walk out of this and go to the police with what you've told me?"

Frustration squeezed MacFarlane's features taut; Anger reddened them. "Haven't you heard what I've been *saying*? We can't fight them, Karen. But if you walk out of this with me now and give them what they want, we can save ourselves."

She stiffened. "I don't think I can do that, Alex."

The hand stayed out there. "You must. Please."

"They may own you. They don't own me."

MacFarlane tilted his gaze briefly into the spill of the

high beams. "You've got to come back to the car with me, Karen. There's no other choice."

She felt her hands clench involuntarily into fists. "They're watching. You brought them here."

"Pl—"

"They shoot me if I don't accompany you, is that it?" MacFarlane just looked at her.

"You know what, Alex? I don't think they will. If they want Lot 35 so badly, I don't think they'll kill me. I think I can walk right out of this park and they won't fire a single bullet."

"You don't know them. *Listen* to me."

"I'm learning fast."

"They'll find you, Karen. They'll find your kids."

Her expression hardened. "I'm going to destroy them, Alex. I'm going to expose them and destroy them."

"You can't. Nobody can."

"We could—together. It's you who should come with me."

"Don't be a fool."

"Trust *me*. We'll turn and start walking together toward the car. When I tug your arm, we make a dash for the woods over there on the right."

"You're mad!"

"We'll be safe. We'll find someone in power who'll listen to what you've got to say. Van Dyne has got to be stopped, Alex. You wouldn't have admitted all this if you didn't believe that yourself. I'm the one who can save *you*."

"You're not alone," he realized.

"Neither are you."

Just for an instant MacFarlane wavered, seemed ready to join her before his expression solidified once more, his eyes like the granite spheres of a park statue's.

"Last chance, Karen. Last—"

MacFarlane's words were interrupted when gunshots erupted their way from inside the limousine. Karen caught the brief flares of orange muzzle blasts as she dove to the ground under the spray.

"What?" MacFarlane blared. "No! *No!*"

He turned back toward the car and began waving his arms. A pair of bullets thumped into his chest and blew him backward. He staggered briefly, puzzled eyes finding Karen's, and then crumpled near her.

The doors to the limousine opened, allowing four figures to emerge. Rifles leveled, they began a slow trot across the park toward her, taking their time. No reason to rush.

Where were the Skulls? Why weren't they firing back?

Fear poured through Karen as she lunged to her feet and started to scamper away.

A pair of the gunmen were bringing their rifles upward. *God . . .*

Karen stumbled and lost her footing. All the gunmen had stopped now, the weapons of the two in the front trained upon her.

And then a pair of pounding roars split the stillness of the night. The two gunmen with rifles ready were blown forward, blood exploding from the chasms ripped straight through their chests by what could only be the Skulls' shotguns. Another series of roars sounded where the remaining pair tried to swing. These two were blasted from all directions, it seemed, not even managing to get a shot off before hitting the ground.

Stuttering automatic fire from the limo raked the Skulls who had moved in the open. One of the bikers fell, whether from a hit or from evasive action, Karen couldn't tell as she continued to hug the ground. The remaining members charged out of the woods and closed on the big car from both front and rear. Their fire peppered the limo in a nonstop barrage that had Karen covering her ears tightly to drown out the sound. Window glass exploded and sprayed the ground nearby. The tires blew out. Stray shotgun pellets punctured the car's white body, leaving black holes from front to back. The firing from within the

cab had stopped early into the barrage, but the Skulls were
not taking any chances. Finally a half dozen of the gang
members converged on the doors, while the remaining pair
rushed toward Karen.

"You all right, ma'am?"

"You hurt?"

She shook her head as one of them helped her to her
feet. The second Skull grasped her on the other side, and
then they were running, her body shielded between theirs.
Karen wanted to tell them to slow down, let her catch her
breath. But there were no words.

There was only the night and the wooded park that enveloped them as they fled.

CHAPTER 17

Harlan Frye had first realized his destiny the day his step-father kicked his dog to death. A week past young Harlan's eighth birthday, the mutt had shit in the house. His stepfather's response was to chain the dog in the backyard and begin kicking. He made Harlan watch the whole thing until the animal lay there bloody and quivering. A lesson in responsibility, he called it.

Harlan Frye stayed up all night praying for his stepfather to die. No matter how stiff he became, no matter how bad the pain got in his knees, he stayed on them, leaning over his bed with hands pressed tight together and eyes squeezed closed. He nodded off a few times, but the knee pain brought him back and he was glad for it.

Please make him die.... Please make him die....

Over and over again.

By morning the flesh covering his knees had become so raw, it was sticking to the fabric of his pajamas. Harlan pulled the fabric away, visualizing his stepfather as the pain jumped through him. His back and legs were all cramped up, and his shoulders throbbed terribly from the strain of digging his dog's grave the day before.

Please make him die, God. . . . I'll do anything if you make him die. . . . I'm yours if you make him die, God.

It was a childhood fantasy of the most self-serving, lurid kind, but in this case it was a fantasy that came true.

The Sheriff brought the news to the Frye doorstep two nights later. Grim and solemn, he held his hat in his hand while he delivered it. Harlan's stepfather, a truck driver, had apparently nodded off behind the wheel and crossed the center line. He plowed into the oncoming traffic, ultimately jackknifing and spilling over, causing a massive pileup in all directions.

An investigation later showed that Harlan's stepfather had polished off one bottle of Jack Daniel's and was halfway through another when he lost control. While his mother wept and cried, Harlan sauntered back upstairs to resume his position of prayer.

Thank you, God . . . I'm all yours.

He meant it, too. God had done him a favor, the biggest favor anyone had ever done him, and he wasn't about to forget it.

There was plenty he would have liked to forget about those years of his youth spent in Haleyville, Alabama. Friendless and painfully shy, Harlan went through childhood alone. But from that day forward he didn't much care because he had God. He wasn't keen on regular church, but he was a regular at the services held by traveling preachers who set up shop in ramshackle tents and ranted about sin, while their assistants passed wicker baskets through the crowd. These men knew the real God, knew how to talk to Him and how to listen back.

Harlan Frye had just turned twelve when he stowed away in the back of a truck belonging to Preacher John Reed. Reed's roadies didn't find him until the next morning when they hit Mississippi to set up shop anew. Harlan had polished off his candy bars in the first few hours of the journey, and that had been it. He emerged pale, sickly thin, and certain Preacher John Reed was going to send him straight on home. So he prayed silently to God to let him stay. Don't make him go back to Haleyville; anything was better than Haleyville.

And, once again, God heard him.

Only it wasn't long before Harlan learned there were plenty of things worse than Haleyville, after all.

Harlan Frye began to believe that God would do things for him if he asked right. But he never wasted the privilege, never asked for anything unless it was something on which his whole young life seemed to hinge at the time. Sometimes God taught him a lesson by giving him just what he asked for. He couldn't have been happier traveling with Preacher John Reed at first, for example. Reed called him his adopted son, let Harlan sleep in a small cot in Reed's own trailer.

Then one night Preacher John climbed into the cot with him.

"It's God's will, child."

Harlan Frye felt John Reed's arms wrap around him and shivered.

"Please . . ."

Reed's arms began to stroke and pet him. "Let it be, child."

Harlan pulled away and stiffened. Those hands locked like simmering ice cubes on his shoulders.

"Refuse the Lord's will and I must turn you out, boy. Back to the world you came from. Turn away from me and you turn away from Him."

Preacher John Reed pressed his crotch against him. Harlan shrunk up against the wall the cot was perched next to.

"That's better, boy. That's better. . . ."

The experience became almost a nightly one. Sometimes Preacher John Reed smelled of liquor. Sometimes he just stank of the day's sweat. For Harlan each night became like watching his stepfather kick his dog to death over and over again. He thought about asking God to help him, but never did. After all, this was happening because God had already granted the request of an earlier prayer. Harlan had nowhere to run and was desperately afraid if he stopped obliging him, Reed at the very least would turn him out, and at the very worst might do far more than that.

He'd have to settle this one for himself.

So one night, lying in the cot all sweaty and rank after Preacher John had finished with him, Harlan slipped out of bed and eased a can of extra gasoline from the trailer's rear storage hold. He sprayed it around the cot's perimeter and the sheets, then sprinkled it atop Reed's frame, careful not to rouse him. Harlan Frye lit a match and waited until the flame had singed his thumb before tossing it.

Preacher John awoke on fire, trapped within a circle of flames. His eyes bulged with terror and rage as he spotted Harlan calmly gazing at the scene in the last instant before the flames swallowed him. Harlan heard his awful high-pitched screaming and loved it.

They were the screams of his stepfather, the screams of Haleyville.

Harlan Frye watched him burn for as long as he could take the heat, then escaped through a window while the roadies worked desperately to douse the flames. He was long gone by the time the trailer had been reduced to ash.

Harlan figured God had granted his prayer to stay with Preacher John Reed for a reason. There was a lesson to take from everything, and especially from this: the world was an evil, wanton place in desperate need of being saved. Maybe God Himself had given up on the process. Or it could be that He dispensed salvation now through a few chosen others. In time Harlan came to believe he had been doing the Lord's bidding the night he had burned Preacher John Reed.

And he could continue to do the Lord's bidding, because the world needed saving.

He apprenticed with a number of men who, like John Reed, traveled the South in big trucks and trailers. He learned the tales of the hopeless lot that filled the tent shows hoping to be saved. He came to know that they were a microcosm of the downtrodden and needy throughout the country. Yet all these people *could* be saved. But he couldn't reach them from atop a rickety makeshift stage when the ones most in need of saving would never even consider passing into the tent.

So Harlan Frye decided to go to them.

He broke off from a long succession of traveling preachers at the age of twenty. His first real ministry began in the South and trekked cross-country, picking up the down-on-their-luck on the way west. Ex-convicts and criminals, men and women in need of a second chance, in need of a man with the key to unlock the door to a better life. In the north woods of California, others who had heard of his work came in dribs and drabs. His success proved he was worthy of more, of moving on to another, higher phase. It was time to branch out, to spread the word God had given him to more of those in need of it. The first years had been good. The next ones would be even better.

But another test, another lesson, awaited him. Not all of his legion agreed to follow. The Reverend Harlan Frye knew what would become of them without him, knew they would lapse back into their old lives without his guidance. He gave them every chance, every opportunity, yet they continued to balk. If they were not with him, they were not worthy. It was as simple as that.

Once again Harlan Frye called upon fire to vanquish those who had disowned him. If hope was to survive, all those who resisted it had to be destroyed. Harlan Frye was true to his own word and teachings. Punishment dispensed justly serves the world well, and he returned to that world from the woods determined to save every soul he could toward its remaking.

Magazines began to take notice of his work. Radio talk shows wanted him to do call-in programs. Men from television began calling regularly.

Television . . .

The progression was as natural as every other step in his

life had been. With television he could reach millions and
millions more with his word, could save anyone from afar
who could flip a switch. Harlan Frye felt certain this revelation had been shown to him because now he was ready
to use it. He started with a Sunday show on a southern religious cable channel. His successful ratings led to a
breakthrough in northern markets as well, making him the
rival of Jerry Falwell and Pat Robertson.

Unlike these contemporaries, the Reverend Harlan Frye
was hardly satisfied. If a program could do this well for
him, imagine what an entire *network* might yield! Inves-
tors were easy to come by, and the Future Faith network
was born. Only five cable systems picked the station up
initially, but Harlan Frye was patient. Within seven years
that number had grown into the low hundreds. And "Sunday Morning Service" was now one of the top ten programs in all of cable. Since the occasion when the true
purpose of his ministry had been revealed to him, Frye had
been broadcasting the service live from a different location
every Sunday; not just ordinary locations, but from an
inner-city back alley, a welfare hotel, a porno theater. The
theme, after all, was rebirth—hope from nothing. Live audiences drawn from locals had become staples as well.
The demand for seats grew so frantic that Frye had
stopped announcing Sunday's site until the Saturday night
before. Word traveled fast. Boy, did it ever. . . .

The Future Faith network was available in all fifty
states and reached an estimated hundred million people.
International negotiations were under way with a number
of countries who wanted to carry it too, the biggest stumbling block being the Reverend Frye's resistance to letting
his words be translated by a stranger. A compromise was
reached whereby the foreign representatives agreed to let
him choose the translators for them from a list provided.
Harlan Frye paid the candidates' way to the United States
so he could interview each and every one of them personally. He was that serious.

The money in terms of donations and advertising reve-

nues began pouring in beyond Frye's ability to keep track
of it. And yet still he wasn't satisfied. Still he didn't feel
he was reaching enough of those who needed help. Then,
as always, when he needed a revelation, it came to him.

Riding the crest of the wave of 900 numbers, the Reverend Harlan Frye opened 1-900-237-2833, or 1-900
BE SAVED. By paying two dollars for the first minute and
one dollar for every minute thereafter, the troubled and
downtrodden could speak to a representative one on one
for consolation and counsel. The average call ran twenty-
six minutes, and hundreds of representatives were on duty
to take them around the clock. It was the crowning
achievement of his ministry and the most successful mar-
keting tool in the history of religious evangelism.

The Reverend Harlan Frye became one of the ten most
recognizable men in the country. The incredible power he
wielded was as terrifying to some as it was mystifying to
others and wondrous to still more, though least of all to
himself. He felt he had merely scratched the surface of the
world's need. The core continued to elude him.

The Reverend Harlan Frye prayed to God for guidance.
Just as he had done that first night so many years ago in
Haleyville, Alabama, he knelt by his bed and cupped his
hands atop the sheets. He prayed for guidance, for a sign
of what he should do. Come dawn, when nothing had
come, Harlan Frye dared to consider that the Lord might
have abandoned him. His faith wavered, and the ensuing
days brought no means to avoid its continued diminishing.

Until Dixonville, a small town in Virginia. Frye was
drawn there when a school collapsed, killing over fifty
children He stood atop the rubble, even as rescue crews
continued to sift through the last of it, and conducted a
service. The minutes that followed revealed the true basis
and inspiration for his being and his ministry. The
thoughts rushed into his mind, the words barely trailing
them. And as they came, he saw, he knew:

This was the sign he had been waiting for! If these children were not worthy to be saved, then who was? The

world as a whole had fallen from any trace of grace. It
needed to be rebuilt from scratch, to rise out of a rubble
only figuratively different from the remnants of the school
upon which the revelation had been delivered onto him.
Those worthy of being saved had to be found, singled
out, before the rubble consumed them as it had these children.

After that, for a day and a night unbroken Harlan Frye
read the Book of Revelation and came away knowing what
he was to be the instrument of.

Judgment Day, as had been foretold.

But he couldn't do it alone. The Book of Revelation had
told of seven great woes, an angel signaling the coming of
each. So it would be for him, the task to find six others
who spoke the Lord's word and possessed the resources,
frustrations, and power that mirrored his own. In Judgment
Day's wake, they and their chosen alone would be left. Toward that end, Harlan Frye would construct a kingdom for
them where they would be able to thrive unencumbered.

The Kingdom of the Seven.

It had taken four additional years to find a site that met
all the specifications. Frye fondly recalled the day when he
had been summoned by one of the teams he had sent off
in that quest to a massive, abandoned salt mine near Palo
Duro Canyon in the heart of the Texas panhandle. The
mine's interior was formed of a labyrinth of various-sized
chambers surrounding one central one that was nearly two
square miles in area, easily large enough to contain the
equivalent in construction of several city blocks. Only a
few of those structures had actually been completed today,
and of these, only the main building was fully functional.
Several additional shells had been finished, and construction crews were hard at work on their insides, even as
more foundations were poured. Other crews had begun
work in the connecting chambers, which were perfect locations for living quarters of various designs. It was like a
beehive, Frye supposed, taking solace in his kingdom's
kinship to nature.

Among the factors that raised it above other potential sites, the salt mine offered solidity and stability. There was plenty of air, and the risk of accidental combustion was significantly less than it would have been in, say, either a sandstone or limestone cavern. Several government agencies, in fact, had taken to storing hard copies of their records in similar salt mines, the expert theory being that their integrity could withstand even a nuclear blast.

Of course, problems of light, heat, and safety were inevitable. First the chambers had to be shored up with huge support beams which were designed to eventually become unobtrusive parts of the finished buildings. Because of the risk of fire posed within any confined space, all construction equipment had to be powered by propane, which was simply not as efficient as oil or gas. And, of course, the work crews' need for light necessitated the installation of massive gaseous lamp rows all across the ceiling. The effect created was comparable to that of an indoor sports arena. It was so bright that Frye could walk about the mine and, if not for its musty, baked air, could have easily convinced himself he was above the surface instead of below it.

Only when the kingdom approached becoming functional did Harlan Frye share with his chosen brethren the true intent of his plan. Lacking the means to impart Judgment Day at that point seemed not to deter the Reverend in the least because he knew the means would be delivered unto him in good time. A second member of the Seven fled in the wake of the first with whom he had shared the truth of his vision years earlier, perhaps prematurely, proving their unworthiness. Frye looked forward to their deaths amongst the rest of the masses when Judgment Day dawned.

But how to find a means whereby the truly worthy could be saved? Destroying civilization meant nothing if it could not be rebuilt in the image God had determined for it. That meant that this means had to allow for the luxury of selectivity—unheard-of and impossible in anyone's

mind except the Reverend's, the only person who had been
made privy to the true word.

Harlan Frye surrounded himself with others who felt as
he did, subordinates and underlings from various arenas
who furnished him with reports on their current projects.
He read them all, searching and waiting. It was easy to be
patient when awaiting the inevitable.

The patience had paid off just three years before, the
means to preserve the worthy while ridding the world of
its refuse shown to be in reach. It was so surprisingly simple. And fitting, wondrous in its clarity.

*God had done it! God had created it for him to make
use of!*

Frye first fretted over not realizing it earlier, then recon-
ciled to himself the fact that he had simply been neither
ready nor worthy. That had all changed. The Reverend had
surmounted the final obstacle en route to the achievement
of his destiny.

Until now. Even as Judgment Day had come within sight,
he found himself under siege. Seated in the back of his theater, Frye could not take his eyes off the still shot on the
large screen picturing Blaine McCracken from the waist up.
The screen's proportions exaggerated the V-shaped torso.
His facial features had been enhanced by a computer into an
almost cartoonlike clarity. His dark complexion showed every crease and line. A jagged scar ran through his left eye-
brow like a train track. McCracken's close-trimmed beard
looked as though it had been stuck on randomly in uneven
splotches. His eyes were narrow and intensely focused,
making it difficult to stare into them even off a screen.

Harlan Frye made it a habit of evaluating a man out of
comparison with himself, primarily on how he would fare
before a crowd of faithful in need of reassurance. Mc-
Cracken wouldn't fare too well because he couldn't lie
with his eyes, couldn't look at people and let them think
they had him fooled.

Frye, on the other hand, could change his appearance as
easily as most people changed their clothes, be what he

needed to be when he needed to be it. Even the mirror could be fooled, never giving back the same image twice. He was a half foot shorter than McCracken and flabby where his antagonist was taut with muscle. The Reverend's face, though, exuded warmth, reflecting what he had been told since childhood was a glowing spirit. It wasn't something he tried for, any more than McCracken tried for his glare of fierce intensity; it was simply there. People's eyes had always been drawn to him. Sometimes the stares were uncomfortable, like the first ones cast his way by Preacher John Reed. But as the years wore on, the Reverend Harlan Frye learned how to manipulate that glowing spirit to his great advantage.

Audiences, both live and television, loved watching him, couldn't get enough. And yet in photographs, he was easily dismissed. Frye's face was strangely soft looking, a morning's shave all he needed to chase back any unwelcome shadows until the next day dawned. His hair was plain and neat. Depending on the angle, he could have looked anywhere from thirty to fifty. In short, the Reverend enjoyed a terribly mundane appearance, so much so that he was almost like putty: able to mold himself into whatever the moment required, even as his faithful molded him into whatever they needed to see. Given the task, no two of them would have painted his portrait the same.

The one constant remained his eyes. They were like an owl's, big and deep-set. They dug into people and trapped them in their own thoughts. People didn't want to look into them, yet once they did, they couldn't break the stare. Strange, Frye reckoned, how McCracken's eyes came to life on the screen, while his remained utterly dormant in stills. The contradiction bothered the Reverend and had led him to refuse posing for standard photographs. The one exception was those shots that caught him in the midst of a service. Then his eyes leaped to life the same way they did from the stage or the pulpit.

"So this is our nemesis, Major," Harlan Frye said, from his accustomed spot in the theater's rear.

Major Osborne Vandal had been patiently waiting for
the Reverend to comment for nearly twenty minutes; he
would have waited twenty years because Harlan Frye had
saved his life. Not in the physical sense, but in the equally
important moral sense.

Osborne Vandal had spent the last seven years of the
Vietnam War in an especially brutal Vietcong POW camp.
He came out with a hand that had been crushed and rendered useless by repeated torture. Doctors told him he'd be
best off to let them amputate; a prosthesis would serve him
better. Major Vandal wouldn't hear of it. He wanted to remain a whole man, even if that meant he'd be a disfigured,
fumbling one.

Vandal gazed down at the hand now, flexing the fingers
that for nearly two decades had formed little more than a
palsied, shrunken claw he kept tucked away in his coat.
He could grasp things just fine now, and besides the scars
and discoloration, his bad hand looked almost no different
from his good, thanks to—

"Major?"

The Reverend's voice drew him from his trance and
Vandal looked up, clearing his throat.

"Sir," Vandal started, unhappy to be the bearer of bad
news, "we have now been able to confirm that McCracken
did come into possession of the list that Ratansky stole
from Sister Barbara."

"How?"

"The IRS computer was broken into earlier today. The
names on the list were fed in."

"Then he knows of me, Major, doesn't he?"

"That is a safe assumption, sir, yes."

"And just where does that leave us?"

"With the need to prepare for McCracken's next move."

"Potentially one from a limitless number."

Major Osborne Vandal didn't seem to agree. "I've studied this man, Reverend. He fought the kind of war over in
Vietnam I wish I'd had the chance to fight. Over there,

and over here, his greatest strength lies in his consistency. But that can be a burden as well as a blessing."

"How so?"

"It creates predictability. Based on what we've learned, I think I know where McCracken is heading next. I intend on having a number of teams waiting to intercept him in several select locations."

"Would you care to elaborate, Major?" Harlan Frye listened as Vandal obliged. When Vandal ceased speaking, he nodded, almost smiling. "I'm impressed. I believe, Major, you are starting to grasp the message in all this."

Frye stepped into the aisle, so that the bulk of the projector's beam was lost. Only the corners of the screen remained alight, the rest casting him in an eerie luminescence.

"This is happening because there are doubters in our realm, Major. The kingdom is not yet pure. We are not yet ready. The sign is clear."

"Sir?"

"McCracken is a lesson, as so much else has been before his coming. He will serve as a test of our mettle, of our true resolve. Did we panic when the calamity in Beaver Falls befell us? No. We responded in kind, searching for another means instead of accepting the loss. I have been to the lab this evening, Major. I have seen the wonder we are about to salvage from his debacle. A miracle, I tell you, a miracle! The time has come to summon the others to us."

Frye took a deep breath.

"And when they reach the kingdom I will inform them that Judgment Day will dawn inside of a week's time. The Lord delivered onto us a great gift in Beaver Falls, but He cloaked it in the robes of disaster. Stripping the robes away was one test. Disabling McCracken is a second. The Raymond woman represents the third. Has there been any progress on that end?"

"I'm afraid not, sir, and we should not take the threat

she poses lightly. She is currently on a path that could take her much closer to us than McCracken."

"Threat, Major? Did you say threat? The woman is not a threat so much as a blessing for the knowledge she possesses and must be convinced to give unto us." Frye's hands stretched outward and open, palms up at shoulder level when they stopped. "Don't you see? Is not the point of this clear to you? We are close. We are oh, so close. Our Lord is truly a demanding one. The obstacles He places in the path of our destiny challenge us at every turn, and yet each challenge is accompanied by an opportunity. He must be sure we are truly worthy to take back the world, to save it from itself while it can still be saved. Truly an awesome task, a terrible responsibility." The slightest of smiles crossed his face. "Don't you see, Major? Our Lord has saved these greatest challenges and opportunities, not threats, for *last*. Once they are overcome, nothing will stand between us and the destiny it is ours to fulfill. Then and only then will His doubts vanish. Then and only then will His faith in us be solidified."

The Reverend Harlan Frye stepped out of the projector light and became a dark specter once more.

"We must pass these tests, Major. You are confident in your strategy pertaining to McCracken?"

"I am, sir."

"Then let us concern ourselves with the challenge posed by the Raymond woman and obtaining from her what it would be to our great advantage to possess."

"We have managed to trace the area from which she made a number of phone calls, sir. I've studied her file. I think I know where she can be found."

"Her children as well, then?"

"Yes, sir."

Harlan Frye allowed himself a pause in which he mouthed a silent prayer of thanks for the understanding he had been granted and vision of what he needed to do.

"Bring Earvin Early to me," he told Major Osborne Vandal.

PART THREE

THE SEVEN

SANPEE, CALIFORNIA:
WEDNESDAY; 8:00 A.M.

CHAPTER 18

"Thing you should do," T.J. Fields advised Karen Raymond back in the trailer park Wednesday morning, "is beat it the hell out of here. Take your kids and run. I'll come if you want and ride shotgun."

The Skulls had driven Karen back to the trailer park in Sanpee after rescuing her from the shootout that had taken Alexander MacFarlane's life the night before in Torrey Pines State Park. She'd been in no shape to talk then, too frazzled and scared. T.J. had eased her into a rocking chair in the same trailer where her sons were sleeping in twin beds. The television was tuned to a music channel. T.J. had closed the door softly behind him and planted his massive frame on the trailer's front steps, shotgun balanced across his knees.

"I can't do that," she said, an hour into a damp, misty morning after a fitful night's sleep. "Before last night, I could have, but not anymore."

"Why?"

"Because I know they can't let me live now. Wherever I go, they'll track me down."

T.J. looked at her from across the picnic table where their coffee sat cooling. "I got some pretty out-of-the-way places even the animals live near 'em don't know about."

"It doesn't matter. They'll find me."   .

"How can you be so sure?"

"Because there's too much at stake," Karen replied. "Look, you told me you've been reading the papers, watching the news."

"Yeah."

"And there hasn't been a single mention of my lab team being murdered at Jardine-Marra, and you won't hear anything about Alex MacFarlane's killing last night. They make things go away, T.J. They can get away with anything they want."

"I don't see another option 'sides running, babe."

"There's one."

T.J. rose at that and glared down at her. "You fixin' on paying these Van Dyne boys a visit, I'll knock you on your head and tie you down to a chair."

"I know someone who works there."

"Someone you trust, that it?"

"I don't trust anyone."

"But you're gonna meet him."

Karen shrugged. "If I can."

"Then we do it my way, babe."

"The *whole tour*, Sister?"

Margaret Rennick, chief organizer of Sister Barbara's church on wheels, looked up from her notepad.

"Every town, Margaret," Sister Barbara elaborated. "Every date."

"I thought perhaps you meant just for the next few weeks or so."

"I didn't. Cancel all of them."

Rennick didn't bother hiding her disappointment and concern. "Yes, Sister."

"And I'll also want you to make sure all those on staff are given a full six weeks severance pay."

"What do I tell them?"

"That I'm not well; no, better to just tell them I've had the sign that another change is upon me and that their efforts have been greatly appreciated."

"You . . . won't be around to tell them yourself?"

"No, Margaret." Sister Barbara's gaze was somewhere between sadness and resignation. "I'm going home."

The appearance of the Reverend Harlan Frye's men last night had given her no choice. She needed to think, to plan. And, by all indications, there was likely little time to do either. She had vastly underestimated Frye's madness and the extent of his vision.

Nearly a decade ago, when her popularity and belief that she could make a difference were at their peak, she had agreed to become one of the original members of the Seven. It seemed the right move at the time, a natural progression of her growth. Frustration over the limitations of what *one* could accomplish provided the attraction to what *seven* might be able to with their resources pooled. The potential seemed limitless.

But Frye had changed all that the first time the Seven ventured down into the kingdom he had constructed for them. It was then that he had shared the truth of a vision of Judgment Day Sister Barbara had never dreamed could actually become a reality. But last night had proven otherwise. Sister Barbara had spent the dark hours following the departure of the Seven's two soldiers reviewing her determined desperation of these past two years. She had left the kingdom resolved to stop Frye by proving him wrong about the fate the world deserved. But now that he possessed the means to became the maker of that fate, everything had changed. Sister Barbara would have to plan carefully; quickly, yes, but carefully. And where better to plan than within the last remnants of her former life of fame and fortune:

The Oasis.

The Oasis was a massive theme park located in the majestic, rolling hills of Asheville, North Carolina, she had built as a haven for neglected, abused, sick, and underprivileged children. Two hundred acres of pure enjoyment in the form of a water park, amusement rides, playing fields and courts, all to take their minds from the lousy lot life had dealt them. There was no charge. Admission was by invitation only, and no weekend slots remained until after the summer. No long lines, no worry about tickets or rationing money between hamburgers and ice cream. Everything was free. A fleeting dream for those whose lives were living nightmares.

The actual home Sister Barbara had seen so little of these past two years was a sprawling mansion built on the outskirts of the rides and games that brought happiness and joy to so many who might not have otherwise known it. When she got back there tomorrow, she would begin to lay the seeds for Harlan Frye's destruction. But the Reverend's soldiers were sure to come for her, waging a war in which time had become the most crucial weapon.

"Yes," Frye called into the speaker from his position behind the desk of his private office.

"He's here," returned the voice of Major Osborne Vandal.

"Send him in."

The knobless door to Frye's private office within the kingdom slid mechanically open and the hulking figure of Earvin Early glided in. Of all of Early's unusual features, the way he moved was the most unsettling to Frye. A man with that size and bulk should be lumbering and awkward. But Earvin Early moved with a flowing, dancelike rhythm, each step graceful and precisioned.

The Reverend Harlan Frye regarded him in the bright light of his office and wanted to look away. Early's stringy, grease-laden hair hung in all directions, partially obscuring his face. The festering sores and boils on those portions not obscured looked more significant than the last time they had met. Early's clothes, though, were the same, as were his bloodshot, yellow-toned eyes that seemed to have leaked red into the whites. The giant held those eyes narrowed like a cat, calm and intense at the same time. Always at the ready.

Earvin Early, his massive frame shrouded in his dark, stitched-together canvas overcoat, stopped ten feet away. The Reverend Harlan Frye smelled the stink coming off him and struggled not to react.

"It has been too long, my brother."

Early's steady gazing was piercing. He spoke in a strangely melodic voice. *"Time keeps all his customers still in arrears. By lending them minutes and charging them years."*

Often Frye could identify the author of the particular lines Early chose for his words. In this case he could not. In all the years they had known each other, from that first night when a half-dead Early was pulled from the river, Frye had never heard the giant utter a normal sentence. At first unnerved, he had long ago grown used to the habit and found himself easily able to interpret the proper meaning.

"I have an important task that awaits you, my brother, one I wanted you to receive directly from me."

"Theirs not to make reply, Theirs not to reason why, Theirs but to do and die."

Tennyson, Frye noted, from "The Charge of the Light Brigade."

"You have been told of the woman who has disrupted our plans."

Early's slight nod was almost lost amidst his wild fall of hair.

"We believe we know where she can be found. We have reason to believe she has enlisted the help of some former friends, members of a motorcycle gang. This gang is protecting her and her children."

The slightest trace of a smile crossed Early's lips at that.

"Children pick up words as pigeons pease, And utter them again as God shall please."

Frye returned the smile, understanding. "Yes, my brother. And know that God has spoken. You know what you must do."

Early nodded again. *"The glories of our blood and state, Are shadows, not substantial things; There is no armor against fate."*

"You *are* fate, my brother. I am counting on you. *God* is counting on you."

"God moves in a mysterious way, His wonders to perform; He plants his footsteps in the sea, And rides upon the storm."

"Yes! Yes!" cried Harlan Frye, beaming. "And now we ride with him, you and I and all the others who are worthy. But we must show ourselves to be worthy. Do this for me, my brother. Do it as none of the others in my legion can."

Earvin Early's face appeared from within his tumbling hair, as if he had pushed it forward. The festering sores had purpled. The boils were oozing whitish pus.

" *'Tis my vocation,"* he said with a faint smile, quoting what the Reverend recognized as Shakespeare. " *'Tis no sin for a man to labor in his vocation."*

Indeed, thought Harlan Frye. Indeed.

CHAPTER 19

"That him?" T.J. Fields asked.

"It's his car," Karen replied, noting the black Lexus 300 coupe inching its way through the dust of the closed-off exit ramp.

She stepped out from behind the cover of a pile of chewed-up roadway and faced the approaching car. The unfinished off-ramp along the Pacific Coast Highway was built on a moderate decline that created a tunnel effect between the gradually diverging overpasses above. The Lexus's driver seemed to see her, and the dust-covered car slid to a graceful stop forty feet away. The driver's door opened and Freddy Levinger stepped out, elegantly dressed in a dark suit that showed every speck of dust the wind tossed at him. He tried in vain to brush it from his suit and kick it off his highly polished shoes, but gave up after a brief attempt. The wind ruffled his fashionably slicked-back hair and he ran a hand through the locks to smooth them back into place.

Karen had gone to graduate school with Levinger at

UCLA for a time, and their rises through the industry were pretty much mirror images of each other, although Freddy's gains at Van Dyne Pharmaceuticals stretched way beyond hers at Jardine-Marra in a relative sense. He was head of development now, which meant if anyone could tell her about Van Dyne's AIDS vaccine, it was Levinger.

Meanwhile, clandestine meetings in the pharmaceutical industry, although not exactly commonplace, were not unusual, either. People at high levels often developed a notion to make a change, for one reason or another, and contact was often initiated in just that way. After all, there was always a chance that someone new to the company might be bringing something *new*; in fact, it was often the only reason that person was invited into the new surroundings. Karen had implied making a change was the reason she needed to meet Freddy, hoping her reputation in the industry, along with their friendship, would be enough to lure him to such a strange meeting place.

"You need me, babe," Karen heard T.J.'s voice call as she started forward, "I'm here."

She could see Freddy Levinger squinting into the sun, missing his sunglasses. "I really hope that's you, Karen, because if it isn't . . ."

She stopped two yards away from him. "Hello, Freddy."

Levinger smiled and tilted his eyes back toward the Lexus. "Wouldn't have a hose anywhere around, would you?"

"Nice car."

"Thanks." He turned sideways to the sun, face gaining confidence. "I hope the subject of this meeting justifies me getting it so filthy. I don't mind telling you, Kar, that Van Dyne's has had their eye on you for some time."

"Someone had more than that on me two nights ago, Freddy; last night, too, for that matter."

The playful glint dropped off his expression. "Really?"

"I'm not here because I'm considering a change. Actually I'm here because of my kids."

"Your *kids*?"

"Two boys."

"I know that."

"Did you know they were almost killed Monday night?"

Levinger's eyes bulged in shock. His mouth dropped.

"And you're part of the reason—at least what you're involved in at Van Dyne."

His whole body had stiffened. He edged back toward the Lexus. "I think I'd better leave."

"I wouldn't."

"If I can back my car up this ramp . . ."

"Bad idea."

"Huh?"

"Look up."

When Freddy looked up, he could see members of the Skulls lining the overpasses, responding to Karen's signal. Their shotguns, rifles, and pistols were showcased plainly before them.

"Who *are* these people?"

"Friends of mine. You can never have too many. Are you still my friend, Freddy?"

"Jesus, Karen . . ."

"I need all the friends I can get right now."

Levinger started cautiously back toward her from the Lexus, eyes reluctant to leave the figures draped in black leather. "What's going on, Karen? What's this all about?"

"You mean you don't know? It's about AIDS, Freddy. Its about an AIDS vaccine that Van Dyne presently has in the testing phase—your domain, if I'm not mistaken."

Levinger's tanned face was going white.

"The main reason I know about your vaccine is because I discovered one, too, something called Lot 35, if that matters. Anyway, I presented my findings to Jardine-Marra's board of directors Monday afternoon. Monday night three gunmen tried to kill my sons and me. They might have

been the same gunmen who killed all the members of my
research team right in our lab at JM."

"*What?*"

"Are you really shocked to hear this, Freddy?"

"God, yes."

"I'm glad, because it might mean you'll be willing to
help."

"Karen—"

"Let me finish first, Freddy. Alex MacFarlane took my
sons and me to his home, where we were supposed to be
safe. But I got this notion that Alex wasn't playing totally straight and took off. I was right. We met last night
and Alex admitted some things to me. He admitted in-
forming your people about our rival AIDS vaccine. Mac-
Farlane claimed he had no choice. You see, Van Dyne
owns JM." She paused. "Did you know that, Freddy?"

"Karen, *Jesus,* I swear this is the first I've heard of it."
Then Levinger was silent for a moment, searching for
something to say that wouldn't reveal how nervous he was
becoming. "Maybe I should be talking to him."

"You can't, Freddy. He's dead. Killed by whoever killed
the eight members of my lab team and would have killed
my kids."

"Karen," Levinger started, shaking his head slowly,
"you've got to believe I know nothing about all this."

"Prove it."

"How?"

"*Whatever's* going on, this vaccine you're testing is the
key. I want you to tell me everything you can about it. I
want to see the files, the paperwork."

Levinger came closer. His eyes swept the twin overpasses where the half dozen bikers stood rigidly at their
posts. "That could cost me my job. You've got to give me
time to think about it."

Karen shook her head. "I know you, Freddy. You'll go
back to Van Dyne and ask some questions. Then, tomorrow or the next day, you'll end up like MacFarlane and my

team. And you know what? Your death won't get reported
either."

They stood there facing each other for what seemed like
a very long time. Finally Levinger spoke.

"What exactly do you want to know?"

"How your vaccine was discovered. The fundamentals
of its function. How it was refined and developed. That
should get us off to a decent start."

"That's *years* of work!"

"Then talk fast. I'm in no rush, anyway."

Levinger's lips trembled as he began to speak. "We
went back to the beginning, Karen, and I mean the *very
beginning* of AIDS as it is known today."

"Enlighten me."

"How much do you know about the work of Hilary
Koprowski?" he started.

Karen looked at him scornfully. "Beside the fact that it
led to a generally discredited theory of the disease's origin?"

"Discredited because people refused to keep an open
mind. It seemed too simple, too pat, so it was disre-
garded."

"With good reason."

"We found reason, Karen."

"Go on."

"You've got to have full grasp of the scenario first.
Koprowski was under tremendous pressure to come up
with a polio vaccine, just as Salk was; even more, since at
one point he was closer to the answer. Koprowski's problem was that by that time India had suspended export of
rhesus macaques, so he began importing green monkeys
from Africa, specifically the Belgian Congo. Typically he
used their kidneys to cultivate his vaccine. Only there was
a problem."

"The green monkeys carried a disease in their blood,"
Karen picked up, nodding. "Something called Simian
Immunodeficiency Virus or SIV."

"Dormant in the greens, just like you said, but not in humans. A few years after Koprowski began testing his vaccine, which had been grown in the monkeys' kidneys, the first African natives began showing symptoms of the disease we now call AIDS. A relatively benign virus in green monkeys mutated and became a killer when incubated in the systems of humans."

"All of this is widely known, Freddy, but not widely accepted."

"Karen, seventy-five thousand African children in Léopoldville became the first to receive Koprowski's vaccine, starting in 1958. A year later we know now that the first detection of AIDS was made there." Levinger looked as if his point had already been made. "We went back to Koprowski's original work with the greens," he continued confidently, "starting with some of the actual cultures that had been frozen for forty years. We re-created the precise conditions that had converged to keep the SIV we believe evolved into HIV dormant in monkeys until Koprowski used their kidneys to cultivate his vaccine. Koprowski couldn't have understood it, because he lacked the technology. Until very recently, so did we." Levinger stopped. "Protein, Karen."

"What?"

"The reason why SIV remained benign in the green monkeys was because it was enclosed by a protein coating the animals' antibodies had formed around the individual cells. When grown in the animals' kidneys, Koprowski's vaccine eroded that coating and released the virus that became HIV into the systems of those inoculated with his vaccine. But Van Dyne successfully isolated the original protein from the frozen tissue samples and formulated its DNA. Once we had the genetic codes, we were able to produce antibodies that successfully recognized and then enclosed the invading cells of the AIDS virus in a similar coating, forming an impenetrable seal."

"Trapping them so they can't spread and destroy the immune system," Karen concluded.

"All our research indicates the immune system destroys itself, begins destroying its own CD4 cells once the virus short-circuits it to promote its own spread. The virus is ruthless but limited. Our antibodies don't totally eradicate it from the system, just render it forever dormant as was the case with the SIV Koprowski's green monkeys had in their systems."

"But if that's true, if it really works—"

"Yes, Karen," Freddy Levinger broke in before she could continue, "our vaccine is therapeutic as well as preventative. It should work in all but the most advanced cases of AIDS."

Karen nodded, strangely calm. "Surely one of the greatest discoveries in the history of medical science."

"If not *the* greatest."

"And most lucrative."

"Of course. But . . ."

"I think you're starting to see my point. We're talking about a discovery worth tens of billions of dollars here. But if there was another vaccine, a rival vaccine, that worked at least as well . . ."

"Yours?"

Karen nodded and explained the parameters of Lot 35 to him. Levinger responded at the appropriate times, suitably impressed until a squint of confusion crossed over his features.

"Okay, Karen, now tell me why, since according to you, Van Dyne owns Jardine-Marra and thus Lot 35, the company would bother to destroy it and murder eight people?"

"Nine," she corrected, remembering Alexander MacFarlane, "and here's the clincher. Van Dyne wasn't trying just to destroy Lot 35 Monday night, Freddy, they were trying to steal it. But they didn't know I've got the only complete files. They sent MacFarlane to make a deal with me, and when he failed they killed him."

Levinger stood before her, motionless. "Tell me what you want from me, Karen."

"What level has your vaccine progressed to?"

"Well into final, large-scale human testing. Several months in. With government approval and support, I might add."

"I want you to go over the staging with me, Freddy. I want to go over every bit of data up to this point, step by step."

"Even I don't have access to *everything*."

"You're Van Dyne's *head* of development."

"Karen, I'd be breaking the law if I helped you. We're partners with the government on this, for God's sake."

She looked at him harshly. "Get me the latest results of the test group, Freddy."

"And just what do you expect to do with them?"

"Use them as proof that Van Dyne's vaccine exists. Hard evidence to convince the proper authorities of what's going on. They'd never believe me without it."

Levinger's eyes flared. His face reddened. "This was supposed to be between *us*! I *trusted* you!"

Karen shook her head. "No, you talked because you were scared. But you're not as scared as I am, and let me tell you, being scared makes you capable of just about anything."

Levinger thought about it briefly. "This will take some time to arrange. I don't have access to all the materials you want."

"You have until tonight to get it."

"Karen—"

"And don't even think about going to Van Dyne's corporate wing with this, Freddy. Don't even think of playing hero to your company." Karen let her eyes drift to the gunmen standing sentry over the scene and waited for Levinger's to follow her gaze. "You've got a wife, Freddy. You've got three kids. If anything happens to me tonight . . ."

"No! That's *sick*! How can you— You can't—"

"Only what was almost done to me, Freddy. When someone threatens your kids, your choices get narrowed pretty fast." She paused. "I think you just realized that. You do what you have to do."

"I'll *do* what I can," he followed, seething.

"Tonight, Freddy. So long as it's by tonight."

CHAPTER 20

McCracken flew from Chicago into Atlanta's Hartsfield International Airport on the first flight out Wednesday morning, after Sal Belamo successfully completed the next stage of his research into the Reverend Harlan Frye's Key Society. Specifically, Blaine wanted the name of the largest donor of all.

"No sweat, boss," Belamo reported first thing Wednesday. "Information wasn't hard to come by. Guy by the name of Jack Woodrow, better known as Jumpin' Jack Flash."

"Don't know him by either name."

"Be different if you lived down in the South. Jumpin' Jack happens to be the most successful automobile dealer in the whole U.S. of A. Got maybe twenty dealerships spread over five states, and all of them rake in a ton. Made his name with trucks, four-by-fours, RVs, and campers, and they're still the source of his primary bread and butter. He operates a dealership outside of Atlanta that's got twenty solid acres of them lined up bumper to bumper, new shipments coming in every day."

"What's Woodrow in for with Frye?"

"Near as I can figure, a hundred easy, boss."

"A hundred *million*?"

"I kid you not. You ask me, Jumpin' Jack must figure he's got a lot of soul to save."

Blaine ran that through his mind briefly before speaking again. "I'll ask him personally when I get to Atlanta. Anything from Johnny?"

"Funny you should ask. Called me last night from Cal-i-for-ni-a. He's been spending some time in the woods. Turns out he ran into some holdovers from a criminal commune Earvin Early literally fell into. You'll never guess who the founder was."

"Harlan Frye."

"I gotta stop underestimating you, boss. Anyway, maybe fifteen years ago Frye tries to burn up the members who don't agree with his plans."

"Nice way to treat your followers."

"Hey, if he ain't changed . . ." Sal Belamo let the thought complete itself. "You want me to tell the big fella to head east?"

"And make sure he keeps calling in."

For Jacob and Rachel the wait was agonizing. Blaine McCracken was surely long gone from Illinois by now, and they needed to know to where. So far, contacts still available to their father had managed to turn up a number of the aliases McCracken traveled under, so the search had to incorporate all of them at both O'Hare and Midway airports.

It was Rachel who answered the phone in their hotel room when it rang.

"Atlanta," the voice of her father said flatly. "McCracken flew to Atlanta."

"Atlanta?" A chill passed through her. "Jack Woodrow," she said to her brother.

"He knows!" Jacob responded. "If he's going after Woodrow, he must have the list Ratansky stole!"

"How large is his head start on us?" Rachel asked their father.

"Several hours."

"We'll make it up," she said, and hung up the phone.

The most impressive thing about Jumpin' Jack Woodrow was that he still involved himself in the day-to-day operation of his business. When the time was there, between shooting commercials and attending benefits, he rotated his days between dealerships. He still took pleasure in every single sale, and the ones he closed himself were especially gratifying. He also busied himself occasionally back in the service department, where he was not above getting his hands dirty on an oil change.

His flagship and favorite dealership remained the Flash Pot on Buford Highway in Chamblee, Georgia, a suburb of Atlanta. It was sprawled over a patch of land directly across from the Church of God Woodrow had pried from the hands of the Gwinnet County commissioners, planting some thick green in their hands in return. Buford Highway was a motor-head's delight, auto body and repair shops crammed along its entire stretch, interspersed here and there with an occasional fast-food franchise. Woodrow couldn't think of a better place for the world's biggest truck and RV dealership. Twenty acres of product right smack between two major access roads to Hot-lanta itself, twenty minutes from downtown and easily accessible from just about everywhere. The Flash loved walking amongst the glistening, sunbaked steel just waiting to be driven off his property and onto some lucky buyer's, especially since these kinds of vehicles carried the biggest markups.

Customers who were shopping at the dealership where Jack Woodrow happened to be at the time were never disappointed. What they saw on television was exactly what they got in real life, right down to the flab-layered belly. That belly had become famous itself on the day Jack

Woodrow couldn't squeeze it all the way under one of his campers' tables in a commercial filmed at the Flash Pot, but bit into the shitty sandwich anyway without the director having to call cut once. He was still running the damn spot. The man known affectionately as Jumpin' Jack Flash didn't mind being laughed at, so long as those doing the laughing came in to buy. He hadn't been seen in years without his signature spur boots, khaki ten-gallon hat, and string tie.

Wednesday was his normal day to enjoy himself at the Flash Pot, and this week should have been no exception, would have been if it weren't for the call from Harlan Frye's people the night before. Seems the old Reverend was concerned an enemy of his might decide to pay the Flash a visit. Not to worry, they told him. Just go about your business and let us handle things. Oh, and if you see a man with . . .

Jack Woodrow wedged his trademark ten-gallon hat on at ten o'clock sharp and emerged from his private office into the showroom, drinking in the luscious scents of fresh steel and rubber. In the case of the Flash Pot, that showroom was half the size of a football field and contained everything from a customized pickup to the flagship of the Winnebago line, a house on wheels that slept five and came complete with a Jacuzzi whirlpool. There were forty to fifty vehicles all told, at least half of them being hawked by eager salesmen to potential customers.

Jack Woodrow was moving through the already crowded showroom when a big, bearded figure slid through the main entrance and looked right at him.

"Uh oh," the Flash muttered to himself.

McCracken took one look at the man he recognized as Jumpin' Jack Woodrow and knew something was wrong. The fat man's eyes spun away from him and scanned the room, Blaine's following.

Almost all the conversations between customers and salesmen had stopped, and too many glances had turned

his way. That instant's advantage was all McCracken
needed to tear his SIG-Sauer free of its holster and nail the
first four of the bogus customers who had managed to
whip submachine guns from inside their jackets. Then he
was in motion, dancing and dodging from behind one vehicle to the next, as bullets from the gunmen blew out the
glass from windshields and windows and punctured tires
along his escape route.

"No!" he was conscious of a voice screaming that must
have belonged to Jack Woodrow. *"Stop!"*

Some of that glass sprayed outward toward his face, and
he threw his free hand up instinctively to block it. He continued firing his SIG, the remaining twelve shots in this
clip reserved for the areas of largest enemy concentration.
He placed the bullets well enough to buy him the time and
space he needed to launch into a dash toward a massive
plate glass window at the showroom's side. The gunmen
responded just as he expected them to, by firing wild barrages in his general direction. One of the barrages shattered the glass of the window he was rushing for, so it
took hardly any effort at all to crash through with his arms
covering his face.

Blaine rolled once upon hitting the pavement and
jumped back to his feet, already running. He briefly considered angling for Buford Highway, but that route would
bring him into the open with no possibility of cover. His
remaining choice was the massive twenty-acre lot
crammed with vehicles.

He lost himself quickly between the first rows of four-
by-fours, arranged by colors and available options. There
was barely room to move between their front bumpers. He
stayed low and rushed for the lot's rear, where escape
might be easier found. But first he calculated he had another two dozen heavily armed men to elude and outwit,
even as they moved to surround him and close in from the
perimeters. All McCracken had working for him, the only
viable advantage he could seize, were the logistics of the
lot itself.

A bullet rang out and clanged off the grille of a midnight blue pickup. Behind him a pair of gunmen were snaking their way down the narrow aisle on his trail. McCracken twisted and fired a trio of shots from the SIG's fresh clip in their direction. When they lunged for cover, he dove behind the four-by-four on his right and continued on from one vehicle to the next.

Maintaining the stalemate, though, meant he was losing. Pinned down, hampered by an obvious lack of firepower, he would inevitably be encircled and closed upon. But the inevitable could be modified. It was a matter of taking advantage of the elements afforded him, weapons created out of what would not ordinarily be considered in that vein.

Gas tanks . . .

The lot had a natural downward grade to it that would send the freed gasoline coasting downward beneath the pickups toward where the Flash Pot met Buford Highway. Blaine pulled the ever-present Riggin knife from his pocket and locked the fid extension into place. The fid, normally used for parting individual strands of rope or line, could puncture steel like butter. McCracken slid under the nearest truck and went to work.

"Where is he? Where the fuck did he go?"

"Under the trucks!" returned the second of the gunmen farthest down the long, narrow rows of jammed-together four-by-fours. "I think he's crawling under the trucks!"

The first man immediately flopped to his knees and squeezed beneath the nearest flaming red pickup. The asphalt was still wet and puddled by the heavy rains from the night before, and he could feel the water soaking through to his legs as he crawled farther along. He could see the whole way to the end of the row.

"No sign of him," he called to his partner. "Not a damn thing."

"He must be *in* one of the trucks!"

The man beneath the truck grunted an acknowledgment and shimmied back out, his clothes covered with grease

and grime. Together they moved in combat fashion down
the long line, each truck checked by one while the other
held a submachine gun at the ready. At the far end of the
row, another quartet of men had begun the same process.
The rest of the assault team members kept their distance in
positions enclosing the long stack of four-by-fours from all
angles. The pair closing from the showroom end of the
Flash Pot lot had just passed the center of the row when
one noticed a fresh, thin puddle snailing along, lapping up
near his loafers and then heading on by.

"Jesus," he muttered, "Jes—"

McCracken popped up from the rear bed of a four-by-
four, eight vehicles down the row, between the two converging enemy groups. His SIG spit rounds at the nearest
pair coming from the other side and felled both of them
instantly. They had barely crumpled when the other two
closing from that direction opened fire.

"No!" screamed the man whose nostrils were now
drinking in the scent of gasoline.

His warning came too late. The bullets from the converging team ignited the gas flowing beneath the fuel
tanks along the row, setting off a series of explosions that
followed one after the other like dominoes.

Blaine had hurled himself from the truck bed where he
had stowed himself in the instant before the blind return
fire commenced. He landed on the asphalt and launched
himself sideways. The explosions became his camouflage,
stealing sight of him from any of the gunmen with the
sense to look. He darted dangerously close to the edge of
the expanding flames in a crouch toward the Flash Pot's
rear and the endless rows of fully equipped campers,
scooping up a pair of submachine guns from the enemy
pair he'd downed en route.

There was no way to count exactly how many of the enemy had perished in the blasts behind him. At least four
more, McCracken guessed, had been in the immediate area
when they struck. Add to that the two he had shot out here

and the four incapacitated in the showroom, and
McCracken figured that still left him with upward of fifteen more to face.

A good start.

The members of the assault team never knew what hit
them. The ones in charge ran about the angry flames trying to restore order and reorganize their charges. Men
were bleeding. Men were staggering and screaming. Men
looked like blackened, charred pieces of wood, wearing
dazed expressions on their features.

The ones in the worst condition were left to seal the
front of the lot off in case McCracken opted to double
back that way. The rest, reasonably unscathed by the
blasts, converged on the rear of the Flash Pot in a wide
arc. The electrified security fence would keep McCracken
from getting out through the back. But having already seen
a demonstration of his work firsthand, few took comfort in
that.

"Keep your spread," the leader barked, his voice turned
ugly and deep by the smoke that had burned his throat.
"Shoot anything that moves."

Thomas J. Bodine woke up with a start. Better known as
the mayor of Buford Highway to those who frequented
this stretch of road, Bodine had been homeless longer in
life than he'd had a roof over his head. Of course, that
didn't mean he had to suffer. Not when he had access to
a lot crammed full of the most luxurious roofs money
could buy.

Thomas J. Bodine, the mayor of Buford Highway, referred to the various Winnebagos in which he made his
ever-changing home as "Win-a-bag-ofs," because that's
what the name sounded like to him. He was sleeping
stretched out on a fully made-up water bed when the shat-
tering series of explosions roused him bolt upright.
Thomas J. had had his sleep interrupted before, sure, but

usually by an enthusiastic salesman in the midst of a pitch who had just entered the camper.

The mayor of Buford Highway needed his sleep, especially after a night that had seen him swipe a fresh bottle of Absolut vodka from the front seat of a car parked near the pizza joint just down the road. After the first few hot swallows, the stuff became cool and smooth. Before Thomas J. knew it, the bottle was gone, and he had found his way onto the water bed to sleep off the effects.

Now, after the blasts had ended, the mayor of Buford Highway did what came naturally.

He curled up and went back to sleep.

McCracken could see the three wires running across the whole length of the ten-foot chain-link fence from ten feet away. He hadn't expected it to be electrified, and their presence threw him. There was no time to short the thing out without leaving himself exposed for an unaffordable length of time, even with his pair of submachine guns. That left him with the campers that filled out most of the rear portion of the Flash Pot's lot in neat rows.

McCracken took cover behind the front tires of a huge Winnebago in the very rear and stooped to peer beneath its frame. He could see the feet of several of the gunmen approaching deliberately in the near distance, steering clear of the smoldering remnants of the Flash Pot's four-by-four inventory. Blaine stayed low and pressed against the Winnebago's frame as he reached up to the driver's-side door. Incredibly, it was open. The keys, however, were not in the ignition nor anywhere to be found in a quick search.

McCracken tucked himself low beneath the dashboard and started on the wires.

The members of the assault team bringing up the front were the only ones to hear the roar of a powerful engine kicking in. But with the sirens of the just-arriving fire trucks blistering their ears, they couldn't pin down exactly where it was coming from, at least not until they saw the huge Winnebago bearing down on them.

It slammed through a row of smaller campers without so much as a waver and rolled forward, gaining speed. The men closest to it opened fire and watched its windshield shatter.

The Winnebago kept coming.

The first line of gunmen dove in desperation from its path, while a trio farther back aimed their fire at the vehicle's tires. One of the Winnebago's front tires blew out. The vehicle bucked one way and then the other, ultimately banking right and surging straight for the Flash Pot's vaunted showroom.

"No!" screamed Jumpin' Jack Woodrow as he stood outside near the befuddled firemen. "Holy . . . *shit* . . . *Noooooooo!*"

His agonized howl ended just before the wounded Winnebago crashed through the remnants of the glass wall on that side and made a shambles of every vehicle in its path. Some of his most prized models piled up before it, collectively driven backward until the line of wrecks had nowhere else to go.

"Shit!" Jack roared, and kicked at the ground. "Shit, shit, shit, shit . . ."

A segment of the assault team followed the Winnebago into the ruined showroom and began firing away. Bullets chewed into its steel sides, obliterating its logo, custom body moldings, and accent stripes. Windows blew out and the optional shades flapped helplessly behind them. The engine was still revving, though the tires had stopped spinning at the end of its charge. The passenger-side front door was hanging off its hinges, and two team members lunged through what was left of it to find the accelerator tied to the floorboard with a rolled-up length of plastic that had previously been protecting the seat covers. They looked at each other, grasping the ruse, and headed back down the steps.

No sooner had they reached the bottom than the still intact center sunroof of the Winnebago blew outward behind McCracken's determined thrust. He held his salvaged pair of submachine guns in two hands and opened up with both barrels simultaneously, firing at anything that moved with virtually no pause. The twin bursts lasted just under five seconds, an eternity when hot death was flying through the air. The enemy barely got a shot off before their target hurtled from the ruined camper and escaped down the hall that ran parallel to the office area.

McCracken sped down the corridor linking the Flash Pot's massive service department to its body shop, both abandoned now due to the fire. Blaine remained nonetheless cautious as he moved through the bays, contemplating his next move. The sharp scent of auto paint found his nostrils as he reached the body shop area. The key now was Woodrow. If he could come up with a way to get the remainder of the assault team out of here, he could deal with Jumpin' Jack alone.

Blaine had barely considered his options when the door to one of the smaller Winnebagos parked in a service bay creaked open. He spun and fixed his SIG on a disheveled lump of a man who looked like he had just climbed out of bed.

"Can't a man get his sleep around here?" murmured a slowly stirring Thomas J. Bodine.

"How'd you like to go for a ride?" McCracken asked him, forming a plan as quickly as he spoke.

The mayor of Buford Highway smiled.

CHAPTER 21

The remaining nine members of the assault team moved through the Flash Pot lot tentatively. The foe they had faced had turned out to be even more formidable than they'd expected. Only a few moments remained before they would have to abandon the property and disappear. The disastrous gunfight inside the showroom had led the few terrified policemen on the scene to summon every bit of available backup, including a SWAT team. Momentarily, the place would be swarming with a well-armed force that would pose an instant threat to them.

None of the assault team were facing the service bays when a small model Winnebago crashed through one of the garage doors and sped through the lot. Its tires spun deftly to avoid all but a few minor scrapes en route to thumping over the front curb and onto Buford Highway.

No tricks this time. This time there was definitely a driver behind the wheel.

The men charged for their own vehicles, McCracken in their sights.

As police cars poured onto the scene, a quartet of the assault force's sedans tore away from it, giving chase to the Winnebago that was weaving its way through typical Buford Highway traffic.

Jumpin' Jack Woodrow took refuge in the back of the Flash Pot's auto body repair shop, trying to lose himself in the clutter amidst the aromas of auto paint and steel. The cops were everywhere, looking to ask questions; looking for him, no doubt. He wished he were anywhere else, and decided to stay hidden until he got his story worked out.

Goddamn fucking Harlan Frye . . .

Thanks to the way the Reverend had chosen to handle this, the fire department was trying to put out the second burning of Atlanta, while cops were arriving from all directions. How was Woodrow going to explain a gunfight involving maybe thirty men, leaving most of them dead or wounded, not to mention an entire row of trucks on fire and a smashed-to-smithereens showroom? Jumpin' Jack had to come up with something that the authorities would buy. Attempted kidnapping seemed his best bet, make himself out to be the victim. Or, better yet, maybe the bodies, plenty of them charred beyond recognition anyway, belonged to terrorists who had tried to destroy the nation's biggest car lot. Found it listed in the *Guinness Book of World Records* and here they came. Made a twisted kind of sense. Jumpin' Jack Woodrow could almost make himself believe it.

Story needed work, though. He needed to ask himself the questions the cops would ask and have enough answers to satisfy them. Boy, had things gone bad.

And then they got worse.

Jumpin' Jack Woodrow, the Flash himself, felt something round and hard jab into the small of his back at the same time a hand closed over his mouth.

"I think we should talk," said Blaine McCracken.

* * *

The remainder of the assault team couldn't believe their eyes. There it was, the Winnebago, wedged diagonally across Buford Highway between the four cars that had slammed into it when McCracken had tried to run a red light just past the on-ramp to Route 285 two and a half miles down from the Flash Pot. They approached its dented shape cautiously, expecting the same type of counterattack their quarry had used back at the dealership. For this reason, a trio crashed through both access doors simultaneously, while the remaining men kept their eyes and guns on the sunroof.

The six heavily armed men burst into the Winnebago to find the driver's seat empty and a shabbily dressed stranger spinning the channels on a television set in the camper's rear.

"Hey," called out the mayor of Buford Highway, "any of you guys know what station Oprah's on?"

"Jesus," Jack Woodrow moaned, as the man who had proven himself to be even more dangerous than he had been warned strapped Jack's limbs into the frame-straightening mechanism. "Jesus Christ . . ."

Blaine gave the control wheel some torque and instantly Jumpin' Jack's arms and legs were drawn in opposite directions, stretched to the near full capacity of his tendons, ligaments, and muscle.

"What do you want to know? Just tell me!" he heaved.

"This is to make sure you don't lie. I haven't had a good morning. I'm running out of patience."

"Jesus, *anything!*"

"You knew I was coming today, didn't you?"

"Frye's people called me last night. Said they expected you. Said they were sending some help—for my own good. I didn't know it would be this many. I didn't know they would do—" his eyes searched out a window "—*that.*"

"Then do you know what Frye's going to do?"

"What are you talking about?"

"The hundred million dollars you invested with him . . . in Judgment Day."

When Woodrow didn't respond, Blaine worked the control wheel another full turn. The fat man's jacket ripped and his pants split. He wanted to scream, but all that emerged was a low rasp because of the strain the stretching placed on his lungs and throat.

"I didn't believe him!" he gasped at last.

"Didn't believe what?"

"What you said before—Judgment Day. He never called it that, though."

"What did he call it?"

"Just told me not to worry about the future. Told me the Key Society would be preserved when the time came."

Woodrow tried to gaze about him, hoping someone outside may have heard something. Maybe the cops were coming now. Fat chance, he realized, with all the commotion going on. Until things got reasonably settled, he doubted they had even noticed he was missing.

Blaine kept his hand on the frame straightener's control wheel but didn't spin it. "Keep going, Flash."

"Frye called it the final sowing of the fields of civilization," Woodrow continued. "Said he was gonna plow over the dead crops and turn the soil so fresh ones can come up. Said I was gonna be one of the ones left whole." Woodrow tensed, as if expecting the tightening wheel to be turned again. "Look, I never paid any attention to that shit. Frye's crackers. Crazy fucking nuts, all right? That hundred mil bought me a lifetime's worth of advertising on his Future Faith channel, got me God-fearing people from all over the South driving a couple hundred miles to one of my dealerships when they coulda gone to the one down the street from them. That's all I was in it for, I swear!"

"Didn't seem strange, the Reverend sending an army here today?"

"I told you, he said it was for my own protection. Told

me I was on one of his enemy's hit list, on account of my support, financial and otherwise."

Blaine felt his spine arch. "Tell me about the otherwise, Flash."

"More crazy shit I didn't bother to find out about. Just another of his whims."

"What?"

"Had me deliver a whole bunch of cars. Told me to make them different makes and models and where to bring them. Even gave me a list of people to register them to. Funny thing was, all the addresses were in the same goddamn town."

"What town?"

"Give me a minute to think about it, okay?" Woodrow's face crinkled in consternation as he pushed his thinking. "*Something* . . . Falls! That's it! An animal name, I think. Badger or, or . . . *Beaver!* Beaver Falls. Beaver Falls, Arizona!"

"How many people?"

"Can't tell you that, and that's the God's honest truth. A little over a hundred cars, though. I remember the pile of registrations. . . ." Woodrow managed to tip his eyes upward. "Hey, wait a minute. You don't think Frye was so rious about all this shit? You don't think he really believes Judgment Day's coming?"

"He does because he's the one who's bringing it about."

Woodrow looked like he was about to say something, swallowed it down, and then looked at Blaine. "There's something else," he started hesitantly. "I never really gave it much thought, but now . . ."

"Go on."

"The paperwork for the car deals, shipping invoices and all that, was routed through a company in San Diego. Van, Van, er, Van something."

"Van *Dyne*?"

"That's it!"

The information sent a slight quiver through Blaine's stomach. Van Dyne was an international pharmaceutical giant, the biggest in the country, if not the world. But how was it connected to Harlan Frye?

"Frye be mighty pissed off he ever finds out what you told me," Blaine advised Jack Woodrow. "Means it would be a real bad idea to run straight to him about our little talk."

"Count on that, mister," the Flash said gratefully as Blaine turned the wheel toward him to release the pressure. Jumpin' Jack felt the pain in his joints replaced by numbness. His limbs felt wobbly and weak. "I never knew about any of this Judgment Day shit. Damn, if he's half as nuts as you say he is, I wouldn't've given him the change in my pocket."

The chains around his legs rattled off and then Woodrow felt his arms being unlaced. Slowly, very slowly, he tried to stretch the life back into them.

"Only wish I could get my money back," he said. "Only wish—"

Jack Woodrow looked up and stopped. The body shop area was deserted.

Blaine McCracken had disappeared.

Wayne Denbo knew what he had to do. He had known it for the long hours recently he had pretended not to be aware of anyone else in the room. They couldn't help him. No one could help.

Only he could help himself.

Even the darkness no longer helped. Every time he closed his eyes, Beaver Falls appeared as he had last seen it: wasting away in the desert and missing its people. He saw himself driving the patrol car in, Joe Langhorn bitching and Frank McBride starting to stir in the backseat. The stop at the sheriff's station, the restaurant, the post office, the bank, and finally the school. People just up and vanished in the middle of their lives. For a time when they got him to the hospital, Wayne Denbo was convinced it was only a matter of time before it happened to him. He was pretty sure now that wasn't going to happen, not with a highway patrolman in his room at Tucson General at all times. But that didn't mean he was safe. Sooner or later, *they'd* be coming.

The figures from the dust.

Wayne Denbo could explain all this to the people who filled their days hanging over his bed, could describe the men in weird suits driving space-age trucks with all kinds of steel sticking up from their roofs. But then the doctors would move him up into the crazy ward, where getting out when the time came would be much, much harder.

Where the darkness had been his refuge, now it became his ally. He used it to map out a plan in his mind. First he stayed calm and quiet so they'd keep the needles away. Needed to be sharp, needed to be quick. No funny juice to slow him down, at least no more than was already pumping through his system. Then he laid the plan all out so he could see. Ran it over and over again just like the Beaver Falls videotape, so when he finally got to it, it wouldn't seem like the first time. Wasn't really going to be that hard, once he got round to making things happen. Hightail his ass out of here and get back to where it started.

Back to Beaver Falls.

Jack Woodrow was still trying to ease the feeling back into his limbs and joints when the two figures entered the body shop area. A boy and a girl, barely old enough to drive.

Woodrow watched them swing their stares about in unison, paying him little heed and seeming disappointed. The boy advanced his way ahead of the girl.

"Where is he?"

"Who?"

"McCracken."

"Never heard of the guy," the Flash said, hoping the police and fire police were still looking for him. "You must have—"

And before he could finish the sentence, the boy had

him by the soft flesh of the throat. Kid moved like a cat, the girl already right behind him.

"I'm going to ask you again," the boy said, so calmly it scared Jack Woodrow. "Where is Blaine McCracken?"

The pain in his throat was worse than anything he'd felt on the frame straightener. He just wanted it to end. "Gone," he choked out. "Just before you got here."

The boy and girl exchanged glances.

"Where?" the boy asked. "Where did he go?"

" 'Ow the fuck should I—"

The next burst of pain made him gasp, filled his eyes with tears. Jack Woodrow sank to his knees, sick to his stomach.

"I know who you are," the boy said from over him. "I know what you're a part of. McCracken knew and I know too. You told him something. Tell me what."

"Beaver Falls," Jumpin' Jack whispered, because that was all he could manage. "Town in Arizona. Told him about a bunch of cars I shipped there, a hundred of them. . . . Let me go. Please."

"My pleasure," Woodrow heard the boy say.

A popping sound followed as a final squeeze severed the cartilage lining his throat and sent the Flash writhing to the floor.

Jacob turned away from the dying man beneath him and faced his twin. "Let's go."

CHAPTER 22

Hank Belgrade was waiting when McCracken climbed the steps of the Lincoln Memorial at two o'clock Wednesday afternoon.

"I missed my lunch on account of you, McNuts," he jeered.

"It's good for your diet, Hank," Blaine said, sitting down next to him.

"And fuck you, too."

Belgrade was a big, beefy man who, like a select few in Washington, drew a salary without any official title. Technically, both the Departments of State and Defense showed his name on their roster, but in actuality he worked for neither. Instead, he liaised between the two and handled the dirty linen of both. He had access to files and information few in Washington had any idea existed. Blaine had once saved his career back in the Cold War days by bringing a Soviet defector safely in after a leak had been detected. In return Belgrade was always there for McCracken when he needed information. They met here on the steps of the Lincoln Memorial every time, Belgrade wearing his perpetual scowl, never looking happy to see him.

"Van Dyne Pharmaceuticals, Hank."

"Boy, you got some sense of timing, you know that? What the fuck you into here?"

"Why?"

"I make a couple calls to get you your background check and all of a sudden my other line's ringing off the hook. You musta found your way into another bee's nest, McNuts."

"My specialty."

"For starters, Van Dyne's got an eighteen percent market share of the domestic business, making it the biggest drug company in the country. Did almost twenty billion dollars in business last year."

"Anything else?"

"Yeah, the company's protected, McNuts, all the way to the top."

"How high, in this case?"

"High as I can reach. Lots of people down Pennsylvania and Constitution didn't like you snooping around."

"You tell them why I was interested?"

"What, tell 'em some nutty preacher's got dreams of Armageddon? I *like* my job. Thing is, the FDA ended up with dibs on you. They got a man waiting now as we speak. Dupont Circle." Belgrade checked his watch. "You're already late."

Dupont Circle was Washington at its lowest. A neatly trimmed, grassy park located at the edge of Georgetown, it was a known gathering point for drug dealers and purveyors of other assorted merchandise. Several homeless called the circle home during the day and loitered there atop the garbage bags containing their life's worth. Many of the benches were occupied by other unkempt figures drinking the day away out of paper bags.

McCracken had remembered that much about Dupont Circle. What he had forgotten was the striking absence of women on its grounds. He could see only men mingling amidst the trees and statues as he entered, was instantly conscious of the interested stares cast his way. Blaine met none of them and just kept walking for the monument in the circle's center, where the man from the Food and Drug Administration was supposed to be waiting. Cutting across the grass, he had to step over a huge, sprawled shape with its face covered by yesterday's *Washington Post*.

The figure pacing impatiently before the monument was the only one in the park wearing a suit. An overcoat was draped over his left arm. He looked extremely uncomfortable. Blaine stopped a yard from him.

"I really like your suit," Blaine greeted with a wink.

"You must be McCracken. I'm Maggs," said the small, fidgety man with nervous, beady eyes and dark, oily hair.

Neither bothered extending a hand.

"Come here often, Maggs?"

"As little as possible. Look, I want to make this quick, if you don't mind."

"Important plans this afternoon?"

"I'm not from the FDA," Maggs admitted.

"I know. This wouldn't be their style. Then who would you be from, exactly?"

"Let's say our concerns closely parallel those of the Food and Drug. You opened a door you shouldn't have."

"Bad habit of mine, Maggs."

"Anyone else, we would have ignored it. But your reputation precedes you. Whenever you start asking about something, that something is usually in for trouble."

"And rightfully, in almost every case."

"Not this one," Maggs said flatly, folding his arms before him around his overcoat. "Van Dyne's protected."

"That's what Hank Belgrade said. He didn't say why."

"Because he doesn't know. We've kept it under wraps, and that's the way it's got to stay. There's a lot at stake here."

"My point exactly."

"I need to know what your interest is in Van Dyne."

"Maybe they're involved in more than you think, Maggs. Maybe you're protecting them for all the wrong reasons."

Maggs nodded dramatically, stretching the gesture out. "You like saving lives, McCracken?"

"Some would say that's what I do best."

"So is Van Dyne. In fact, they're on the verge of being able to save *millions*. If we leave them alone. That's my job."

"To leave them alone?"

'To make sure people like you do." The little man took one step closer and lowered his voice. "I'm talking about something the government has an extremely important interest in. I'm talking about an AIDS vaccine Van Dyne is on the verge of submitting documentation to gain FDA approval for."

Blaine tried not to show his surprise. "And you're worried that's what I'm threatening?"

"Van Dyne doesn't need any attention, any exposure. That's what you *always* threaten. Look, I don't know what trail brought you this far, but it stops right here in this park."

McCracken looked at Maggs suspiciously. "Why is the government so interested in the workings of a pharmaceutical company? No, don't answer that. Just let me guess. Under the new AIDS research coordination and funding policies, you would have been involved with Van Dyne's progress every step of the way. Bedmates."

"We prefer to call it partners in a newly defined democratic-capitalist system."

"Whatever you call it, this is about *AIDS*, an international epidemic that has merely brushed this country, while it ravages and decimates others. And that makes everything come back to power, and the government wants a piece of the action. Imagine, taking charge of dispensing and allocating a vaccine that—"

"That's enough!"

"Am I close? Of course I am. Whoever in our illustrious

government sent you here today must see Van Dyne's vaccine as a bargaining chip, a means toward other ends."
Blaine shook his head, a humorless smile of disgust traced across his face. "It figures."

"It's the way the world functions today, McCracken. Like it or not. And we can't let you screw this opportunity up by fucking with Van Dyne on one of your crusades."

"Strange you haven't asked me about this particular crusade yet."

"I don't have to. Van Dyne isn't involved."

"And if they were?"

Maggs remained silent.

"There's a man out there who's ready to turn tomorrow or the day after into Judgment Day, and I think Van Dyne's connected. I don't give a shit about your plans for their AIDS vaccine, Maggs, but I mean to find out what else they're into that links them to one very scary dude named Harlan Frye."

Maggs took a step backward and straightened his shoulders, "I'm afraid I can't allow that."

"I wasn't aware I needed to ask for permission."

Maggs was having trouble looking straight at him "We're going to take a walk now, McCracken. You don't have to be hurt. You *won't* be hurt. You'll just be asked to relax under cover for a few months until approval for the vaccine is finalized."

Blaine glanced around him. "So that's why you chose Dupont Circle, the crowds, lots of people mingling. . . ."

"You don't know where all of my people are, McCracken. Oh, maybe you'll be able to spot a few— maybe you already have—but it only takes one, if you try to run."

McCracken nodded. "One of the eight, Maggs?"

The little man's eyes bulged and followed Blaine as he turned toward the east entrance to Dupont Circle. The large sprawled shape McCracken had stepped over en route to the monument was kneeling now, yesterday's *Post* still clothing his shoulders beneath a gray-flecked black ponytail.

Johnny Wareagle!

"I figured you wouldn't know them, either," Blaine continued. "It's the way men like you work, Maggs. But Johnny over there knew them. Stuck out eight fingers when I stepped over him. They're in the park, all right, but they won't be moving anytime soon."

Maggs stood there frozen, eyes scanning Dupont Circle desperately, searching for the accomplices who had preceded him here. Prone and passed-out forms were scattered everywhere across benches and ground, a few leaning up against trees. The eight men could have been any of them.

"Don't worry, Maggs," McCracken continued, "I'm not going to hurt you. You've told me what I needed to know. The fact that Van Dyne's secured protected status means they can get away with anything, *have* gotten away with whatever they needed to."

He started to back away. Behind him Johnny Wareagle had risen to his feet.

"Trouble is, Maggs, they're about to get away with more."

Blaine continued to look at Maggs as the distance widened between them, wondering if the little man might draw the gun that made a bulge near his right armpit.

"Where to now, Blainey?" Johnny asked when McCracken reached him.

"San Diego, Indian. Van Dyne Pharmaceuticals."

CHAPTER 23

The private side entrance to Van Dyne Pharmaceuticals slid open to reveal Freddy Levinger peering out through the crack.

"Hurry," he whispered urgently, motioning for Karen Raymond to enter as his eyes darted about the courtyard.

She was inside almost before he had finished speaking. Levinger closed the door behind them.

"When we're done tonight," he followed nervously, "no matter what we find, my role in this is finished. I want your word on that."

"You've got it," she said softly back.

She had followed the instructions Levinger had given her that afternoon exactly. Van Dyne had outgrown their facilities in Torrey Pines Industrial Park years before and had moved out to their own private complex off the freeway heading north out of La Jolla. The complex included not only the company's corporate headquarters and research wings, but also a self-contained manufacturing facility on the grounds that allowed Van Dyne the luxury of private production and distribution.

A pass Freddy Levinger had provided got Karen through the main gate, and his own identification card had permitted her access to the underground parking garage. The air of this parking garage smelled peculiarly clean, not anything like that of other such garages she'd walked through. Karen moved quickly yet warily toward the exit door he had indicated, anticipating the possibility of another car arriving or rattling footsteps that would force her to take cover. Neither intruded and she climbed up a staircase back to the surface. She emerged inside Van Dyne's processing plant near its main entrance. She crept down another corridor toward a less obtrusive exit sign that took her out into the night.

The distance separating her from the courtyard contained within the U-shaped office and lab complex was considerable. But she could see no guard patrolling, and the spill of lights could be easily avoided. Karen covered the distance fast, stopping and pressing her shoulders against the cream-colored Van Dyne facade just before the open part of the U. She made sure to peer around the corner before entering the courtyard. When again there were no guards in sight, Karen dashed toward the door in the back right corner of the complex Levinger had directed her to.

She reached the door a minute early and waited, eyes scanning the courtyard frantically. This locked door had no specially tailored slot to accept the card Levinger had given her for easy access. Instead, she'd had to wait in this spot until he appeared to let her in.

"There's a room upstairs they've converted into the nerve center for all data concerning the test group," Levinger told her, leading the way down the corridor.

"Sounds like you're not very familiar with it."

"With good reason: I've only been inside once."

"Even though you're head of development?"

"This testing was considered too important for anyone other than a select few to handle. I've been briefed regularly on the test and documentation status. Beyond that, I couldn't really tell you what's been going on there."

" 'There' as in *where*, Freddy?"

Levinger took a deep breath as they reached the top of the stairs. "The test group for our vaccine, numbering one hundred and eighty, has been confined to a single town, situated smack-dab in the middle of the Arizona desert where not many are likely to ask questions when so many new residents appear on the scene. That number includes entire families, and don't ask me how Van Dyne came up with the volunteers. We moved them in about six months ago. Story went they were all associated with a fabricated water development project "

"In the Arizona desert . . ."

"Fabricated, like I said."

"But not the town."

"No, the town's real enough." Levinger paused, as if to collect his thoughts. "It's called Beaver Falls."

McCracken pulled the Pacific Coast Security Services van up to the main gate of Van Dyne Pharmaceuticals. There had been no time to obtain a detailed schematic of the complex's layout. The best he was able to come up with were some broad, overview photographs contained in a stockholder's annual report he had obtained from a Washington brokerage firm following his meeting with Maggs.

If the Reverend Harlan Frye really did have Judgment Day in the offing, the pharmaceutical connection made perfect sense. The possibilities were endless. Since Van Dyne dominated the over-the-counter, nonprescription drug business, the number of people just in the United States they reached per year likely stretched well beyond a hundred million. But speculation was futile at this point. The answers would be inside Van Dyne, somewhere, leading ultimately to the company's connection with Harlan Frye.

McCracken had expected security would be increased

around the complex in the wake of his meeting that afternoon with Maggs. A picture in Van Dyne's full-color annual report showed one of the guards clearly enough to read the label on his sleeve. Accordingly, upon arriving in San Diego, Blaine had driven out to Pacific Coast Security and "borrowed" one of their minivans. The original driver, a sergeant, was tied up in the back, certain to wake up in the morning with a terrible headache. He was about Blaine's height but outweighed him by fifty pounds, making his clothes a poor fit.

The increase in security personnel on the grounds led the gate attendant to wave him in after only a cursory check. Blaine nodded and slid the van through the gate, heading it toward the underground parking garage. The minivan was equipped with a small drawer where the ashtray should have been, filled with clearly marked electronic access cards to a number of buildings on the company's patrol. The only one for Van Dyne was marked GARAGE.

Recalling the complex's layout from the overhead shot found on the cover of the company's annual report, McCracken pulled his minivan up to a ramp built on a steep decline. A slot awaited him before the drop-off, easily accessible by simply extending his hand out the window. Blaine slid the access card in. The machine gulped it down briefly, then coughed it back out. The automatic door below began to rise, and McCracken headed the Pacific Coast Security minivan into the garage.

It thumped softly off the decline onto the macadam surface, the door falling again almost immediately. McCracken parked amidst the other PCS vehicles and climbed out of the minivan. He had barely closed the door behind him when he heard footsteps rattling his way from the west end of the garage. Confident in his disguise, Blaine paid them little heed until a familiar voice echoed his way.

"Nice to see you again."

McCracken stepped away from his van and saw Maggs, a triumphant grin spreading across his face.

"It's about time somebody cracked *your* balls, Mc-Cracken. I don't think even your Indian friend would be able to spot all my people this time."

The room Freddy Levinger had been referring to was located at the darkened end of a hallway on the building's third floor, the only room in the general area. The door featured another electronic slot on its right and lacked a knob.

"I'll need my access card back," Levinger told Karen.

"Does it work up here as well?" she asked, handing the card over.

"It will," he followed, and produced a strip of what looked like gray tape wrapped in cellophane from within his jacket pocket.

He carefully peeled back the cellophane and lifted up the tapelike strip over a nearly identical one that covered the entire lengths of both sides of his card. Levinger gazed back at Karen before easing the tampered card haltingly into the slot.

No light flashed this time. There was no beep, just a barely audible click as the door to the room parted electronically from its seal. Levinger pushed it the rest of the way open and entered, with Karen on his heels. The room was equipped with a heat sensor that automatically triggered the lighting upon their entry. The sudden brightness stole a breath from Karen, but it was Levinger who gasped audibly.

"My God," was all he said.

The room was empty.

"What does it mean?" Karen demanded.

"I . . . don't know."

"You've got some ideas. You *must*!"

Levinger looked away from her, then back again. "All data was collected and collated in here. There were computers, state-of-the-art communications links."

"What about the information?" she asked him.

"Wouldn't it still be somewhere in Van Dyne's main data banks? You can find it, Freddy, I know you can."

Levinger didn't bother denying it. "There is one way."

"Use it."

"We find nothing and I'll still end up losing my job if the intrusion gets noted."

"But we know there's *something*, don't we? Something must have gone wrong in Beaver Falls, something they're not telling you about. And whatever it is happened at almost the same time someone at Van Dyne decided they had to get their hands on *my* vaccine. Doesn't that make you the least bit angry, the least bit suspicious? Look, I know you've been resisting everything I've said. I know you don't want to believe it. Ask yourself for one moment, though, what happens if it's all the truth? What does that say about Van Dyne? What does that say about their real methods and motivations?"

He nodded grudgingly. "It'll take a few minutes before the computer notes and reports the intrusion. I'm giving you five, Karen, and that's it. After that you can do anything you want to me."

Freddy Levinger's office was located in another wing of the corporate section of the Van Dyne complex, outfitted for a busy executive rather than a man committed to science and research. Clearly Levinger's role as head of development had been redefined by Van Dyne's upper echelon to fit their needs. He was a figurehead more than anything, a man whose job it was to travel the country giving update reports on new and exciting products to stockholders' meetings and medical conventions.

Levinger closed the door to his office and pulled his chair over so it faced the computer sitting on his L-shaped desk. He didn't offer Karen a chair and she didn't bother to take one.

"Okay," he started, "this will take a few minutes."

"You sound nervous."

"To get on line, I'm going to have to shut down all the

power in the complex, except for the manufacturing plant, for several seconds, long enough to make the machine reboot. Big chance to take. Makes it too easy to identify where the intrusion originated from." He called up the proper command sequence on his screen. "Here we go, Karen."

Five armed men, none of them wearing Pacific Coast Security uniforms, converged on McCracken's position. Blaine looked fast toward Maggs, but the little man was smart enough to keep his distance this time.

"I know what you're thinking," he taunted. "Stop. You'll never get all of them. I haven't even *signaled* all of them. It would be a senseless waste if you fired. Get rid of the temptation, McCracken: Drop your gun, a SIG-Sauer nine, I believe."

Blaine let it fall to the floor. "I'm impressed."

"Don't be. Two men are going to come forward to search you thoroughly. After they're done, we're going to take a little walk."

Maggs's two henchmen searched him with surprising restraint, finding nothing. One of them held his wrists behind him, while the other moved to fasten on the hand-cuffs.

The steel had just grazed McCracken's hand when the lights died, plunging the parking garage into utter darkness.

Levinger left the power off for ten seconds before reactivating Van Dyne's internal power grid. As the mainframe-based computer system started to reboot, Freddy logged on to the Beaver Falls file in the midst of the process.

Levinger checked his watch before beginning his scan of the material. Karen tried to read over his shoulder, but the data on the screen were changing too fast for her to keep up with.

"Doesn't look like there's anything here out of the ordinary," Freddy said as he scrolled through the material.

"Nothing's out of place. Everything just as they told—" His voice froze in midsentence as he halted his rapid scrolling.

"What? What is it?"

He ignored her and continued scrolling until the screen locked on a half-empty page, the data at its end. Levinger sat there with his finger still on the PAGE DOWN key. Even in the black starkness of the CRT screen, his face reflected back ghost white. Karen could see him trying to swallow.

"What is it?" she asked.

He turned and looked at her. "The entries, all the data, end on Sunday. There's been nothing since."

"What's it mean?"

He was still looking at her, his stare considerably harder. "Something went wrong, something big."

"With the test group. That's what you're suggesting, isn't it?"

"I don't know what I'm suggesting. All I know now is that everything was status quo up until Sunday when—"

Levinger broke off his words when the screen in front of him went dark. He lurched up from his chair, fear blazing over his features.

"They've isolated the intrusion into the network! We've got to *get out of here*!"

CHAPTER 24

McCracken seized the advantage the darkness gave him instantly. He pulled from the stunned and weakened grasp of his captor and bolted away.

"Shoot him!" he heard Maggs's voice order. "Shoot him!"

Gunshots erupted, echoing, identifiable only as orange muzzle flashes. Blaine chose the widest path between the gunmen available, which had brought him to the start of a corridor when the lighting returned. He thundered down the hall and burst through a heavy fire door at its end. A stairwell lay before him, and McCracken took it two steps at a time and charged straight for another heavy door marked PLANT ENTRANCE. He threw his shoulder into it and surged into Van Dyne's massive drug manufacturing center.

Virtually all of the company's drugs, both over-the-counter and prescription, were produced within this plant. In one section cough and cold liquids were dispensed automatically into the proper-sized bottles, then sent to another station to be fitted with child-guard caps before being labeled and boxed. In another powders were sifted and refined by machines en route to being pressed and molded into tablets, or packed into capsules. Some of the tablets were sent on to a machine that sprayed a microencapsulating coating over them to make them time-release. From there the pills and time capsules were automatically apportioned in foil push-out packs, and then shrink-wrap was fastened tightly around the completed packages.

McCracken ran swiftly into the very center of this mammoth manufacturing complex. He hoped to avoid the eyes of the token shift that monitored the process. They wore earplugs to guard them from the pounding racket kept from the rest of the complex by the specially reinforced walls. It was those earplugs that kept them from hearing the staccato bursts of gunfire aimed at McCracken when Maggs's team entered the plant on his trail.

Avoiding the bullets was as easy as ducking beneath one of the huge lines of machinery, but Blaine knew now that reaching an exit door under the circumstances was impossible. He had to neutralize this enemy force first, and for that he had to figure out a way to use the only weapons available to him: the machines themselves.

McCracken hunched low. The cover of the machinery was serving him well. As he neared the center of the floor in a crouch, he spotted a pair of legs emerging at the end of the row visible beneath a machine that spun thousands of pills at a time in order to dry their bonded coatings. McCracken froze and slowly started to turn.

A bullet clanged off the machine just above him. He pressed himself tight against the floor, thankful for the deafening roar of the machines that kept the gunmen from shouting signals to each other. Blaine pushed himself under the shrink-wrapping machine and emerged along the next row. He was halfway to his feet when a man catapulted over the rolling tread of a conveyor carrying finished packages of an over-the-counter cold medication and slammed into him. Blaine's hand locked on his pistol and shoved it skyward. He felt the trigger go and a bullet sped upward for the lights. The cavernous room darkened ever so slightly as one of the huge fluorescents twenty feet up was shot out and showered down jagged shards of thick glass.

The man's free hand found Blaine's throat, while McCracken continued to keep the gun under control. But the man's back was pressed up against the shrink-wrap machine, giving him the leverage he would need to strip his pistol from Blaine's determined grasp.

The gunman's head brushed against the outlet that dispensed the shrink-wrap over the packages thrust beneath it by a robotic arm. A noise like popcorn popping sounded every time a fresh package was sent on its way to be heat-blasted for final seal. McCracken managed to follow the motions of the robotic arm and saw the opportunity the shrink-wrapping procedure provided.

Keeping hold of the gun as best he could, he drove his right shoulder sideways into his assailant. The blow, barely a graze, was still enough to force the man's face under the rectangular dispensing spout, just as the robotic arm was swinging the next package into position. The machine regarded his face as that package and spit out the proper segment of plastic with the usual *pop!*

Then another, and a third as Blaine kept his face there, the machine continuing to dispense its plastic wrap. The man began flailing with his arms, the gun lost, desperate to tear the shrink-wrap from his nose and mouth. He might have succeeded had not McCracken's final thrust wedged his face against the dispensing spout itself, catching it between motions and jamming it in place. The machine rattled and started to whine. The robotic arm froze in midmotion. The spout continued to spit out shrink-wrap in machine-gun fashion.

McCracken released his hold and the gunman slumped to the floor. A breakdown alarm began sounding in cadence with a flashing red light atop the machine to indicate the source of the problem to the monitors on duty. The massive machine sputtered one more time and shut itself down. The boxes of cold medication that had backed up behind it had already begun to spill over onto the floor. McCracken headed for the next row, the next bit of his strategy suddenly clear to him.

Freddy Levinger grabbed Karen's arm as they hurried from his office, propelling her toward the elevators at the end of the corridor where a pair of shafts rested directly across from each other.

"You take one, I'll take the other," Karen said, the fear driving the numbness from her mind. She hit the down arrow on one side and then the other. The soft whir of the machines' approach sounded instantly.

"We should stay together."

"Not if it means reducing the odds of at least one of us getting out."

"You'll never make it without me."

"Like I said, Freddy, one of us."

When Karen's elevator arrived just ahead of his, she stepped in wordlessly and pressed G for garage. Before her doors had closed completely, she watched Freddy's compartment begin to slide open.

A barrage of bullets poured out nonstop from inside. The last thing Karen saw before her doors closed completely was Levinger's body spiraling backward, turned into a pincushion. The bursts banged off the steel doors of her compartment in the last instant before it began its descent.

Karen shoved herself against the compartment's rear. The G button glowed alive, the elevator descending fast. For all she knew, more gunmen would be awaiting her once it stopped.

The elevator ground to a halt. Karen froze in place, tensing in anticipation of the barrage she felt certain was to come.

The doors opened.

She nearly screamed.

No bullets poured into the compartment. No one was waiting outside it. Karen rushed down the hallway leading to the garage.

A circuitous route brought McCracken to the station that poured alcohol-rich cough medicine into bottle after bottle before sending them along the line to the capping station. He ducked beneath the dispensing unit and, as expected, located the drain pipe on its underside. The steel cap holding back the overflow contents rested directly over another drain that dropped into the floor. Blaine tore out a piece of his jacket's lining to use as a plug for the floor drain and then twisted the cap off the machine. Instantly cough medicine spilled outward, pooling across the floor now that entry to the drain was blocked off.

McCracken sopped up some of the medicine in his handkerchief and then pulled a lighter from his pocket. He ducked quickly beneath the next row of machinery and waited as patiently as he dared. When the first sign of approaching footsteps reached him, he touched the lighter's flame to his alcohol-soaked handkerchief. The *poofl* of heat singed him an instant before he tossed it into the spreading spill.

He saw the flames catch and rise and was rushing farther away when the resulting explosion of jagged steel and glass shook the entire room. He had no idea how many of the killers had been in range and he didn't wait to find out; the screams he heard told him the move had been successful.

The fire alarm had begun to wail maddingly when Blaine lunged back to his feet and sped toward a gunman near an exit door whose attention had been drawn to the explosion. McCracken knew he couldn't close the gap fast enough to prevent the man from firing on him, so he rushed instead toward the huge steam hoses that extended down at various angles throughout the plant from the ceiling. Used to clean the machinery, the hoses pushed steam out at incredible pressure. The gunman had just turned toward him when Blaine leaped for one of the thick black hoses and yanked it downward, tearing it from a feed pipe.

Steam gushed out in a hot, white stream. McCracken managed to hold the black rubber steady long enough to catch the gunman right in the face before he could open fire. His piercing screech bubbled Blaine's ears, rising above the din of the machines and the wailing of the fire alarm. Weaponless, McCracken elected to go for the automatic rifle dangling from the gunman's shoulder. He was still trying to strip it free when the remainder of Maggs's men converged, firing. The burned man became a convenient shield long enough for McCracken to steady the rifle that remained strapped to the man's shoulder. Blaine fired in a wide arc, hoping to catch all of Maggs's remaining killers in its spread.

The gun clicked empty. Blaine drew a Beretta nine-millimeter from a holster on the dead man's belt and let him slip to the floor. He rotated his eyes, searching for motion. He found none in the processing center, but heard sounds of approaching feet thudding from outside toward the exit door he had hoped to utilize. The sprinkler system had activated over the medicine-dispensing station he had destroyed, replacing the angry flames with coarse, dark smoke. Again his options narrowed to one. Holding the pistol before him, McCracken rushed through the thickening cloud toward the door on the far side that led into Van Dyne's corporate offices.

For Karen, the run was agonizing. It seemed to take forever to negotiate her way to the garage. Panic stole her breath away and left her gasping before even one corridor was behind her. She grew dizzy and had to hug the wall for support. Her feet felt like lead. She listened fearfully for any sounds of pursuit from Freddy Levinger's killers.

The thumping of footsteps clamored in her direction from in front of her. She had started to back up when more sounded from her rear.

They were coming from both directions!
She was trapped. It was over.
The first figure rounded the corner of the hall just ahead of her and dropped into a crouch, the pistol that would end everything angling up in his hand.

McCracken had heard someone approaching clumsily just before he reached the end of the hall accessing Van Dyne's corporate wing. Maybe it was that fact that kept him from firing once he had the gun steady. Maybe it was the look in the woman's eyes, the look of the hunted and not the hunter. Still, the moment of hesitation lingered into a long second as he stayed in his crouch.

"Help me," she pleaded in a strained, terrified voice.

A trio of armed figures crashed through a fire door twenty yards behind her. Blaine resteadied the Beretta.

He wasn't sure how many of the seven shells he fired found their targets; enough to drop them, and that was all that mattered. The woman was sliding down the wall she had been pressed against for support. At first, he thought one of his or their errant shots had struck her. But another gaze into her eyes told him panic was to blame.

Blaine hurried over and pulled her to her feet.

"Come on!" he ordered.

"Thank you," she said emotionlessly. "Thank you . . ."

Blaine dragged her forward, supporting her entire weight, as he retraced his steps back toward the manufacturing plant. She was gasping, her weight starting to hold him back.

"Run!" he instructed flatly. "If you want to live, run!"

Spurred by his words, the woman picked up her pace. She seemed recharged, and now had no trouble keeping up with him.

Blaine yanked her behind the cover of an open fire door just before another trio of gunmen tore out from the plant area. The men passed by without taking notice of Blaine and the woman, Maggs stumbling at their rear.

"That should clear us the path we need," he whispered.

"They were after *you*," Karen Raymond said, realizing it for the first time. "I thought it was . . . me."

"Why you?"

She was about to answer when more footsteps thundered their way down the hall.

"Christ," Blaine muttered.

Karen felt him take her hand. He pulled her the last stretch of the way into Van Dyne's manufacturing center, and together they raced through it and lunged out the nearest exit door into the night.

Karen didn't bother resisting or arguing. She ran as fast as she could across the open field that rimmed the manufacturing center's rear. A chain-link fence enclosed the entire complex, and she hurtled toward it with the man she now regarded as her savior. She was only a few yards away when a hail of bullets erupted behind her.

"Keep going!" Blaine ordered as he released his hold.

Before she could respond, he had steadied himself with knees bent and shoulders squared forward. Karen heard the bullets burst from his gun as she approached the fence. She didn't think of climbing it, she thought of *leaping* it to generate the momentum she needed to carry her. She landed just a few feet from the top, and a single hoist was all it took to get her prone body over the top. Karen hit the ground on the other side hard, was stumbling back to her feet when the bearded man came over the fence with an effortlessness that defied understanding. He hit the ground moving and grabbed her on the way.

"Don't look back!" he ordered. "Just run!"

He led her up and over a hill, then down a light slope toward a side road that intersected with the freeway.

"They're coming!" she noted desperately.

The words were barely out of her mouth when a car running without its headlights pulled up before them. The passenger-side window slid down.

"You're early, Blainey," said the huge shape of an Indian from the driver's seat.

* * *

McCracken shoved the woman into the backseat ahead of him. "That's because I ended up with her instead of what I came to Van Dyne to get."

"Van Dyne has surprises for everyone," she said, having recovered her breath.

"Spoken from experience, it sounds to me," responded Blaine as he slammed the door behind him.

"Bitter experience," she sighed.

"Doesn't surprise me in the least," he said. The car thumped back onto the road, and Johnny Wareagle screeched away into the night.

The woman suddenly lurched forward in her seat. "I've got to meet them!"

"Meet *who*?" Blaine demanded.

"No one in pursuit," Wareagle announced when the car neared the freeway.

"Take a right," Blaine said, looking away briefly from the woman.

"No!" she insisted. "Left! *Please!* I've *got* to meet them!"

Wareagle's eyes found McCracken's in the rearview mirror.

"Make that a left, Indian."

CHAPTER 25

Earvin Early was invisible. Even if he hadn't arrived at the trailer park in the cover of dark, no one would have seen him. Even if someone had happened upon him in his hiding place back in the woods, they would not have seen him. So long as he stayed still and concentrated hard enough, he was invisible.

There had been no trace of the woman in the hours since he had arrived. Early had never met her, of course, but he could imagine her scent, and sniffing the air told him she was not here.

It didn't matter. The Reverend Harlan Frye's orders had been clear to him in this case. If the woman could not be found, he was to go after her two boys the motorcycle gang was guarding. That way the woman would have no choice but to concede. To save her children, she would do anything. They would already be dead, of course, but she wouldn't know that.

Invisible, Earvin Early hung back and watched over the scene. He studied the placement of the gang members and

the weapons they carried with them, weapons that would
be useless against him. He charted the position of all the
trailer homes the bikers resided in. An old lame one with
a ponytail, an eye patch, and a face that looked like tanned
leather seemed to be in charge. Early saw him several
times, walking with a pair of pit bulls by his side and a
shotgun slung over his shoulder as he moved about, checking the security he had set up. Once when the old leader
was patrolling, the door to one of the trailers opened and
a young face peered briefly out.

Earvin Early had found his targets.

He measured everything off in his head. The armed bikers
were well spaced and positioned to watch for intrusions at
all vantage points within the park. Early understood now
why the Reverend had needed him. They would never expect to be attacked by a single man, never mind one they
could look at and not see until he materialized before them.

The first biker he reached after emerging from the
woods several hours later when the time was right was the
biggest and most alert, accounting for Early's choice.
Early came at him from the rear, his footsteps not even
ruffling the soft ground underfoot. The man didn't so
much as turn. Early swallowed his head in two massive
hands and jerked it hard. The snap was loud but quick.
The man crumpled and Early caught him before he hit the
ground and hauled him behind some cover.

The next closest biker watching the perimeter was fifteen yards away, smoking a cigarette. Early sniffed the air
and could tell it was a Marlboro. He approached from the
side this time, the rear blocked by a trailer. The man
turned at the last moment, tried to bring his gun round.
But he had to discard the Marlboro first, and the delay
proved fatal. Early stripped the rifle out of his grasp and
smashed the stock into his mouth before he could scream.
The man's teeth shattered and his eyes bulged with pain
and shock. Early continued to shove the rifle butt down
the man's throat. The biker's cheeks stretched obscenely
and his breath was choked off. There was a loud crack and

he went limp. His eyes weren't moving anymore. Early shoved him beneath the trailer.

The next two were huddled together. Early smelled the strong aroma of beer on them. One burped. The other rested his shotgun against a tree and stretched, yawning loudly.

"Shit," he exhaled, "shit on this night . . ."

He brought his arms down and reached back for his shotgun to find it was gone, fallen probably.

The biker was feeling about on the dark ground, attempting to retrieve it, when a huge, stumplike hand closed on his wrist and yanked. The last thing the biker felt was another hand closing on the back of his head and slamming him forward. A mushing sound followed as his face was driven through the tree bark.

"What the fu—"

The second biker had lunged round the big tree to see his friend wedged there, face a flattened, bleeding mess incised into the bark.

"Hey!" he called. "Somebody!"

Earvin Early swung the shotgun toward the second biker's head. The biker never saw the blow coming, even when he turned toward it. The stock cracked his skull wide open upon impact and sprayed blood and brains into the air. The first of those responding to his call got there just as the second biker was falling into a portion of what used to compose the contents of his skull.

"Jesus," the first one on the scene muttered, "Jesus . . ."

Another pair were not far behind. Earvin Early waited until all three were standing in a group, easily within his killing range. Then he drew the knife. The knife was old; the knife was rusted. But the knife was his chosen instrument and he whirled into the center of the group, letting himself become visible.

Most had time to see nothing, though, as the knife slashed and cut, ripped and tore. Not a single shot was fired in defense or retaliation. The men died puzzled by the shapeless thing that had killed them, not really sure of what was happening.

When he was finished, Earvin Early headed for the trailer where he had spotted one of the boys earlier. It sat three down the row, sixty feet away. The lame old man who was the leader could still be a nuisance. There might be others nearby who could cause problems, as well, if he got too noisy in his work.

But Earvin Early was confident about his abilities to work quickly and quietly. The trailer was just up ahead, and its contents belonged to him.

Karen Raymond had begun her tale tentatively while the big Indian drove, waiting for a disbelieving scowl to appear on Blaine McCracken's face. Instead, though, his eyes encouraged her to keep going, clearly astonished by her words but accepting them.

"So first they go all out to kill you," he concluded before she had quite finished, "and then they decide you've got something they want."

Karen nodded. "Because they couldn't get Lot 35 any other way. None of the computers they pilfered contained all of the information they needed. Collating what they stole would have taken months. I made sure of that."

"Then, even though Van Dyne had their own vaccine, they suddenly needed yours."

"I told you, because theirs didn't work. Something went wrong; in the testing stage, by all indications," she said, explaining Freddy Levinger's discovery that all data had ceased as of Sunday.

"Tell me more about this test group."

"Heterogeneous in virtually all respects. One hundred eighty in number, an unusually low number for this kind of test. They were all placed in a single town; also unusual, if not unheard-of."

"Not a good idea from a secrecy and security standpoint either," Blaine noted.

"The town's isolated nature in the Arizona desert allowed Van Dyne to pull that part off," Karen explained.

McCracken felt a chill pass through him. Johnny Wareagle stole a glance back his way,

"Arizona *desert*?"

"Yes, a town called—"

"Beaver Falls," Blaine completed for her.

Karen's mouth dropped. "How did you know? How *could* you know?"

"I think it's time you heard my story, Doctor."

Papa Jack came down the trailer's steps awkwardly, sawed-off shotgun held in a single hand.

"What the fuck," he muttered to himself in a voice that sounded like he spoke between chomps on gravel. Both hands now gripped the sawed-off.

A huge shape spun out before him, charging. Papa Jack emptied both barrels. The force of the twin blasts knocked him backward and nearly toppled him. He was sure he had scored a hit and was looking for the body when something grabbed him from the side. He felt fingers wrap tight around his face and squeeze mightily at his temples. Papa Jack gasped, struggled back. He tried to scream, and the breath he drew for the effort brought an awful smell of rot and death that nearly made him gag.

The stench got heavier still, and then Papa Jack felt nothing.

Earvin Early released the old man's crushed skull and discarded his limp frame before moving for the door to the trailer. His work was almost at its end now. The two boys would be inside. They belonged to him. He had never Freed a child before and wondered how it would feel. They would thank him if they knew everything of the world; if they understood. They didn't, of course, but that didn't matter.

> *"A simple child*
> *That lightly draws its breath*
> *And feels its life in every limb,*
> *What should it know of death?"*

Early finished quoting Wordsworth softly to himself and reached up for the doorknob. It gave easily. He pushed the door inward, ready to spring after it.

And the dogs lunged upon him. A rank stream of brown fur and flashing teeth pushed him hard off the steps and snapped for his flesh.

"Judgment Day," McCracken started, after a brief pause.

"What about it?"

"That's what drew the Indian and me into this. We're following the trail of someone we believe is committed to making it happen."

"But you knew about Beaver Falls. That trail led you to Van Dyne."

"Because they're both connected somehow to what Frye's got planned."

"*Harlan* Frye?"

"Apparently you've heard of him."

"I don't know anyone who hasn't. Like him or not, he's always in the news, and he's a terrifying bastard to everyone except the extreme religious right."

"I think you're starting to see my point."

Karen shivered, the car suddenly seeming very cold. "But where could Van Dyne possibly fit into his plans?"

"My guess, Dr. Raymond, is the answer to that has got plenty to do with their AIDS vaccine. Discovery's been conveniently sealed up tight by government types who figure they've got a pretty big stake in the outcome."

"But they don't know something went wrong with the test group."

"And neither Frye nor Van Dyne is about to tell them."

"Then that's all we have to do!"

Blaine shook his head. "Forget it, Doctor. You can bet we were already the enemy in Washington's mind even before we trashed Van Dyne's complex tonight. The bad guys will have everything turned all inside out. Believe me, I've been here before."

"And Washington won't help us until we turn them right again."

Blaine nodded. "Call it the government's rules of engagement, or at least certain parts of the government you probably never could have imagined existed until tonight."

"Parts you must be quite familiar with."

"All too familiar."

"Then you're saying we're on our own."

"Don't forget the Indian, Doctor. Between us, we make a pretty good team, and with you on our side, we might just get lucky and come up with something that changes Washington's mind."

"Like what?"

"Can't tell you that. Can tell you where we might find it."

"Beaver Falls," Karen realized.

"There you go."

Early made it to the woods, despite the excruciating pain from the bites and wounds inflicted by the dogs. He'd killed or crippled them all, but not before they'd taken their toll. His left arm hung bloody and limp where the shoulder had been mangled. His right forearm, used for defense, was marked with bite gouges that oozed thick blood. He'd killed two dogs that wouldn't let go and then had to pry their jaws open to free what they'd left of his flesh. When he wiped the pools of blood away, he could see the teeth patterns briefly before the blood covered the marks again. His legs were torn and sliced, his face ripped up horribly, especially on the right. The eye on that side was already half-closed, and a wide, pulsing gash stretched across his neck, little more than a hair's distance from his jugular.

This kind of pain was a new sensation to Earvin Early; he had seldom felt it in his new life since being rescued by the Reverend Harlan Frye. But he welcomed it for giving him something to take from this night to remind him of his failure.

> *"Nothing begins and nothing ends*
> *That is not paid with moan;*
> *For we are born in other's pain,*
> *And perish in our own."*

Early mumbled the words through the blood frothing from his mouth. His upper lip had been split in two and hung grotesquely over his lower one. Early coughed more blood out, but he didn't intend to perish as Francis Thompson suggested in the last line of her poem. He intended to grow stronger, to will his body to heal itself so he might venture out once more.

After the woman.

After her children.

After anyone who stood in his way.

"Something's wrong," Karen said, as soon as Johnny pulled into the gas station and eased the car toward the three bikers parked in the far left corner.

She flung her door open and lunged out of the car before it had come to a complete halt, scurrying across the dark pavement for the grim-faced biker in the center. Blaine followed patiently, making sure that the three bikers who were part of the gang protecting Karen Raymond's sons could see his hands.

"What is it?" Karen asked T.J. Fields, dreading the answer. "What happened?"

"They got Papa Jack," came his reply. A scowl formed of both sorrow and rage stretched across his face.

"Oh God . . ."

"Six others, too. *Six!*"

"What about my kids?" Karen demanded, feeling like a hand of cold steel had closed over her heart. *"What about my kids?"*

T.J.'s eyes were watery. "Papa Jack got them out. Said he had a feeling early in the night. Had a few of the others split with your boys in tow, just in case. Lucky thing. Otherwise, he'd have gotten 'em."

"He?" Karen repeated, shocked.

"Was one man that did it," T.J. told her, not seeming to believe it himself.

"He wasn't fucking human," a Skull with a long red beard on T.J.'s right said. "Shaves is still alive, not by much, but he's holding on. Said it was some kind of fucking monster that did it, a giant."

"But old Papa Jack, he left a surprise for the fucking bastard," T.J. picked up, his face trapped between a fond smile and a frown. "Giant opens the door to the trailer he thinks the kids are in, out come the dogs. . . ."

"Others followed the blood far as they could," started Red Beard. "All the way to the road. Looked like somebody picked the giant up there."

T.J. Fields seemed to regard McCracken standing ten feet from them for the first time, sneering. "Where'd you find him?"

"He found me. Saved my life, actually."

T.J. looked Blaine over, sizing him up. The sneer didn't go away.

"Yeah, well, let's get you back to your kids."

"No."

"Huh?"

"I said no," Karen told him, forcing the words up through the heaviness in her throat. "It's better for them if I stay away. It's better if you don't even tell me where they are." She tried to compose herself, failed, and continued through trembling lips. "I've got to stop Van Dyne, T.J. It's the only way to save my kids."

"Van Dyne what got Papa Jack killed?"

"What they're involved in, yes, but there's—"

"Then you're forgettin' something, ain't you? I'm in for a big piece of this now." The look in his eyes was death. "They shouldn't't've killed Papa Jack, babe. Bad idea on their part. Was Papa Jack who brought me into the Skulls, looked after me since I was still havin' wet dreams. That gives me a score to settle."

"You can't help me, T.J., not against Van Dyne."

T.J. cast a cold glance McCracken's way. "And he can?"

She nodded slowly. "Yes, I think so."

"What if I go over there and kick his ass?"

"I saw him work tonight, T.J."

"Yeah, so?"

"Two of you are a lot alike."

T.J. seemed to like that.

"And you got one thing in common, anyway: You both saved my life."

He pointed toward himself. "Twice, by my count, you go back a few years."

"And now my kid's lives are in your hands. That says it all, T.J. That's everything."

"Not quite." T.J. glanced at McCracken briefly and then fixed his stare back on Karen. "Got myself a debt to Papa Jack, babe, me and all the others who wear the colors. When the time comes, I just want my shot to pay it off."

Two highway patrol squad cars were already outside Tucson General Hospital with their dome lights slicing through the last of the night when Captain Ted Wilkerson screeched to a halt. He charged right through the entrance past a patrolman on watch who stiffened as Wilkerson approached.

"Premises been searched yet, son?"

"Sergeant Harkness is supervising a second sweep now, sir."

"Second?"

"The first sweep turned up, er . . ."

"Shit," the captain said under his breath, and brushed past him.

Bart Harkness was standing in the middle of the hospital lobby near the reception desk, listening to the report of two hospital security guards who had just come up from the basement. He stopped nodding when he saw Wilkerson approaching.

"You better have an explanation for this, Bart, and it better be good."

"I'm taking responsibility, Captain," Harkness said staunchly, leading the way toward the elevator. "The fault's all mine."

"What the fuck good's that do us now? I don't give a shit who's responsible. I don't give a shit how it happened. I just want him found. Christ, in his condition . . ."

They stepped into the elevator and headed toward the third floor.

"Doctors figure now he may have been duping us. Knew everything that was going on around him and just pretended not to."

"What the fuck for?"

"They . . . don't know."

"What about you?"

"I think Wayne had his reasons. That's all."

The doors slid open and the men started down the corridor together.

"How'd it happen, Bart?"

"I went to get some coffee. I was out of the room six, maybe seven minutes. When I got back . . ."

They reached the room and Harkness stopped talking. Captain Wilkerson could read the sights better than he could explain them. The rumpled bed was empty, the covers thrown back almost reaching the floor. The door to the small closet was open and the patrolman's uniform that had been hanging there was missing. A hospital gown lay in a shapeless pile on the floor.

"Well, fuck me," muttered the captain.

Wayne Denbo was gone again.

PART FOUR

RETURN TO BEAVER FALLS

THE KINGDOM:
THURSDAY; 11:00 A.M.

CHAPTER 26

Harlan Frye held the test tube in both hands, barely able to restrain his smile. Tears of joy filled his eyes.

"This is *it*, Doctor? You're telling me you've *done it*?"

The frail-looking, bespectacled man standing before him in the front of the kingdom's sprawling main laboratory nodded. "Once we had the subjects here, it was a relatively simple process. Merely a matter of isolating the proper cells in their blood chemistry and then extracting those cells for harvesting." He paused. "Of course, the manner of delivery you specified required a rather powerful concentration that could be diluted beneath the ability to achieve expected parameters."

"A problem?" Frye anticipated.

"Just a complication. We needed to find a catalyst the concentrated formula could bond to and thus spread in the geometric pattern needed to achieve your desired results. The logistics involved made the choice of one quite easy."

Frye held the test tube almost tenderly. "You're telling me you're finished? That this is all you need?"

"No, sir. We still need ten times that amount to achieve the concentration required. Another forty-eight hours should be sufficient to produce it. And beyond that, well . . ."

"Go on, Doctor."

"It's rather complicated, sir. Your mandated timetable required us to take certain liberties with the formula that render it too easily susceptible to neutralization by a number of natural elements, light and heat for example."

"Surmountable?"

"Simply a matter of delaying release until they are no longer a factor. I think we have everything worked out."

Frye could have cried with joy. This news was almost enough to make him forget the disaster that had occurred at Van Dyne the night before. His enemies, joined up now, were drawing closer in their search for the specifics of his master plan. He wondered what would have happened if not for the turn of events in Beaver Falls. First thought to be a disaster, he now realized it was a godsend—literally— because had it not occurred, McCracken would have been able to stop him. Now, thanks to the contingency developed in this very lab, no one could stop him.

"Excellent!" The Reverend beamed. "Truly excellent. God has let us perform His work for Him, and we have proven ourselves worthy at every turn. Our task is so great, so humbling. And here, nearing the finish, our challenges have multiplied to the point they've become nearly overwhelming. But we have not failed or lost ourselves in the scope of those challenges. We have met them, turned them aside."

The Lord's final stamp of approval, that's what this represented, he thought. God helping him the last bit of the way. Judgment Day would have its own spot on the calendar now, just seventy-two hours from now.

On Sunday. The Lord's day, *his* day. Only one problem remained, one spoiler to his reverie.

"What of your progress with Lot 35, Doctor?" he raised.

The man in the white coat before him shrugged. "Collating the material has proven as difficult as I had feared. Without a firm formula from Dr. Raymond—"

"Assume that will be the case."

"Six months."

Harlan Frye nodded resignedly, aware of the ramifications. "So much has gone our way, more than we could reasonably hope. We cannot expect everything, and perhaps less will actually become more. We must accept His will in this matter, His guidance. Major Vandal," he said, turning slightly, "you will summon the others to me. Tomorrow, at the latest."

"Of course, sir," Osborne Vandal replied, feeling the taint of his Vietnam experience at last begin to wash off in the face of this certain victory. Osborne Vandal was one of only thirteen survivors, and the sole officer, from the prison camp in which he was interned. There were originally perhaps seven times that many prisoners. In accordance with procedure, and totally without merit, the major was investigated for possible collaboration with the enemy. No charges were ever leveled, but the damage had been done. Vandal was guilty because the antiwar furor said he was. Advancement beyond his present rank became impossible. Any decent command or post was out of the question. Osborne Vandal was disgraced for no reason whatsoever.

For ten years he shuttled from job to job and base to base; never wanted, barely bothering to unpack sometimes. But then one day the Reverend Harlan Frye heard his sad tale and sought him out, stared at Vandal's ruined right arm when the major reached his left out to shake. Looking back at that moment, Vandal would remember that stare more than anything, the stare and the strange smile that crossed Harlan Frye's face as he grasped the limp arm gently.

The next morning Osborne Vandal awoke to find that he could use the hand again; not totally, but at least squeeze his fingers enough to perform everyday tasks. Even the wrongly healed bones looked straighter to him. His hand seemed to have re-formed itself overnight. Osborne Vandal dropped to his knees and prayed.

Then he went looking for the Reverend Harlan Frye.

Frye was waiting for him, expecting him. He said nothing about the arm and refused the credit Vandal was convinced was due him, but asked the major if he wanted a commission in the most wondrous army of all.

God's army.

The Reverend started moving for the spiral staircase that led to the level above. "And now you must accompany me in a needed task. I wish to thank those truly responsible for what has been achieved here this morning."

Major Vandal turned his gaze fearfully up the staircase. "*There,* sir?"

"A great debt is owed them, more than we could ever repay even if time and opportunity availed itself. I must do this much, Major."

"Sir—"

"Join me, Major," Frye said, waving him forward. "It shouldn't take long."

The man holding the cane looked at Sister Barbara as if she were crazy.

"Are you sure, Sister?" he asked again. "Are you quite sure?"

"Was there something vague about my instructions, Roland?"

"No, Sister, not at all," he said apologetically. "It's just that, that . . ."

"Go on."

"Canceling a group on such short notice will cause disappointment to so many people." Roland Bagnell, manager of the sprawling Oasis grounds that held her famed amusement park, shifted the cane from his right hand to his left. The cane had been a gift from Sister Barbara herself on the day he finally abandoned the crutches that had been necessary since a factory accident had almost taken his life. He had come to the Oasis broken and beaten. He was less broken now and not at all beaten.

Thanks to Sister Barbara.

He stood with her in the midst of the park he had been managing for the past three years, in the center of what was aptly named Hope Avenue. "Children, Sister, we are talking about *children*."

"Don't you think I know that?"

"Well, of course . . ."

"Then you know I must have my reasons."

"Forgive me, Sister, but—"

"It is for their own good. Let's leave it there."

Bagnell wasn't ready to do that. "Sister, is there something you're not telling me, something I can help you with?"

"You are helping, Roland: with this. And there's something else. I want all residents cleared from the Oasis by eight o'clock tonight."

The manager's mouth dropped in shock. "But maintenance, security . . ."

"We can do without them."

"A skeleton staff at least, *please*."

"There is no need. And, Roland?"

"Yes, Sister."

"That includes you."

Sister Barbara turned and walked away before Bagnell could protest further. It took all the will she could muster not to look back at him, to meet his bufuddled gaze with the tearful one she had managed to hide until now. She so loved this place, loved strolling amidst its playing fields and courts, amusement rides, sidewalk concession stands, and water park. The favorable climate of North Carolina had allowed her to make that water park the Oasis's most dominant attraction. Six swirling slides wound down steep, slithering courses toward a lagoon-shaped pool below. The water was crystal blue, refreshing just to look at. Behind the expanse of slides was a second, much larger pool capable of generating its own pounding waves to mimic the actions of the ocean. Beyond that was a man-made pond holding the bumper boats on one side and the pedal boats on the other.

Sister Barbara walked along the waist-high chain-link fence that enclosed the water park, smelling the chlorine and imagining the happy screams and shouts of children. The last group had left only yesterday just before her return, and another had been scheduled to arrive tomorrow. Roland Bagnell was right about the tremendous disappointment the last-minute cancellation would cause. But there was no choice.

The wind shifted and ruffled the streamers lining the sidewalk concession stands that never charged Oasis patrons a single penny for their wares. The Ferris wheel shifted slightly. She passed the merry-go-round, and the animal-shaped seating seemed to smile her way. She imagined them bobbing up and down to the rhythm of the music, while happy children laughed and grinned their way through a wonderful day. Children who were sick, abused, or poor. Children who might never have known a place like the Oasis or, if they did, could never have sampled all of its wares. For a day, or two or three, Sister Barbara lifted them out of their pain and heartache and gave them paradise. Footing the bill for the operation and upkeep of the Oasis was made possible by the millions of dollars she still had put away from the days when fund-raising was a key element of her ministry. It warmed her spirit to see so many made happy by that money, so many benefit.

She would miss them so much. This was her Oasis, too, and that made it the fitting place to plot her strategy for bringing down Harlan Frye. But if his soldiers arrived before she could be successful, she could accept no loss of innocent life. There was enough blood already threatening her hands; she had, after all, been party to the Seven's formation, having succumbed, however briefly, to the same lust for power and self-importance the Reverend had.

Sister Barbara headed back to the stately mansion situated on the eastern rim of the property, built up slightly on a hill just beyond a huge flower garden. On the way she passed the three-story complex of hotel-like buildings that had been home to both her visiting children and, on a more permament basis, her most avid devotees. A hundred or so of the latter were here now, earning their keep by performing odd jobs around the park and recharging their spirits in the process. Roland Bagnell would see to their safe departure. Sister Barbara took great solace in the fact that they would leave here much better people than they had come in, content and at peace, which at the moment was far more than she could say for herself.

The drive southeast from Tucson International Airport was approaching ninety minutes when a sign indicated the proper access road for the town of Beaver Falls. Blaine was driving, Johnny Wareagle taking in everything from the passenger seat while Karen Raymond fought against sleep in the back.

"Slow down, Blainey," Wareagle said all of a sudden.

McCracken worked the brakes. "What is it, Indian?"

"Something on the side of the road, over there on the right."

"Christ," Blaine followed, seeing the dust-shrouded shape on the shoulder, lying halfway on the embankment.

He pulled the car over and climbed out an instant after Johnny. The big Indian knelt down next to what Blaine now recognized as a man, at least what was left of him. Beneath the blanket of dust, he made out a wrinkled, sweat-soaked highway patrol uniform.

"Seems like he's a little off his beat. Hit by a car, you figure?" McCracken raised. "Maybe dumped here by somebody?"

Wareagle enveloped the man's wrist in his hand to check for a pulse. "He's still alive, Blainey. And look."

Blaine followed Johnny's eyes to the man's feet: He

was wearing socks, but no shoes, and the socks had worn through, leaving his flesh blistered and raw.

"He walked a long way."

"Many hours," Johnny acknowledged. "Many miles."

"I'll get the canteen."

Karen Raymond stepped forward and handed it to Blaine when he was halfway back to the car. She accompanied him in silence over to the thin strip of shade cast by their car into which Johnny had dragged the highway patrolman. McCracken crouched down on the other side of the man and touched the canteen's spout to his lips. After balking initially, those lips parted and accepted some of the water. Then the patrolman's eyes fluttered open and he seized the canteen from Blaine's grasp, gulping its contents.

"Easy," McCracken cautioned, holding the canteen back by the strap.

The patrolman's mouth opened. His lips quivered, gaped, and then closed again.

"He's trying to say something, Blainey," said Wareagle, and he lowered his ear to the patrolman's mouth.

Blaine heard a muffled rasp, the shadow of a word lost before it reached him. Johnny moved his ear away and gazed upward.

"What'd he say, Indian?"

" 'Gone,' Blainey. He said 'gone.' "

Neither Johnny nor Blaine paid the dazed highway patrolman much heed until the next words slid out more audibly between his freshly moistened lips:

"Beaver Falls."

"Indian, did he say—"

"Yes!" Karen Raymond blared. "I heard him!"

The patrolman rasped out something else.

"What?" McCracken prodded.

The man swallowed and tried again. "There . . . I was there."

"You *came* from Beaver Falls?"

His eyes were turning wild, mad. "Must get back there . . . Must stop them."

Blaine and Johnny gazed at each other, then back at the figure at their feet, who was gathering his wits.

"Maybe we can help," offered McCracken.

They got the patrolman into the car and turned the air conditioning on high to help him cool down. His breathing steadied quickly, but the furtive madness continued to skirt through his eyes, making all of them wary. McCracken had traded places with Karen in the backseat.

"What's your name?" Blaine asked him.

"Denbo. Wayne Denbo."

"Well, Wayne, what was it you saw, exactly?"

The story of what Denbo and his partner found when they drove into Beaver Falls the previous Monday emerged in fits and starts between grateful gulps of water. Ultimately he clutched the canteen to his chest, where it trembled and throbbed to mirror his own agitation. It shook as he sketch-ily detailed finding that all the inhabitants of Beaver Falls had suddenly vanished in the midst of whatever tasks they were performing. But the water did not begin to jump out until he got to the part about exiting the school after his partner's disappearance.

"I was talking on the mike. That's when I saw them."

"Saw who?" McCracken quizzed.

"The figures from the dust. Whiter than the sun. They came for me and I jumped in the car. Must not have known I was in the school, too. Musta missed me." He swallowed hard and the canteen settled against his chest. "Didn't miss anyone else, though. Whole town was gone, I tell ya, the whole town!"

"Describe them," Karen Raymond urged.

"I did already."

"Again."

"All white, that's what I remember most." Wayne Denbo stopped and seemed to be thinking. The canteen went still in his grasp. "Holding things and ... driving things."

"What kind of things?" she pushed. "What kind of things were they holding?"

"Machines I never saw the likes of before. They came out of the dust everywhere. In their suits."

"White suits," Karen said for him. "Almost like what astronauts wear."

Denbo leaned forward. "Yes! Yes! And they were coming after me!"

She looked at McCracken. "Decontamination suits to keep the wearers safe from all possible toxins. Standard procedure when entering a potentially contaminated setting."

"Contaminated as in ..."

"Diseased, usually. The machines he's describing are used to take samples of the air or, in the event you know what you're looking for, they can be programmed to tell you instantly if the toxin is still active."

Denbo looked confused. The canteen began to throb again. "What about the vehicles? Like campers, with spindly things twirling on their tops."

"Tracking devices?" Blaine raised to Johnny.

"Or motion sensors to track down the positions of all residents, Blainey."

"To make sure they didn't miss any."

"One of them could have been a mobile lab," Karen pointed out. "It would have probably been in the rear, the largest."

"What about the *people*?" asked Wayne Denbo.

"They must have been evacuated before you got there," Karen told him, "before the decontamination team got there."

"And my partner?"

"He's probably with the others they brought out."

Denbo's face grew determined. "That's why I was going back. I've got to find him."

McCracken looked at Karen Raymond. "How does all this tie in with Van Dyne's AIDS vaccine?"

"Well, it explains why Freddy Levinger and I found the project center empty last night: Van Dyne had already covered their tracks, making sure no one else learned that something went wrong."

"How much of the town was part of the test group?"

"Only about a fifth. They may have evacuated everybody else for precautionary reasons, or because they witnessed something no one could know about."

"And if we drive into town now?"

Karen swallowed hard and drew her field bag closer to her in the front seat. "I may be able to learn something, I may not. It's been four days."

"Then we'd better not waste any more time."

They stopped a half mile out of Beaver Falls and parked their car near a slight rise beneath a larger overhanging hillside that overlooked the center of town. Wareagle had brought binoculars with him and fished them from his pack. He handed them to McCracken as they approached the small ridge. But Blaine did not need the binoculars to see what Beaver Falls had to show him. The primary structures along the main avenue, as well as the homes that dotted the perimeter and outskirts with greening lawns, were a study in the mundane. Like something out of a painting; Rockwell working in a desert southwestern motif of beige, cream, and terra-cotta stucco, with adobe finishes adorning a town that could have been sliced from a century back, if not for its tar black roadways.

And something else.

McCracken looked at Wareagle. Karen Raymond squinted and cupped a hand upon her brow. Wayne Denbo sank to his knees, shaking his head.

"No," he muttered, casting his eyes fervidly about the scene beneath him. "*No! . . .*"

A few cars inched their way along the town's central

road. Women walked with handbags dangling from their arms. A man emerged from a shop holding an ice cream cone. At the far end of town, children spent the last of the afternoon on a playground adjacent to the school building on the outskirts of town.

Beaver Falls, it seemed, wasn't gone at all.

CHAPTER 27

Wayne Denbo took the binoculars from McCracken and pressed them to his eyes. Blaine and Johnny could see his face tighten as he took in a closer view of Beaver Falls. They watched him move the binoculars in an arc from left to right, stopping a few times en route.

"Are you sure this is the place? Are you sure this is where you were?" Blaine asked him.

Wayne Denbo's hand edged slightly toward his empty holster the way an amputee reaches for a missing limb. "Oh, yeah. Beaver Falls. Gone no more."

Johnny and Blaine looked at each other, trying to make sense of it. Maybe Denbo was crazy. Maybe he had made the whole business up; but neither thought so.

"Right people can get an awful lot done in four days, Indian."

"Replacements, Blainey?"

"It won't hold up long, but maybe it doesn't have to. If it works in the short term, that's good enough. You can't keep a disappearing town secret. But now . . ."

"I've still got to go down there," Karen Raymond insisted.

"Doesn't the fact that people are alive tell you what you need to know?" Blaine asked her.

"It tells me things are safe now. It doesn't tell me what led to the evacuation. But the town itself might be able to." She touched the handle of her field bag, which looked like a large black makeup case. "There's still the soil, the roadbed, the storm drains or sewers, where I can get samples of water that's been standing since Monday."

Blaine didn't look convinced. "And if anyone sees you . . ."

"Who said anyone had to? I can get my samples from the outlying homes and streets as easily as the town center. And don't tell me you can do it," Karen said, anticipating Blaine's next proposal. "It would take me a month to teach you how to use the equipment in this bag."

"Guess we don't have quite that long," McCracken agreed.

Taking a roundabout route to be safe, Karen reached the outskirts of Beaver Falls in half an hour. She had to work fast, but not at the expense of thoroughness. Her priorities were air, soil, vegetation, and standing water, especially the latter three. Long after a potential toxin or contaminant had disappeared from the air, its residue remained on leaves, in dirt, or water pooled for some time.

She approached a house that had all of its windows closed and most of its blinds drawn, figuring that indicated no one was home. To be at least partially accurate, Karen knew she would need to duplicate the sample-gathering process in at least two other locations in Beaver Falls, preferably as far away as possible from this one.

She started with the air, employing a small vacuum pump to fill a thermally sealed container with a sample. The soil came next, five separate samples taken and cataloged from five different depths along the house's backyard. She then clipped a hefty section of grass and vacuum-bagged it. She took tree leaf samples, a section of a cypress tree branch, and sliced off the outgrowth from some sort of fern growing in the garden in front of the house. Karen imagined she would look like a gardener to anyone who happened by.

On the side of the house she found a moderate hole in the ground that seemed to be waiting for a tree or shrub to fill it. The hole was half-filled with murky, thickening water coated with a light film on top. Muttering a silent prayer of thanks, she reached into her field bag for three small vials. She used an eyedropper to fill the first two vials with the standing water before her and then skimmed some contents from the very top to fill the third. She stowed the vials in the tailored slots within her padded field bag and set out writing labels for all three. She was halfway through the third when a shadow suddenly blocked the sun.

"I think you better come with me, miss."

Startled, she turned and squinted up into the eyes of a short, uniformed figure wearing a gun.

"Uh-oh," McCracken said, as through his binoculars he watched a patrol car return to the sheriff's office.

He didn't have to see the figure in the backseat clearly to know it was Karen Raymond. An officer waiting near the curb reached in to help her out. The driver emerged holding her field bag by its shoulder strap, letting it dangle low toward the ground.

"Trouble, Indian," he told Johnny.

"More than you realize, Blainey."

"What?"

Wareagle's naked eyes were fixed on a figure that had just emerged at the head of Beaver Falls' main street.

"Denbo," Blaine realized, before he had even rotated his binoculars. "Son of a bitch!"

"Let her go!"

Karen swung round and saw Patrolman Wayne Denbo

standing in the middle of the street, a hand poised over his noticeably empty holster. The officer who had picked her up on the outskirts of town nodded to the deputy on her other side. The deputy drew his gun and stepped down off the curb.

"I want to know what you did with the *real* people who live here!" Denbo demanded. "Do you hear me? I want to know where they are!"

"No!" Karen screamed when she saw the deputy's gun coming up.

She broke free of her captor's hold and slammed into the deputy. He reeled sideways and grabbed hold of her hair, pulling hard when she rushed him again.

Wayne Denbo had closed to within ten yards by then. Before he could draw any closer, though, one of the apparent bystanders charged in from his rear and smashed Denbo over the head with a club. Karen watched him crumple to the street.

"Get her inside," Karen heard someone yell to the deputy who still had her by the hair.

"We've got to get them out of there," McCracken said, lowering his binoculars.

"Their captors will be expecting us, Blainey."

"Because they were advised of the possibility," Blaine followed, something occurring to him. "Then why did they let Denbo get so far? They must have seen him coming, right?"

Wareagle understood his point at once and, looking about him, seemed to sniff the air. "We must get out of here, Blainey."

McCracken nodded.

Before they could reach their car, a dozen armed figures appeared atop the larger hillside overlooking the small rise where the two of them were standing. Most had their hands already poised on the triggers and eyes pressed to the sights. Their spacing was good, certain to deny Johnny and Blaine victory even if they had been able to reach their guns.

"Hands in the air!" a voice shouted down, and then repeated itself, words turned into a scattered echo by the surroundings.

"Tried to arrest them," Wayne Denbo muttered near the door to the small root cellar, his unshaven face pale and flaking. "Tried to arrest them."

They had all been gathered here rather than taken to the three cells of the Beaver Falls jail. Karen and Denbo were already inside when Blaine and Johnny were shoved through the door. McCracken saw them briefly before their armed escorts yanked it closed again, slamming a bolt lock into place. The meager light available came only from what was able to sneak feebly through the thin cracks in the wood.

That was enough for Blaine to see Denbo curled up on the floor in a ball. A portion of his hair was matted with blood. Streaks of it were visible on his forehead.

"What happens now?" Karen Raymond asked McCracken.

"I suspect we'll be taken elsewhere."

"Why not just kill us?"

"Because Frye will want to be sure we haven't involved anyone else. He knows I was asking questions in Washington. He doesn't know of whom."

"You still think he's behind all this?"

"I know he is, Karen."

"You're forgetting that the real key is Van Dyne, and so far there's been no hint of any connection between the Reverend and them."

"There wouldn't be; he would make sure of it."

"You sound like you know him."

"Not personally, just his type. That's enough."

She moved a bit closer to him in the near dark. "So all this is nothing new for you."

"Not new, just different."

"How so?"

"Well, I've met up with more than my share of mad-men, but never one who thought he had God speaking to him, that he was speaking for God. All fanatics believe they're right, but what they're capable of, how far they'll go, is determined by how well they can justify their actions. Not just to others, but also to themselves. Harlan Frye can justify *anything*. He can do anything and accept anything because he'll honestly believe he's doing the work of the Almighty. That strips him of fear, and a man who fears nothing is the hardest opponent of all. Makes him less likely to make the kind of mistakes that helped me take down others who came before him."

"You'll think of something."

"I'd better."

What little light they had at first vanished with the fall of night, nothing left to slither through the slight cracks in the heavy wooden door. An hour had passed since sunset when McCracken and Wareagle heard footsteps approaching outside. Karen Raymond could feel them glance at each other in the darkness, certain their positions had been strategically chosen.

Karen tensed as the door was opened. She half expected McCracken and his Indian friend to surge into motion at that instant, but they held their ground, and it wasn't long before Karen saw why. Beyond the door, beyond the flood of light pouring into the root cellar from a number of flashlights, she distinguished shapes and some movement.

The street beyond was teeming with gunmen, each with his weapon drawn. Three of the men, carrying flashlights, approached the prisoners and beckoned the small group to accompany them back to the surface. One reached down to grasp the dazed form of Wayne Denbo. Karen noticed all three of them were unarmed and could sense Blaine McCracken's disappointment in that fact. It seemed every move their captors made was designed defensively to keep McCracken from seizing the advantage.

Back on the street, the true scope of their predicament

became obvious. The gunmen rimmed it in a wide circle, all with guns held ready at eyes or hips. Their unarmed escorts prodded the four of them into the center of the circle and cast their eyes upward to the night sky. Karen also noticed that only a select few streetlights in the center of Beaver falls, the bare minimum, had been switched on—another defensive measure on the part of their captors.

The gunmen possessed an incalculable advantage over them in all respects, yet Karen could sense their tension as clearly as her own. These men had obviously been warned what McCracken was capable of. She looked his way in the darkness and saw his face was expressionless, emotionless. The Indian's was a virtual mirror image. They might have appeared to be nonchalant, even indifferent. But their eyes missed nothing, waiting for an opportunity to present itself. Karen knew she would have little warning when it came and made herself ready to respond with only a heartbeat's notice.

Suddenly the night sky was split by a wash of light and sound. A helicopter surged in low over the sheltering hillside. It slowed into a hover above the center of Main Street and then began to descend deliberately toward ground level. Its rotor wash kicked dust, street debris, and paper into the air, forcing most of those present to raise their hands up to shield their faces. McCracken's hands stayed down. Karen thought in that instant of distraction Blaine was going to move, but instead he squeezed her arm tenderly, reassuringly.

"Not yet," he whispered.

Blaine noted the helicopter was a Chinook troop carrier, military issue repainted in civilian colors, its twin main rotors just now slowing to a complete stop. With no airfield nearby, he had been expecting the arrival of some form of chopper to spirit them off to another destination. They couldn't be killed until the enemy knew how far its opposition extended; who else, in other words, Blaine and/or Karen Raymond had taken into their confidence.

He and Johnny had held off making any move yet because they knew the chopper would offer their best opportunity. Once they were airborne inside it, the confined space and limited enemy numbers would work in their favor. He was certain the Indian and he would be tied down, but he was confident he could deal with that eventuality somehow.

The Chinook finally settled uneasily into the center of the street, its rotors continuing to cough debris in all directions as the blades slowed. Two gunmen moved toward the chopper and threw open its rear hold, exposing a single troop ramp. On cue, their unarmed escorts eased Blaine and Johnny forward, Karen Raymond and Wayne Denbo walking just ahead of them.

They were halfway to the Chinook, walking straight into the spill of its most powerful floodlight, when Blaine felt the man at his side go rigid and then drop. The second went down in rapid fashion and then the third, as if the street had been yanked out from under them.

McCracken hadn't heard the gunshots and didn't bother considering their origin; he simply took Karen down safely to the ground, as Johnny Wareagle did the same with Patrolman Wayne Denbo. For all they knew, they could just as easily be the sniper's next targets. Suddenly, though, the remainder of the guards placed strategically in the street began to drop, felled by fire from the unseen gunman. Those left standing lunged for cover and fired wildly in all directions, hoping to at least keep their mystery enemy at bay.

"Who, Blainey?" Wareagle asked, crawling next to him.

"No clue, Indian," McCracken returned. "But I think I'll lend them a hand. . . ."

He had just slid away from Karen, ready to rise to his feet, when a grenade blast near one of the opposition's heaviest concentrations sent him diving back to the asphalt. Two more explosions sounded in rapid succession, keeping Frye's troops pinned down, which left Blaine and the others absurdly safe in the field of fire's center.

"The chopper!" Blaine screamed. "Get to the chopper!"

Johnny led the way in a fast crawl toward it beneath the sporadic, random spray of bullets fired desperately their way by Frye's gunmen. McCracken hovered over Karen and Wayne Denbo, urging them on. Wareagle had almost reached the Chinook when a pair of dark figures emerged from the narrow slot between a pair of buildings diagonally across from the chopper. The two figures ran side by side, black mirror images spinning off one another as they fired nonstop barrages at any of the enemy gunmen who dared showed themselves. Blaine noted the latest M24 sniper rifle dangling from the shoulder of one of them. Black head masks left only the darkened flesh of their faces exposed.

Johnny Wareagle led Wayne Denbo up the Chinook's troop ramp, while McCracken did likewise for Karen Raymond. The black figures had just reached the chopper, swinging to face the ravaged battle zone. One hurled another grenade skyward while the second turned and rushed into the passenger hold with the grace of a cat.

"Go!" the other screamed. "Go!"

McCracken hurried through the rear hold into the cockpit. The pilots had been the initial targets of the snipers and lay sprawled in their seats as a result, neat holes punched in their foreheads and the glass of the windshield spiderwebbed before them. Blaine yanked their restraining safety harnesses off and pulled them from their seats. He caught a glimpse of Johnny Wareagle offering return fire from the ramp with a rifle he must have gotten from one of their rescuers. One of the figures in black entered the cockpit. The other one, sniper rifle dangling behind, moved out of Johnny's shadow and hurried after the first. Wareagle followed last and dragged the ramp back in after him. The rear door thumped closed. The first figure to enter the cockpit opened the passenger door long enough to shove the bodies of the pilot and copilot out.

McCracken had squeezed himself into the pilot's seat and begun to work the controls.

"Get us out of here!" screamed one of the masked figures.

CHAPTER 28

A cascade of bullets shattered the top of the windshield, and one of the black-suited figures twisted to return the fire through the still open passenger door. The other took the copilot's seat and yanked off its head mask.

Neat hair tumbled down past her shoulders, and the figure shook it back.

It was a woman! No, *a girl*, who looked to be in her late teens.

"Hurry!" the other masked figure ordered, a boy's voice.

Blaine pulled back on the throttle, working the pedals, and the Chinook fluttered into an uneasy rise. He steadied the chopper and drove it forward over Beaver Falls. Muzzle flashes from ground level continued to track it, but the fire, thankfully, was errant. Blaine felt his hand relax.

"Who the hell are you?" McCracken demanded of the strangers sharing the cockpit with him.

The second figure had just shed his head mask as well.

The hair beneath it was shorter than the girl's, but the face was virtually indistinguishable.

"You're *twins*!" Blaine realized, and then he remembered. "The children of Preston Turgewell, no doubt."

"Very good," said the girl.

"We're impressed," added the boy.

"Jacob and Rachel," Blaine recalled from Sal Belamo's research. Johnny Wareagle and Karen Raymond stood together and peered in through the doorway leading from the hold.

"And you're Blaine McCracken." The boy was ogling him as a Little Leaguer would his major league idol.

"I'm equally impressed. Now tell me where the two of you fit into all this. Where does your dead father fit in?"

"He's not dead," said Rachel.

"He only needed to appear dead to fool them," picked up Jacob. "It worked. For a while."

"And just who exactly is 'them'?"

"The Seven. When they tried to kill him after he dropped out, he let them think they were successful."

"Wait a minute, what's 'the Seven'?"

The twins looked at each other.

"You know about Harlan Frye," Rachel interjected.

"You learned of him through your discovery of the Key Society in the papers Ratansky obtained," said Jacob.

McCracken felt his hand tighten on the joystick control. "He was going to deliver them to you!"

"To our father," Rachel confirmed. "He planted Ratansky where he'd be able to get the list, in return for his freedom."

Jacob was nodding. "The list included all of Frye's most generous and powerful supporters. Eliminate them and the damage done to his plan would be catastrophic."

"You mean *kill* them? *All* of them?"

"We had no choice."

"What about targeting Harlan Frye himself?"

"He has become virtually unreachable," Rachel explained. "And even if we were successful, there were others prepared to step forward and replace him."

McCracken held the Chinook steady. "Don't tell me, kids, the other members of the Seven . . ."

"The name comes from Frye's obsession with the Book of Revelation," Jacob explained. "The number seven appears constantly through it. The seven signs of the apocalypse, the seven trumpets, the seven angels, the seven woes. When Frye determined that he couldn't save civilization, he decided his destiny was to destroy it so it could be reborn."

"And to help him in that task," added Rachel, "he gathered six other powerful religious leaders who he thought were equally committed to changing the world."

"But your father, for one, changed his mind, right, kid?"

Jacob nodded. "Because Frye was willing to destroy society if that's what it took to save it."

"But he wasn't planning to destroy *all* of society, was he?" challenged Karen Raymond, speaking for the first time.

"No," Rachel replied. "The Seven was founded to devise and follow through with a plan that would allow them to destroy civilization, while at the same time saving those they judged deserving to help them establish a new order."

"And thus the Key Society," Blaine interjected.

"Ratansky stole the list from another member of the Seven who walked away and became a rogue, as our father had," explained Rachel. "The list had been that former member's insurance, keeping Frye from dispatching his soldiers to dispense with her."

"Her?" Karen Raymond raised.

"*Another?*" followed McCracken immediately. "Then the Seven is now short *two* of its original number."

"So far as we know."

"They why didn't they join forces?"

Jacob looked at Rachel. "Because the means our father chose to pursue were considerably different from those the woman opted for."

"Meaning more violent, of course."

Rachel's expression tightened. "What was at stake called for it. Frye took our father into his confidence very early on, early enough for him to realize Frye had every intention of destroying the world as it is known today."

"And, don't tell me, Frye made your father one of the original number because of his control over the Fifth Generation."

Jacob nodded. "They were to become the Seven's centurions, riding herd over the weak and undeserving lot who manage to escape Frye's wrath. Common killers, in other words."

"The size of an army."

"Yes."

"And with all these soldiers at his command, your father couldn't even save Ratansky. With all these soldiers, it's the two of you he sent to do this job?"

"We volunteered!" insisted Jacob.

"We are the last ones left," said Rachel.

"What happened?"

Rachel looked at her twin brother before replying. "Our father's control over the Fifth Generation was not as strong as he thought. Various factions became apparent after his departure from the Seven. Groups splintered off, some sticking with our father, others moving to Frye. Still more embraced neither and went off on their own. By the time he faked his death, only a select few he could trust remained, and now even these . . ." A shrug completed her thought.

"Where does—er, did—Arthur Deek fit in?"

"He renounced my father and desperately wanted to become part of the Key Society. But Frye wanted no part of him."

Blaine was nodding. "So when your father decided to spring Ratansky, he made the late Arthur Deek think the request had come from Frye. The dearly departed son of a bitch thought he was getting himself into the Reverend's good graces by helping."

"Exactly!" from Rachel.

"How did you know?" asked Jacob.

"It's the way I would have done it, that's all."

Jacob looked suddenly proud. "I know that. I've studied you, everything my father could obtain."

"Starting when?"

"New York. Ratansky's death brought us there. We had no idea of your involvement until we secured the police report," Jacob explained, and gazed at his twin.

"We've been tracking you ever since. Always a step behind. New York, Illinois, and then the Flash Pot."

"But you finally caught up. What changed?"

"Jack Woodrow," said Jacob. "He was kind enough to talk."

McCracken didn't like the confident sneer that had spread across the boy's face, making him look younger instead of older. "He have coaxing?"

"Some."

Blaine looked in the boy's eyes and knew. "You killed him, didn't you?"

"He knew where we were going. He knew where *you* were going."

"But he wouldn't have talked. Jesus, he *couldn't*. Then *they'd* have killed him."

Jacob looked at him emotionlessly. "We couldn't take that chance. Besides, he was one of them. I was merely following through with the intended plan. We'd have done the same if Ratansky had succeeded in delivering the list to our father."

"But since he didn't, how did you know to come to Atlanta and Jack Woodrow's Flash Pot?"

"Woodrow was publicly known to be his largest donor by far. When we learned you were en route to Atlanta, the connection was unavoidable. We knew you must have had the list in your possession and had chosen to start at the top."

"But you would have killed all the people on it right

down to the bottom. So why not take Woodrow out before?"

"We were afraid of alerting the rest before their identities were even known to us," answered Rachel.

"This is a war," her brother added. "You must see that; you, of all people."

McCracken looked away from the controls long enough for the Chinook to waver in the dark air. "What I see is a boy who thinks he's doing a man's work. Well, let me tell you something, kid, killing's got nothing to do with being a man."

"Was it all right when it helped us save *your* lives tonight?"

"That was different."

"Why?"

"Because they were trying to kill us *and* you. They had guns. Jack Woodrow didn't."

"But his money helped pay for what we're facing here, for the Judgment Day Harlan Frye is soon to enact. Doesn't that count for anything?"

"It might have if Woodrow had been a willing and knowing participant."

"How were we supposed to know whether he was or not?"

"You find out. You make damn sure you find out before you kill a man." Blaine lowered his voice. "Listen to me, kid, I've got a pretty good notion of what kind of person you fancy yourself as, so I'm going to give you some advice—call it partial payback for saving my life. Everybody thinks their side is right—the bad guys and the good guys. And the only thing separating them, the only real determining factor, is how they feel about people, how they feel about life. You don't kill anyone you don't have to and you never kill anyone who isn't about to do the same to you."

Jacob stayed crouched between Blaine and his sister, looking suddenly like a scared and lonely seventeen-year-old boy.

"Otherwise, it gets to you. You become like what it is you're fighting, and once there's no difference, well, there's no reason. Got it?"

It was Rachel who spoke. "We could not become what we're fighting here."

Blaine looked at her briefly before he spoke. "Nobody ever thinks they can, young lady."

Chastened, Rachel gave a conciliatory nod. "We need you," she said to McCracken. "We need your help and we need your skills."

"We also need your contacts," Jacob added, glad for the change in subject.

"Contacts usually mean Washington, and we can forget about that in this case," Blaine told them. "I misbehaved out there yesterday afternoon and then again in San Diego at Van Dyne Pharmaceuticals last night."

The twins looked at each other.

"What brought you to Van Dyne?" Rachel asked.

"An AIDS vaccine they had discovered," Karen responded before Blaine had a chance to speak. "Van Dyne was testing it on part of Beaver Falls' population. But something went wrong, and whatever it was forced the need for a replacement. My treatment was the only alternative."

"But what could an AIDS vaccine have to do with Frye's Judgment Day?" Rachel asked.

"I don't know," sighed Karen.

"Neither of us does," McCracken added. "But we do know the entire town was evacuated on Monday morning."

"Then who captured the four of you tonight?" asked Jacob.

"Replacements," Blaine explained.

Jacob shook his head, unconvinced. "How long could Frye have hoped such a strategy to work?"

"Long enough for him to bring on Judgment Day."

"If only we knew how," Rachel sighed.

"Where would do just fine," said Blaine, "as in where Frye can be found."

"If we knew that . . ."

"We don't," Rachel picked up from her brother. "But we know someone who might."

They flew on through the desert night.

"There's an airfield two hundred miles northwest," said Jacob. "A jet is waiting for us."

"To take us where?" Blaine raised. "No, don't tell me: to that other former member of the Seven."

"The woman," added Karen.

Rachel smiled briefly at Karen. "Her name is Sister Barbara."

"The jet will take us to Knoxville, a few hours' drive from her home in Asheville, North Carolina," added Jacob.

"Sister Barbara can fill in the holes we have been unable to. She stayed with Frye for several years after our father fled, until just over two years ago."

"The Reverend is building a kingdom for himself and his legion," Jacob expanded, "but our father left the Seven before construction had started. He never learned of its location. Sister Barbara did, though. She can tell us where it is."

"But she hasn't told you before because she doesn't approve of your methods, right?"

The twins looked at each other. It was Rachel who spoke. "We tried to satisfy her. She has never proved very cooperative. She never believed Frye was actually capable of bringing on Judgment Day."

"Of course not. Otherwise you wouldn't have had to send Ratansky to steal the list of the Key Society from her. Bottom line is that you took from her the very thing that insured her safety, and now you want me to convince her to tell me what she's never shared with your father."

"Things have changed," said Rachel.

"*Everything* has changed," added Jacob.

"Without the list as insurance, Frye will kill her. She will be desperate. She will need us."

"All we need to do is convince her that Judgment Day is about to dawn."

"So she can tell us the location of the Kingdom of the Seven."

"That's the hope," said Jacob.

"The fear, too, kid."

"You've seen our work."

"Impressive to say the least, but carried out with the element of surprise on your side. That's gone now. We make it into this kingdom, they'll be ready for us."

"There is no choice."

"Let's see what Sister Barbara has to say, son, before we pass judgment on that," advised McCracken.

Wareagle took the pilot's seat from Blaine minutes later to complete their flight to the airfield where the jet was waiting. The twins stayed in the cockpit with him, Jacob in the passenger seat. He had grown committed to his father's effort to destroy what Preston Turgewell had once been part of. No other concerns had entered in. The boy had been born into a purpose, and that purpose now dominated his very being. Blaine wondered if there was a life for Jacob and Rachel beyond the Seven, no matter how all this turned out. There was so much he could tell them if they were willing to listen; he'd been there himself, after all, and had lived long enough to learn the lessons on his own. But Jacob and Rachel weren't ready to accept any more than what lay before them right now, the only world they knew.

McCracken retired to the Chinook's passenger hold and sat down next to Karen Raymond.

She looked at him with a calm he hadn't expected. "I'm not scared anymore."

"Congratulations," Blaine said, without any trace of celebration in his voice. "You've crossed over. Welcome to my world, Doctor."

"I wouldn't have entered, wouldn't have been able to do all this, if it weren't for my kids. Frye's animals would have killed them." She shivered, as much from emotion as the chill of the hold. "They still might."

Blaine wrapped an arm around her shoulder and drew her closer to him. "Not if I can help it."

Karen trembled in his grasp. Her eyes drifted toward the cockpit. "That boy and girl, their father sent them into this. He *trained* them for it. I think of how I feel about my kids and I find that repulsive."

"He did what he felt he had to, same thing you're doing now. Different perspective." Blaine paused. "Different world."

"Yours?"

"Pretty much, yes."

"No," Karen said, and looked up at him. "I heard what you said to Jacob about killing that man in Atlanta. He didn't have to, yet he still did. But that didn't bother you as much as the fact that it didn't bother him."

Blaine smiled ruefully. "Very good, Dr. Raymond."

"He emulates you, wants to be like you."

"I suppose."

"He never will, though, because he doesn't *feel*; he just believes and acts accordingly. But he'd be a difficult man to face for that same reason."

"You've got that right."

"I'm learning."

"Then let's try another lesson. My contacts may not be able to help us with Frye and the Seven, but there's an ugly little man back east who can be of immediate service to you and your kids."

"What are you suggesting?"

"You trust me."

Karen let her face brush his shoulder and stay there. "Of course. Did you have to ask?"

"I didn't ask; I said. And when we reach this airfield, I'm saying now you shouldn't go on. Let me make a call.

Get you and your kids someplace where even Frye won't be able to reach you."

"For how long?"

"As long as it takes."

She shook her head and pulled away from him. "No."

"You won't do it?"

"Because you *can't*."

"I'm offering you a ticket out of my world, Dr. Raymond."

"That's not what I meant," she told him. "I don't doubt you can keep me safe from Frye's killers, but can you keep me safe from what he's about to unleash on the world? Beyond that," Karen continued, before Blaine had a chance to respond, "you *need* me. Judgment Day's got something to do with Van Dyne's AIDS vaccine, with whatever went wrong in Beaver Falls. I'm the only one in this group who'll be able to explain how, if the chance ever comes. Tell me I'm wrong, Blaine McCracken, I dare you."

Blaine tried. Briefly. "Sorry. I can't."

"Of course not. What I was after and what you were after led us both to Van Dyne for a reason. Now the trick is to find out exactly where the connection is."

McCracken glanced at Patrolman Wayne Denbo, who seemed to be sleeping, his head against the hold's near wall. "Along with what happened to the real residents of Beaver Falls."

CHAPTER 29

Sister Barbara came awake early Friday morning to the unexpected murmur of voices outside her open window. She rose from the chair where she had taken what little sleep the night would give her, stiff and cold.

More voices reached her, dozens of them.

She moved to the window and threw back the sheer curtain blown inward by the breeze. Below, her followers who called the Oasis home for as long as they desired were at work in the sprawling, lavish flower garden that separated her mansion from the rest of the theme park.

But she had issued orders for them to leave! Roland Bagnell was to have made sure those orders were carried out by this very time!

As if on cue, a knock rapped on her door.

"Come," Sister Barbara called.

Bagnell entered, his cane tapping the floor with each step.

"What's going on, Roland?" she demanded. "I was very clear in my—"

"Yes," he interrupted, "and our residents were equally clear in their refusal to leave."

One of Bagnell's principal duties was to coordinate the Oasis's residential services. The people who came seeking spiritual fulfillment or recharging needed to be boarded, fed, and given work assignments throughout the park. Roland Bagnell himself had been one of the first residents of the Oasis, walking in as a crippled alcoholic who never walked out after shedding his crutches and the bottle. He had supported Sister Barbara through all the various stages and swings of her ministry, including her never-explained decision to forsake the huge television revenues and return to the road. In her upper echelon of trusted directors, Bagnell was the most loyal of all. And yet she had never shared even with him her dealings with the Seven.

"You don't understand, Roland," Sister Barbara scolded. "I ordered them to leave *for their own good*."

"But I do understand, Sister, and so do they. They know you're scared. They know there's something wrong. They want to help. *I* want to help. *Talk* to me."

She looked at him with as much anger as she could summon. "I want the Oasis evacuated, Roland. Leave a skeleton staff in place if you wish, but I want them in a position to flee at the first sign of . . ."

"Sign of what, Sister?"

"Get them out of here, Roland. Get them out of here now."

If anyone had bothered to ask Warren Thurlow what he thought of all this, he would have told them it was nuts. Chief federal marshal for the state of North Carolina, Thurlow had been awakened in the midst of a deep sleep just hours before with instructions to serve Sister Barbara with arrest warrants at her Oasis complex as soon as possible. The warrants arrived by courier while he was dressing, alleging that a huge drug ring was operating out of the theme park. Thurlow didn't know what bullshit the allegations were based on, but he did know there was little he could do to brush them aside at this end.

He also knew Sister Barbara; not personally, but he'd seen her enough times on television and knew enough about her work to be certain she could not be capable of such a thing. Nor could she be capable of letting it go undetected right under her nose. The problem was that Thurlow was nothing more than a messenger boy. Bring a few deputy marshals with him and serve the warrant, and then get the fuck away with his tail tucked between his legs. Leave Sister Barbara to chew up her accusers and spit them out.

Thurlow roused the top three deputies from the on-call list and told them to pick him up at 6:30 A.M. sharp. He wanted to be done with this as quickly as possible.

The car picked him up right on schedule, and he sat in the backseat through the duration of the ninety-minute drive, doing his best to doze. He couldn't even keep his eyes closed, and his head began pounding up a storm by the time the car reached Asheville, a town he'd always dreamed of living in. Set in the heart of the Smoky Mountains, Asheville was green and beautiful. Even the smaller homes boasted picturesque and elegantly manicured settings, with views of rolling hills. Plentiful trees dappled the yards and streets with shade, and the lawns were a uniform dark green. Thurlow thought of his own browning grass and chewed his teeth.

His mood had grown even more foul by the time the car pulled up before the main entrance of the Oasis. He ordered his deputy marshals to hang back and started for the gate before they had all climbed out. Halfway there, Thurlow saw an informally dressed man appear from within the guardhouse that was set inside the high, white stone wall that enclosed the entire complex.

"Warren Thurlow, federal marshal," he announced, fishing for the warrant in his jacket pocket. " 'Fraid I need to see Sister Barbara. Course, if she isn't presently on the premises . . ."

The man didn't take the hint. "No, she's here," the guard said, feeling for the phone inside the guardhouse. "What'd you say your name was?"

"Warren Thurlow."

"And you've come here to . . ."

Before Thurlow could respond, the guard's face vanished in an explosion of blood and bone that sprayed up against the federal marshal's best suit. He heard his deputies screaming and swung in time to see a fusillade of bullets rip into them and drop their bodies to the ground. Before he could take cover himself, one bullet hammered his shoulder and another struck him like a swift kick to the ribs.

"Fuck," Thurlow muttered as he collapsed, feeling warm life spilling out of him, thinking with absurd calm, *I'm shot!*

There should have been pain, but there wasn't. Thurlow managed to pull himself behind the cover of some thick azalea bushes and tried to steady his breathing.

What had happened? What was going on?

Crawl back to the car, he told himself, get on the radio.

Before he could do anything of the sort, though, he heard the sound of heavy vehicles screeching to a halt nearby. Peering out from his cover, he saw three large, olive green trucks dwarfing the department's Crown Victoria. Warren Thurlow had enough presence of mind left to pull himself into the deeper cover of the thick bushes rimming the front of the Oasis as the men began to spill out from the rear ends of the trucks.

Thurlow saw their rifles first, shiny black in the morning sun. Mind slowing now, he realized that he recognized them, that they were *familiar* to him. Then he saw why: The black windbreakers some wore over their flak jackets and matching black caps were labeled STRIKE.

They were dressed in the standard garb of the Federal Marshals Strike Force.

The residents of the Oasis had ignored Roland Bagnell's halfhearted instructions, going about their daily chores as if the park would be up and running in a few hours' time. Sister Barbara strode through the magnificent gardens fronting her house in search of Bagnell, finding him finally leaning on his golf cart in the center of Hope Avenue, which ran the park's entire length.

Bagnell had a half smile on his face, looking almost pleased. "I did the best I could."

"They're still here."

"They aren't leaving, Sister. They wish to stand by your side, just as you stood by theirs."

"You don't understand, Roland. *They* don't understand."

He limped closer to her, cane left inside the cart. "They understand obligation, loyalty. They understand what you have taught them."

"No! *Listen* to me. Please!"

Bagnell's smile stretched a little wider. "I have, Sister, and I— *Sister!*"

With that he threw himself at her, twisting her around, his eyes bulging in fear and disbelief. Sister Barbara felt her ribs contract on impact and then tumbled over with Bagnell's weight pinned atop her.

"Roland," she said, trying to get her wind back. "Ro—"

Her hands came away bloody from his back. She looked at his face and saw more blood dribbling from his mouth and nose.

"Roland!"

He'd been shot! Sister Barbara had no sooner realized that than she heard the din of staccato bursts echoing through the park. She rose into a crouch and dragged Roland with her behind the meager cover of the golf cart.

"No," he rasped, blood frothing from his mouth, "leave . . ."

His eyes locked open and sightless, dead. Horrified, Sister Barbara pulled away from him. The bursts of gunfire continued to blare around her, and now her clearing senses recorded another, much worse sound:

Screams.

Her people were being massacred!

A group sped down Hope Avenue directly before her, and Sister Barbara watched three of them being cut down when bullets fired by unseen gunmen stitched up their spines. One who was still alive tried to claw her way for the grass, as if to flee harm's way, and Sister Barbara lunged to her aid.

"Why, Sister, why?" the woman muttered fearfully when Sister Barbara reached her. "Why? . . ."

Because of me, Sister Barbara thought as she yanked the woman toward the cover between a pair of refreshment booths. *It's my fault. . . .*

Sister Barbara was smoothing the woman's hair when her eyes closed. She was still breathing, but clearly there was nothing else Sister Barbara could do for her. But there were others, so many others. . . .

The gunfire was constant and widespread, evidence of an inordinately large group of gunmen on the premises. The Reverend Harlan Frye's gunmen, here to end the threat she posed to him once and for all.

As Sister Barbara made her way through the park, pressed as close as possible to an assortment of buildings for cover, she caught glimpses of figures in black moving in commando fashion behind their erupting muzzles. They fired at anything that moved. A longer look at the water slide attraction showed the bodies of more of her followers floating in the huge lagoon-shaped pool, the crystal blue water dirtied with stringy beads of red.

Sister Barbara could hear herself moaning, crying deep inside. Her sorrow was so vast that every step was becoming an effort, her feet slowed by having to carry the weight of all that was happening around her. She felt rage building within her, a fury that burned at the surface of her skin replacing the chill of her sorrow.

She would destroy Frye and the Seven. If her followers were to be sacrificed, then let there be some worth in their deaths, something salvaged. But she had to survive herself first, and that task at present seemed daunting, if not impossible.

She crept behind the cover of an empty kiosk and waited for an approaching complement of the enemy to pass before pressing on.

"Gunfire," Blaine said as their crowded van approached the isolated hilltop setting for Sister Barbara's Oasis.

"We're too late," muttered Rachel. "Frye's people have beaten us here!"

"Faster!" her twin, Jacob, ordered Johnny Wareagle, who was behind the wheel. The Indian merely glanced at him before he eased the van to the side of the road out of sight from the complex's entrance.

They had arrived in North Carolina after their near cross-country flight landed in Knoxville, Tennessee, just two hours before, leaving no time for rest. They had rushed to pack their gear into the van and drove swiftly to reach Sister Barbara's complex in the hills of Asheville.

"You told me you were good, kid," Blaine said to Jacob.

"I am." Then, as he gazed at his sister, "*We* are."

"I hope so, because with the numbers we're about to go up against, you're gonna have to be." He looked toward Johnny Wareagle, whose ear was tuned out the driver's-side window. "Indian?"

"Between thirty-five and forty men, Blainey."

"Christ . . . And four of us, not counting Dr. Raymond here . . ."

Patrolman Wayne Denbo, curled up in the van's rear seat, spoke from his prone position.

"You got five, mister."

Blaine looked at him, but didn't speak.

Denbo sat up. "Look, I went a little nuts, thanks to Beaver Falls and all the shit they pumped me full of in the hospital. But I think I got my senses back now."

"You good with a gun?"

"District target champ three years running with a nine and a rifle."

"Ever shoot a man, Officer?"

Denbo lowered his eyes. "No."

"There's a first time for everything."

They drove off the road into the line of thick brush buffering the woods less than a quarter mile away, the van sufficiently camouflaged. McCracken, Wareagle, Denbo, and the twins geared up as Blaine laid out the plan for them. Not surprisingly, Jacob hung on his every word.

The twins' cache of weapons allowed a pair of automatic weapons for all of them except Denbo, who would make do with one. Blaine and Johnny each carried an M16 along with a smaller nine-millimeter Mac-10 submachine gun. The twins had M16s as well, but in Jacob's case the arsenal was complemented by an M79 grenade launcher, which fired 40mm grenades out a thick, shotgunlike barrel. Rachel, meanwhile, carried a semiautomatic twelve-gauge shotgun known as a Street Sweeper, equipped with a twelve-shot cylindrical magazine.

The twins led the approach to the front gate of Sister Barbara's Oasis. At the fifty-yard mark, they waited for Johnny and Blaine to catch up, while Wayne Denbo hung back at the group's rear. Inside the Oasis the gunshots continued, though more sporadic and selective. Blaine took that as a bad sign, wondering if Sister Barbara was among the many who had fallen to the hundreds of rounds that had already echoed back their way.

McCracken and Wareagle took the lead in approaching the front gate. Three troop-carrying trucks blocked the street in all directions, squeezed around a single Ford sedan. Johnny moved on ahead to recon the trucks. Finding them all empty, he nodded to Blaine, who waved the rest of the group on for the main gate. Seconds later the five of them were clustered against either side of the stone fence for cover. Blaine was set to lead them in when a low sound made him pause. It sounded like a moan and it was coming from a nearby set of bushes. He signaled the others to hold fast and threaded his way in to find a man whose suit was dirtied by loam that clung to the bloody areas of his midsection and shoulder.

"It's not us," he said between labored breaths. "I don't know who they are, but they're not us."

Blaine looked back at Wareagle. "Not who?"

"Federal marshals. Our strike force. Dressed just like them, but don't be fooled. Kill the bastards, you hear me? Kill them!"

"Sounds like an order."

Warren Thurlow winced in pain. "This is the U.S. government you're talking to here."

"Then just keep your head down, Uncle Sam, and leave everything to us."

McCracken backed away and returned to his original position. When he was certain the immediate coast within was clear, he nodded to Rachel and Jacob. The twins surged past him and slid through the main gate, heading toward the east side of the Oasis where Sister Barbara's private house was located. A moment later Blaine and Johnny entered with Wayne Denbo, and headed west to where the rides and water attractions of the theme park were centered.

They started forward, sweeping the well-manicured front grounds with their eyes, as the sound of gunshots grew even louder ahead of them.

CHAPTER 30

The minutes spent dodging across the Oasis were agonizing for Sister Barbara, full of brief panicked stops behind whatever cover availed itself when the gunmen drew near. Her original thought had been to seek refuge inside the mansion, but sight of the thick, sprawling flower garden set before it provided a better alternative. Taking cover amidst its mazelike confines seemed the best option available. Making sure none of the attackers could spot her, Sister Barbara waded through a bed of flowers and sank quickly into the thicker foliage toward the garden's center. For the moment, she stopped beneath the lavish and tangled growth of some giant dahlias, secure from any eyes that might be searching for her.

Blaine, Johnny, and Wayne Denbo came upon the first bodies seventy yards past the front gate: four corpses, two women and two men. All unarmed. Cut down as they were approaching the front gate.

As they advanced cautiously along Hope Avenue in the

center of the Oasis, Blaine and Johnny saw more bodies everywhere. They'd been shot down in cold blood with no chance to defend themselves. It made McCracken feel sick, revealing to him all at once the lengths the Reverend Harlan Frye was prepared to go in order to complete his agenda.

All the more reason why he had to be stopped. But to do that they needed to find Sister Barbara, alive and unharmed.

A trio of black-clad figures darted out from an aisle separating the slide complex from the wave pool. They saw Blaine and Johnny an instant after Blaine and Johnny saw them. The instant might as well have been an eternity. McCracken and Wareagle's M16s spit out simultaneous short bursts that dropped the men as they stood before the waist-high chain-link fence.

Two more gunmen emerged from behind a T-shirt shop to check on the source of the commotion and opened fire when they spotted Blaine and Johnny. McCracken dove and rolled in Wareagle's shadow behind the cover of a concession booth whose position eliminated their own angle of fire.

A rapid burst from a weapon nearby dropped the enemy pair before they could continue their assault. Wayne Denbo had entered the fray. By lingering behind McCracken and Wareagle, he had remained unseen until he chose to reveal himself.

"Thanks," said a grateful Blaine, now back on his feet with Johnny next to him.

Denbo's response was a rueful smile, glad he'd had the opportunity to prove his worth. He felt alive again, the fog of the last several days, since his fateful visit to Beaver Falls, cleared away for good.

They pressed on toward the rendezvous point with the twins at Sister Barbara's mansion.

The first stretch of Jacob and Rachel's sweep through the Oasis was uneventful. Since they were the only ones who could recognize Sister Barbara, their role was to track her down, while the others dealt with the bulk of gunmen concentrated in the theme park. Still, some of Frye's soldiers were sure to be searching for Sister Barbara as well, if she was still alive. They had to be neutralized if the twins' part in the mission was to be successful.

As they reached the outer edge of the lavish garden fronting the mansion, Rachel grasped her brother's shoulder to get his attention. Turning, Jacob nodded and watched her glide down a narrow aisle between the unbroken reach of the multicolored flowers. She knew her task, just as he knew his. It had been McCracken's idea, and for that reason alone, Jacob had embraced it. He and his sister had made only some minor refinements in the plan, in order to utilize the layout of this section of the Oasis.

The black jackets and caps labeling them as part of the Federal Marshals Strike Force made those in the opposition easy to spot. But Jacob took no action against those who passed by his temporary hiding place in the garden amidst a series of sprawling lilies on their way to the mansion itself. He could just barely see what was going on by gazing through gaps in the thick flora. Rachel had long passed out of his sight and would just be reaching the structure now. Jacob tensed, readied.

Suddenly a burst of gunfire erupted from within the mansion. Glass shattered. A woman screamed. More gunfire followed.

Jacob ducked lower to make sure he wasn't seen.

His strategic positioning allowed him to glimpse a concentrated charge toward the mansion on the part of Frye's soldiers. The sudden bursts, coupled with the screams, had attracted a large bulk of them to the area. Everything was going just as planned.

Jacob pushed through the lilies to obtain view of the mansion's front steps, waiting for his turn to come.

* * *

Wayne Denbo had drawn up even with McCracken and
Wareagle, keeping pace with them. They came to a photo
booth, and Blaine stopped within its cover.

"Expert marksman, right?" he said to Denbo.

"Hundred feet with a pistol. Up to five hundred yards
with a rifle."

"What about a 16?"

"Not my favorite."

"Not what I asked you."

Denbo shrugged, not entirely confident. "From three
hundred, yeah."

"Then we'll keep the window at two-fifty," Blaine said,
and briefly detailed the rest. "We'll cover you."

"No need. Keep moving. I'll get there on my own."

Blaine and Johnny watched and waited until Denbo slid
out of sight. Then they started on again, the past at once
frighteningly close. Neither had seen the likes of this since
entering burned-out Vietnamese villages during the war.
The Cong were very thorough in their work, as borne out
by the number of bodies left compared to the few who
managed to survive. The bodies here lay in the same
twisted, misshapen heaps of limbs and dead stares. They
continued on in search of survivors, hoping to move on
Frye's gunmen before those gunmen could turn their guns
on whoever was left.

Up ahead a woman dragging two children of nine or ten
emerged from the cover of the merry-go-round and scampered toward the recreational area featuring fields and
courts. She gazed back fearfully just as a pair of gunmen
sped out from another of the roads bisecting Hope Avenue.
They leveled their rifles and took aim.

Blaine and Johnny fired bursts into their backs. The
woman kept running, arms like chains attaching herself to
her children and keeping them at her pace.

As others watched their escape, they, too, began to
emerge, desperate and terrified, into the open. They fled
toward the open fields, believing this offered the best
hope.

McCracken and Wareagle moved protectively in their wake, clinging to the side of Hope Avenue that featured the amusement rides because of the additional cover they provided. A number of black-clad figures charged onto the fields, trying to close the gap with the fleeing throng before opening fire, not looking back. Their heedlessness enabled the wild-eyed Indian behind them to drop to one knee, draw a bead upon each black suit, and fire his M16 in single-shot fashion. The enemy gunmen began to fall like shooting-gallery ducks that pop up for the next pass.

McCracken hung back and waited for the expected enemy wave to converge on Wareagle. As anticipated, a small force rushed for the field. Their charge brought them straight into Blaine's line of fire. The first four or five went fast, the others managing to find cover and snap off random bursts at their unseen assailant. Blaine fired back nervously, worried about Johnny being left alone in the fields. It was up to Denbo now to cover him.

Denbo had used a ladder to reach the top of the Oasis's tallest building, a three-story movie theater 250 yards from the field where the Indian knelt. The highway patrolman had just sighted through the M16's scope when eight black-jacketed gunmen rushed Wareagle from the west. The Indian swung and fired a burst their way. A pair went down as Johnny ejected a spent clip and dove to reduce himself as a target while he jammed home a fresh one. The remaining six gunmen surged toward him, firing, widening their spread. No way even the Indian could get all of them.

Wayne Denbo centered the first in his crosshairs and fired. The man's head snapped sideways and he crumpled. Instantly Denbo turned the rifle on the next nearest gunman. Sighted. Aimed. Fired. The man's arms flapped like a puppet's before he collapsed.

The other gunmen swung desperately around now, enabling Johnny to lunge to his feet and take three of the remaining assailants out, while Denbo put a bullet into the skull of the final one. The highway patrolman turned his sight on Wareagle to make sure he was all right.

The big Indian gave a little wave and a nod, then hurried on to meet Blaine McCracken, who was waiting warily at the edge of the field. In all, the three of them had cleared an escape route for upward of fifty people.

"Let's get to the mansion, Indian," McCracken said when Johnny reached him.

Hidden within the garden, Sister Barbara could hear the bursts of gunfire coming from inside her house. It made no sense. Who could possibly be in there that the enemy was shooting at? There were screams, too, a *woman's* screams.

Could a few of her followers have managed to take refuge within the mansion? The enemy must have thought so; over a dozen black-clad gunmen had surged by her in the past few minutes. Sister Barbara had just begun to slide out from her position of cover when she saw another figure emerge from another section of the garden, keeping low. She pushed herself back into the thick shrubbery and caught a glimpse of a teenage boy as he passed by her. He wasn't dressed like the other attackers, nor did he look like one. Sister Barbara watched him stop and bring a strange, thick-barreled weapon down from his shoulder. Then he started on again, closing the gap to the house.

Jacob noted the bursts of gunfire coming from inside the mansion and settled himself between a pair of bushes over a hundred feet away. Rachel's shotgun blasts were easily discernible from the rest, and the intervals between them indicated her winding journey through the mansion was proceeding just as they'd planned. Jacob would have preferred to draw closer, but the 40mm grenades he was about to fire took thirty-five meters to arm themselves by their rotation through the air.

He broke the M79 launcher's breech and inserted the first of his shells, then snapped it closed and brought it to his shoulder. Steadying it before him, Jacob aimed and fired. The grenade thumped out and he had breeched the launcher and reloaded before the explosion sounded.

Sister Barbara heard the ear-rattling blast and instinctively covered her ears. Even so, a second thumping, almost like a pop of air, reached her an instant before the second explosion.

In the next few moments, she counted three more thumps. An explosion followed each one by a few seconds, the sound of exploding glass clear to her now as well. Between the next thump and its accompanying explosion, she slid to a thin enough part of the garden to gain clear view of what was happening.

The mansion was a shambles. Flames flicked out from generous layers of black smoke. Entire windows, along with the areas of walls containing them, were gone, none of the mansion's three floors spared. After another two explosions rocketed wood and glass into the air, the entire house looked as though it were ready to crumble in concession.

Viewing the destruction of her home only brought Sister Barbara additional confusion. She watched a number of black-jacketed killers stagger from the house and tumble down the front steps. A few crashed through the remnants of windows, their bodies in flames. Others emerged reasonably unscathed and tried to drag their fellows to safety. But the next explosion blew their refuge on the steps apart, turning the meager front lawn into a blood-soaked graveyard.

Sister Barbara couldn't believe her eyes. Her entire being was besieged by a welter of emotions. Her house, her *home*, was being destroyed. And yet the teenage boy she felt sure was responsible was obviously acting *against* the force that had invaded the Oasis. Did that make him her ally? Should she approach him?

She moved farther on through the garden's thinner reaches until the boy was directly before her, his eyes riveted on the ruined mansion. Sister Barbara watched as a

final figure emerged from within it: a girl, her clothes
and face soiled by soot, a hand pressed against her mouth.
She reached the boy coughing, nearly gagging. The boy
cupped an arm around the girl's shoulder for support, and
when they finally turned away from the mansion, Sister
Barbara stepped out before them.

"Hello, Sister," the boy said after a brief pause, still
bearing the girl's weight.

The clatter of rapid footsteps made Sister Barbara swing
round to see a tall, bearded man hurrying toward her with
a large rifle shouldered behind him and a smaller one in
hand. Behind him, half watching the rear, advanced a huge
Indian who towered over the highest of her plantings.

"Sorry about the mess," said Blaine McCracken.

Feeling confident now, Wayne Denbo of the Arizona
Highway Patrol protectively followed the progress of
Wareagle and McCracken across the Oasis complex toward the huge flower garden and mansion beyond it. He
was rotating his rifle routinely when the magnified sight
caught something wedged against the rear of the
dormitory-style building. The rectangular mound's cream
color made it stand out from the red brick. Denbo had
never seen this kind of stuff before, not for real anyway,
but where pictures left off, his imagination had no trouble
picking up.

Plastic explosives!

The enemy force must have wired the entire complex,
he thought, realizing his role had just changed abruptly. He
had to get word to McCracken about what he had seen.

Denbo shouldered his rifle and rushed across the rooftop
for the ladder. He descended it quickly, ignoring the resulting clamor and reached the ground to find none of the enemy in sight. He started off, bringing his M16 back
around, when he heard the brief flutter of footsteps to his
rear. Denbo swung his M16 around but wasn't quick
enough. A burst fired by one of the men in the black jackets burned into him just before he found the trigger. The

M16's bullets chewed up the black-jacketed man's midsection and dropped him where he stood. Denbo staggered sideways and leaned against the nearest building, not far from what he recognized as another of the deadly mounds of plastic explosives. Sight of it reminded him that he had to get moving, had to reach McCracken and the others before it was too late.

His breathing came in rapid, shallow heaves. He stumbled the first stretch forward, slowed by the M16 clacking against his body. He shed it from his shoulder and pushed himself on, keeping both hands pressed tightly against the fire-hot wounds in his side and chest.

Jacob kept an arm wrapped around Rachel's shoulder for support as he dragged her toward Blaine McCracken. She was still coughing, her throat burning dry, and tears were pouring from her eyes. But her spirits lifted when she saw Sister Barbara heading their way between McCracken and his giant Indian friend.

The twins' part in the plan had gone off perfectly. After Rachel had successfully drawn the enemy force clustered in this area into the mansion with gunshots, Jacob had opened fire with his grenades. They had worked out the placement and order of his shots in advance, allowing her to shift her position through the mansion to steer clear of the blasts.

"Hello, Sister Barbara," Rachel greeted, separating herself from Jacob.

"I know who you are!" she snapped, while looking at both of them. "Turgewell's children, his famous twins!"

Rachel nodded. "We have much to tell you. And now that—"

She stopped when the sound of heavy footsteps pounded their way. McCracken and Wareagle spun an instant ahead of her, guns leveled and ready.

Wayne Denbo stumbled forward and collapsed, his hands drenched in the blood that had soaked through his jacket all the way down to his thighs. Wareagle got to him first, lifted him carefully and propped up his shoulders, as the highway patrolman fought to speak through quivering lips.

"Got . . . got to get out of . . . here . . ."

"Indian?" Blaine raised.

Wareagle looked at him long enough to shake his head slowly.

"Get out of . . . here now . . ." Denbo's dying eyes burned with fear. He swallowed hard, couldn't complete the motion. "Whole place wired . . . wired to explode . . ."

"Of course, of course," Sister Barbara muttered, as if the enemy's plan suddenly made perfect sense to her.

She joined the others in looking down at Denbo in the hope that he would elaborate further. But Johnny had already closed his eyelids and eased him to the ground.

Blaine swung toward Sister Barbara. "What's the fastest way out of here?"

"Over the fence at the rear of my mansion, or what used to be my mansion." Referring to it brought Sister Barbara's eyes back upon her ravaged house. It didn't look real to her, more like a toy; a young girl's ravaged dollhouse. The remnants continued to char and burn. The explosions themselves had left jagged, blackening punctures that gushed smoke and flames.

McCracken turned that way. "Let's go!" he urged them all. *"Move!"*

The Reverend Harlan Frye watched the series of explosions on television, courtesy of the closed-circuit monitors spread throughout the Oasis theme park. Those monitors had been broadcasting their pictures digitally back to him for months now, one of several means he used to keep track of the traitorous Sister Barbara. Unfortunately their reach did not extend all the way back to her mansion, stealing his chance to see it vanish into oblivion along with the rest of the compound.

The explosions had been rigged to provide the impres-

sion that the invading team of his soldiers, dressed as federal marshals, had triggered the Oasis residents' last desperate line of defense. They would die before allowing
themselves to be taken, the story would go. The madness
of David Koresh and Waco from years before enacted on
a much larger scale.

Minutes before, Harlan Frye had looked up and thanked
God when one of the monitors clearly showed Blaine
McCracken and his Indian friend. That undoubtedly meant
Turgewell's cursed twins were on the premises as well,
perhaps even Karen Raymond. He took the presence of all
his enemies at once in the place of their undoing as a sign
that he had passed the final challenge God had set before
him. The next stage of his plan could go forth unencumbered.

No more distractions. No more tests Judgment Day
would go forward without incident come Sunday morning,
just forty-eight hours from now.

The blasts had been planted to off at staggered intervals
over the course of fifteen wonderful seconds. The Reverend Harlan Frye thanked God again for the gift of being
able to watch Sister Barbara's famed Oasis rupture one
part—and one monitor—at a time. The last thing he saw
before the final monitors went dark was a wall of freed
water from the park's slide and pool attractions being engulfed by a massive sweep of relentless orange flames. A
cloud of black filled the screen briefly, but then the inferno
flared anew, glowing off the monitor toward Frye in the
last moments before the transmission broke off.

The Reverend rose, hands clasped in the position of
prayer, and again looked to the sky, envisioned it beyond
the ceiling of his theater in the Kingdom of the Seven.

"I can begin Your true work now," he promised. "Your
faith in me will be rewarded."

CHAPTER 31

Karen Raymond had felt the power of the blasts from her position by the van parked well off the road. This vantage point precluded view of the Oasis itself, though not of the flames and smoke that rose in billowing waves over it. The shock of seeing them terrified her.

She walked the brief distance to the road. From there the flames were clearly visible and strengthening. The smoke formed vast clouds that swallowed everything they could reach. She could smell the smoke now, all sharp and acrid and full of death.

Karen shivered. There was no sign of McCracken or the others. Had they been inside the Oasis at the time of the explosion? Had the blast consumed them?

She started back for the van. If any of her party managed to survive, it was to the van they would return. Karen even let herself hope McCracken would be there when she got back, wondering where *she* had been.

No such luck. The van was just as she had left it. The air felt hotter, but Karen wrapped her arms about herself to stem the shivers that would not abate. Seconds passed, crawled into minutes. No one emerged from the woods. No one came in from the road. There was only the wail of sirens drawing closer. The dark smoke was starting to thicken at the tops of the tallest trees, obscuring them from view. She backpedaled toward the van; whatever refuge it would provide was more than she had now.

Karen heard a rustling sound in the woods and turned to see Blaine McCracken emerge ahead of the others.

"I'm sorry to have kept you waiting, gentlemen," the Reverend Harlan Frye apologized as he entered the chamber where the Seven traditionally held their meetings. His voice echoed slightly in the hall's spacious confines. He moved down the center aisle past rows and rows of empty pews. The chamber had been laid out in the form of a cathedral, complete with ornate paintings and sculptures, as well as stained-glass windows lit from behind with artificial illumination. "It couldn't be helped," he continued, "and the news I bring is well worth it."

Frye had reached the dais by that point and mounted the five steps leading onto it. Though the many seats in this chamber had never once been occupied, Harlan Frye envisioned a day when they would be. As it was now, the four men waiting for him atop the dais were the only ones to share the chamber with him. Seven chairs were still set around the hand-carved mahogany table that rested upon the dais, though never more than five of them had been filled for two years now.

" 'Bout time you had somethin' good to tell us," snapped Tommy Lee Curtisan, thumbs wedged in the vest of his trademark white linen suit. Tommy Lee was founder of the Right Way, a five-million-strong group of fundamentalist Christians, one of whose major aims was to influence elections from coast to coast. At fifty, his hair as white as his suits, Tommy Lee had become a popular attraction on the political stump circuit, a role he relished since it provided him with public forums by which to expand his audience.

"I would hope that you can provide an end to the problems confronting us," said a rail-thin, pale man with a thin mustache named Arthur Burgeuron. Burgeuron published a monthly newsletter appropriately called *Apocalypse Now*. His subscribers were made up exclusively of the most radical religious elements for whom the end of the world was a foregone conclusion. The only question, in addition to when, was how those chosen to be saved should prepare for civilization's rebirth. They had a survivalist mentality and had gathered on at least a dozen separate occasions to await the world's end.

"McCracken is dead," Frye reported to them, barely able to restrain his glee. "The woman, too."

"Praise the Lord!" screeched Louis W. Kellog. Kellog had invented the concept of the satellite Sunday service. Nearly three hundred churches nationwide now carried his video service in lieu of their own. For those communities lacking the resources to support all the professional and lay personnel needed to run a complete church, the satellite services made perfect sense. For a parish priest or minister too lazy to organize his service and write his sermon, it was made to order.

But Kellog's system wasn't just downlinked pictures. The system was interactive, allowing Kellog to be able to hear any participating congregation he chose at the touch of a button. A different one was featured on live television every Sunday morning. The only constant remained the magical satellite in the sky that allowed him to do God's work. His program would have made keen competition for Frye's "Sunday Morning Service" had they not run at separate hours.

"Hallelujah, hallelujah, hallelujah," recited the Reverend Jessie Will, with little emotion. Will was a baptist minister who had become the radical right's prime spokesman on the issues of abortion, homosexuality, and family values. Jessie Will's views made Pat Buchanan's seem liberal by comparison, and as a result, he had become a most sought after speaker for the caucuses the extremist members of the Republican party had already begun to hold. There was talk that if one of the so-called moderate Republicans seemed on the verge of getting the presidential nomination of 1996, the true conservatives would hold their own convention and put forth their own candidate and platforms. And none other than Jessie Will would be the keynote speaker when the convention opened, waving his arms dramatically as he ranted, his thick brown, wiglike hair frozen magically in place.

The thing these five men, including Harlan Frye, had in common above all else was the undying and unrivaled faith of huge segments of the nation's populace. Beyond that, they all also had active organizations in place, the resources of which would be put to full and good use once the Seven's control was achieved and their power absolute.

These were the men the Reverend Harlan Frye had chosen to secure and rebuild the world following Judgment Day. Frye had never replaced the two who had betrayed the work of the Seven, because there seemed something wrong with disturbing his original vision. Even though Sister Barbara and Preston Turgewell were gone, their contributions—the lessons they had taught the other truly devoted members—remained. In that respect they were still present, while at the same time removed as threats to the attainment of the Seven's final goal. So seven chairs remained at the mahogany conference table, two of which would never be used again.

"We should not let our rejoicing distract us from the other matters at hand," cautioned Tommy Lee Curtisan.

"Indeed," agreed Louis W. Kellog.

"The complications caused by McCracken and the woman may be gone," said Jessie Will to Frye. "But we still have the equally pressing concerns raised by the occurrences in Beaver Falls."

"That is the main reason why I summoned you here, my

brothers," Harlan Frye told them. "You see, we don't. Not anymore."

They waited for the bulk of the police and rescue vehicles to scream past en route to the burning remnants of the Oasis before pulling the van back on the road. During this time the twins used a small first-aid kit to tend to Sister Barbara, who had been carried from the woods by Johnny Wareagle. The force of the initial explosion had come just as she reached the top of the wall enclosing the complex. She had fallen off and struck the ground hard, cutting her head. Unconscious when Blaine reached her, she had begun to show signs of coming around during the last stretch through the woods.

"Shock, mostly," Jacob reported. "Her concussion is minor."

"She'll be all right," added Rachel as she finished bandaging the nasty gash that ran across Sister Barbara's forehead.

They drove to a motel they had passed not far from the North Carolina hills where the last remnants of the Oasis lay smoldering by now. McCracken felt strangely secure and at ease. At least a few of the Seven's soldiers, after all, would surely have escaped to tell the tale of doing battle with his group. It was reasonable to think that these men would report that McCracken and those who had accompanied him had been caught in the massive explosion. Harlan Frye would thus conclude they were dead, providing Blaine the edge he needed once Sister Barbara pinpointed the location of the Kingdom of the Seven.

Jacob and Rachel went out for food and additional medical supplies to tend Sister Barbara. By the time they returned to the room, she was already sitting up in a chair, her eyes regaining clarity and color. They clouded up with tears as the reality of what had occurred at the Oasis struck her hard and fast.

"What have I done?" she muttered. "What have I done?"

"You weren't responsible for what happened today," Rachel said, as Jacob began unpacking the supplies and McCracken looked on.

Sister Barbara's expression remained flat. "People who were loyal to me are dead. People who believed in me are dead. I let them down. They came to me for another chance at life, and today I brought death to them at the . . . Oasis." Saying the final word drew a grimace of pain across her face.

"The Reverend Harlan Frye's doing," Rachel persisted.

"And was I not a part of his work and thus this? Was not your father?"

"He has tried to atone, as you have."

"But we failed, both of us, I more than he since I refused to believe in Frye's ability to bring on Judgment Day. I couldn't let myself believe because believing meant accepting I had been party to it. And today happened because I couldn't let myself believe he would go as far as he did or strike as quickly."

"Where is Frye, Sister?" McCracken asked. "Where is the Kingdom of the Seven?"

"It's too late to stop him, isn't it?"

"That depends on how much you're able to help us," Blaine told her.

"What has he done? What is to be the instrument of his Judgment Day?"

"We don't know. We have pieces, clues, but how they fit together, well . . ."

"It all starts with a vaccine for AIDS," said Karen Raymond.

Sister Barbara's expression seemed to perk up at that. "Did you say vaccine?"

Karen nodded. "Developed by a company called Van Dyne Pharmaceuticals, but—"

"Of course," Sister Barbara interrupted.

"That means something to you," McCracken realized.

"Oh yes. Plenty. Because Harlan Frye *owns* Van Dyne Pharmaceuticals."

* * *

The four remaining members of the Seven had all taken their seats by the time Harlan Frye completed his report. Surprise and doubt had taken the place of triumph and celebration on their faces.

"Can this truly be done?" asked Jessie Will.

"Most certainly," returned Reverend Frye, who alone had remained standing.

"In spite of what happened in Beaver Falls?" challenged Arthur Burgeuron.

"As I explained," said Frye, "*because* of it." He strode confidently closer to the table. "Can't you see it, my brothers? What we first interpreted as disaster was actually a blessing—a final blessing God has bestowed on our works. He has shown us a better way, my friends. He has given us the means to accomplish His work in the manner He has chosen."

"Through a *single* city?" from a skeptical Tommy Lee Curtisan.

"Not just any city, my brother. The visitors will come and they will go and they will take the end of the world with them."

"What of our followers?" asked Louis W. Kellog. "Our own chosen who were to survive?"

The Reverend Harlan Frye laid his palms on the hard wood table and shrugged. "Some will have to be sacrificed for the greater good, but within six months we will be able to produce the means to save the majority of them."

"How?" asked Jessie Will.

"Did I not tell you? We are fortunate enough to have in our possession a vaccine. . . ."

It took a few moments for Sister Barbara's revelation about the true ownership of Van Dyne to sink in.

"Actually," she continued, "we all owned Van Dyne, a huge block of it anyway, thanks to a pool of our collective resources worth nearly a billion dollars. That list you have of Frye's Key Society, check it again. You'll find Van Dyne's founder mentioned prominently."

McCracken began pacing the room, trying to put it all together. His gaze fell on Karen. "Assume Van Dyne's vaccine worked as advertised. Assume no complications sprang up in Beaver Falls."

"FDA approval within a year or two."

"And then?"

"Worldwide distribution and inoculation. Vaccinating *everyone* would be the only way to be sure of stamping out the disease. Like polio."

Blaine stopped and ground his feet into the carpet, his point made for him. "So I figured."

"I don't understand. What are you getting at?"

"You just said it yourself: Frye's vaccine would have been used to inoculate the entire world."

"Oh, my God," Karen muttered through the chill rising through her.

"That's right." Blaine nodded.

"The vaccine Frye was testing in Beaver Falls . . ."

"Not a vaccine at all," McCracken said. "Quite the opposite, in fact: Everyone inoculated will become infected with the disease."

Karen Raymond leaped to her feet. She wrapped her arms about herself to try to still her shaking. "The pathological alterations in the vaccine would have to be very subtle. Van Dyne's vaccine was based on the body's ability to form a permanent, genetically based protein coating around invading HIV cells, after it recognized them. Only, Frye's scientists must have designed this protein coating to erode over time, probably through some form of cellular encapsulation. And as the coating eroded, the virus would be freed to attack the immune system and turn it against itself at all levels—AIDS, as we know it today." Her eyes flashed back to life, aimed McCracken's way. "But something went wrong."

"Beaver Falls . . ."

"Yes! It's clear, everything's clear! The disease must have begun to metastasize long before it was supposed to; the microencapsulated protein coating broke down years ahead of schedule."

"And Frye's volunteers ended up coming down with AIDS."

Karen nodded. "Based on what Wayne Denbo told us he saw, that's the explanation that fits. It also accounts for the procedures Frye employed to evacuate the town."

"But why evacuate the whole town, Dr. Raymond?"

"My guess would be because evacuating only the test subjects would cause too much attention. In any case, this is reason for hope. The vaccine didn't work like it was supposed to. Frye stands no chance of gaining approval, which means widespread inoculation isn't going to happen. That explains why he so desperately needed my vaccine. Since his didn't work, his only hope was to replace it with an altered version of Lot 35. And when I refused to hand over the formula, chances are the Reverend got stopped in his tracks, at least until he's able to collate the computer disks he managed to steal."

McCracken shook his head, unconvinced. "You're forgetting something, Dr. Raymond. When Beaver Falls went sour on him, Frye didn't just empty the town; he filled it with new people. A short-term cover to buy himself the time he needed."

"Time he needed to what?"

"Come up with a new means of unleashing Judgment Day, salvaged from the remnants of his work in Beaver Falls and not from Lot 35. He needs your vaccine, all right, but even if he had the formula, it couldn't do him any good in the time frame we're looking at based on everything he's done. And the only way we can find out what the Reverend is up to now is to find him." McCracken turned to Sister Barbara. "And that's where you come in, Sister. Where can we find Harlan Frye? Where is the Kingdom of the Seven?"

Sister Barbara sighed. "An abandoned salt mine in the

Texas Panhandle. Frye is in the process of building an entire underground community within it, his kingdom."

"Perfect," said McCracken, sounding almost complimentary. "Isolated enough to keep such a massive construction project secret, but possessing the elevators, air shafts, and general framing to take years off the project."

"And security," Sister Barbara reminded. "Don't forget about security."

Blaine looked over at Johnny Wareagle. "Just tell us where to find it, Sister."

PART FIVE

JUDGMENT DAY

THE TEXAS PANHANDLE.
SATURDAY; 10:00 A.M.

CHAPTER 32

The convoy of supply trucks rolled through the Texas Panhandle on sleepy roads that had begun to buckle under the strain. This one had lagged several hours behind the two that preceded it toward Palo Duro Canyon, because of a delay en route caused by a stubborn bridge stuck in the up position over the Colorado River.

That incident, though, was anything but random. Blaine McCracken and Johnny Wareagle had arranged a subtle bit of sabotage in order to create the opportunity to hide themselves within the covered cargo compartment of the third convoy's rearmost truck. They climbed in after the twins and Karen Raymond. All five tucked themselves into gaps amidst the cargo, a tight squeeze made even more discomforting by the darkness that dominated once Wareagle got the canvas flap back into place.

McCracken found a seat on the cargo bed floor next to Karen. He had resisted letting her join in this trip only as long as it took to realize that he still needed her. She was, after all, the only one capable of understanding and interpreting whatever they found within the Kingdom of the Seven. In the wake of Beaver Falls, Harlan Frye had come up with a new means to bring on Judgment Day, a means they were committed to uncovering.

Of course, knowing the kingdom's location didn't necessarily make gaining access to it any easier. Toward this end, McCracken put in a call to an antsy Sal Belamo, who was champing at the bit to get back into action. Sal was able to uncover the precise route taken by a number of large supply convoys that had been departing Amarillo almost daily over the past few months for destinations unknown. That route took them over a bridge spanning the Texas leg of the Colorado River, a revelation that allowed the rest of McCracken's plan to fall into place. The same private jet that had brought his small group to Knoxville served as transport into Texas. McCracken had a list of needed supplies he would have passed on to Belamo if the twins didn't have virtually everything available already.

Sister Barbara had wanted to accompany them as well, but here McCracken refused to bend. One of them *had* to stay back, and she was the most obvious choice.

"This small group of ours is composed of the only people in the world who know everything the Reverend Frye is up to," he had explained when they were alone. "That means we need insurance, Sister, and you're our best bet, because you've got credibility. You can reach people, powerful people. If the rest of us don't make it out of that kingdom, contacting them will be the only chance left to stop Frye."

Sister Barbara didn't disagree, but looked at Blaine long and hard. "You like this. You enjoy it."

"Are you asking me?"

"Telling you."

"Am I supposed to deny it?"

"I wouldn't expect you to."

McCracken returned her gaze with apparent indifference. "You good at what you do, Sister, saving souls and all that?"

"I wouldn't know."

"Yes, you would. You'd know by your followers' faces as they left your tent or whatever. You'd be able to tell if you touched some part of them that forgot it still could feel. You'd get an idea whether they were better people, at least more content, than when they walked in."

Sister Barbara said nothing, waiting for him to continue.

"Oh, you're good, all right, Sister. But you can't be good unless you like it. Doesn't mean you totally understand why you're doing what you do; some things you just accept. You serve a purpose and you know it." Blaine paused. "See, we've got more in common than you realized."

Sister Barbara sighed somberly. "I did realize. That's why I brought it up."

"The likeness bother you?"

"Only because I wonder how different my methods are from yours. I'm worried that I want so badly to succeed that I don't care how I do it anymore."

"Why bother?" McCracken challenged her. "You and me, Sister, we both help people. That's our business. Maybe they're better people because you stepped into their lives. Maybe they're still alive because I did. You fight the one devil; I fight a lot of his surrogates."

Her stare knifed through him. "Who's the real devil, Mr. McCracken?"

"Hey, if it helps me get closer to them . . ."

"I was talking about how you see yourself, not how others see you. Can you accomplish good if you do not perceive yourself as good?"

"I don't view what I do as good or bad, Sister, only that it's necessary."

"I was referring to who you are, not what you do."

"Same thing."

"Are they, Mr. McCracken?"

"For me they are. That's what keeps me going. That's what keeps me from asking myself the kind of questions you're asking me. I believe in what I do, Sister. That means I believe in who I am."

Sister Barbara realized what had been bothering her so much in that instant. Blaine McCracken might be guilty of many things, but he had never strayed from the truth of his ideals, never let them consume him. Her years spent with the Seven made her weak by comparison. She had wanted something so badly, she had let it change her, and now she was doomed forever to strive to find the person she had been. It hadn't happened on the road. It hadn't happened when she returned to the Oasis to face Harlan Frye's wrath. It had happened only in the midst of the rage roused in her by the massacre of her people yesterday. Violence had tapped the well or her true emotions and commitment. Only in the world of Blaine McCracken had she found herself again.

After the bridge was finally operable again, the convoy continued on through the Panhandle. The supplies forming the group's camouflage were made up entirely of the component parts of high-tech solar displacement units. Once fully assembled, these would be capable of providing a huge measure of the Kingdom of the Seven's energy needs by storing energy channeled from huge solar receptors upon the surface.

"Once we're inside the kingdom, Johnny will help you find the laboratory," Blaine reiterated softly to Karen.

"While you . . ."

"Do a little exploring. Find out exactly what Frye's got in store for the world. You may uncover the how in that lab, Dr. Raymond, but not the where and the when."

"You won't have much time," Karen said, recalling the roles of Rachel and Jacob in the operation. "Neither will I."

"Two hours from the time we disperse. We'll have to make do."

"Do we have to be so firm in that deadline? Can't the explosives be set off once we're safely out of the kingdom, instead of by timer?"

"That assumes one of us with a detonator will be alive

to set them off, Doctor," McCracken pointed out. "We can't take the chance of that not being the case. If all else fails, the Kingdom of the Seven and everything inside it has to be destroyed. And if we fail there as well, then it's up to Sister Barbara to convince the world about Judgment Day."

The convoy took Route 287 into the heart of the Panhandle, heading toward Palo Duro Canyon. Along the way the broad, flat plains, formed of limestone caprock, were interrupted occasionally by low, rolling hills. Brown grasses, cacti, and tumbleweeds owned the land that was also known as *Llano Estacado*, or the Staked Plain. When a peek through the canvas flap showed the deep canyons beginning to dot the landscape around them, McCracken knew they were drawing very close to the site of the Kingdom of the Seven.

Twenty minutes later, McCracken felt the truck shimmy slightly as the brakes were applied. Its pace slowed to a crawl and then stopped altogether. Blaine didn't dare risk peering outside again, but he guessed the convoy was approaching its destination. They had probably come to a security fence closing off the area on the false pretext of some government-connected project. Way out here, who was going to challenge or question?

Their truck began to inch its way along, progress choked off by maddening stops and starts. Several more minutes passed before it slid at last through a security gate and approached the entrance to the salt mine. McCracken glimpsed the guards fronting the gate after the truck was waved through, rattling and clanging atop the uneven ground.

"What now?" Karen whispered.

"The supply trucks and construction equipment must be ferried down into the mine by hydraulic platforms, kind of like large-scale elevators. They don't move too fast. This could take a while."

In fact, it took thirty additional minutes before their truck slid inside a garagelike bay and thumped onto one of three enclosed platforms. A huge door slid closed behind it and the platform jolted into a slow, steady, and whining drop. Once the platform finished its descent, Blaine guessed they would drive to a central unloading depot. At that point he, Johnny, and Karen would head for the main building Sister Barbara had designated on her detailed map of the kingdom as it existed two years ago. In all likelihood that building would be the only one fully operational at this point. That meant the laboratory Karen sought would be contained within it, as well as what McCracken had come in search of.

Rachel and Jacob, meanwhile, would work their way about the kingdom itself, planting powerful plastic explosives at key stress points and within the shells of uncompleted structures. There would be no need to plant charges in the connecting chambers as well; the resulting blasts would cut them off or destroy them.

The platform finished its descent with another slight jolt. In the cab before them, the driver revved the engine and shifted into gear. The truck thudded atop a scaly, uneven surface and edged its way along. It rumbled to a halt after five minutes. Blaine moved to the truck's rear and cracked the flap slightly. As expected, they had come to a stop in a line of trucks waiting to unload their cargoes at a central depot. The area around them was packed with trucks, heavy construction equipment, and a number of corrugated steel sheds of varying sizes undoubtedly used for storage. The nearest ongoing construction project was forty feet away where a pair of cement trucks hovered over a sixty-foot-square foundation form waiting to be poured; a central storage drop-to-be probably, judging by the location.

McCracken lowered himself from the back of the truck first and reached up to help Karen Raymond follow. Then he stood watch while the twins and Johnny Wareagle emerged through the flap. Wareagle led the way to the cover provided by a huge John Deere 744E loader parked near the foundation hole, the top of its cab nearly twelve feet off the ground, with its tires alone making up almost half that height. The loader's front end was composed of a sharp-toothed excavating shovel with a massive four-cubic-yard and nearly two-ton capacity. Given time, the 744E was capable of moving mountains and, in point of fact, very likely had done just that through the course of the kingdom's continuing construction.

McCracken allowed himself a brief gaze about their surroundings. The Kingdom of the Seven was everything Sister Barbara had indicated it might be: an underground city. Unfinished streets wide enough to carry even the largest of the construction equipment crisscrossed between the buildings. At first glance the symmetrical layout of the structures gave Blaine the impression they were all interconnected, or meant to be. But a second look showed him the design was more like an ultramodern city block with no wasted space whatsoever. The whirring, pounding, and slapping sounds of construction, meanwhile, dominated the thin air. They combined to form a rattling din he blessed for the added cover it would provide.

Up to this point, Blaine had taken the kingdom's lighting for granted. More comfortable with the surroundings now, he turned his gaze up at the massive solar-powered gaseous lighting built into the mine's ceiling. The huge fixtures, ranging from twenty square feet to as much as fifty, were laid out in no discernible pattern, their randomness, he judged, being due to their placement within workable areas of the ceiling. These supplied upward of fifty percent of the mine's light, the rest emanating from powerful floods mounted upon the completed shells of buildings.

The sight was altogether mesmerizing, the costs to turn this underground world into a reality incalculable. From his vantage point, McCracken was able to glimpse only a few of the additional connecting chambers Sister Barbara had mentioned and used his imagination to conjure up pictures of their unfinished residential structures. The Kingdom of the Seven as a whole was still years from

completion, but its mere existence served as testament to
the depth of Frye's commitment and the madness of his
vision.

The kingdom headquarters Sister Barbara had described
was located beyond three taller unfinished buildings several hundred yards away. It was five stories in height, with
an additional three located beneath the mine floor. The
layout was comparable to a medium-sized office building,
though the inside had been built to Frye's unusual specifications. Blaine couldn't see the building from where he
stood, but the route to reach it was clear from the map she
had drawn. He looked back at the twins.

"Set your detonators for two o'clock sharp," he told
them.

"Just over two hours from now," noted Jacob, after a
gaze at his watch.

"Plenty of time," said Wareagle.

Blaine and Johnny waited for the twins to move away
from the huge loader before setting off themselves in single file, with Karen Raymond between them. The various
construction equipment, debris, and partially completed
structures afforded plenty of cover on their route to the
kingdom's main and sole totally functional structure. The
building itself was a simple rectangle, dotted with windows in apparent haphazard fashion. It was cream-colored
to make best use of the mine's lighting, its finish creased
with an unfinished, stuccolike quality.

McCracken was surprised to find security virtually nonexistent in the area around it. Then again, Frye would
never believe an interloper could get this far, especially
now that he believed the Seven's most dangerous adver-
saries were dead. He noted only an occasional guard, patrolling either on foot or in a motorized golf cart, and easy
to evade in either case.

Entrance to the building, though, was another matter.
The doors had no knobs and required either a special identification card or keypad code to access. Blaine knew they

could not force their way in and risk tripping an alarm system. What, then?

The answer was revealed moments later when a guard riding one of the golf carts pulled up near a side entrance. McCracken saw him move toward the keypad and nodded at Johnny Wareagle, who sprang into motion instantly. The guard saw nothing of the big Indian other than the arm that looped around his throat, after the door had popped electronically open. Blaine led Karen across the brief stretch of open ground and lifted the guard's unconscious body into the golf cart before Johnny pushed it toward the nearest position of cover.

They entered the building, moving quickly and cautiously, and proceeded down a narrow entry hall to a set of glass doors just beyond a staircase. Sister Barbara had seen the first two floors of this building before leaving the Seven, and nothing resembling a laboratory had been contained on them. That meant the kingdom's scientific facilities were on some higher floor.

Blaine pointed upward when they came to the staircase, and Johnny motioned to Karen Raymond to accompany him. When they had disappeared up the stairs, he crept along the main corridor, the layout Sister Barbara had provided recalled in his mind. She couldn't be sure where the information Blaine sought could be found, since the building had no command post or planning center when she had left. The closest thing to it might well have been the small private theater that Harlan Frye had designed to the last chair. He was obsessed with media and video. A master manipulator of both, the Reverend relied on visual input far more than anything else.

"He needs to see *everything*," Sister Barbara had said, further explaining that the theater had been the first completed interior project in the entire kingdom. It took up an entire corner of the building and rose three stories in height.

Blaine moved quickly toward the theater, still alert to the possible presence of guards. He reasoned that Frye would entrust the kingdom's existence to as few people as possible. The more individuals he utilized, the higher the odds that the true nature of the kingdom would leak out. Despite the lack of guards, the Reverend would feel safe and invulnerable down here in his domain.

The theater was exactly where Sister Barbara described, accessible through a door that rested apart from the others at the end of a hall on the first floor. The door was open. As Blaine approached, a shadow fell across the hall floor in front of it, signaling him to take cover within a small alcove. Four men emerged and strode stiffly past him. The quick glance he managed to grab was enough to identify the four from the descriptions provided by Sister Barbara as the remaining members of the Seven.

Blaine was tempted to overpower the four evangelists and do away with them on the spot. He restrained himself by recalling that his only meaningful target here was Harlan Frye. Risk exposure by slaying these men and he ran the very real chance of forfeiting his opportunity to get to the Reverend. Obviously a briefing of some sort had just taken place within the theater. Unless Frye had taken a different route out, he would still be inside.

McCracken detected no signs of activity when he drew closer to the open door leading into the theater. He stopped just before reaching it and pressed his shoulders against the wall. Peering in, he could see connected rows of chairs neatly arranged upon a sloping rise before a screen that covered a portion of the front wall's length. A still image was projected upon that screen now, unidentifiable from this angle. The door provided access to the front of the theater, near the screen.

McCracken dropped down to all fours and crawled into the theater on his belly, pulling himself along with his hands and letting his feet drag behind him. He wormed his body beneath the bottom rows of seats for cover and curled his frame tight, once he was all the way under. The vantage point still precluded view of the screen, and Blaine had started to angle himself for the aisle in an at-

tempt to better that view when a *click* sounded. Instantly
the screen went dark and soft lighting lit the theater to replace the still image that had been projected. Footsteps
rapped his way down the central row of stairs. McCracken
froze and looked upward, catching a glimpse of a pair of
small feet encased in expensive velvety loafers before the
face of Harlan Frye slid by above him.

Blaine had known the Reverend only through poor photographs and a single brief appearance on the Future Faith
channel he'd seen while inside a hotel room earlier that
week. Frye was a short man of medium build who seemed
average in every respect and detail, except for his face. That
face seemed ageless, unmarred and smooth even without the
aid of makeup. Blaine hadn't glimpsed him smile here in the
theater, but he knew that smile would be incredibly warm
and reassuring. People looked at Harlan Frye and trusted
him, and McCracken found himself briefly questioning how
such a man could be responsible for the coming of Judgment
Day. He shook himself as if from the effects of a spell. The
Reverend had that effect on people.

Another man descended the stairs a few steps behind
Frye, his left arm hanging stiffly by his side. Blaine followed both sets of steps until they had almost reached the
open doorway. The door closed with a *whooooosh* after
the pair exited, and Blaine cautiously waited a few extra
minutes before snaking his way into the single aisle. He
rose into the theater's half-light and retraced Harlan Frye's
steps up the stairs. At the very top a remote control device
had been left in a specially tailored slot within a chair arm
at the end of the row. McCracken picked it up and pressed
the ON button, eager to see what the Reverend had just
shared with the other members of the Seven.

The still image reappeared on the huge screen below
him, slightly fuzzy due to the lighting in the theater. Holding the remote control in his hand, Blaine began to descend for a clearer view of what could only be Harlan
Frye's plan for Judgment Day.

CHAPTER 33

•

The laboratory was located on the building's fourth floor, easily identifiable thanks to a sign in bold view on a windowless steel door:

RESEARCH WING
RESTRICTED ACCESS
NO UNAUTHORIZED PERSONNEL

Johnny Wareagle eased Karen Raymond behind him and tried the security guard's identification card in the slot. The two of them remained tightly pressed against the wall as the door slid open. The Indian spun away from it and lunged through the door in a blur Karen's eyes could barely record. Barely a yard inside, he froze and motioned Karen forward with the submachine gun gripped in both hands.

The huge laboratory was deserted. Desks sat unmanned, the computer screens atop them dark. A series of separate glassed-in booths and cubicles were empty as well. More, though, was missing than just people. None of the lab equipment looked in any way operational. Everything seemed pristine, virtually untouched. Karen had expected to find a lab teeming with activity. She had expected Johnny Wareagle would need to hold everyone at bay while she inspected its contents.

Her eyes locked on a single grouping of test tubes placed on a waist-high platform that ran the length of the side wall beyond the cubicles. She approached and lifted one of the tubes carefully. The plastic tube nearly compressed in her hand, because it was composed of a gelatin-plastic mixture similar to that used in the manufacture of time-release capsules. The test tube was thicker and stronger, but equally pliable; and, as with the thinner time-capsule version, it would dissolve gradually in any liquid, thereby freeing its contents.

Before Karen could consider the ramifications further, Johnny Wareagle quickly drew her back against the wall. The test tube slipped from her hand and plopped to the floor, rolling away. Her eyes darted to the center of the lab where a pair of figures was descending a staircase that spiraled upward for the next floor. They were wearing white lab isolation suits, complete with individual oxygen supplies. The Kevlar gloves on the figures' hands perfectly traced the contours of their fingers to allow for delicate manipulations.

Karen had used such suits herself, usually to avoid contaminating an unstable mixture, or in situations requiring quarantine procedures. Her eyes followed the suited figures as they approached a set of inner security doors constructed of glass rather than steel. The glass doors slid open and the suited figures continued toward the main entrance. They stopped near a series of hooks to shed their suits, turning toward their unwelcome visitors in the process.

Johnny Wareagle sprang.

Karen Raymond had never seen a man move so fast, didn't think a man *could* move that fast. He covered most

of the ground separating him from the figures before they
had even recorded his presence. One turned and grabbed
for the other's shoulder. Karen could see the panic in his
eyes under his faceplate.

The big Indian pounced, huge arms stretching outward.
He took a head in either hand and smashed them viciously
together. The suited figures crumpled to the floor, helmets
shattered. Johnny looked back at Karen, and then dragged
their unconscious frames into one of the cubicles.

"Let's go, miss," he said when he reemerged, eyes dart-
ing from her to the stairwell.

"There could be others," she pointed out.

"There aren't."

"How can you be so—"

Johnny was already approaching the glass doors leading
to the stairwell. They parted automatically when he drew
close enough, and he remained between them until Karen
was safely through. He climbed the stairwell ahead of her,
and Karen hurried to keep his pace. Her boots clanged
against the metal steps. She reached the top just behind the
Indian and saw that a glass wall lay twenty feet before
them, running the floor's entire width. Wareagle took a
few steps forward and froze. Karen could feel him go
tense and drew up even to share his view.

"Oh, my God," she muttered at the sight before them.

The twins' work was progressing smoothly. Although
the amount of extrapotent plastic explosives contained in
their packs was not nearly enough to cover the entire expanse of the kingdom, it was enough to topple a huge
measure of it. Beyond that, the stifling and poorly venti-
lated confines of the mine would facilitate the spread of
flames, an inferno certain to be raging in no time.

Preston Turgewell had spoken often of such a day to
Jacob and Rachel through the last several desperate years.
But everywhere they turned their efforts at penetrating the
Seven had been stymied. Their resources and contacts
dwindled. The Fifth Generation itself had been compro-

mised, so many members turned against them that they could no longer trust its ranks. With Sister Barbara's continued refusal to involve herself, Benjamin Ratansky's pilfered list became their best chance to deal Frye's grand scheme a crushing setback by executing all the people whose names it contained. But now, thanks to Blaine McCracken, the twins were in position to do far more than that.

Destroy the Kingdom of the Seven here and now, and the Reverend Harlan Frye's plans for Judgment Day would be canceled forever.

Jacob and Rachel split up to maximize their effectiveness. They started at the darkest, outermost reaches of the kingdom, in shells of buildings at the earliest stages of construction. From there they worked their way toward the congestion of nearly and partially completed structures where work was ongoing. Their sweep was precise, routes designed to converge at a point closest to Frye's command center where they would rendezvous with the others.

The setting of each charge was as simple as wedging a brick-sized mound of plastic explosives against a structural stress point and activating the detonator. Each timer was set for two o'clock sharp. Rachel had just planted her ninth mound of *plastique* and was readying her tenth when she heard what sounded like a light footstep scuffing the rocks and gravel here in the Kingdom of the Seven's outer reaches. She remained perfectly still as she traced the sound in her mind, gauging distance and direction; swung, finally, with pistol held tight and ready.

No one was there. She relaxed briefly, then heard a similar sound from the exact opposite side. Again she twisted. Again her eyes found nothing.

She was being stalked, toyed with!

An unfamiliar jolt of fear stung her, and Rachel raised the walkie-talkie to her lips, one of the only two they had brought with them on this journey.

"Jacob," she said softly.

"Yes," he replied.
"Someone's here."

Normal accommodations were impossible to conceive
of for Earvin Early. He had lived virtually without structure ever since renouncing his physical self. Without a
physical self to be concerned with, shelter was more a burden than a luxury. Of course, within the kingdom there
was little to choose from, though Early made the best of
things in the dark recesses of the shells of buildings in the
kingdom's rear. He felt reasonably at home in them, although sleep had become little more than a memory since
he had returned.

He recalled the sensation of pain from his previous life
and imagined that was what his bulky shell must be feeling. The wounds in his arms inflicted by the dogs had begun to leak brown ooze through the makeshift bandages
holding his flesh together. The last time he had changed
them, he noted that the flesh had taken on a greenish tint.
He could not see his split lip, but the feel of it was enough
to tell him how puffy it had become, swollen to the point
of peeling away from his mouth to expose his upper teeth.
Each breath from his nose drew in thick gobs of something that felt like resin and smelled like death. The ripped
side of his face had become one big oozing scab, festering,
and his only vision was through his right eye.

My shell is rotting away, he thought, and tried to imagine that he might exchange it for another.

Earvin Early was contemplating that feat when the girl
passed within sight of the unfinished doorway where he
was huddled. He slid his great bulk out and followed her
for a bit, memorizing the spots where she placed a number
of explosive charges. After watching her set a fourth, he
decided to move in, taking his time, wanting to see what
she would do. Her use of a walkie-talkie told Early she
wasn't alone. Have to use her to draw the other one in,
then. Early found the brief exertion had tired his legs. This

shell was indeed dying, but the business at hand needed taking care of.

He grew weary of the game after the girl gave up on setting her explosives and turned her focus solely on locating him. He was impressed with the way she moved, the quickness in her feet and eyes. Of course, Earvin Early didn't mind letting her see him because he wasn't there, not to her, not until he was ready to push his physical self into the world he preferred to shun.

The girl stopped and started to raise the walkie-talkie to her lips again. Earvin Early crept out behind her and slid into motion.

"It's him," Rachel whispered into her walkie-talkie.

"Who?" Jacob returned.

"The man from New York, the one the Indian spoke of. The monster."

"How can you be—"

THUD!

Jacob heard a gasp on his sister's end.

"Rachel," he called. "Rachel? . . ."

The sound in his ear died, nothing but static in its place. Jacob turned cold, was willing the strength back into his quivering limbs when a voice that was little more than static itself emerged through the speaker.

"*Stay for me there; I will not fail, to meet thee in that hollow vale.*"

"No," Jacob moaned. "No . . ."

And then he was running.

Behind the huge glass wall, Karen Raymond and Johnny Wareagle saw what might have been a large hospital ward; rows of beds lined up on the floor, surrounded by clusters of IV packs and monitoring machines. One entire wall of the anteroom they stood within was made up of a massive LED board that constantly accepted the data from within and displayed it in upward of a hundred separate readouts. Seeing the dancing grids made her edge closer to the glass.

Many of the beds beyond it were empty. The occupants of the rest turned her blood cold.

Their bodies were decaying, wasting away, little more than slight bulges beneath sterile, white bedsheets. Rows and rows of men and women in the last stages of life. The limbs she could see were little more than bones tinted the color of withered flesh. The faces exposed above the bedsheets were marred by sores, lesions, and purplish blotches known as Kaposi's sarcoma. And the stares on the faces she could see were blank and dazed, emanating from eyes that seemed made of glass. Karen knew well enough what she was looking at: This was the last stage of AIDS at its most cruel. Bodies reduced to mere memories of human beings. As she continued to peer into the chamber, some of the eyelids trembled and a few of the heads turned feebly toward the glass.

They were still cognizant, still aware!

Karen shivered at that thought, kept shifting her eyes to avoid meeting any of their stares.

"You'd better look at this, miss."

Johnny Wareagle's voice broke her trance. She turned and saw he was holding a steel medical clipboard out to her, already open to a page early in the recordings that looked like a master list.

"What was the name of the man Wayne Denbo found in the desert?" she asked him.

"McBride," Johnny recalled. "Frank McBride."

Karen scanned the list, eyes stopping with a thump to her gut. "He's here," she said, looking up. "These are the residents of Beaver Falls."

She flipped through the next series of pages frantically, skimming their contents, stopping when a passage demanded special attention and narrating as she went.

"The first symptoms of this appeared only, my God, a week ago on Friday night. The evacuation took place at nine A.M. Monday morning, five hours before Denbo and his partner got to the town with McBride in their backseat." She stopped to gaze through the glass. "This log records the rate of deterioration in the town's residents in the five days since."

Karen slowed her flipping, eyes bulging in intensity.

"There was no trace of HIV anywhere in their blood until the first symptoms began to show up, escalating at a geometric rate when compared to the standard course of the disease—eight years in eight days wouldn't be far from accurate. The rate of deterioration has apparently continued to advance beyond the ability of their machines to track—" Karen suddenly went pale. "My God, wait . . ."

The pages in the logbook flew backward and then forward again, Karen seeming to calculate something in her head.

"No," she muttered. "No . . ."

"What's wrong?" Wareagle prodded.

Her voice remained muted, distant. "Seven hundred twelve total residents in Beaver Falls. Seven hundred twelve advanced cases of AIDS monitored here, over six hundred of which have already resulted in death."

"Just as you said before."

"*Not* as I said before, not at all." Karen slid her front teeth over her lower lip, hoping to stop it from quivering. "The *entire* town was infected, the *entire* town is dying. But Frye's test subjects numbered only a quarter of the population. . . ."

As he descended the stairs to get a better look, McCracken realized the still image projected on the huge screen was a map. By the time he reached the bottom step, he could see the markings and notations on it clearly. His eyes scanned the entire image and came to rest on the most prominent marking of all in the map's northwest portion where a single location had been enclosed by a bright red box. Squinting, he was able to identify the site enclosed by the box and then follow a thick black line that originated at the bottom of the red box and ran southeast to a large number of sites denoted by small black circles. The thick black line cut through each of their centers in no discernible pattern, looking like the bizarre results of a connect-the-dots game.

Blaine took a final step down to floor level. His heart was pounding as the individual sites contained within those circles and linked together by the black line originating at the red box became clear to him.

Red for a reason: for blood, for death.

In all, over fifty sites in the southeast were circled, each of them different.

Yet the same.

And all part of Harlan Frye's plan for making Judgment Day come to pass.

CHAPTER 34

Jacob found Rachel sprawled on the ground in the twilight brightness of the kingdom. She lay facedown covered by construction debris that looked to have tumbled atop her, leaving only her long hair exposed.

"Rachel?" Jacob probed as he advanced, submachine gun sweeping the area in cadence with his eyes. "Rachel . . ."

She stirred slightly. Alive! *Thank God!*

Jacob shouldered the submachine gun and drew his pistol in its place to give him a free hand. Then he leaped over the debris closest to Rachel and reached down. He touched her hair and started to ease her over.

"What happened? I- "

Her hair came away in his hand. A huge coiled shape, its head previously buried beneath it, sprang upward. Jacob tried to bring his gun around, even as he recorded a face of rotting flesh and brown, decayed teeth that smiled at him. He found the trigger at the same time he nearly gagged at the stench emanating from the monster. Before he could fire, though, a sizzling blow stung his wrist and sent the pistol flying.

As Jacob reached for the machine gun slung from his shoulder, the giant's huge hand whipped toward his face. The boy flinched involuntarily, focus on the Mac-10 lost for a few precious instants.

Block it! Block it!

Instinct took over. Jacob's free arm shot up in a defensive posture. He deflected the blow and completed the process of freeing his Mac-10 at the same time. He brought it around, thinking he could fire before the monster could strike again. But suddenly the gun was being turned back on him, a thick, soiled finger closing over his on the trigger. Jacob had never felt such strength. *No* man was this strong.

He felt the finger pushing his inward, fought against it until the bone cracked. The pain exploded through him, but was nothing compared to the burst of agony that slammed into his midsection and turned everything hot. The heat lasted only briefly before a strange and terrifying cold overcame it with the return of the staticky, frothy voice:

"Fare thee well for I must leave thee, Do not let this parting grieve thee."

Earvin Early watched the boy die and then slid away.

"What's it mean?" Johnny asked her.

Karen's thoughts tumbled over one another fast and furiously. "That the disease, the HIV virus, mutated into a form never witnessed or conceived of before." She pointed a trembling hand at the glass. "What we're looking at in there could only be the result of airborne transmission—spread of the contagion no longer limited to sexual or blood contact. The residents of Beaver Falls caught AIDS from Frye's test group merely by breathing or touching."

Karen backed up and turned away from Wareagle as she continued.

"The whole basis of Van Dyne's—Frye's—vaccine is a

genetically disposed protein coating that traps the HIV virus and prevents its cells from spreading. Starved for sustenance, they eventually die. That was the essence of the vaccine: Train the body to defend itself against HIV and give it the weapons it needs. In Frye's original plan that protein coating would dissolve after a number of years, thereby freeing the cells to infect the host with HIV. But not only did that coating dissolve long before it was supposed to, it also appears that it released a mutated and infinitely more virulent strain of the disease." She turned back to the isolation ward, stretching her hands upward but holding them there as if afraid to touch the glass. "The results of which we're now looking at."

"They were studying this in the labs downstairs," Wareagle reflected.

Her eyes stayed on the glass. "That's for certain."

"Gone now," Johnny continued, "because their work was finished. Because they found what they were looking for."

Karen looked at him, thinking briefly of the set of pliable test tubes left in the lab downstairs. "The mutant strain . . ."

He nodded. "They found the means to concentrate it first, then the means to—"

"*Release it!*" Karen completed. "The means to achieve widespread infection without the mass inoculation Frye was counting on! And that—"

She stopped when Wareagle spun suddenly toward the spiral stairwell. His eyes remained riveted upon it as he spoke.

"Someone's coming."

McCracken was standing only a yard from the screen now, mentally cataloging each of the sites enclosed by a black circle. They were all hotels located in the downtown district and outskirts of a single city:

San Antonio, Texas.

The bold red box from which the connecting line originated in the northwest, though, was etched within the city of Boerne. McCracken had to move right up to the map to identify the specific site centered in that box as a waste-water treatment facility.

What could that possibly have to do with the circled hotels?

Water, it had to have something to do with water. . . .

Blaine felt himself shiver slightly as he began to comprehend Harlan Frye's revised plan. It must involve contaminating the water supply of San Antonio, a convention center that often catered to tens of thousands of guests from all over the country and world at one time. In small print, the circles also contained numbers ranging from the high hundreds to the low thousands: the total number of guests expected at each hotel over a period of several weeks, no doubt, commencing sometime in the near future. McCracken did some quick addition of the numbers in the fifty or so circles. He stopped counting when the sum had stretched to nearly a hundred thousand.

And they would all drink the water.

Blaine's mind continued to speed ahead of him. Somehow Harlan Frye must have come up with a way to poison the water extracted from sewage in Boerne before it was discharged back into the system. Once the treated water was discharged, it would seep into the Edwards Aquifer, from which the entire city—and therefore all of those hotels—drew its supply. Since Frye's original plan had failed, he was going to infect a hundred thousand visitors to San Antonio with the disease, thereby using them as unwitting carriers.

But something was missing. Under that scenario, the contagion process would be much too slow to suit Frye. Nothing like what widespread distribution of his bogus vaccine would have accomplished. So there was more; there had to be.

McCracken turned his attention back to the map. The Reverend's entire plan depended mostly on one element and one location for its success. If McCracken was able to—

"It's beautiful, isn't it, Mr. McCracken?" Harlan Frye asked him from the rear of the theater.

He started to turn slowly, his drawn SIG-Sauer swinging with him and ready to fire. McCracken twisted his shoulders in a quick burst at the end, aiming.

At nothing. No one was there.

"Come now," said the Reverend Harlan Frye, "you didn't expect me to make it that easy for you, did you? Drop the gun now, Mr. McCracken. My men respond well to orders, but even I may not be able to control their nervousness at a moment like this."

They appeared from the darkened rear corners of the theater, three on each side, well spread and well armed. Blaine's eyes searched for Frye and still couldn't find him.

"With God on your side, Reverend, what do you need with common soldiers?"

"To help me in pursuit of His work. Help me remove the final obstacles thrust in my way. The gun, please. Now."

The SIG hit the floor with a thud.

"Much better. Now, make sure you continue to let my men see your hands. You have made for a worthy challenge, Mr. McCracken, but one my foresight has allowed me to overcome, just as it has so many others."

McCracken left his hands in view, the remote control device he still possessed tucked halfway up his sleeve. "You were expecting me, then."

"I allowed myself to briefly believe you had been killed at the Oasis because I wanted to believe it. But I feared all along you had escaped the explosion because a man like you can walk through flames and feel not their heat."

"I'm not much for walking on water, though. You mastered that one yet, Reverend?"

"I knew you would be coming here. I knew it was my destiny to face you as one last challenge before the way is cleared to my ultimate destiny. As soon as I was informed someone was inside the theater, I knew it was you. I have already dispatched men to find those who accompanied you."

"I came alone."

"Please do not insult me. A man like yourself is as good at keeping others alive as he is at surviving himself."

"Precisely what brought me here."

"Unfortunate since I know that trail as well as you. I've walked it my entire life to get to the destination I am about to attain."

"Keeping others *alive*?" Blaine raised, with a strain of incredulity plain in his voice.

"Keeping *mankind* alive. Mine is the only way. It is God's way, Mr. McCracken. I don't expect you to fully understand that or believe it. Your abilities are impressive, but your emotions are crude and primitive." Frye's voice turned almost sad. "Quite a shame, considering we fight the same enemies: greed, injustice, immorality."

"Our methods are considerably different, Reverend, and I'm the last one with a right to judge anyone's morality."

"So my research about you indicated. I must say I found it fascinating. I find *you* fascinating."

McCracken continued to scan the room. Not spotting Frye, he began to think he was speaking from another room altogether. He kept the remote control device within easy grasp up his sleeve. "I wish I could say likewise, Reverend. Trouble is, massacring innocent people makes you about as loathsome a sort as I've ever run into."

"You speak of the events at the Oasis, no doubt."

Blaine made sure Frye could see him cock his eyes toward the map of San Antonio. "Not just there."

"Circumstances mandated my actions at the Oasis, just as far more overreaching circumstances mandated the destiny I have been chosen to bring about. All great causes require sacrifices, I'm afraid."

"How many sacrifices, Reverend? A world's worth?"

"If necessary, yes."

"And it *is* necessary, isn't it?"

"You, better than anyone, should know that it is," Frye said, with what sounded like regret in his voice. "The battles you have fought, the rampant decay you have been unable to check. You plug holes in a dam I seek to remake from scratch over a world flooded by its own excesses and hate. There is no other choice, Mr. McCracken. If there was, I would welcome it."

"As judged by you, of course."

"By God, Mr. McCracken. I am His messenger just as Jesus was, and Moses before him. I am the instrument of the delivery of His chosen destiny."

"Getting tough to tell yourself apart from Him, isn't it?"

"But we were talking about *you*, Mr. McCracken."

"Boring subject."

"Not to me," said the Reverend Harlan Frye. "I've dedicated my life to saving souls. But you, you are one of those rare individuals who found the strength to save his own. I know what you evolved from. I know what you evolved into. Your dedication, your belief, your loyalty . . . You exemplify everything I hold dear. But you, like all classic heroes, see yourself able to do more than any man can. If you could save all the world at once, you would do it, would you not?"

"Like I said," Blaine said flatly, "that's what I'm here for."

The Reverend Harlan Frye sighed. "And still you bicker, still you doubt. Even if you stopped me, Mr. McCracken, the world wouldn't be saved—only the lives of those who are determined to bring it down. The tragedy of your life lies in that dichotomy. You fight to save those whose existence perpetuates the need for you to fight again and again. Truly tragic."

"Is this the part where you ask me to sign up and I say no, Reverend?"

"I wouldn't belittle you with such a request. You and I are too much alike to coexist peacefully. You know it and I know it."

"You've got that much right."

"I felt I owed you this much. That is why I spared you this long. I wanted you to hear, to *see*."

"See what?"

"Watch," said Harlan Frye, as the theater lighting dimmed slightly and a new image replaced that of the map of San Antonio on the screen.

Rachel could not believe the pain. The monster had torn her insides up with a blade and, while she lay there, he leaned over grinning and sliced off her hair to the scalp. Left her for dead and melted away after her brother.

Jacob, Jacob . . .

She tried to call out to him and failed. Where was the walkie-talkie? Rachel tried to remember. It was no use. She could save him if she could make herself move, drag herself along in the monster's wake.

Rachel began to do just that, pulling with one hand while the other did its best to hold her ruptured innards in place.

Find her brother, save her brother . . .

Time lost meaning and then direction. She felt as though she were floating. Then she heard the sudden burst of rounds from Jacob's Mac-10. A single burst, that was all.

"Jacob," she tried to call, but barely a whisper emerged. "Jacob . . ."

The next sound Rachel heard was a maniacal giggle. She knew it was over, knew Earvin Early had killed her brother after he had just missed killing her.

She stopped moving and rested her mangled body against a shack, wanting to close her eyes and for it to be over. But some instinct made her raise her eyes to a sign posted upon the shack:

DANGER!
HIGH VOLTAGE TRANSFORMER!

This shack, she realized, must hold one of the kingdom's central power junctions. With the last of her strength, Rachel managed to pull an explosive charge from her pack. No way she could push it accurately into place. No way she could do anything but press herself against the building, wedging the *plastique* in between her body and the foundation. The pressure-activated detonator was automatically set to the two-minute mark.

Rachel used every ounce of her remaining strength to hold herself against the building.

McCracken had intended to use his remote control device as soon as the lighting dimmed, but the images unfolding on the screen stopped him. He wanted to watch, *needed* to watch.

He recognized Beaver Falls instantly. The shot of Main Street was slightly shaky, picturing the town in its last throes of normalcy. Then the scene changed to a shot of a long line of white, windowless buses rolling into Beaver Falls one after the other. The angle from another camera turned on dozens of armed figures in contamination suits fanning through the center of town, toward the business establishments along the main drag and the school at the street's end. The residents were herded into the buses at gunpoint, prodded along like cattle. The camera's shifting angles caught none of their faces long enough to see the terror they must have felt.

The suited figures were continuing their sweep through the town when Frye spoke. "I wanted you to witness the beginning, Mr. McCracken. Of course, at the point this film was being made, I thought it was the end. Strange, isn't it, how curses become blessings. When I learned of the fate that had befallen Beaver Falls, I thought I was beaten. But it was merely the Lord's means of showing me a better way."

Blaine turned halfway to the theater's rear and eased the remote control device into his hand. "San Antonio, Reverend?"

"Those who come to the city will depart as His unwitting messengers."

"While you and however many others you can squeeze in wait down here to reclaim a world turned wasteland."

"We won't have to wait down here at all. And we won't have to squeeze anywhere."

McCracken could sense the smile beneath Frye's voice. And then he realized.

"Karen Raymond's vaccine, Lot 35 . . ."

"Very good, Mr. McCracken. My faith in you is restored. She could have saved us much trouble and allowed us to save far more of our brethren had she simply turned the formula over. No matter. Our scientists are collating the material salvaged from her lab. In good time we will regenerate Lot 35. A few months, a year at most."

"Inspired."

"Yes, inspired by God and given His blessing."

"Time I gave you one of my own."

Blaine pressed the OFF button on the remote control. Instantly the picture on the screen before him died, plunging the theater into total darkness.

"Shoot him! Shoot him!" Frye screamed.

Bullets from the gunmen he had stationed through the back of the theater rained down almost instantly, but not before McCracken propelled himself up and into the white screen itself. The flimsy material tore under his forward thrust and he rolled beneath the wave of bullets that followed him through the fabric. Momentum carried him to a hatchway built into the stage and he yanked it open to reveal a ladder. He thrust his feet down and began a rapid descent that ended in a large storage room equipped with a single door. Blaine flung it open and burst into a corridor on what must have been the first sublevel.

Pursuit would be closing already, from in front as well as behind him. He had bought himself a bit of time, but weaponless, there was little he could accomplish. McCracken was considering the few options he had when suddenly the corridor was plunged into dead-silent darkness, even the soft whir of the building's air system gone.

The kingdom's power had died.

Karen Raymond waited for Johnny Wareagle to tell her they were safe before moving. Only a few minutes earlier, when Johnny had detected the footsteps approaching the level below, Karen had spotted white protective suits and helmets hanging on the side wall. After each had pulled one on, Johnny's very tight on his massive frame, Karen activated his oxygen supply as well as her own and then led the way into the isolation ward holding the residents of Beaver Falls.

As they expected, the guards who stormed up the stairs seconds later did not dare enter the ward to search for them. Their cursory check through the glass didn't reveal Johnny and Karen in their concealed positions beneath unused beds.

"They're gone," he said, voice muffled behind the faceplate of his helmet.

Karen rose from her perch near the big Indian in the isolation ward's rear and fell in step behind him back toward the entry doors. Outside the ward again, they removed their helmets and stripped off the suits.

"What now?" Karen asked him.

"They will be after Blainey as well."

"So?"

"We have what we came for. We must find him. Then—"

The lighting died suddenly, totally.

"Frye," Karen muttered.

"No," corrected Wareagle, "the twins."

"But—"

She felt his powerful grasp close on her arm.

"Let's go."

And then the Indian was leading her down the stairs through the blackness.

* * *

McCracken blessed what could only be the work of the twins and continued down the pitch-black corridor, pressing himself against the wall for support and bearings. To a great extent the darkness neutralized the advantage of familiarity his pursuers had of these halls. Blaine snaked his way forward in search of the first stairwell that would take him upstairs, where he hoped to find Johnny Wareagle and Karen Raymond.

As he hoped, the end of the hall gave way to a staircase. Blaine grasped the railing and climbed upward.

Wareagle heard the single set of steps coming toward Karen and him from below when they reached the first floor on the staircase Johnny had found. A small glass plate in a nearby exit door allowed thin slivers of light to pass through from outside. The light helped him find the door to the stairwell.

"Blainey," he called softly, after opening it.

"Figured I'd be running into you soon, Indian."

Johnny handed him one of his submachine guns, a British Sterling with collapsible stock. "There is much to tell."

Flashlights pierced the darkness at the top of the staircase Johnny and Karen had just descended. Wareagle and McCracken spun toward the beams simultaneously, waited for them to begin a wobbly descent, and then fired into the source of the light. The beams rolled wildly, flashlights stripped from the grasp of their holders. The magnified sounds of their shots echoed and reechoed in the confined stairwell.

"More will be coming, Blainey."

"Best not to wait for them, Indian," McCracken followed, and threw his shoulder into the exit door.

The solar-powered gaseous lighting strung from the sandstone mine's roof had not been affected by the power failure. The illumination allowed some of the waiting gunmen to greet them with a hail of automatic fire. Wareagle countered with a token burst and then ducked back inside. Blaine resealed the door and the darkness returned instantly, save for what little light could sneak through the glass plate at face level. Johnny, meanwhile, spun partway back up the stairwell, expecting another attack from that angle any second. Karen Raymond pressed her shoulders against the near wall, frozen with fear.

"Not a great place to make a stand," McCracken whispered.

When none of the Reverend's soldiers appeared on the stairwell, Johnny edged back down. "Give me twenty minutes, Blainey."

"To do what?"

"Acquire us a taxi."

CHAPTER 35

There was no time to elaborate further, and Wareagle
didn't bother to. McCracken waited for Johnny to take position by the door before he shouldered it ajar yet again.
He fired a burst from his Sterling into the darkness, then
stopped long enough to allow Wareagle to dash across his
field of fire. Johnny squeezed his trigger in short, con-
trolled bursts that were swiftly supplemented by Blaine's.
Their fire was returned, but they had succeeded in pinning
down the enemy and throwing them briefly on the defensive.

"Blaine!"

McCracken heard Karen's scream just ahead of a fresh
barrage of gunshots originating at the other end of the corridor where another group of Frye's guards had massed.
McCracken drained the remainder of his first clip at their
positions and then snapped home the second and final one
Johnny had given him.

"We've got to head down!" Blaine ordered, feeling for
Karen's arm to guide her.

She felt his hand find her shoulder and slide down to her elbow.

"Careful," Blaine cautioned, easing her sideways and then forward into the stairwell he had climbed moments before. "The first step should be right in front of you."

She crossed over the threshold of the top step and quickly grasped the railing with her left hand. McCracken glided down the stairs toward the first sublevel sideways, most of his attention focusing on the doorway behind them. He stopped at the bottom and drew Karen to him.

"Keep going," he whispered. "Wait for me at the bottom of the next stairwell."

"But—"

"Do it!"

Blaine heard the footsteps thundering his way from above just after Karen slid stiffly away in the darkness. He yanked from his belt one of the two grenades the twins had provided and hurled it upward. It rattled across the ground floor as Blaine pressed himself against the wall.

The explosion was dizzying, deafening, the darkness broken for that brief instant. The screams above were piercing, but brief.

"Karen," McCracken said through the ringing in his ears.

"Here," her voice called to him from halfway down the next stairwell.

He caught up and eased an arm around her shoulder. "Let's go."

Karen fell into an uneasy step beside him as they plunged deeper into the darkness.

For Johnny Wareagle, surviving the present was as simple as utilizing the past. The circle kept repeating itself; the same thing, a different place, a different time.

In the hellfire there had been minefields he had crossed more than once. The first instance, though, had been the most precarious. A pair of soldiers lay wounded and taking fire on the other side, giving Johnny no time to pick his way. He simply had to rush across the mud, trusting the spirits to choose the darts, turns, and twists required to keep him alive. On that day, twilight actually, the ground had spoken to him, the slight imperfections and ridges betraying the planting sites of the mines.

Dashing across the enemy machine guns' field of fire today was much the same. His path was erratic, seemingly random, forming a nonsymmetrical zigzag. He used the shadows and places where the light was held back. The bullets never found him. Johnny fired until all three of his clips were exhausted, and discarded the Mac-10 with little regret; at this point, his muzzle flashes would serve only to alert the enemy to his position.

Wareagle knew where he was headed, just as he knew the best route there would be the one that lost his pursuit in the process. Here, too, Johnny trusted his instincts, his mind like a supercomputer that, once programmed, would get him to his destination without requiring further consideration. The route he took brought him to the mine's edges, where the darkness was most pronounced.

Along the way he came upon a double row of trucks and cars parked within what looked like a darkened alcove. Two of the cars were limousines, leading Johnny to realize that Harlan Frye must have had another route constructed to allow nonconstruction vehicles to access the kingdom without being detected. Where, though, would the origin of such a route be? He moved between the vehicles and saw that the alcove actually extended well into the earth in the form of an underground tunnel that must spill out unnoticed into the Panhandle miles away. Accordingly, the presence of Frye's guests need never be noted entering.

Johnny spent a few precious minutes moving one of the trucks to a new location, a task he felt would come in handy later, and then continued on to the area where the truck that ferried them into the kingdom had stopped. The giant John Deere 744E loader loomed before him, its six-foot tires black against the dark scene. Its bright yellow frame reflected the light that reached it from overhead. Johnny skirted the perimeter of the open foundation for the soon-to-be-built depot center en route to the four-rung ladder that facilitated climbing up into the loader's cab. Once behind the wheel, he would head the massive machine back toward the kingdom's main building where Blaine McCracken would be waiting. Standing upon the ladder's lowest rung, he was able to reach up and grasp the door latch. It opened with a slight squeak and Wareagle started to hoist himself up the remaining rungs.

The shape waiting inside crashed into him with enough force to strip away his grasp and send him tumbling backward. The stink that flooded his nostrils was the first indication of the identity of the shape searching for firm purchase on him now. Both of them plunged downward for the gravel below, Johnny's eyes locked on the evilly grinning face of Earvin Early.

The Reverend Harlan Frye had taken refuge in his private office, escorted there by the six guards who had lost their chance at McCracken when he plunged through the screen just seconds before the whole of the kingdom lost its power. Frye had tripped the breaker in order to force the electronic door to his office open, but there was no way to get it closed again. The guards had remained with him in its stead, forming a human wall that provided the Reverend virtually no comfort whatsoever.

Major Osborne Vandal appeared in the doorway, letting part of his flashlight's beam find his face for identification.

"Reverend?"

Frye turned his flashlight in the direction of the voice. "Come in. Be quick about it."

"We have found the source of the blackout, sir," Vandal reported after entering. "A transformer was blown in the western sector of the kingdom. Fortunately we were able to contain the resulting fire. The remains of a body were found in the same vicinity."

"A body?"

"Tentatively identified as one of the Turgewell twins. Traces of a second body were found in the area of the transformer."

"Early," Harlan Frye realized, feeling suddenly hopeful. "It must have been. . . ."

"I'm afraid there's no sign of him, sir."

"You misunderstand me, Major. Early is out there, and he is to be the instrument of our deliverance, he *alone*. You must find him and bring him here."

"We are trying, sir. In the meantime we are also working to bypass the blown transformer and reroute power to this building."

"What about the guards I requested?"

"I have stationed an additional dozen along this hallway and two at the doors to all stairwells and elevators leading onto it."

"Take charge of them yourself, Major."

"With all due respect, sir, I—"

"You fool! Do you think if McCracken wants to get me, all your guards would be enough to stop him? . . . They wouldn't. I'm not sure a thousand would be sufficient. Until Early is found, I want you to take personal charge."

In the years of the hellfire and beyond, Johnny Wareagle had never felt a strength like that of the man over him. Impact on the thankfully soft ground hammered the Indian's insides, enough of the brunt taken on his side to be absorbed by what were now severely bruised ribs. He rolled, trying to seize the advantage from Early before the manmonster could bring the full force of his strength to bear. For an instant Johnny was actually on top, until a pair of meat-claw hands found the soft flesh of his throat, thumbs maneuvering into killing position. Johnny twisted with all his force and tore free of the grasp. He rolled away gasping and turned back.

Early was gone. Wareagle lunged to his feet and swung to the right.

Early stood there, head cocked slightly forward like a

stalking predator. Waiting, only the broad outline of his bulk clearly visible in the thin light from above. But Johnny's sharp eyes recorded the bearded, mangled countenance dominated by his one bulging eye and recalled the tale of Early's encounter with a motorcycle gang's pit bulls. The bandages upon his arms had unraveled and dangled in the dark air to the ground, revealing thick, oozing sores that seemed to pulsate. His breathing sounded labored, hissing when it passed through his hideously swollen upper lip.

The monster carried the feel of recent death on him, fresh blood from the kill worn over his person like a pelt. It showed in his one functioning eye as well. The twins, Wareagle realized. Early must have found them well before they had finished laying their explosives, the charges they had managed to set sure to be deactivated by now. The kingdom would no longer be falling; escape was all Johnny could hope for. But escape—saving Blainey and Karen Raymond—meant getting past Early.

The man-monster exploded forward, a rusty knife in his hand glinting faintly in the dim light. Johnny managed to deflect the blow at the last, and the blade clanged against the frame of the giant payloader. Wareagle slammed his free hand twice into the side of the decaying face even with his own, but Early grunted away the pain and slashed sideways with his blade.

The swipe caught Johnny across the chest and pushed a thick streak of blood through his clothes. Johnny backpedaled and arched his spine to avoid the next slash. Earvin Early's mad, rotten toothed grin widened as he kept advancing, the knife swiping ahead of him. Wareagle moved in perfect rhythm, a mongoose to Early's cobra. His feet struck a shallow depression in the earth, which began to drop off suddenly. Turning slightly, Johnny could see he was nearing the foundation frame for the soon-to-be storage depot. Earvin Early loomed over him as he neared the churning shape of a cement truck that had been ready to drain its contents when the power failure sent the crew

manning it, as well as all other construction workers, scurrying to find the source of the blackout.

Johnny slid under the spout, heels precariously close to
the edge of the foundation's forms. Early slowed slightly.
The rotten-toothed grin flashed again. He pounced, knife
surging inches ahead of him.

Wareagle pulled the handle that opened the cement
spigot. The gray flow captured Early and swallowed him.
Johnny saw his open mouth, gasping for air, before the
thick river took him with it down into the form, settling
and piling in rapid fashion. He gazed down into the muck
trying to see Early captured within it.

A gray-coated hand grasped his ankle and tugged. Johnny's balance was stripped away in the same instant he saw
Early's other hand clinging to the top. He fell over the side
of the forming foundation and into the leveled pit that
would become this building's basement. He staggered to
his feet and watched as the cement-encrusted shape of
Earvin Early crashed through a section of the wood and
steel foundation forms, and freed the gray flow to spill out
in his wake. The man-monster swiped his face free of the
coating that slid down the rest of his frame.

Wareagle had started toward him when Early reached
back and pulled an exposed steel support form from the
ruined section. The remnants of the wood buckled. Early
held the steel rod effortlessly overhead and lunged toward
Johnny. A stack of similar supports were laid on the
ground near the Indian's feet and he managed to get one
up just in time to block Early's wild strike.

Early whirled in again, and this time Wareagle stepped
inside the blow's force and dropped his rod into a vertical
position. There was a furious clang as steel met steel. A
numbing vibration surged up Johnny's right arm. Immediately Early brought his support up overhead and sliced
down with it. Wareagle twisted from its path and brought
his steel form down hard atop it. Before Early could react,
Wareagle jerked his weapon on an upward angle. Early
managed to turn enough to take the brunt of the blow on

his shoulder, but staggered backward, wincing briefly before the rotten-toothed grin returned to his face.

Johnny felt the steel rod's bulk starting to tell on him. He knew another blow wielded now would be too weak to bother with, so he backpedaled instead. Early held his own steel rod as if it were made of wood, looking no weaker for the effort, as blood from his mangled arms began to mix with the cement coating them, turning the color from gray to light brown.

The man-monster lashed out wildly with his support again. Wareagle ducked under the blow this time, and it slammed through a section of wooden forms on his right. Early came at him with another overhead strike that whistled by Johnny's ear and crashed through the top of the same forms. The pooling concrete began to bulge out from this second gap as well.

Early brought his rod down to waist level and began to poke it at Wareagle, toying with him and smiling through the sores festering over his face.

"One thing is certain and the rest is lies," he rasped through the saliva frothing from his mouth, quoting the *Rubaiyat* of Omar Khayyam, *"The Flower that once has blown forever dies."*

Johnny managed to deflect each of the thrusts, but the muscles in his arms were beginning to seize up. When Early mounted a quick lunge forward next, Wareagle was late with his block. The front edge of Early's support rammed him in the stomach and drove him backward. The weakened wood shattered on impact and the cement flow grabbed Johnny, parting to make a place for him. His hands lost their grasp on his support rod and it clamored to the flattened dirt surface beneath them.

When Early thrust his support savagely forward to shove him all the way into the oozing gray wall, Wareagle twisted sideways. The steel cut the air adjacent to him and sank deep into the wet concrete. Early tried to extract it, and Johnny locked both hands on the rod's shaft in what he wanted the man-monster to think was simply an effort to restrain him. Actually he was seeking to gain leverage for his legs. With that leverage gained, he kicked upward, feet scissoring together, and caught Early square in the chest. The man-monster gasped and flew backward.

His steel rod lost to the cement, he lashed out toward the advancing Wareagle with a wild flurry of blows, using both hands and feet that Johnny just managed to stay ahead of. His blocks and deflections came with the same blinding motion that Early's attacks did.

Wareagle mistimed a block and his cheek exploded in agony. Early went for the same spot again, but Johnny ducked under the blow, which shattered the top portion of another section of forms. Behind Early now, he slammed an elbow in his ribs and then threw all his force against him. Impact drove Early through the remnants of the wood and into the heightening cement, which parted to accept and then engulf him.

Johnny could feel the viscous cement pouring over his arms and face as well, but he held fast to the pressure, holding Earvin Early in the thickening flow. He took a deep breath when it reached his own face, his grip never slackening on the desperately struggling shape lost before him. Wareagle maintained his hold even after the man-monster's movement stopped and he began to sink. Johnny kept it up until his own lungs could take no more and he had to lurch away in order to clear the tumbling cement from his nose and mouth.

Woozy and dizzy, Wareagle dropped to his knees. But his eyes never left the section of forms where Earvin Early had been entombed. He waited for several moments just to be sure, and then rose to his feet as the monster's grave began to harden.

The rooms on the third sublevel were unfinished, all lacking doors and many having not been wired. Mc-Cracken and Karen had finally taken refuge in one at the midway point, equidistant between exit doors on either side of the hall.

"I've got to tell you what we found!" Karen insisted, heaving for breath when they finally came to a halt along a corridor in the darkness. "I've got to tell you what was up there in the lab!"

"Time for that later, Karen."

"What's wrong with *now*?"

"Now we get moving again." He paused. "Back to the first floor and the door where the Indian and I parted company."

"Why?"

Blaine looked at his watch. "Because that's where Johnny will be coming back for us."

The lights had just come on again in Harlan Frye's private office when Major Osborne Vandal reappeared in the doorway. Memories of Vietnam had been awakened in him again, this time the bad ones. Memories of frustration, loss, and ultimately capture. The darkness of the kingdom was too much like that of the prison camp where he had spent seven years of his life. Strangely, his bad hand had begun to throb and stiffen again.

"Sir, the repair crew dispatched to the power station reports some commotion in the area of the supply depot."

"Commotion . . . That's how they described it?"

Before Vandal could respond, his walkie-talkie began to squawk and he raised it to his ear. His eyes widened as he listened intently.

"What is it, Major? . . . Major? . . ."

"Suspend all search of the grounds!" Vandal barked into the mouthpiece. "Concentrate all troops back at central. Do you hear me? *Do you hear me?* . . . Send squads one and three to the Reverend's office. *Now!"*

"Major!" Harlan Frye demanded. "What happened out there?"

The major took a deep swallow of air before he spoke. "Early has been found, sir. . . ."

* * *

McCracken and Karen's climb had brought them one level directly beneath the exit door Johnny Wareagle would be returning to when the lighting snapped back on.

"Stay behind me," he ordered when they turned onto the final staircase.

Blaine ran swiftly up the staircase, holding the Sterling poised before him. Just over half his last clip remained. Karen followed a few steps behind.

"Down!" he screamed when a burst of footsteps stormed their way.

Blaine never stopped, firing the last of his bullets on the move. A half dozen men were cut down in the rush that left him only a single grenade to fight back with.

"Let's go," he said to Karen, and tossed the Sterling away.

She didn't hesitate, trusting his judgment and side-stepping the bodies without a second thought. They reached the ground floor, to be greeted by a barrage from an ambush team stationed just down the corridor. Blaine shoved Karen behind the cover of his body and hurled his last grenade in the direction of the gunfire. They reached the exit door in the wake of the deafening explosion and pressed against its steel. Blaine had bought the two of them some time, but there was no more to be had at any price and nowhere to go in any event.

"Blaine," Karen Raymond started. "I think I hear some—"

McCracken pushed himself back against the door, hearing it too. He peered out through the glass plate in the exit door that had been shattered by one of the grenade blasts.

And saw the giant John Deere loader steaming their way, its sharp-toothed shovel extended straight out before it.

Wareagle slammed the 744E through the wall to the right of the door where he had left McCracken, teeth slicing through the frame effortlessly. The loader's unique electric downshift allowed him to shift instantly from second to first to attain the traction he needed. Blaine anticipated Wareagle's strategy in time to yank Karen safely away from the expected shower of rubble. The shovel continued its neat slice across the body of the main building of the kingdom, Johnny working the wheel to bring the cab up even with the exact spot he expected McCracken to be. For the last stretch the 744E ran half in and half out of the building. Its shovel tore aside everything in its path. Its massive tires rolled over whatever dropped before them. The loader ground to a halt, engine still revving, and Wareagle leaned across the front seat to throw open the door on the passenger side.

Blaine boosted Karen up the ladder and lunged after her as quickly as possible, shoving her rigid frame through the open side door. Bullets trailed them the last stretch of the way, clanging off the steel rungs and drawing dangerously close in the final moments that saw Karen Raymond reach cramped safety behind the operator's seat, where Wareagle was.

The loader's windshield exploded, forcing Johnny to duck beneath the dashboard as Blaine closed the passenger door behind him and squeezed into the cab next to the Indian. The interior smelled mustily of damp cement, and Blaine gazed up to see Johnny's frame encased in a crackling layer of gray, making him look like a statue that had broken free of its bonds.

The passenger-side window exploded into shards as automatic rounds burned into it. Johnny instantly banked the loader to the left, tearing out another huge chunk of the wall as it made its break. Gunfire continued to pepper its frame and tires, to no avail. The 744E pulled away from the building and thumped onto the unpaved street.

"What now, Indian?" Blaine asked, still squeezed next to him in a crouch beside the shot-out passenger-side window.

"We complete our escape."

With that, Wareagle flipped a switch marked POWER BOOST into the on position. Almost immediately 250 horsepower kicked in, and Johnny shifted from second into third, working the floor pedals madly.

"The twins?" Blaine raised.

Johnny shook his head somberly. "Early," was the Indian's only spoken reply.

McCracken felt honest regret. "I assume the favor's been returned."

"That circle is complete, Blainey."

"And the explosives?"

"Early found the charges; I'm sure of it."

"So how do we get out?"

"I'll show you."

McCracken saw the dark alcove in the mine wall just before Wareagle barreled the John Deere 744E right into the line of vehicles jammed before it. He had lowered the shovel to slightly above ground level, and it swept them into each other with barely any resistance as it cleared a path for itself. The ride ended when Johnny wedged the shovel's teeth tight into the far tunnel wall. The result was to place the loader diagonally across the only entrance to the secret tunnel, effectively blocking any other vehicles from entering it in their wake. McCracken watched Johnny strip the ignition wires free, rendering the 744E inoperable until time-consuming repairs were carried out.

"Must be a long walk back to the surface, Indian," Blaine realized.

"I pulled one of the supply trucks parked in the entrance farther down into the tunnel for us, Blainey."

McCracken smiled at Johnny, no more amazed than usual. "Then let's get the hell out of here, Indian."

CHAPTER 36

The drive up the darkened ramp was broken only by the spread of the truck's headlights. Blaine had taken the wheel. Johnny's eyes never left the truck's rear on the chance that Frye's guards had somehow managed to follow them into the tunnel. Karen Raymond, breathing somewhat easier, was wedged between them in the cab, far more comfortable than squeezed behind the operator's station in the John Deere.

The tunnel banked into its steepest rise yet and Mc-Cracken saw the blackened end of it opening like a huge mouth. An electronic eye must have triggered the mechanism automatically, saving them the trouble of ramming their way through or tripping the wires.

"I've figured out what happened in Beaver Falls," Karen said, after the truck had thumped onto a hardened dirt roadbed. Their hope was that somewhere up ahead it would join Route 287 through the plains of the Panhandle. "I think I know everything now."

McCracken turned and looked at her.

"It's worse than I thought," she continued, "worse than I could have imagined. Frye's test subjects weren't the only ones infected by AIDS in Beaver Falls; the *whole* town was infected!"

McCracken's gaze tightened.

Karen stole a swift look at Wareagle. "We saw what was left of the town in an isolation ward above the kingdom's laboratory. There were beds full of residents who'll be dead in a matter of days, if not hours."

"Of *AIDS*?" Blaine asked, knowing that ran counter to everything known of the disease.

Karen nodded slowly. "When Frye's scientists tampered with the disease's genetic makeup, they laid the foundation for its mutation beyond a strictly blood-borne virus, into one that is water-borne or droplet-spread."

"As in *air*?"

"Air, touching, breathing, mucous membranes—almost anything."

Blaine slowed the truck. "The AIDS virus being spread like the yearly strain of flu . . . But it's not the AIDS virus as we know it now."

"Not at all. The residents of Beaver Falls didn't just begin showing signs of AIDS prematurely; they began showing *advanced symptoms* of the disease within a matter of days after being evacuated. Three or four years of immune system breakdown in barely that many days."

"That explains it."

"Explains what?"

"The Reverend Frye is planning to poison the city of San Antonio's water supply, Dr. Raymond. And all the people who visit the city in the month or so after are going to leave with the disease in their systems. Infected by drinking the water."

"His scientists must have used what happened in Beaver Falls to create an extremely concentrated version of his 'vaccine,' " Karen responded, trying very hard still to sound professional.

Blaine was nodding. "To be introduced through a wastewater treatment facility in Boerne, which discharges its purified water into the aquifer that provides San Antonio with its drinking supply."

"Why San Antonio?"

"Because the city's one of the convention capitals of the country, Doctor. I'm surprised you were never invited to one for research and development types."

"I think I was, actually. I didn't go."

"Plenty of other people do, from every state and plenty of countries. A hundred thousand in the next month. And instead of bringing home presents, they return with a time bomb stuck in their system."

"If Beaver Falls is an accurate indication, it will take six months for the contagion to begin its spread. After that, everyone the carriers come into contact with become carriers themselves." She shook her head. "Frye's followers included. It makes no sense."

"It does if a large number, even a majority, of those followers can be protected."

"But there's no way they—" Karen felt herself grow strangely calm. She squeezed her eyes shut. "Lot 35 . . . That's why Frye needed it. . . ."

"Within six months he may well have figured out your formula, Dr. Raymond."

"Thereby salvaging the original intent of his plan. He'll only need to produce enough of Lot 35 to supply the chosen followers of the Seven." Karen's mouth sank, her face going dreadfully pale. "My God, I'm a party to what he's done. I *helped* him."

"Karen—"

"Wait! There's something else!" Her mind was working feverishly, churning information both new and old at a desperate clip. "There's something else. Frank McBride, the man Wayne Denbo found by the roadside, was inside the isolation ward," she explained. "That means Denbo might have become a carrier, along with everyone else he in turn came into contact with. You see what I'm saying."

"No."

"The disease may *already* be spreading. Frye's divine function may be playing itself out without him doing another damn thing."

"But you're not sure."

"No. It would depend on when McBride actually contracted the disease. It could have been after he had been placed with the others. But if not . . ."

"Go on, Doctor."

Karen swallowed hard. "We were around Denbo, too. All of us. We could be infected. We could be carriers. And there could be hundreds more, thousands by now. Ten times that many by tomorrow."

McCracken remained maddeningly composed, his voice flat and precise. "You're saying Judgment Day might already be inevitable."

"No, there's another way we can stop it," Karen said, sounding sure, "a way we can reverse the process. Frye's bogus vaccine works on the genetic level by teaching the body to recognize and effectively imprison HIV cells. But remember, his protein coating was programmed to erode over time. Change that genetic programming and the cells remain trapped."

"Are you saying you could change it?"

"If not me, someone with more expertise in this specific field. But they'd need a sample."

"And there's only one sample we know about for sure, and Frye's got it."

Karen nodded. "A sample he plans to release into San Antonio's water supply." She recalled the test tube she had found within the Kingdom of the Seven's lab. "Using a dissolvable test tube."

"Which means the Indian and I have to do more than just stop Frye from dropping his poison into the wastewater treatment center in Boerne: We've also got to come up with this test tube."

"I'm afraid so."

McCracken's expression wavered just a little as he gave the truck more gas. "I'm afraid, too."

* * *

"You assured us McCracken was dead!" Jessie Will ranted, speaking for all four of the men seated before the Reverend Harlan Frye.

For reasons not yet explained to them, Frye was holding the meeting in his private theater. He addressed his audience standing directly before the screen that had been ripped and torn when McCracken plunged through it.

"I erred and I admit that," the Reverend conceded. "I saw the tapes of the explosions. I responded with my head instead of my heart because my heart told me that McCracken is somehow blessed. He couldn't have survived in his world as long as he has if he wasn't. Only one of equal purpose can defeat him."

"You mean kill?" Tommy Lee Curtisan elaborated.

Frye looked dismayed by his use of the word. "His previous opponents have made the mistake of attempting to do just that. But in doing so, they place themselves in the world he has mastered. No, defeating him means accepting his presence but believing in the sanctity of our mission over that of his in God's eyes."

"Well, God seems to have been about as unable to stop him as we've been," Tommy Lee Curtisan said almost whimsically, behind the slightest of smiles. "We're beat, Reverend. Now, I'm not laying the blame with you and I'm not saying you're not worthy. But it's plain as day that we got to wait a time before we put your plan into effect."

"And the rest of you," Harlan Frye raised, "do you echo these words?" He looked at the other three members of the Seven. None of them could meet his gaze. "Your vision has been corrupted, my brothers. You stand to be defeated by something far more powerful than Blaine McCracken: your loss of faith. Don't you see what's going on here? The Lord would *never* trust the destiny of His world to anyone whose faith was not absolute. Let yours waver now and you risk losing His grace as well as your place in the kingdom."

"This isn't about faith," said Curtisan. "This is about reality."

"And all reality is based on our obligation to the Lord. Leave here now if you wish to shirk yours, but do not expect me to cower before mine." Frye paused and looked each one of them in the eye. "Think of the shape of the world as we evisioned it," he continued. "Think of your role within it. Are you willing to forsake that now, to concede that you were never worthy to enter this kingdom?"

"McCracken knows where the kingdom is," Louis W. Kellog reminded. "He will return here or send others in his place. They will destroy everything we have built, everything that is so crucial to the fulfillment of our vision."

"Perhaps they will," Frye conceded. "And if we dwell on the material, then we will lose sight of what is truly important: serving Him by fulfilling our destiny."

"McCracken will be waiting for us in San Antonio, Reverend," Jessie Will said flatly. "We have entered *his* kingdom now. Do we dare believe ourselves capable of battling at this level, no matter how many guns and guards accompany us?"

"Indeed we can believe it, brother," Frye assured them, "but only if we believe our purpose to be more resolute and our resolve to be stronger than his. As soon as we delay or defer, we truly enter his realm where desperation fuels defeat and despair." He paused and let them see the confidence brimming in his eyes. "But there is a way we can keep McCracken from interfering, while at the same time letting the whole country witness our blessed work, so those who are worthy might understand what they are to be a part of."

"Whole *country*?" raised Jessie Will.

"Witness?" followed Tommy Lee Curtisan.

"Let me show you," Frye told them, and stepped away from the screen.

"They didn't make it," McCracken said upon noting the distant look on Sister Barbara's face that followed her realization that Jacob and Rachel had not returned to the Amarillo motel room with the others.

She digested the recounting of all that had transpired and then demanded that McCracken tell her exactly how the twins had died. Blaine deferred to Johnny Wareagle here, who was typically brief in his tale.

"I must go to their father," Sister Barbara said when he was finished. "He must hear of this from me personally."

"Spoken like a person who feels responsible for their deaths," Blaine responded.

"I refused Turgewell's overtures. I wouldn't help him destroy the Seven when I clearly should have. And now, because of that, his children are dead. Senselessly. Needlessly."

"I don't think you knew them as well as I did, Sister."

"That doesn't matter."

"I think it does, because they weren't in your world anymore and hadn't been for some time; they were in mine. That's where they wanted to be."

"But they were merely *children*!"

"Raised by Turgewell to be his soldiers, not his heirs. They grew up in an environment of hate and desperation."

"Your world," Sister Barbara followed flatly, in what had started as a question.

"It's what I am, Sister. It's what the twins were. You didn't make them that way, and you can't blame yourself for their deaths."

"What about the deaths of my followers at the Oasis? Am I to shrug off responsibility for them as well?"

"You couldn't have known Frye would go that far."

"Oh, but I did, and have for some time. I thought myself above it. I foolishly believed faith would be enough to hold him at bay, perhaps even defeat him. It never is, is it?"

"Not in my world, Sister."

"Is there room for vengeance in your world, Mr. McCracken?"

Blaine nodded. "Biblical *and* otherwise."

"Frye must be stopped."

"I think he may have provided us with the opportunity," said Johnny Wareagle suddenly.

"What do you mean, Indian?"

"That."

Johnny's single-word response was punctuated by a finger aiming at the muted television screen where a commercial featuring the Reverend Harlan Frye himself had just begun playing.

"I'll be damned," muttered McCracken.

The commercial had ended by the time Johnny turned up the volume, but they'd seen everything they needed to.

"He's one bold son of a bitch," Blaine continued. "I'll give him that much."

"And that may be what allows us to destroy him, Blainey," Wareagle put forth. "We fear Frye because he can convince himself and others that anything he does, no matter how destructive, is God's will. But that very arrogance leads him to believe he is invincible. He won't care if we show up in Boerne or not. His plan is meant to take our presence into account."

"Why bother with this whole charade at the treatment plant, anyway?" Blaine wondered. "Why not just dump his poison into the water system in San Antonio itself?"

Karen Raymond looked up from a guidebook she'd purchased in a store on the way here. "Because there isn't one. San Antonio has no centralized water treatment facility per se. Instead it relies on dozens of individual wells to pull the water up from the Edwards Aquifer."

"Which is what the Reverend plans on contaminating."

She nodded. "Almost as simple as draining the contents of his test tube into the purified water at the Boerne treatment center before it's discharged into Civolo Falls, which drains into the aquifer."

"You said 'almost.' "

"Because Frye needs a catalyst to saturate the entire system in a relatively rapid time frame."

"What do you mean by catalyst?"

"Something his toxin can bond to in order to spread." Karen sighed. "It could be anything, or some combination of things."

"But it would have to be connected somehow to water, something he knows is already present in the supply."

"The possibilities are endless."

"Narrow them down for us, Doctor."

"Well, that test tube I found in the kingdom's lab was made of gelatin-plastic compound made to dissolve slowly in water."

"So?"

"So that indicates Frye doesn't want his toxin to actually be released until it's inside the system. It means the toxin must be light- or even heat-sensitive, and that means he can't risk releasing it into the treatment process before the final stage."

"Which is . . ."

Karen Raymond's eyes widened. "Chlorination! Of course! *Of course!*" Excited now, barely able to keep her words up with her racing thoughts. "Frye's scientists were limited by time, as well as what was going to be available to them."

"Like chlorine," Blaine realized.

"They must have programmed his toxin to require exposure to it in order to become active. And once that exposure takes place, the toxin will expand a millionfold, easily enough to infest the entire system."

"But chlorine dissipates. Otherwise we'd taste it in every glass."

"Microscopic, virtually immeasurable levels remain present in every glass. Safe under ordinary circumstances."

"But under these circumstances, assuring that everyone who takes a drink will become infected."

Karen was still thinking. "If Frye is able to somehow introduce his toxin into the stage of the treatment process in which chlorine gets injected, he'd be able to saturate the system as soon as the poisoned discharge reaches the aquifer."

"What do you mean by 'stage'?"

"There are three basic stages in the treatment of waste-water. You start with sludge and extract the water, which is filtered and then treated. Chlorination is part of the last stage before the final product is released back into the system."

"But Frye needed this dissolvable test tube because exposure to heat or light would likely destroy the toxin if he simply poured it into the tank."

"Yes," Karen acknowledged. "You're learning. He has to make sure the toxin isn't released until the treatment water has already begun its journey underground."

Blaine smiled faintly. "I think you just gave me an idea of how to stop him."

"Sal's on his way," Blaine reported. "Couldn't sound happier. Guess he likes to be needed." He looked at Karen. "Trouble is, we may need a lot more to pull this off. The Reverend Frye isn't likely to be fooled for very long, maybe not even long enough for us to get out of the parking lot."

"Then we need more help," Karen concluded.

"Tough to come by these days."

Karen started for the phone. "Maybe not."

"What the hell?"

David Martinez shined his flashlight at the huge clumps of asphalt resting atop the stone floor of the Alamo. When he had made his last pass through the shrine twenty minutes before, they hadn't been there. His first thought was that the unusually wet spring had soaked into the ancient walls to the point where one had cracked. Martinez had seen the magic the Alamo maintenance staff could work. By noon tomorrow it would be as good as new.

But a pass with his flashlight along the walls showed all

in the vicinity to be intact. Martinez then followed a plopping sound with his flashlight to a puddle of water rippling
with fresh droplets. But how—

Martinez turned his beam upward.

"Uh-oh."

David Martinez had been an Alamo ranger for only six
months. Being low man on the totem poll, he pulled a
great number of late night duty rotations. He much preferred the day shifts when a small measure of the three
million tourists who visit the Alamo pass through. He
liked to watch them as they strolled leisurely around the
exhibits, hovering about the various memorabilia and lingering near the painting of Davy Crockett making his last
stand.

In the quiet, dark, air-conditioned cool of what had been
built as a Spanish mission, history came to life in the
minds of the tourists, and in Martinez's. The chapel had
been built in 1744 only to be abandoned in 1762 after its
roof collapsed. The mission remained vacant until Spanish
and then Mexican troops occupied it. Rebellious Texans
seized it from Mexican hands in 1835 and a year later
made their fateful stand against Santa Ana that ended in a
fierce twenty-minute battle just after dawn on the thir-
teenth day.

Few realized, Martinez reckoned, that this chapel shrine
the rangers patrolled twenty-four hours a day was one of
only two original structures that remained from those
years, the other being the long barrack. The bulk of the
famed thirteen-day stand, in which 189 held back nearly
4,000, was fought behind long-vanished walls in a plaza
now occupied by Pizza Hut and K-Mart, among others,
stretching all the way to the Hyatt Hotel.

The restored chapel, though, was more than enough to
bring the feeling of those days back. Martinez never tired
of listening to the standard recital of the famous tale, was
still learning something new almost every day.

Not when he was pulling the graveyard shift, of course.
Nothing much happened. Ever.

Until tonight.

Martinez's flashlight had illuminated a large, jagged chasm in the Alamo's ceiling. The rain that had just started up again found easy passage through it, as more layers peeled away right before his eyes.

"Jesus," he muttered, feeling for the black walkie-talkie that linked him up to the maintenance office. "Jesus."

For the second time in its storied history, the roof of the Alamo was about to collapse.

Guns and Ammo claimed to be not only the largest retail seller of weapons in the Southwest, but also the entire country. Open twenty-four hours a day, it had supermarket-style rows that contained every handgun, rifle, and semiautomatic rifle imaginable. Special display counters featured whatever was hot, and huge bins carried cheap, bag-it-yourself target ammunition sold by weight.

A buzzer went off when T.J. Fields entered the store flanked by a Skull on either side. The proprietor had done business with the Hells Angels themselves for a time, so he knew the kind of men who were approaching the front counter and sensed a big sale.

"Morning," greeted the proprietor, a balding man with a massive belly extending well over his belt.

"Morning," returned T.J.

"Name's Carson, boys. Friends call me Car. You come to the right place. I got the best sawed-offs you ever did see, damn good buys on semiautos, and I'm running a special on the Desert Commando, biggest handgun currently available."

"I was thinking more of your private stock."

Carson's smile vanished. "Huh?"

T.J. pulled a crumpled slip of paper from his pocket and read it off like a shopping list. "Five LAW rockets, a dozen M16s, an M79 grenade launcher and ammo, two dozen hand grenades. Oh, and did I forget to mention an M60 machine gun?"

Carson's eyes shifted frantically to make sure no one else was nearby to overhear. "Are you out of your fucking mind, man? You want that kind of hardware, I got to check references. Cash or not, I never move the big stuff without knowing who I'm moving it to."

T.J.'s .45 was out of his pants and against the proprietor's forehead before he could blink. "We're friends now, Car. Make an exception."

CHAPTER 37

The Future Faith network's number one program, "Sunday Morning Service," was scheduled to be broadcast this week from the wastewater treatment facility in Boerne, thirty miles northwest of San Antonio. Since the day the cameras had caught his sermon atop the rubble of that school in Dixonville, Virginia, the Reverend Harlan Frye had made a practice of holding his service live in places least expected. The commercials advertising the fact that Boerne was next on the list had begun running throughout Texas Saturday afternoon, and Harlan Frye knew, as always, he'd be turning away more people than he could seat. By the time the Reverend got there thirty minutes prior to the 11:00 A.M. live broadcast, several thousand unfortunate but placid faithful who'd arrived too late to be seated were waiting outside the complex's chain-link fence. The crowd cheered Frye and parted respectfully to allow his limousine to snail through them up to the front gate.

The Reverend shook a few of their outstretched hands

on the way in and tousled the hair of children near his path. A touch on the shoulder soothed those who were crying, hands clasped in pleading prayer before him. They all wanted something, and Harlan Frye today was fully prepared to give them what they needed.

"Praise the Lord!" someone shouted.

"You're the greatest, Reverend!"

"Love you, Reverend!"

Before entering the complex, Frye turned and spread his arms before them triumphantly. A swell of applause and cheers rose from his followers.

His director, Stu Allison, was waiting just inside the gate alongside a short man wearing a name tag and a white hard hat.

"Everything is all set, I trust," Frye greeted, after he had stepped through the gate.

Allison shrugged. "As much as can be expected under the circumstances."

"Circumstances?" Frye raised.

The short man slid in between them. "This place wasn't exactly built with Sunday school in mind."

"Sunday *service*, Mr., er . . ." Frye read the name off the tag. "Randall."

"Nice to meet ya. I'm the plant manager, case you didn't figure that out."

The Reverend noticed Randall's nose was mashed in the center and bent to one side, like a boxer's. He seemed to be favoring his right shoulder.

"You ask me, Father, the city park 'cross the street'd be a better place to hold your service."

"It's *Reverend*," Frye corrected. "And I have my reasons."

"Yeah, I'm sure you do," said Sal Belamo. "I guess we better get to it."

The Daughters of the Republic of Texas have been custodians of the Alamo since 1905, responsible for the shrine's maintenance, upkeep, and day-to-day operations.

The four-and-a-half-acre plat lies between two major San Antonio streets, much of it enclosed by a combination of fully restored walls and black wrought-iron fences. The chapel shrine and the long barrack share the grounds with a combination museum and souvenir shop and a library that have been constructed to blend perfectly with their neighboring structures.

The chief of Alamo maintenance, Lantz Lecolt, was on the premises fifteen minutes after Bob Martinez's call had come in the night before. The repair job was under way half an hour later, but by dawn it was obvious the Alamo would not be able to open today, much to Lecolt's dismay. Christmas and Christmas Eve were the only days it was traditionally closed, and Lecolt had long prided himself on keeping the Alamo open through flood conditions, air-conditioning failures that ballooned the temperature in the chapel to a sweltering 110 degrees, and other crises.

This, though, was different.

"How bad?" asked Clara Marshall, head of the Daughters, upon returning just after ten-thirty Sunday morning.

Lecolt looked down from his perch on the recently erected scaffolding thirty feet above her. The chasm in the roof started a yard back from the chapel's front facade and ran in jagged fashion virtually its entire length.

"Bad," Lecolt shouted back, his reply drowned out by the sudden swirling of a circular saw. "But we can handle it."

In the scant few hours since he had been called, the head of maintenance and his men had already begun the process of erecting a wooden restraining structure, essentially a truss placed under the imperiled section of the roof for support. One of his crews had put the scaffolding together, while another set about constructing the individual components of the truss under bright floodlights trucked in to permit work in the dark chapel. From where he was standing, Lecolt could reach up through the chasm. He crept along, his hand exploring the jagged remnants of the ceiling. They'd have to be neatly filed down before the patching process could begin. Lecolt had already obtained the specialized equipment he was going to need before the day was out, including a sand-blaster, a portable cement mixer, and commercial-strength heat lamps to quicken the drying process.

"What caused it?" Clara yelled up to him, walking at his pace to keep up.

"Can't be sure." Lecolt stopped and leaned over. "Could be the weight of those damn air-conditioning compressors."

"Structural engineers assured us the roof could hold them."

"Hold them, sure. But the vibrations they make mighta damaged its structural integrity enough for the heavy rains to finally split it."

"You check the rest?"

Lecolt nodded. "Sound for now."

"When can we reopen?" Clara asked, dreading the answer.

"Tomorrow, if you don't mind my people livening up the place and . . ."

Another whirling saw drowned out the rest of his words. Clara Marshall waited until the sound had ceased before responding.

"Awful lot of noise to put up with."

"In two days I can have the hole patched."

Clara breathed easier. "I guess the tourists can live with it."

"Sure," Lantz Lecolt agreed. "Just tell them the hole was made by cannon fire."

As in the case of all "Sunday Morning Service" broadcasts, the logistics for today's program had been worked out by Stu Allison in advance, based on the parameters Harlan Frye gave him. This morning that meant broadcasting from inside the plant where the third and final treatment stage took place, which disinfected the aerated water with chlorine. From there the resulting purified water would be discharged into the underground casements of Civolo Falls, which drained directly into the Edwards Aquifer.

"Where have we got the congregation set up?" Frye asked, ignoring the plant manager.

"A field around to the side," Allison told him. He gestured in the field's direction, and the Reverend glimpsed the rows and rows of his faithful waiting patiently before a platform that held tower speakers in lieu of his personal presence.

"Hey," the plant manager interrupted, "you really need this many people on the grounds?"

Frye followed his gaze to the dozens of casually dressed Fifth Generation soldiers who had taken posts around and within the entire complex, according to Major Osborne Vandal's specifications. Though none of their weapons were in evidence, their presence was nonetheless noticeable and intimidating.

"We've had problems crop up at some of our other services," Frye explained. "Those men are a deterrent against anything unpleasant happening on these grounds, Mr. Randall."

"Hey, Father, I'm all for that."

Frye's face reddened as he fumed silently. "I think we can go inside now."

"Whatever you say."

The inside of the plant was more open than Frye had been expecting, a labyrinth of pipes running in all directions connecting tanks of varying sizes to each other. A glassed-in control room that looked like something more fit for NASA lay in the center of it all. Since it was Sunday, a crew of only three was at work inside, monitoring gauges and adjusting knobs and buttons. Along with the pug-nosed Bob Randall, these were the only men who seemed to be here other than his own. This surprised Harlan Frye. After all, he had the county and city of Boerne's permission in writing for this shoot and had been expecting the usual bevy of local officials desiring to partake in the festivities.

"Over here," Harlan Frye heard the plant manager say, as he led the way to the plant's largest tank, located close to the right-hand wall.

The tank rose three of the four-story height of the building, rimmed at the top and across the center by dual catwalks accessible by a steel ladder. The only place Frye could conduct his service was high atop a semicircular platform at the tank's south end where the ladder was positioned. Allison had done the best he could with the dim lighting by setting up some powerful floods upon the platform.

"Reverend."

Frye turned away from the ladder and watched Major Osborne Vandal approach him. Vandal had had the premises thoroughly searched prior to his arrival to insure that McCracken and his cohorts were not lying in wait.

"The grounds are clear, sir," he reported confidently.

"Keep the men on their guard, Major," Frye cautioned. "McCracken *will* be here—I know it. I know his tricks, how he's overcome comparable challenges before. The men posted are all in visual contact?"

"Of course, sir."

"They are required to check in at regular intervals?"

"Yes, sir."

"We'll need men in the surrounding fields, woods, and buildings—*atop* the buildings as well."

"Already taken care of, sir."

Frye looked away from Osborne Vandal and spoke to his director.

"Let's get up there, Stu."

The Reverend Harlan Frye completed his sound check at three minutes to eleven. He stood uneasily atop the grated steel platform adjacent to the chlorine-rich disinfection tank, barely able to gaze over into the clear water churning within it. The Reverend had been advised to wear goggles to prevent his eyes from being burned by the chlorine, but had discarded them because they made him look foolish and played hell with the lighting. People wanted to see his eyes, people *needed* to see his eyes. Otherwise, how could he expect them to believe? Every week the live broadcast of "Sunday Morning Service" was watched by eight million Americans, and Harlan Frye wanted them all to believe.

"On my mark," said Stu Allison, eyes on his watch. "Ten, nine, eight, seven . . ."

". . . six, five, four, three . . ."

Outside, the assistant director cued the congregation seated in the makeshift pews set in the plant's field that they were about to go on, just as Allison was cuing Harlan Frye. There would be no applause at the eleven-o'clock mark when the six cameras set up around the audience began their sweep. The participants had been told to simply do what came naturally; and since all were devoted followers of the Reverend Harlan Frye, this meant looking intently reverent and worshipful.

Allison pointed to Frye.

The assistant director pointed to the audience.

At the signal a sober, well-modulated voice filled the airwaves of America, emanating at the same time from the tower speakers set before the congregation in the field.

"Welcome to the 'Sunday Morning Service,' a presentation of the Future Faith television network. Today's service is being broadcast live from Boerne, Texas. And now, speaking for the Lord, the Reverend Harlan Frye."

Stu Allison cued Frye again, while his surrogate in the truck chose the proper close-up of the Reverend upon the platform, using the disinfection tank as a backdrop.

"Good morning, brothers and sisters, and I hope this as all Sundays finds you reflecting with family and loved ones on the successes and failures of the past week as we begin the next one. Each week is its own journey, friends, and we must strive not to submerge ourselves in regret over ground lost or become complacent over ground gained. A fresh start must be made with the coming of every Sunday, and fresh starts is what today's service is all about."

Frye started deliberately forward, Stu Allison ordering his surrogate in the truck to use the pause for a series of crowd shots. As planned, the sequence would finish with a full view of the treatment center itself that slowly pulled in on the single sign posted just outside the fence announcing what this site was. He cued the Reverend again when the sequence was complete.

"Every Sunday, brothers and sisters, the Church of the Redeemer takes its service and its message outside the walls of a traditional chapel into the world of people like yourselves. Today I speak to you from a place that symbolizes renewal; the renewal of hope out of hopelessness, of something from nothing."

Television screens across America filled with various angles and shots of the treatment center's interior, as the Reverend Harlan Frye continued.

"This facility, brothers and sisters, exists to salvage water from waste—the very essence of life from what has been discarded as refuse." He smiled slightly, confidently. "What no one wants anymore, what no one sees any need for. How symbolic, friends, for does not this describe so many of our lives? . . ."

"Amen," the congregation outside chanted, hands ringing the air, and cameras cutting to shots of it all.

"Are we not forever burdened by the wasted hours and wasted opportunities that weigh upon our lives every day?"

"Amen!" Louder.

"And so many of us never seek to salvage any part of what we have lost. We give up, we concede, convinced that nothing good can be gained from something bad."

"Amen!" The loudest yet.

Televisions across the country were now filled with

close-ups of congregation members, as the Reverend
Harlan Frye continued to speak.

"And yet this facility takes what has been discarded and
returns it to life. This facility takes what is ugly and re-
volting and squeezes, I say *squeezes*, something wondrous
and life-giving from it."

Stu Allison cut back to Harlan Frye, who had squeezed
his fingers so tight that his fists were trembling. He
stepped closer to the camera.

"On this Sunday, at today's service, I come before you
to say we must take heart in what happens in this place
that is as holy as any I have ever stood inside of."

Crowd shots again, the emotion beginning to show on
the congregation members' faces, many kneeling now at
their seats in positions of prayer.

"Instead of accepting our mistakes and our misjudg-
ments, we must recognize them and seek to take from
them, to—" back to Frye squeezing his hands once more
"—*squeeze* from them what we can so our own happiness
may be salvaged and we might find meaning where we
had thought there was none."

Harlan Frye took a deep breath and withdrew from his
pocket a test tube measuring nine inches long by one inch
in diameter and filled with a clear liquid. Knowing congregation pans and close shots were being featured, he scanned
the treatment plant's interior, still half expecting Blaine Mc-
Cracken to appear at any moment. The Reverend held the
specially formulated test tube up to the camera when the
focus returned to him. Minutes after sinking into the darkness of the tank, its contents would be released to mix with
the chlorine injected into the system. By the time the water
was discharged back into the system through another section of the plant, his poison would be spreading rampantly.
Expanding until in a few days not a single faucet in San
Antonio would be spared unleashing it.

"Brothers and sisters, this is a simple chemical called
chlorine," he lied, grasp tightened on his test tube. "Simple and yet, when dropped into the tank behind me, it

purifies the soiled water within so it can mix again in the world that tossed it aside. Purified once more, it gives life and sustains life." The Reverend took two steps closer to the camera before him on the platform. "How many who have given up on life, who have become the spiritual equivalents of the sludge the soon-to-be-cleansed water in this tank was born from, cannot believe their lives can be made clean and pure again? How many would not gulp down a magic fluid such as this were it placed within their grasp?

"But there is no magic fluid for our lives as there is for the contents of this tank." The Reverend Harlan Frye backpedaled until he was nearly against it. "There is no magic potion we can drink to soothe our ills and the wrongs of our lives." His eyes fell on the test tube grasped in his hand, the camera zooming in on it. "And yet there is a way we can do for our lives what the contents of this does for the water."

And with that, Harlan Frye reached over the edge of the holding tank and dropped the test tube in. He kept talking, barely able to discern his own words, which were spoken with a fire and intensity that represented new heights even for him. He did not lack for motivation today.

Judgment Day had dawned. The camera had recorded the precise instant for the Reverend to replay as often as he desired.

But no camera captured the moment when one of Frye's Fifth Generation soldiers forced open the door to a storage shed on the outer rim of the complex to find six fully bound and gagged shapes inside. He had passed off the incessant tapping as the sound of water draining from a leaky pipe, until he drew close enough to realize it sounded like someone inside was trying to get his attention. The tapping, it turned out, was the result of one of the captives managing to work a hammer into his bound hands and rap it against the shed's frame. He removed this man's gag first.

"Who are you?" Frye's soldier asked, still befuddled.

"Bob Randall," the man answered hoarsely, "plant manager. Now, untie my hands and tell me *what the hell is going on here!*"

All morning Karen Raymond had been holding on to the hope that the dissolvable test tube would withstand the waters long enough to deliver its contents to her intact. Otherwise, hope of stemming Frye's deadly pestilence would be lost.

She stood in the drainage ditch that had been dug just that morning in Boerne City Park across the street from the wastewater treatment facility. Her feet sloshed in the water spilling out into the ground around her through the screen Johnny Wareagle held over the severed pipe. Without being able to see Frye, or hear him clearly, they had no way of knowing that he had dropped the test tube into the tank until something plopped up against the screen wedged against the pipe.

Johnny Wareagle pulled the screen back and grasped the test tube that was propped against it. He handed it to Karen Raymond, and she clutched it frantically. The test tube's already dissolving plastic made it feel like a Baggie full of water in her hand. But, miraculously, its contents had remained intact thus far. She placed the limp remnants of the tube inside a larger plastic test tube and firmly screwed on its cap.

Karen took a deep breath and nodded at Wareagle.

Not only had they prevented Harlan Frye from poisoning San Antonio's water supply, but his formula, at the same time deadly and potentially lifesaving, now belonged to them. . . .

Wareagle brought the walkie-talkie from his pocket up to his lips.

"We have it, Blainey."

"Sunday Morning Service" was just about to go to commercial when the previously bound occupants of the storage shed were delivered to Major Osborne Vandal inside the plant. Halfway through their tale, he signaled frantically for Stu Allison to get the Reverend's attention. From floor level he could see Frye grab a walkie-talkie from the hand of a Fifth Generation soldier stationed upon the platform.

"What is it? What's going on?"

"Six men were just found tied up in a storage shed, sir. One of them is Bob Randall. I'm sending him up."

Harlan Frye went cold. Stu Allison ordered the control truck to stay on commercial.

"Randall? But he's right—" Frye searched for the pug-nosed plant manager on the platform. He was gone. "My God," the Reverend followed, utterly confused. "But, but . . ."

By that time, a tall, muscular man had reached the platform. "Bob Randall, Reverend. We spoke briefly last week."

"Then who was . . ."

"I don't know what the devil's been going on here, Reverend, but somebody's made you look like an honest-to-God horse's ass."

"Excuse me?"

"You told me you wanted to film near the disinfection tanks, but this is the effluent discharge tank."

"I don't . . . understand."

"This tank contains fully purified water, Reverend."

Frye felt himself go numb. "What about, what about the chlorine?"

The real Bob Randall pointed to the smaller tanks across the plant. "Disinfection takes place over there. That's where the chlorine gets injected. Once purified, the water makes its way over here to be returned to the system."

"Returned?"

Randall nodded. "Constant cycle. Whatever was in here five minutes ago is already on its way to Civolo Creek. You're on the wrong goddamn side of the plant!"

"Reverend!" Major Vandal's voice barked through the walkie-talkie Frye had forgotten he was holding.

He raised it dimly, but didn't speak.

"Reverend, the Future Faith helicopter is taking off from the city park across the street!"

"Helicopter? We didn't bring the heli—" And then, with a shudder that shook away his numb shock, everything became clear. "McCracken! It's McCracken!"

CHAPTER 38

The chopper, painted with the seal of the Future Faith network, surged forward through the air as McCracken kicked in the throttle.

"You outdid yourself with this one, boss," congratulated Sal Belamo, who had reached the city park just as Blaine was landing.

"I haven't done anything until we reach San Antonio International, Sal," McCracken reminded. "Congratulate me when we're on that private jet bound for Washington."

"Washington, boss?"

"National Institute of Health," Karen Raymond told Belamo, tapping the carrying case in her lap. The case had a spongy interior that conformed to the shape of whatever was placed within it—presently a single test tube containing the contents of another that by now would have dissolved entirely. "That's where this belongs now."

"Ten minutes to the airport, people," Blaine interjected. "Keep your fingers crossed."

* * *

Those tuned to the Future Faith network's "Sunday Morning Service" had the broadcast replaced by a TECHNICAL DIFFICULTIES announcement across their screen. Still on the platform, the Reverend Harlan Frye had made contact by cellular phone with Commanding General Luther Gaines of Lackland Air Force Base and the military training center contained there.

"The worst has happened, General," Frye said, as calmly as he could manage. The fact that Gaines was one of the primary members of the Key Society had allowed the Reverend to set up one final bit of insurance for his plan. "There's a helicopter in the air with Future Faith network markings. It's probably headed for San Antonio International. I want you to have your airborne chopper shoot it down."

Gaines hesitated, clearly flustered. "Reverend, this is an open line."

"I haven't got time to worry about open lines, General, and you haven't got time to protest. Bring down that chopper! Do you hear me? Blow it out of the sky. And I need those troop carriers you've got standing by, enough to ferry seventy, make that eighty, men."

Gaines relented with a sigh. "There's going to be hell to pay for going through with this, Reverend."

"A worse hell if we don't, General."

San Antonio International Airport was clearly in view, their helicopter just minutes from landing, when Johnny Wareagle shifted uneasily.

"Company, Blainey."

McCracken turned to the rear and saw the growing speck closing on them from the southeast.

"What we got, Indian?"

"An OH-47 reconnaissance chopper."

"Two .30-calibers?"

Wareagle nodded.

McCracken quickly calculated the remaining distance to the airport against the rapidly diminishing gap between them and the gunship. No way they could possibly touch down safely before the OH-47 was upon them, especially since it was closing on a trajectory that would take it over San Antonio International.

"What's her top speed, Indian?"

"Two twenty-five to two fifty, depending on ammo load."

"And the best we can manage is one-eighty. Doesn't leave us much choice, does it?"

And with that Blaine banked their chopper around toward downtown San Antonio.

T.J. Fields, fuming over being stuck in traffic on Route 487, heard the distinctive slicing whir of a helicopter rotor and looked up to find a pair of choppers heading toward the city. The one with air force markings seemed to be in pursuit of the other.

"You don't think that could be . . ." He turned away from one of the fifteen Skulls who had accompanied him on this journey for another gaze at the steel birds descending on the city. He was still watching when the air force chopper opened fire with its dual bottom-mounted machine guns.

"Fuck me," T.J. muttered to himself, and then swung to face the tightly knotted group of bikers behind him as the choppers soared over them for the city. "Boys," he yelled, "it looks like we're headed in the wrong direction."

With that, in unison, the Skulls spun their bikes around and rode off, weaving eastward through traffic in the westbound lanes.

McCracken was bringing the chopper over the center of San Antonio when the sizzling flashes zoomed past it on both sides.

"Looks like he's in range, Indian."

No sooner had Blaine uttered that pronouncement than their chopper buckled slightly, jarring its passengers. Coarse black smoke began to spill from the area of the oil tank on the helicopter's rear flank, and McCracken felt the controls instantly go stiffer in his hands. The chopper wavered and then began to dip, the oil pressure gauge making a determined slide toward zero.

"He's attacking from the left, Blainey!"

"Trying to finish us off, boss," picked up Sal Belamo, reaching for his M16. "Let me see what I can do."

Blaine stole a quick gaze back at Karen, who was silently clutching the case containing Harlan Frye's deadly toxin. "Let's try something more subtle first. Hold on."

McCracken stopped fighting the chopper and let it drop. It took all his strength to maintain even the semblance of control as it flitted through the air and then angled nose-down for the buildings below. The maneuver successfully brought them out of range of the OH-47's .30-caliber fire, though at the expense of forfeiting any chance of pulling back into a climb.

"He's starting to close again, Blainey," Wareagle reported.

Belamo, gun in hand, had stripped off his harness and was sliding toward the door, a hand ready to thrust it open. "Just let me have a shot at him, boss."

"Strap yourself back in, Sal. The roof of that parking garage down there just became our landing pad."

Belamo got his harness rebuckled just as McCracken succeeded in settling the smoke-belching chopper into a wobbly auto rotation. He pulled up with everything he had at the end. Even so, the result was a jolt that shook his insides once the landing pods touched down on the concrete rooftop. He cut power to the rotor blades and exited the chopper last after Sal, Karen, and Johnny, all of them racing for the stairway door on the rooftop.

The OH-47 was soaring in after them, a blistering metallic clang emanating from its pulsing .30-caliber guns mounted on either side of its pods. Belamo fired a token spray upward before following the rest of the group into the roof-perched stairwell.

"Where the fuck are we?"

"Rivercenter Mall," McCracken answered.

"Great," Belamo moaned. "You ask me, we can do something 'sides get our shopping done."

"We will, Sal. Trust me."

The San Antonio River slices through the whole of the city's downtown district in a twenty-foot-wide channel below street level. A sidewalk promenade called the Riverwalk lines its entire five-mile loop with easily accessible hotels, souvenir and novelty shops, and, especially, eating and drinking establishments. Riverboats jammed with tour patrons cruise along the five-mile loop from morning well into the night, some equipped with tables for drinking or dining. The resulting effect is that of a commercially modernistic Venice, albeit along a narrower and more tunnel-like channel.

One of the Riverwalk's newer additions, the four-story Rivercenter Shopping Mall, has become a true centerpiece and one of the walk's most popular attractions. Eighty percent glass, it has more than one hundred stores and restaurants, forming Riverwalk's symbolic beginning.

McCracken, Belamo, Karen Raymond, and Johnny Wareagle surged onto the third-floor level of the mall, Blaine and Sal making only a token effort to conceal the M16s they were holding. The Riverwalk patrons in the crowded aisles parted to make a path for them. They reached the center of the mall and gazed downward at the figurative start of the Riverwalk, beyond the deep blue girders enclosing the mall's massive panes of glass.

"The nearest down escalator is to our right, Blainey," Wareagle noted, having grasped McCracken's intentions.

McCracken had just turned toward it when the lunchtime crowd seated on the walk-level promenade abandoned their tables and lurched away. An instant later the OH-47 dropped down before the glass directly in front of Rivercenter's third floor. McCracken grabbed Karen Raymond's arm and dragged her to the floor before it opened fire. The sound of exploding glass pierced their

ears and sprays of it blew everywhere, scattering patrons
in all directions. The front windows of the designer clothing shops behind them blew inward, creating a stereolike
crescendo. The helicopter hovered sideways, and fired off
another burst.

"Go!" Blaine screamed, when it had soared well past
them.

He lunged back to his feet and ran through the chaos,
Johnny bringing up the rear behind Sal Belamo and Karen.
Her case bounced against her, and she was terrified that
the test tube inside would be smashed and its contents lost
forever in spite of the padding.

The chopper looped its way back toward them, still firing incessantly. More glass shattered and Rivercenter's entire steel frame seemed to buckle under the strain. Blaine
led the way through the panicked throngs huddled on the
escalator leading down to the first floor and then dashed
for another that would take them out onto the Riverwalk
itself.

The damage inflicted by the OH-47's .30-caliber machine
gun traced their path, yet more glass blown out everywhere
in their wake. They found cover on the Riverwalk level
within Tony Roma's Place for Ribs. The chopper had
stopped firing and had risen slightly before settling into an
insectlike hover, waiting to spot its targets once more.

McCracken looked beyond the wide pool of water that
rimmed Rivercenter's semicircular outdoor promenade. A
dark green speedboat marked RIVERWALK RANGERS sat
moored between a pair of the tour boats.

"Indian."

"I see it, Blainey."

They glanced at each other.

"The wheel's all yours," McCracken told him.

"You gotta be fuckin' kidding me," Sal Belamo uttered,
following their stare.

"The boat," Karen realized.

"Let's go!" McCracken ordered.

They darted out from the cover of Tony Roma's and rushed for the speedboat. Johnny reached it first and lunged in. Blaine worked the rope mooring free, while Sal helped Karen.

"Go!" Blaine ordered as he hurtled over the gunwale and thumped onto the deck. The boat rocked slightly, but that didn't stop Wareagle from shoving its throttle all the way forward.

The engine was an Evinrude 55, capable of maybe twenty-five miles per hour with four passengers. The occupants of the OH-47 didn't spot them until the speedboat had passed under the second of two enclosed walkways linking together different wings of Rivercenter. It swung all the way round and dipped low toward the Riverwalk to give chase as the speedboat passed the already long line of patrons waiting for a seat on one of the Riverboat tour barges.

Johnny swung the speedboat to the right when they hit a wide pool of water and surged into the tunnel-like, tree-lined channel. He swerved between a pair of oncoming tour boats, eliciting screams of terror and wide-eyed fright from the passengers. Their eyes bulged even wider when the chopper appeared overhead and commenced firing, forcing many of the tourists to lunge from their seats and jump into the murky five-foot-deep water.

The chopper's fire spit water high into the air. McCracken and Belamo opened up with their M16s to keep the pilot from dropping low enough to insure an easy kill. Their speedboat surged beneath a hundred-foot-long overpass just after traveling past San Antonio's chamber of commerce building. As expected, the OH-47 beat them to the other end, and Johnny spun the speedboat hard to the left at the tunnel's close, hoping to dodge their pursuers. Blaine and Sal popped fresh clips into their M16s and opened fire again just as the chopper angled for a steep drop. Riverwalk's shroud of overhanging trees was keeping the OH-47's pilot from chancing a deeper descent that would have further increased its already distinct advantage. As it was, he did a masterful job of steering the chopper with the curving form of the Riverwalk.

The speedboat surged past the gleaming cream structure of the Hilton Hotel and continued its zigzag pattern. Sidewalk café patrons and Riverwalk strollers passing before the hotel, splashed by the boat's wake, scattered desperately at the chopper's appearance. It rode agilely with nose angled down, pace sacrificed to permit better aim of its machine guns. The thus-far-errant bullets coughed plumes of water into the air, the effect not unlike that of giant raindrops.

Up ahead Blaine could see the outdoor, tiered seating for free performances at the Arneson River Theater directly across the narrow channel. The structure triggered the beginnings of a new escape plan in his mind. Race up those combination seats and steps, and escape could be gained through La Villita, a collection of old-style shops and stores forming what is traditionally known as Old San Antonio.

"Johnny!" he shouted.

When the Indian turned, Blaine pointed forcefully at the Arneson Theater. Wareagle aimed the boat toward it as a walking bridge just past the theater came into view.

The gunmen concealed upon the bridge rose and opened fire. Johnny just managed to spin the speedboat back around, but a few of their bullets slammed into its engine. The boat sputtered a few times and died.

"Out!" Blaine screamed. "Move!" He glanced at Karen, then at the bag draped over her shoulder. "Get her out of here, Indian."

He kept the gunmen on the bridge at bay with the remainder of his M16's clip, long enough for Johnny to lead Karen into the brown-green waters of the channel. Sal Belamo did his best to hold the chopper back, but the pilot had lifted over his effective range, biding his time. McCracken grabbed Belamo and pulled him into the water.

They waded hurriedly for the promenade lining the

channel's far bank. Much to his distress, he saw Johnny and Karen huddled behind an abutment where the river broke into a sharp curve before reaching the Arneson Theater. Fire raining down from East Market Street above had stopped them from chancing an escape in that direction, or any other for that matter. Blaine and Sal, meanwhile, had no choice but to squeeze atop the small promenade as well, their presence forcing Johnny and Karen's backs up against the vine-shrouded wall.

Blaine pulled a pistol from his belt to join the M16, one in each hand, a fierce scowl frozen on his face. The chopper danced through the air above as if to taunt him. Belamo emptied the last of his clip futilely into its frame.

"Crouch behind me!" McCracken ordered Karen as the OH-47 hovered lower.

He found himself staring straight into a pair of .30-caliber barrels. He raised his M16 in one hand and pistol in the other, started to squeeze the triggers of both.

The helicopter exploded in the air, engulfed in a huge fireball that drove it upward, spun it around, and sent it crashing down in shards upon East Market Street above.

"What the fuck," Sal Belamo started.

The answer came back in a sudden roar of revving engines as a black wave of motorcycles rolled down the grass-covered seating tiers of the Arneson River Theater.

The Skulls! Karen Raymond realized. Tears of joy and relief flooded down her cheeks. *It was the Skulls!*

She picked out T.J. Fields riding at the head of the procession that thumped down the stairs, firing toward the positions of Frye's gunmen, both those on the bridge and the ones stationed above on East Market Street. A biker at the top had stopped to bring a second LAW rocket to his shoulder. It thumped out and blew the bridge into concrete fragments that splashed into the river channel, Frye's posted gunmen lost with it.

McCracken watched as the motorcycle gang members hurled grenades toward the rest of the opposition's largest concentrations and answered their automatic fire accordingly. One biker was pumping round after round from his M79 grenade launcher. The small brown and white building that was part of the Arneson Theater stage erupted into flames. Bodies toppled out its fake windows.

"Time for a swim," Blaine signaled, and the four of them plunged from the promenade into the greenish water past their waists, and waded quickly to the other side under protective fire from the Skulls.

A larger contingent of Frye's Fifth Generation gunmen took up positions at the wall behind the Arneson River Theater and opened up with a relentless hail of automatic fire. A trio of Skulls went down, but not before one of them managed to hurl two of his grenades dead on target. The resulting explosions silenced the gunmen and split a water storage tank, its contents washing down over the stage and spilling into the channel.

"Let's go!" T.J. Fields screamed, revving his bike.

Karen Raymond lunged behind him. Johnny, Sal, and Blaine picked up three of the bikes belonging to Skulls lost in the battle.

T.J.'s tires screeched away in the lead, the front one lifting into the air while the back one drew a black stitch across Riverwalk's stone-inlaid promenade. The rest of the bikes fell into line behind him in a single-file surge down a walkway barely large enough to accommodate a trio of strollers. In spite of this, Blaine managed to bring his bike alongside T.J.'s as they thundered past a sidewalk restaurant.

"Keep going straight. Toward River Square!" he instructed.

"River *what*?"

"Just follow me!" McCracken shouted, and took the lead down the promenade.

He followed Riverwalk's path up four steps and thudded back down another four. The tangle of covering vines and the branches of cypress trees knotted thickly above him, then cleared briefly as they sped across an overpass just beyond the Hilton Hotel. Enemy fire rained down from gunmen following their pace above on East Market Street. Skull riders kept one hand clinging to their throttles and clutches, while returning fire with whatever weapon the free hand of each was holding. Explosions dotted the upper reaches of the promenade, and two more Skulls fell to opposition gunfire.

"Shit," T.J. Fields muttered, and Karen tightened one arm around him, while clinging doggedly to the satchel containing the deadly toxin with the other.

The bikes roared off the overpass and clambered down the stairs on the other side. The Skull riders sped into River Square in tight formation. Totally contained on both sides, with no clear access from any street, River Square and its assembly of eating and drinking establishments provided an instant respite. But the distance separating the bikers from the start of the tables shrank to barely a yard, and the Skulls had all they could do to avoid slipping over the edge into the river channel as they dodged stunned pedestrians. They passed multitiered restaurants containing both interior and sidewalk tables and featuring all manner of food from Mexican to Cajun, from Italian to Texas steak. Tables and diners alike went flying as the bikers sped along beneath the tight shroud of overhanging branches that formed a protective umbrella over this stretch of the Riverwalk.

McCracken jerked his bike to a halt just past Jim Cullum's Jazz Club at the Riverwalk entrance to the Hyatt Hotel.

"This way!" he signaled.

"Where?" T.J. Fields wanted to know.

McCracken's response was to tear off straight into a sublevel of the Hyatt, the only hotel in San Antonio that actually contained part of the river channel beneath it. He sped across the welcome flat tile, past the water that had turned miraculously crystal-clear from murky green. The crystal clarity remained as Blaine headed outside into a lavish patio lined with rolling waterfalls that created a tropical feel. He thudded up four series of steps, each with a brief gap in between, that ultimately brought him to street level in the plaza fronting the Hyatt, the Riverwalk abandoned behind it.

By the time T.J. Fields and the others had caught up, large squads of enemy gunmen could be seen closing on the plaza from both directions.

"Okay," T.J. raised, desperate, "where to now?"

"Only one place I can think of," McCracken told him.

Blaine kept his engine revving while his eyes gestured at the old structure a hundred yards directly in front of them.

"You gotta be fucking kidding me, boss," muttered Sal Belamo, who had drawn up even on his bike.

McCracken's gaze fell upon the converging troops of Harlan Frye. "Not much choice I can see, Sal."

And with that he gunned his bike across the street toward the Alamo.

CHAPTER 39

The lack of the usual tourist crowd on a Sunday mystified Blaine until he slammed his bike through the main entrance of the chapel facing the Grand Hyatt. Scaffolding rimmed the interior of the building's entire front section. A work crew was busy installing what looked like a supportive truss under the structure's crumbling roof.

Lantz Lecolt heard the commotion despite the steady whirring of saws and pounding of hammers. He had just finished working the sandblaster himself and was just about to refill it when a fleet of motorcycles roared into the shrine. He watched thunderstruck as a muscular bearded man and a huge Indian both swung off their bikes. The Indian moved quickly to close and lock the thick, heavy double wooden front doors.

"Hey!" Lecolt roared at the two of them. "What the hell do you think you're doing?"

"Repeating history," said the bearded one. "Only hopefully this time the good guys are gonna win."

"*What?*"

"Listen, friend. What's outside now could wipe out Santa Ana's thousands in a heartbeat. So get your men out of here. Get them out of here now. Use the back. If you're lucky—"

An explosion rocked the front section of the chapel facade, showering fragments of the restored structure inward. Another portion of the roof caved in and the workers scattered beneath it. The parts of the supportive truss they had managed to get in place gave way, the wood splintering on impact with the stone floor. The scaffolding shook but held.

"You're not lucky," McCracken told Lantz Lecolt.

General Gaines had kept three troop-carrying Blackhawk helicopters ready on the chance Harlan Frye would need them. All of the choppers had already dropped off the Fifth Generation soldiers who were now massing in the plaza fronting the Alamo complex. Major Osborne Vandal looked up to see one of the Blackhawks hovering in search of a spot to set down.

There had been throngs of people strolling about Alamo Way when he had arrived with the first of his troops. Their befuddlement had turned to terror as soon as the gunfire and explosions began. Even the most curious fled the scene, a few stopping to snap pictures when they reached a safe distance.

The Blackhawk settled uneasily onto the plaza. Harlan Frye leaned out from the passenger hold and waved Osborne Vandal to him.

"I can't afford to be seen here!" Frye yelled above the rotor wash.

"I understand, sir!" the major returned.

"You know what has to be done! Kill them all! Bring down the building if you have to, but kill them all! That test tube *cannot* leave here!"

"Yes, sir!"

"God is with you," he said solemnly, and disappeared back inside the helicopter.

In his mind Harlan Frye had already worked everything out. All the helicopters used in the raid would be reported stolen by a renegade terrorist group that had chosen the Alamo for a target. General Gaines would likely be stripped of his command, but his complicity would remain a secret. So, too, would Frye's involvement. The story would hold, because there would be no one alive to refute it.

With the test tube's contents destroyed and Alamo's inhabitants killed here and now, he would be free to utilize the formula another day. The Reverend did not expect ever to be able to return to the majestic kingdom he had built. He also knew the Seven were finished. But he wasn't ready to give up. He still believed that God was behind him. He would rebuild from scratch, salvage what he could and move on.

Another day, another time . . . .

Turning the Alamo into the grave of Blaine McCracken and his cohorts would insure it. God works in strange ways, and the Reverend Harlan Frye would accept this as His will, as he accepted everything else.

He strapped himself back into his seat and signaled the Blackhawk pilot to take off as a convoy of blue and white San Antonio police cars streamed boldly onto the scene. Heavy fire turned most of them back, and a pair of RPGs blew two of the ones that kept coming into flaming hulks.

"Get ready to move on the building!" Major Osborne Vandal shouted, and his command was passed down the line.

Instinctively, and in little more than a few seconds, McCracken cataloged what lay before him around the interior of the Alamo. The chapel structure had been converted into a museumlike shrine to the famed battle when fewer than two hundred defenders had managed to hold back an army of four thousand. Various display cases dotted a floor that stretched sixty yards from front to back. Plaques memorializing various participants in the battle and portraits of the defenders, along with scenes frozen from the battle, were hung upon the stone walls. With the exception of the floodlights moved into place by the workmen, the shrine's sole light came from a trio of dangling, period-accurate chandeliers.

The reconditioned building was far stronger structurally than its predecessor, of course. Instead of adobe, it was built of concrete and stone with a yellowed stucco finish eerily close to that of the original. The building's remaining windows were simple, yet majestic. Blaine counted seven in all, including the three mounted in the alcove wings that widened the structure from a hundred feet to a hundred twenty at its center. He also cataloged fortified inner rooms in three of the chapel's four corners, one of which, he recalled, had been the hiding place of the women and children who lived to tell the original tale of the Alamo.

McCracken called Karen Raymond over to join him with the man in charge of the repair crew.

"You can still get out through the exit on the left there," he insisted, pointing to it. "I want you to take her with you."

Karen's eyes swung toward Blaine in disbelief as rounds of gunfire continued to pepper the front facade of the shrine. "I'm stay—"

"No, you're not, Doctor. Saving what you've got in that case is what this stand is all about. You make it to safety or we fail. Period. Stay with him."

Blaine pointed at Lantz Lecolt, whose attention was locked on the eight leather-jacketed bikers taking up defensive positions under the direction of the big Indian. Toting their weapons with them, the bikers used the ladders to scale the scaffolding his work crew had been using until moments ago and rushed to their posts. Lecolt watched as they smashed through the grate-covered windows on the chapel's front and sides and steadied their weapons on the resulting sills.

Strangely, all he could think of was that in the original battle of the Alamo, this was the only structure to survive reasonably intact. Time and destiny, it seemed, had caught up with it.

"Get her out of here!" the bearded man was ordering him, thrusting the woman his way. *"Now!"*

"Lantz," one of his men called, "come on!"

Lecolt backpedaled slowly toward the shrine's rear, as if reluctant to leave. More explosions and gunfire rocked the building, sending huge chunks of roof and walls downward, obliterating many of the display cases that featured the memorabilia of the Alamo's original defenders.

"Lantz!"

One of the workmen finally grabbed Lecolt's arm and hustled him and the unknown woman toward the door built into the left alcove that spilled out near the museum and souvenir shop. The first three in his crew had surged outside when a barrage of automatic fire sounded just ahead of their screams. Two more of his men were wounded and had to be dragged back inside. Lecolt himself got the door resealed and locked, while the big Indian charged over and hurled three grenades through the window over the door. The explosions sounded instantly and the bearded man ordered a ladder to be brought over so one of the bikers could be stationed at that post. Then Lecolt watched the two of them rush forward.

"How many outside, Indian?" McCracken asked during their run to the front of the chapel. T.J. Fields had almost finished getting an M60 machine gun set in place atop the scaffolding, its barrel perched just over the top of the angular facade.

"Nearly a hundred, Blainey."

"You, me, Sal, and eight bikers makes eleven."

"Similar odds as the last time here," Johnny reminded.

"Somehow I don't think we'll be able to hold out thirteen days against Santa Ana Frye."

As if to punctuate McCracken's pronouncement, a deafening blast blew out the right-hand portion of the front facade. The pair of Skulls who had been pouring a nonstop barrage of grenade and automatic fire from that vantage point crumpled, along with a chunk of scaffolding they'd been standing upon.

"Fuck!" T.J. Fields screamed, and opened up with the M60 from the other side of the facade.

Standing atop the highest point of the scaffolding brought his head through the portion of the roof that had collapsed the day before. Another pair of Skulls climbed fast up the ladders and joined Fields, peering over the jagged facade just enough to steady their M16s toward the congestion of troops firing from covered positions within the plaza. Sal Belamo joined them and added the clout of the M79 grenade launcher he had salvaged from the pile of rubble when the central scaffolding had collapsed, the process of breeching, loading, and firing repeated in incredibly rapid fashion. Skulls posted before windows on both flanks drained clips as quickly as the bullets could surge out their barrels, evidence that the enemy was now closing from the sides as well.

"We need an equalizer, Blainey," Wareagle said, cataloging what was available to them.

McCracken was already moving toward the sandblasting machine Lecolt had been poised near when they entered. The main tank had fallen over and was partially covered by the remnants of a display case.

"How's this, Indian?" he asked, already checking the hose connecting it to the compressor for holes.

Wareagle smiled.

"Buy me some time, Johnny. Buy me some time."

The San Antonio police had given up the effort of joining the battle for now, regrouping elsewhere to assess what exactly had befallen their city. No matter, thought Osborne Vandal: By the time they returned, the battle would be long over.

He slid along the back of his attack lines, watching his men take up positions ever closer to the front of the Alamo chapel. Fire from within continued to hold them reasonably at bay, especially that of the M60, but the supply of the enemy force's grenades and LAWS rockets was being rapidly depleted. When certain the men inside the punctured and crumbling fort were out of ammunition, he would order his men to attack from all flanks, just as Santa Ana had done back in 1836. They would storm the front entrance and side exits simultaneously, obliterating everyone inside. No one could escape, no mercy shown.

The rebuilt facade of the old Alamo chapel was crumbling a piece at a time. Four large chasms had been dug along its upper reach, each impact widening the breaches all the more. Vandal's ears rang from the incessant fire of his troops.

One of his men missed the top arch of the facade with a missile, but the grenades of two more rattled atop the sloping roof structure. The explosions coughed twin plumes of debris into the air. Osborne Vandal couldn't see the roof from his vantage point, but he imagined another gash torn within it, the rubble crunching downward upon the opposition below.

For the second time in history, the defenders of the Alamo were going to fall.

Sal Belamo had just climbed down to find fresh weapons when the grenade blasts sounded. He threw himself to the floor with arms tucked around his head.

"Fuck me," he moaned, shoving the rubble off himself as he reclaimed his feet and hurried back to the ladder.

The front section of scaffolding had all but collapsed, T.J. Fields and his M60 alone clinging to what remained. The most recent blasts had crushed one of his legs beneath a shower of debris, but he continued to answer enemy fire without pause.

"I'm coming back up!" Sal yelled to him, steadying the ladder. The scaffolding wobbled under the pressure of his climb.

Johnny Wareagle, meanwhile, had thrown himself through a window on the chapel's right flank where the enemy had mounted a determined charge that had nearly

penetrated their meager defenses. He surged forward with
a pair of M16s spitting fire at a stream of troops thrown
suddenly onto the defensive. He took brief cover within a
rectangular, unroofed parapet and spun out to cut down the
gunmen who had tried pursuing him.

Inside the crumbling chapel, McCracken had yanked the
top off the sandblaster's main tank to find it fortuitously
empty. Karen Raymond rushed to join him as he wheeled
the tank across the floor, with inch-and-a-half-wide rubber
hoses that ran both in from the compressor and out to a
nozzlelike end dragging like snakes behind it. He stopped
the tank at a huge pile of sawdust, refuse from the recently
constructed supportive truss that now lay in broken pieces
across the floor.

"Help me," he ordered as he began piling the sawdust
inside the tank.

"But what, what are . . ." She gave up on the question
and started helping him pack the sawdust in.

Seconds later, Johnny Wareagle, his face and arms a
mass of cuts and lacerations dripping blood, rushed over to
McCracken. Explosions rocked the chapel on both flanks.
The Skulls firing down through the windows there were
hurled from their posts as glass and rubble showered inward.

"We're out of time, Blainey."

Despite Blaine and Karen's desperately hurried work,
the sandblasting tank was only three-quarters full.

"This will have to do," he told her, already screwing the
cap tightly back into place and making sure the fittings for
both hose extensions were fastened in.

The added weight of the sawdust made the tank much
harder to wheel and impossible to carry. McCracken managed to drag it toward the punctured front facade, where
sunlight streamed in through the many fresh cracks and
chasms. He coiled the nozzled end of the hose about himself as Johnny switched on the generator that powered the
compressor. A shrill whine echoed through the stark confines of the chapel.

Blaine reached the façade and mounted the ladder, looking up to see Sal Belamo crouching over the wounded T.J. Fields upon what remained of the scaffolding. Sal had replaced him behind the M60, offering resistance to the troops poised to attack as soon as its ammo belt was expended. Johnny held the ladder in place, and Blaine climbed it quickly with one arm held to the hose that stretched out behind him.

He reached the top just as the M60 machine gun clicked empty, its third belt exhausted. Johnny lunged onto the scaffolding ahead of him and opened fire with another M16 he had salvaged from the platform.

Blaine looked at the wounded T.J. Fields. "Get him down from here, Sal."

Belamo slammed the M60 in frustration. "Hey, if the two of you are staying—"

"The Indian's not staying, either. Just me. The rest of you are getting out. *All* of you."

Belamo stole a brief glance down at Karen Raymond at the bottom of the ladder. "Jesus, boss, Jesus . . ."

"Get going." Blaine saw the pair of grenades clipped to Sal's belt. "But leave me one of those."

Belamo handed over one of his grenades. They traded places gingerly upon the precarious scaffolding. McCracken eased the wounded T.J. Fields onto the top rung after Sal, so Belamo could help guide him back to the floor. Johnny Wareagle snapped a fresh clip into his rifle and gazed back at McCracken.

"They're massing, Blainey."

McCracken looked at the ladder. "Your turn, Indian." And, when Wareagle's response was to fire another burst downward, "The others won't be able to make it without you."

Wareagle waited until the M16 clicked empty again before giving in with a nod. "I'll see you on the outside."

"Give me thirty seconds, Indian," Blaine said, tightening his grasp around the neck of the hose running from the sawdust-filled tank like a fireman about to battle a blaze.

"Then you'll have the distraction you'll need to make it out of here."

McCracken turned his attention back to the front and opened the nozzle.

Major Osborne Vandal had arranged his troops in three separate phalanxes, ready to charge the Alamo chapel's front, as well as both sides. He knew the fire emanating from within had all but ceased and could only guess as to how many in McCracken's party remained alive. A fourth, smaller phalanx had the Alamo complex's rear effectively enclosed, waiting for whoever had survived within the chapel to launch an escape.

In Vandal's mind Vietnam was being fought all over again to a dramatically different result. No wasting away in a Cong prison camp for seven years. No return home to ostracism and disgrace. This was his second chance, and he wasn't about to squander it. He could taste the victory he'd waited twenty long years to sample.

Vandal lifted his walkie-talkie to his mouth to give his unit commanders the go signal. Before he could speak, a shower of what looked like thick yellow dust flooded out through the broken roof of the chapel in a constant stream. It spread into a nearly unbroken blanket over the plaza knoll his men were concentrated upon, hovering virtually motionless over and around them.

The major stopped short of giving the order to attack; his spine snapped rigid and his entire body had gone cold.

The hose was alive, a snake in McCracken's hand. For cover, as well as optimum angle, he held it while standing three rungs down on the ladder, the sandblaster's nozzle aimed over the facade's central battlement on slightly more than a forty-five-degree angle. Since the thick, humid San Antonio air hung breezeless, the resulting cloud of finely milled sawdust barely moved at all. Each layer forced the one before it farther forward, until at the point the tank was finally empty, sawdust covered the entire area of the plaza across South Alamo Road to the city's Bureau of Tourism.

McCracken abandoned the hose and clambered rapidly down the ladder. Halfway to the bottom, he heard the clacking of gunshots originating from where Johnny was leading the escape of Karen and the others, a number of whom were wounded and had to be dragged or carried. Besides T.J., six of the Skulls had managed to survive, but only half of those were still fit to fight. Immediately upon reaching the floor, Blaine yanked the pin from the grenade supplied by Sal Belamo and hurled it skyward through the largest chasm in the roof.

"Seven, six, five," he counted out loud as he sprinted toward the rear of the building, keeping his mouth open to prevent damage to his eardrums from what was coming. "Four, three, two . . ."

The deafening explosion literally stole his breath as the blast ignited the blanket of sawdust hovering over the front of the Alamo chapel. The results amounted to a localized fuel-air explosive blowing downward on an unfathomable scale of pressure. Frye's troops beneath it in the plaza were either crushed or shredded, virtually vaporized by the tremendous heat and percussion. Those at the fringes were horribly burned and mangled. Death for them, though, came as a result of the rupturing of their internal organs before the flames had a chance to catch them.

The incredible percussion of the blast shattered every window in downtown San Antonio for a three-block radius, raining glass down in all directions. Huge shards of it floated atop the San Antonio River with the currents along Riverwalk. Yet the Grand Hyatt across the plaza, built atrium-style with no windows across its front, survived almost intact.

The impact of the blast hurled Blaine through the air as he neared the exit in the left-side alcove. Airborne, he could feel the structure shaking around him and landed with enough control to cover his head with his hands.

The front half of the chapel collapsed like a neatly

stacked pile of blocks. It caved in on itself, leaving nothing but rubble where the shrine had been just seconds before. The long barrack, meanwhile, caught more of the brunt of the blast and left barely any rubble where it had stood, the explosion either melting the stone or pulverizing it beyond recognition.

McCracken felt the shower of stone enclose him with painful thuds and thumps, but he clung to the hope that this part of the chapel would be spared. When the rumbling stopped, he realized he could still breathe. His jaws ached and a hollow throbbing plagued both his ears, but at least he could hear. Moving his frame shifted the weight that had piled atop him, and Blaine began to push, shove, and drive his way out. He climbed back to his feet atop a yard-high pile of rocks and rubble within the back shell of the chapel. Despite many cracks and fissures, this portion of the building had somehow remained standing.

The front two thirds of the structure, though, was gone entirely. Nothing remained of the memorial to another great battle 150 years earlier but a huge, irregular pile of beige, cream, and gray rocks. A thick dust cloud had carried over the front plaza knoll, preventing McCracken from seeing the vast carnage beyond.

He climbed down from the pile of rubble from which he had extracted himself and limped toward the exit whose door no longer existed. Reaching it, Blaine turned back for one last rueful glance at the ruined chapel.

"Remember the Alamo," he heard himself say.

EPILOGUE

"What about Frye?" Karen Raymond asked McCracken during their flight to California from San Antonio.

"Maybe he was killed with the others at the Alamo," Blaine responded, aware that the tremendous force of the explosion had made it impossible to identify the remains of all the dead.

"You don't believe that. I know you don't, and neither do I. The question is, what are you going to do about it?"

Blaine took a long look at her. "What do you think I should do?"

"Go after him. *Stop* him."

"We already did that, Doctor."

They had, indeed. In the twenty-four hours since the Alamo had fallen for the second time, albeit with dramatically different results, troops from the 7th Light Infantry Division had seized control of the Kingdom of the Seven. Although Frye and the others had drained the computers and filing cabinets of all pertinent information, enough remained to prove the Seven's existence and identify its primary members. Beyond that, if the Reverend had survived the Alamo, none of the resources of the kingdom would be available for him to salvage in attempting to continue on the same path.

As for the others, Tommy Lee Curtisan and Jessie Will had already turned themselves in. Louis W. Kellog had disappeared, while Arthur Burgeuron was last seen boarding a flight to South America. General Gaines, who had been party to Frye's siege at the Alamo, had been arrested and would face a military court-martial.

Ever since the aftermath of that blast, when McCracken was reunited with the group ushered from the chapel by Johnny Wareagle, Karen Raymond had been disturbed by his apparent disinterest in Frye's fate. After assiduously briefing the proper authorities on everything that had transpired, he seemed to give no further thought to the Reverend's whereabouts. And yet Blaine had insisted on accompanying Karen back to California and her sons personally.

"If you're not at all worried about Frye," Karen persisted, "why did you insist on coming out here with me?"

"Because if the Reverend is still around, I know how he'll think, what he might do."

"My *kids*?" She shuddered.

"Only if you were with them at the time. That's the way men like Frye work."

"And you still aren't going to go after him."

"If I go after him, I might as well go after the other ten thousand or so who've got the same mad dreams he does."

"Frye's different."

"Not really. The contents of that test tube you sent on to the National Institute of Health are what made him different."

"He'll find something else, maybe the contents of another test tube."

"He'll try, Kar, they'll all *try*. Each and every one of these maniacs is scary in his own right, but they only become dangerous when they latch on to something that makes their vision achievable. The distinctions are based in what they're holding at the present time. You saw that firsthand."

Karen grasped his point. "And that's where the true fear comes in."

"More than ever now, because technology is providing more and more means for them to latch on to and carry out their schemes. Every wondrous discovery scientists like you come up with has a dark side that can be twisted and subverted. You saw that firsthand, too."

"You're blaming *me* for this?"

"Of course not. Men and women like you are driven by an insatiable urge to find ways of helping a world that often seems unable to help itself. But along the way you don't always close all the doors you open, and there are men like Frye who are waiting to use what you leave behind to their own advantage."

"There have always been men like Frye."

"But never this many doors, Karen, not even close."

McCracken followed T.J. Fields's directions down the long, winding desert road to where Karen's sons had been hidden under guard. He breathed as big a sigh of relief as she did when they arrived at the small cabin to find the armed Skull members in place and waiting.

"I'm having more traditional protection for you set up now," Blaine assured. "It will be in place in another twenty-four hours."

Karen looked at him in a way she hadn't before. "Be nicer if you could handle it yourself."

"I'm not much good in the kitchen and I travel a lot."

"Lots of doors to cover; I know." She started to reach for his hand, then stopped. "That doesn't mean you can't have a single special one to come back to."

"No, it doesn't."

"The thing is—God, I'm screwing this up." She took a deep breath and steeled herself. "The thing is, I'm afraid when I step out of this car, you're going to drive out of my life. Do I have to stay in here with you with the doors locked until you promise not to?"

Blaine smiled and grasped her hand. "Wait and see how you're going to feel more than a day after the finish, after things have settled down. Right now we're still too close to all we've just gone through, and that was quite a bit, in case you've forgotten."

"I don't want to forget." Karen squeezed his hand back tighter. "I know how I feel now and I know how I'll feel then. I'm asking for a chance, Blaine McCracken, not a phone number." She didn't want to let go. "At least meet my boys. That much, please."

After a pause, he nodded. Karen stepped out of the car and rushed up the slight hill toward the cabin. Blaine watched the door open. Taylor and Brandon charged out of it into their mother's arms, Taylor forgetting he was nearly twelve, and Brandon feeling ten would never end. The hug lasted forever, which wasn't long enough. Then Karen eased them away and started to turn back to the car.

"There's someone I want you to—"

She stopped. The car wasn't there.

Blaine McCracken was gone.

"I couldn't stay," McCracken explained to Johnny Wareagle in the Maine woods a week later.

"And that bothers you, Blainey."

"What bothers me is that I wanted to, and I *still* couldn't." Blaine paused. "It's what Karen said about having something to come back to, isn't it, Indian?"

Wareagle nodded with his eyes and poured McCracken a second cup of his homemade tea. "If there is something to come back to, Blainey, there is also something to leave. The way we have chosen is the way of the warrior, and the way of the warrior is constant. No demarcations. No beginning, no end. Opening the door you speak of implies the acceptance of both."

Blaine sipped the steaming brew. "I could have at least met her kids."

"Why didn't you?"

"Didn't want to make leaving more difficult."

"Understand this, Blainey: Passing through a door does not mean having to always remain on the other side."

"No, Indian. I couldn't walk in and then walk away. It's either all the way through or not at all."

"Then if you pass through that door someday, it will be because the time has come. And when it does you will know it. A different way, but ultimately yours just the same."

McCracken frowned. "Tough to see myself changing that much."

"The alternative is trying to have things both ways."

"And we both know that's impossible, of course."

Johnny shrugged.

"I don't know, Indian. I just think sometimes that I'm missing something."

"You can turn away from what you do, Blainey, but not from your passion for it. Calls would come. You would answer."

"Like the old firehouse dog that jumps up at the sound of a bell . . ."

"Quite, Blainey."

McCracken reached up and tugged an imaginary string. "Ding-a-ling, Indian."

The weeks after the fall of his kingdom stretched into months, and Harlan Frye waited for a sign of how he should proceed. It came in the middle of the night, came in the sultry warmth cheap fans in a cheap room could not case. He woke up sweating between the sheets, bounced out of bed and fell to his knees.

"Yes, Lord! Yes!"

Harlan Frye cut his hair and dyed it white. He added contact lenses to change the color of his eyes and learned how to use makeup to lighten his skin to a pale, ghostlike pallor. He rented an abandoned church with some of his remaining funds; it had chairs and a pulpit, and that was all he required. The crowds started out small but grew quickly. Volunteers began coming in the afternoon to get the old church in order, patching leaks, repairing the broken chairs, so when the crowds built to standing-room level, all available space could be utilized. These volunteers evolved into Frye's handlers and had even begun to speak of larger battles waiting to be fought.

God had told him to go back to the beginning, to start again, to build from nothing. A new name. A new place. So he had.

And it was happening.

He had eternity, he had time immemorial to finish his work for the Lord. The Kingdom of the Seven was going to rise again. That inevitability fueled him, charged him. Soon, so very soon, Harlan Frye would have it all back.

"I feel a healing coming on tonight!" he shouted to tonight's congregation of worshipers, his largest crowd yet. He preached without benefit of microphone. His throat ached from the strain, his voice going raspy, but he didn't care. "I feel a lot of healing coming on tonight!"

Harlan Frye stepped down from the pulpit.

"I feel healings of the body that are going to take place!"

"Praise the Lord!"

"I feel healings of the mind that are going to happen this night!"

"Praise the Lord!"

"And especially, *especially*, I feel healings of the *soul* that are going to be yours tonight!"

"Amen!"

Harlan Frye started down the center aisle, reaching out in random fashion to bless the faithful. Those nearest the aisles crowded toward him, eager for a touch of his hand upon their heads or shoulders. He obliged as many as he could and came finally to an old man bent with the agony of arthritis, needing the support of an equally old woman just to stand up.

"Heal thyself, brother! Reach deep within, deep into the

power of your soul, and transfer it to heal your broken body. You can do it, brother! You can do it!"

The Reverend brought his hand to the crest of the man's skull and kept it there. The man shuddered.

"Yes, brother, yes! Feel the strength, feel the power. . . ."

The man's eyes came up slowly and found Frye's: not old eyes at all, narrowed and purposeful.

"Give yourself up, brother! Give yourself up to the power of—"

Frye lost the rest of the sentence in the center of his throat as the man's head rose all the way, neck joints seeming to straighten miraculously.

He was missing the lobe on his left ear.

Preston Turgewell smiled. "For my children," was all he said.

The silenced pistol spit a single time. The bullet ruptured Harlan Frye's heart and left him just enough time to contemplate his own death. By the time he crumpled, the pistol was already back in Sister Barbara's handbag. The old couple melted into the ensuing chaos and slipped out of the building, the last vestiges of the Kingdom of the Seven vanquished forever behind them.

Coming soon from Tor Books . . .

THE FIRES OF
MIDNIGHT

A Blaine McCracken Novel

by Jon Land

Enjoy the following preview!

Susan Lyle gazed out the window of the helicopter as it hovered over Commercial Avenue. The rotor wash kicked up dirt and debris on a normally bustling Cambridge thoroughfare that sat deserted save for the Massachusetts State Policemen making a concerted effort to keep the milling crowds back.

"Setting down now, Doctor," the pilot called to her from the cockpit.

Susan felt the chopper begin its straight drop and checked her watch: barely three hours had past since the alert had come in and she'd issued the appropriate orders. How well they'd been followed she would know soon enough, though initial view gave her reason for high expectations.

The entire block, from the Sonesta Hotel across the length of the Cambridgeside Galleria mall and Monsignor O'Brien Highway, had been blocked off by sawhorses and yellow strip barriers. A ring of officers in riot gear fronted the primary mall entrance on the chance that the efforts of their fellows holding the lines went for naught.

The suspended traffic lights bounced as the chopper settled down in the center of Commercial Avenue in front of the Royal Sonesta Hotel. Susan saw a man in a police uniform approach with one hand raised to shield his eyes, while the other kept his hat pinned to his head. She climbed out of the chopper and started forward, watching the officer lower the hand from his eyes, clearly surprised by her appearance. She wore brown slacks and a cream-colored blouse beneath a slight summer-weight jacket. Her blond hair bounced as she approached the state policeman, flung randomly by the rotor's slowing spin. Her skin was fair and firm, her eyes a shade hovering between blue and green. She looked to be of average height, until she straightened her knees once confidently free of the blade's reach and looked the officer almost straight in the eye.

"Doctor Susan Lyle," she greeted, right hand extended and voice raised to carry it over the chopper's whirring engine. "Firewatch Command."

"Captain Frank Sculley, Massachusetts State Police," he returned, lowering the hand that had been shielding his eyes to take it. "Got a command post set up just over here."

"Have my instructions been followed, Captain?"

"*Your* instructions?"

"The quarantine."

"Best as we could manage."

"And the witnesses?"

"They're still together."

"On scene?"

Sculley gestured toward a trio of coach buses parked down the block and enclosed by cruisers. Beyond them the steadily increasing crowd continued to look on. "I commandeered those from a tour group. Figured that was as good a place to hold them as any."

Some of the tension eased from Susan Lyle's face. "What about the hotel guests?"

"Trouble there. We lost some of them."

"Some . . ."

"Dozens. Lots actually. Sorry, Doctor. By the time I got here—"

"They've got to be tracked down and isolated, do you hear me? There's another chopper en route with men inside who can handle the details. I'll want you to coordinate things with the hotel personnel."

Captain Sculley shrugged, not looking very happy.

Dr. Susan Lyle's eyes fell on a Mexican restaurant located on the Galleria's ground floor, but accessible via its own off-street entrance. "I assume that was open."

"Until the local police closed it."

"And the patrons?"

Captain Sculley said nothing.

"My instructions were to secure the perimeter, Captain," Dr. Lyle snapped. "No one allowed out."

"Too late by the time your instructions all came through. In case you haven't noticed, things have been pretty crazy around here the last few hours."

Susan Lyle let it go. She had been expecting too much of the local Cambridge and Massachusetts authorities who knew nothing of Firewatch Command's existence, or of the helicopter on constant prep outside the Center for Disease Control in Atlanta. Whoever was standing watch could be anywhere in the country within six hours of an alarm being sounded, whisked there in a jet that was fueled and ready twenty-four hours a day at Hartsfield International. In the fifteen years since Firewatch's formation, there had been only two such alarms before today: one false and the other easily passed off to a leak in a chemical storage tank a few miles from the afflicted area. If the initial reports were borne out, the Cambridgeside Galleria would mark the first incident of high confidence potentially warranting full-scale alert status. That decision would be Susan's to make.

"How many people have actually entered the mall?" she asked Sculley.

"I haven't counted. The Cambridge patrolman first on the scene, the sixty or so witnesses we've got in those buses."

"Have any of them displayed any effects or symptoms?"

"Whatever happened in that mall, the symptoms are pretty—"

"Just answer my question, Captain."

Sculley's neck turned slightly red. "Not that we've been able to detect, no."

"And the equipment that was supposed to arrive from Mass General?"

Sculley gestured toward the command post. "In that rescue wagon." Susan Lyle wasn't looking at him as he continued. "I'm going to assume, Doc, that whatever's in that truck is something the hospital keeps just in case somebody like you from out of town needs it."

"That's correct, Captain," she said and started across the street.

"Probably means lots of other hospitals are similarly supplied."

Halfway across the street, Susan turned back his way. "In every major city."

"Like you were expecting this."

"Prepared for it, more accurately."

"You got your problems, I got mine," Sculley said and planted himself in front of her, stopping. "For instance, you haven't asked me about the next of kin of the people who were inside that mall. We got damn near a full-scale panic on our hands. I haven't got enough men on detail to hold all these people back from the perimeter. Plenty have pushed their way through. A few got close to the mall."

That got her attention. "But not inside."

"No," Sculley said, "not inside."

"What about the National Guard?"

"Governor's calling them up. It takes time."

"And the media?"

"News blackout, as per your orders. There've been

some leaks, rumors. You can't keep word of something like this quiet. If you ask me—"

"I didn't," Susan said. "We do nothing and say nothing until we determine the level of contamination."

Sculley's eyes gestured toward the nervous throngs gathered at the heads of both Commercial Avenue and Monsignor O'Brien Highway. "You wanna tell *them* that, Doc? That's where the next of kin of plenty of those inside are gathered. Parents mostly. Sunday at the mall, loaded with kids, you get my drift."

"Why don't we wait until we have something intelligent to tell them? Why don't we wait until I've had a chance to inspect the inside?"

The isolation suit was a poor fit, a generic medium when Susan could better have used a small. She pulled it up over her pants and blouse, and checked the miniature camera built into the helmet just over the faceplate. The camera's controls were built into the right wrist area of the suit, deceptively simple with a continuous run switch that would insure continued recording even if the wearer was incapacitated. Sculley helped Susan pull the double-tank backpack over her shoulders and then escorted her wordlessly to the security line set up before the Cambridgeside Galleria's main entrance.

"I'll be waiting for you when you come out."

Susan's response was a noncommittal smile. She snapped her faceplate into place. Then she squeezed between a pair of sawhorses and approached the vacuum seal portal that had been installed in front of the glass doors. The primary goal was to maximize containment, both by quarantining those exposed and by isolating the supposed point of origin.

The thick airtight plastic of the prefab unit wavered a bit in the wind. The "door" to the vacuum seal was actually a zipper running up the plastic. Susan stepped inside and then resealed it before proceeding through the closed double glass doors onto the first floor of the Cambridge-side Galleria.

She was aware of each breath echoing in her helmet as she advanced. The rhythm of her heart came as deeper, quicker riffs in her head, seeming to expand the confines of her helmet with each throb. She activated the camera's wrist control and made sure to rotate her helmet sideways as well as up so the tape would capture the entire scope of the mall. Later computer enhancement and magnification would be able to lock onto and enlarge any specific point or area her visual inspection might miss. The microphone built into her helmet sent a delayed, scrambled transmission to Firewatch Command which would evaluate her analysis and pick up with the decision-making should transmission break off suddenly. Initially she was silent, letting the pictures of a similarly scrambled video speak for her. Those pictures along with her words reached Atlanta via a digital translink.

Outside Susan had managed to remain detached when Sculley broached the issue of the victims and their next of kin. At that point they were nothing more than theoretical concepts. But now the victims, or what was left of them, became reality. She felt her throat clog up. Drawing breath became a struggle, and she sought to calm herself by focusing on the task before her.

Susan waited until she reached the second floor before beginning to transmit her report. Her initial estimates based on what she had seen so far put the count of victims in the 1,500 range conservatively. The condition of the bodies seemed to be identical. There was no reason to describe that condition in detail, since the video transmission would more than suffice.

"Condition of remains confirmed," she started, speaking into the microphone located just below her misting faceplate. "Confinement of exposure confirmed. Fatality rate from exposure . . . one hundred percent."

Susan moved on across the floor, stepping over what

had been a hand and turning away from what had been a face.

"Confidence of hostile action very high," she continued. "Fire danger is clearly Level One. Full alert status recommended. All—" Susan cut herself off suddenly. A sound had caught her ear, something moving, rustling.

Something alive.

"Wait a minute," she continued. "I think I heard . . ." She aimed herself in the direction the sound had come from. When she heard it again, louder, she turned toward a store on the right, miniature camera turning with her. "I think the sound came from inside that—"

A shape hurled itself toward her, rising for her faceplate. Susan threw a gloved hand up instinctively. The broadcast picture scrambled, then died. A crack sounded just ahead of her garbled screaming that faded into oblivion as the transmission ceased abruptly.

If you would like a longer, personalized preview of THE FIRES AT MIDNIGHT, send your name and address to:

Jon Land
c/o Tor Books
175 Fifth Avenue
New York, NY 10010